PASSION'S PRIZE

BARBARA ANKRUM

ZEBRA BOOKS
KENSINGTON PUBLISHING CORP.

ZEBRA BOOKS

are published by

Kensington Publishing Corp.
475 Park Avenue South
New York, NY 10016

First printing: August, 1990

Printed in the United States of America

To David — my love, my hero

Chapter One

Independence, Missouri
May 1854

"Kierin!"

The angry voice rumbled through the din of the crowded, smoke-filled saloon and echoed off the rich, flocked walls like thunder through a rain-swept canyon. The whiskey glass slipped from between Kierin McKendry's fingers and crashed to the floor, shattering into a thousand splintered pieces and dousing the lanky ranch hand who stood beside her.

"Dad-blast-it!" he howled and leaped sideways, swiping at his sodden pantleg with his hand. "Aw, hell! Now look what you done!"

"Oh, Jeb!" Kierin cried, color staining her cheeks, "I'm — I'm so sorry. I . . ." At a loss for words and reluctant to explain the cause of her sudden clumsiness, she bent quickly to mop up the mess with a rag from her serving tray. What good would it do to tell Jeb that she'd been jumpy ever since her run-in with her boss, John Talbot, this morning. Or that hearing the ire in his voice just now had nearly undone her. She'd learned to give Talbot a wide berth when he was angry. And right now, he sounded very angry.

Kierin patted hopelessly at Jeb's wet pantleg, then made an attempt at the glass-strewn whiskey puddle, only to cut herself painfully on a razor-sharp piece of glass.

She bit back a cry and frowned at her bleeding hand. *Perfect,* she thought to herself. *What else can go wrong tonight?*

The cowboy rubbed at the gray-speckled stubble on his chin, and looked down at the slender, auburn-haired girl. "Good God, Miss Kierin," he murmured finally, leaning down to help her up. "This just ain't yer night, is it?"

"No," she answered, smiling ruefully at the old man, "I guess it's not at that."

"Now, looky here—" He pulled a surprisingly clean handkerchief from his pocket and wrapped it gently around her injured hand. " 'Tain't nothin' to worry yer-self about. I'll get the barkeep to clean up this mess." He gestured at the burly Irishman behind the polished oak bar. "You'd best be seein' to that cut after you find out what yer boss over there is a'shoutin' about. He ain't the kind of man who likes to be kept waitin' long. Especially when he's been at the losin' end of a deck of cards all night."

Kierin took a deep breath and swept an out-of-place strand of coppery hair from her eyes with the back of her wrist. She glanced warily over at John Talbot's table.

"Losing?" The very idea of Talbot getting his come-uppance at his own poker table satisfied her sense of justice, but she carefully squelched the smile that rose at the thought.

"Yes, ma'am. Some feller in buckskins over there's beatin' the pants off him an' everbody else who sits down at the table."

"Is he cheating?"

"If he is, he ain't been caught at it," Jeb replied, chuckling. "Cleaned my cayuse and that's a fact. Just a lucky so-and-so, I guess."

"Thanks, Jeb." She held up her bandaged hand. "For

everything." Jeb nodded with an understanding smile and then turned, almost reluctantly, back to his drink.

The Independence was unusually crowded considering the lateness of the hour. The discordant notes that rose relentlessly from the tinny piano in the corner created a constant backdrop of noise as Kierin shouldered her way past the crowds to Talbot's table. She had an uneasy feeling as she approached, seeing the malevolent smile on Talbot's face. She knew that look. It was the one he wore when he hit her. Absently touching the still-tender bruise on her left cheek with the back of her hand, Kierin straightened her shoulders and pushed back that errant wisp of hair again. She'd be damned if she'd let him see the fear in her eyes. It had simply become a matter of pride.

"What kept you, my dear?" Talbot asked with a lascivious smile. He slipped his fingers around her wrist, tightening them in a viselike grip. His dark eyes traveled the length of her immodest red satin gown and back up again.

Kierin had no doubt Talbot's look was aimed at embarrassing her and she found she was, indeed, unable to stop the blush that crept into her cheeks as his dark brown eyes raked her. She lifted her chin, painfully aware of the pressure he was exerting upon her arm. Her green eyes locked with his in a silent struggle of wills.

"I came as quickly as I could," she told him evenly, ignoring the stares of the other men.

"Good. Good. Well, down to business then, gentlemen." In an impatient gesture, Talbot smoothed down his sandy-blond mustache with his fingertips. "I'm about to make the stakes in this game a bit more interesting."

A prickle of fear ran through Kierin. What did *she* have to do with their game? She looked back at Talbot, trying to guess what he had in mind for her. He was as unpredictable as a rattlesnake and just as dangerous.

John Talbot was a deceptively handsome man with clean even features which, she knew, turned many a young woman's head on the streets of Independence. His vanity was reflected in the fit of his perfectly tailored clothes, always cut in the latest Eastern fashions. Everything about him, down to the small silver derringer she knew he kept hidden in a vest pocket, was aimed at keeping up the pretense of refinement. He appeared to the world to be a man who had everything. Everything, Kierin amended silently, but a conscience.

The saloon owner slipped his cigar between his teeth and reached into his coat pocket. Withdrawing a sheath of papers, he laid them open upon the pile of wagers at the center of the table. "I believe that most of you know Kierin, my indentured girl," Talbot began, giving her a familiar pat on the behind.

She flinched at his touch and squeezed her eyes shut as a blue cloud of smoke from his cigar circled her head, stinging her nostrils.

"All save you, Mr. — ?" His questioning look was directed at the stranger in buckskins whom Jeb had mentioned.

For the first time Kierin noticed him. He was indeed a rough-hewn man of the frontier. His appearance was not far different from any of thousands who drifted through Independence on their way to or from the West except that he was unusually clean and well kempt. He was tall — towering over the other men at the table even though he was seated. His skin was a golden, tawny brown — from the sun, she imagined. Dark, wavy hair spilled rakishly over straight dark eyebrows which hooded startlingly blue eyes. *Eyes, the color of the Missouri sky after an April shower.*

One ebony eyebrow cocked in arrogant acknowledgment of her perusal of him and she quickly averted her eyes, shamed that he had caught her looking.

"The name's Holt," the stranger answered finally.

10

"Clay Holt."

John Talbot blanched, then choked on the last puff of his imported Cuban cigar, seized by a coughing fit.

"I say there, John," sputtered Percy Thrumball, the overweight banker who sat opposite Talbot at the table, "are you all right? Jessup!" Thrumball ordered. "Get your boss a whiskey."

Kyle Jessup, the hard-looking henchman who worked for Talbot, had not strayed far from his boss's side all night and now hesitated uncertainly at the fat man's request.

Talbot waved his hand as his coughing abated. Clearing his throat, he laughed with uncharacteristic nervousness.

"I think I'm going to have to change my brand of cigar. Damn Cubans never could make a decent smoke." He crushed the tip into his spent whiskey glass. "But Mr. Thrumball's right. We could all use a drink, couldn't we, gentlemen?"

Jessup snapped his fingers at a short, plump girl who scurried off for a trayful of drinks.

"Now then, as I was saying," Talbot continued, pulling Kierin closer to him, "I have a contract here that makes this girl worth a considerable sum to me, say — five hundred dollars. But I'm willing to add her contract to the pot if any of you think you can meet my wager. Winner take all."

Kierin sucked in her breath and bit the inside of her lip to keep from crying out. *No! He couldn't do this to her. Her father's debt had been nowhere near five hundred dollars! What about the ten months she had already worked for him? Didn't they amount to anything?*

There was an uneasy silence at the table as the men stared at the girl, considering Talbot's words.

"You — you mean to wager with the girl?" Calvin Bennett asked incredulously. The young man swept his hand through his straight blond hair in agitation. "This is a free state, man! If it's slave trade you're looking for, it's done in the South."

Talbot chuckled at the youth's insolence. "Hardly slave trade, this. No, I own her papers as you can see by my signature. She is my property to sell, trade, or wager as I wish. It's the law, Calvin, like it or not. Let's not bring your Freesoiler arguments into a friendly poker game. All we're doing here is separating the men from the boys."

"Friendly?" blurted Calvin, outraged by Talbot's cavalier attitude and stung by the slur on his age. "Well, being a man has nothing to do with what's going on here tonight, Talbot. I dare say that you're a—"

His brother Micah, who had been sitting next to him, laid a firm hand on Calvin's shoulder, silencing the words the young man would have surely lived to regret.

"I think what my brother Calvin here is trying to say," Micah interrupted, "is that the stakes in this game have just gone a bit too high for us. Ain't that right, Calvin?" Micah Bennett's question to his younger brother was punctuated by a dark, warning look.

Calvin shrugged his brother's arm angrily from his shoulder, but wisely kept his mouth shut as Micah bent to retrieve what was left of their stakes.

"We'll just be callin' it a night then," Micah mumbled. "Evenin', gents." He retreated from the table with his brother firmly in tow.

Kierin watched them go, grateful to Calvin for trying to stand up against the man who held her future in his hands. She had gone to school with the Bennett brothers during those few years she had been able to attend—when her mother had been alive. She and Calvin had been friends once. As she watched him walk away, she decided they still were.

A sense of unreality descended upon her, and she wondered if this could truly be happening. In its way, Talbot's scheme to humiliate her here was no more astonishing than the fact that her father had left her here

12

in the first place and taken her younger brother to California. She wished impulsively that Calvin could have taken her with him. Bitterly, she wished that her worthless father could see what she had come to, and in the same moment, she was grateful that her mother never would.

As the Bennetts disappeared through the louvered saloon doors, Talbot turned once again to the men still seated. His expression said that he was pleased to have narrowed the competition so easily.

"My bid stands, gentlemen. Shall we get on with it?"

God knew, the time she had worked for John Talbot had not been easy, but at least she had Lily—Lily who had become her protector, and more importantly, her friend. But this—to be wagered away like an unwanted pocket watch—was one last humiliation she wasn't sure she could bear.

"Please don't do this," Kierin begged him in a choked whisper.

"It's done, my dear," Talbot returned.

Kierin curled her fist into a ball and tried to break free of his grasp. "If Lily were here, she wouldn't—"

"But she's *not* as you can see," he snapped in a low voice, tightening his steely grip on her. "Keep your counsel, my dear, or you shall certainly regret it when I win this hand."

John Talbot's words had been barely audible, but Clay Holt had not missed their tone. The son of a bitch was terrorizing the poor girl. He looked at her more closely. She was young—perhaps eighteen—and had the look of a frightened deer ready to bolt for higher ground. Somehow, she didn't seem to fit in here. The rouge on her cheeks looked utterly out of place against the natural blush of her fair complexion. Her thick auburn hair was swept up in a careless chignon and wispy curls framed her delicate oval face. Dark, thick lashes lined a pair of the most incredible green eyes he had ever seen.

13

His gaze was drawn to a purplish smudge on her left cheek — a nasty bruise, partially concealed by the flour she had evidently dabbed on it. Anger washed over him like a wave as he realized who had undoubtedly put it there. With an effort, he kept his expression blank. Yet he couldn't pull his hungry gaze away from the girl.

She was slender as a willow, with soft curves hidden beneath the ill-fitting red gown. Still, something in her expression defied the delicate look about her and triggered a feeling deep in his gut that he couldn't quite put a name to. Maybe it was the flash of anger in her stunning green eyes or the way she stood proudly with her chin tilted up that way —

Damn! What are you thinking about? There is no room for a woman in your life, you fool! Holt told himself, tearing his gaze from the girl. *Not now. Not ever again.* He cursed his own stupidity for getting involved in this game in the first place tonight. He should have listened to Jacob and gone back with him to the wagon. Daybreak would find them on the trail west to Oregon, with no room for this wisp of a girl who looked like she might blow away in a strong prairie wind.

Yet — his gaze found her again — Talbot meant to bid her whether he stayed in the game or not. He knew Talbot's type well enough to know that his goal was to humiliate the girl, not lose her in a small-stakes poker game. He guessed that Talbot must have a strong hand to have risked a girl like her here.

Holt ran a hand across the tight muscles at the back of his neck. He was a fool even to consider playing for her — though the logic of that line of reasoning, as Jacob would say, had never stopped him before. Still, the thought of leaving her to Talbot stirred up an unreasonable grinding anger in him.

The quiet voice of reason which niggled at Holt's impulsive nature like a worrisome pest told him to fold his hand. Fold and get out before he got tangled up in this. But another voice — the one which he admittedly listened to more often — dared him to stay. Holt picked up his hand and fanned his cards again. It was a long shot, but what the hell?

"I'll see your five hundred, Talbot," he announced, pushing a stack of coins toward the center of the table.

"I'm in, too," Thrumball gushed. He mopped his brow with a white handkerchief, his breath coming in short, rapid gasps of excitement.

Talbot smiled amicably as the plump girl returned to deliver the round of drinks Jessup had ordered. Talbot lifted his in a toast.

"To the best hand."

Thrumball clinked his glass with Talbot's, but Holt simply nodded and slugged down his drink.

"Cards, gentlemen?" Talbot asked, finally releasing Kierin's arm and picking up his role as dealer.

Thrumball looked nervously at his cards. Again, he wiped his sweaty palms on his waistcoat, staining the fine fabric with splotches of moisture. "Two," he requested.

Talbot dealt Thrumball the cards and looked expectantly at Holt.

"I'll take one."

Talbot flipped the card with a practiced gambler's hand onto the table in front of Holt and laid the deck down.

"Dealer stands pat."

Beads of sweat dribbled down the sides of Thrumball's face and he dabbed continuously at his face with the now limp hanky.

Kierin watched the game with growing trepidation, a knot of fear and anger twisting within her. *Damn you John Talbot!* she swore silently. *Damn you all.*

"Call," said Holt. His eyes flickered up to Kierin's, where he caught and held her angry gaze briefly, then looked away.

John Talbot grinned confidently and slowly laid

down his hand, face-up.

"Four lucky nines. Read em' and weep, boys."

Thrumball threw down his full house and let out an exasperated sigh.

"Tarnation, John! I thought I had you for once!"

"Luck of the draw, Thrumball," Talbot drawled. Turning to the man in buckskins, he smiled.

"Mr. Holt?"

Holt looked at the girl. She stood, barely breathing, clutching the edge of the table, her eyes wide with fear.

"Well, now. Four nines," he said, tearing his gaze from her face. "That *is* a lucky hand. It occurs to me, though, that there's one lucky card you seem to be missing there."

Talbot closed his eyes with exaggerated impatience. "And just what card would that be, Mr. Holt?"

Holt laid his cards on the table: an ace, king, jack and ten of hearts. He held in his hand one last card—the one he'd drawn. "The queen of hearts, of course." A confident grin curved his lips and he threw the card down on top of the others. His gaze returned to Kierin's face.

A murmur arose around them. A crowd had gathered near the table and the men jostled for position to see the royal flush that had won the girl for the stranger. The spectators cackled like old hens.

"Cain't hardly remember the last time I see'd an inside royal flush draw'd before," stated Henry Potter, the town's resident blabbermouth. There were nods of agreement as well as slaps on the back for Holt, who leaned forward to begin collecting the pot.

Instincts, honed to a fine edge in the wilderness, warned Holt not to let his guard down yet. He had seen the color drain from John Talbot's face as he had played his cards. Now, Talbot's expression, once coolly confident, said he thought Holt had cheated.

Talbot rose slowly from his chair and Holt's arm moved instinctively to the gun strapped to his hip.

16

Watching the play of emotions on the other man's face, he glanced around, mentally tabulating the odds in Talbot's favor. He had watched the saloon owner's men gravitate toward the table as the game progressed and knew he was greatly outnumbered. But the size of the crowd could work in his favor. Talbot was an impulsive man, but not a fool. He would never try to call him out in front of all these witnesses. Talbot was too much of a coward for that.

Holt looked at the girl. She stood rooted to the floor next to an angry John Talbot, a dazed look of confusion on her face. Already the crowd, sensing what was in the air, had started to retreat from the table, looking to put plenty of room between themselves and a possible gunfight. Slowly, deliberately, Holt picked up the contract and handed it to Talbot.

"I believe you owe me a signature on these papers, Talbot."

Talbot stared icily at Holt, then managed a smile that crossed his lips but did not reach his eyes.

"So I do," he replied hoarsely. The saloon owner motioned to Kyle Jessup to bring him a pen. The man obliged quickly and Holt saw a nod of understanding pass between them as Jessup leaned in close to his boss.

Talbot bent over the paper, scribbled his name, and released Kierin to Clay Holt with an angry scrawl. Then he straightened and handed the paper to the tall buckskin-clad man. Turning on his heel, almost nose to nose with Kierin, Talbot snarled something that was only for her ears and stalked away from the table.

Kierin lowered her head, closed her eyes, and let out a long shuddering sigh. Her whole body was gripped with a tremor so violent that she feared she would fall if she did not sit. But even as she felt her legs giving way underneath her, a strong arm pulled her back up again. Her eyes focused level with the long fringe on his buckskin shirt.

17

"Don't faint on me now, lady," Holt murmured, leaning down close to her ear. "Show me which room is yours. We don't have much time."

The room whirled by as he dragged her through the throngs that had crowded around them. *Stop it!* she wanted to scream, but it was all happening too fast. Anger blossomed from the fear that had paralyzed her only moments ago. The indignity of it all suddenly became too much. Who did he think he was dragging her up to her room to do God knew what with her?

She knew what. She knew just what he thought she was.

Kierin dug her heels into the floor and yanked back on his arm with all her might.

"I'm not going *anywhere* with you!" she screeched. "Let go of me!" Kierin worked desperately to pry the stranger's fingers from her arm, managing only to rake him with her nails.

Holt winced and tightened his grip. Her pitiful struggle wasn't much more than an annoyance to him.

"You'll *go* wherever I *tell* you to go," he warned through clenched teeth. "I *own* you now. Remember?"

Her green eyes snapped with anger. "You have no right—!"

"Look, don't fight me on this, lady. If I have to throw you over my shoulder and carry you there, I will. But one way or the other, we *are* going to your room." The icy tone in his voice held a clear challenge.

Panic welled in her throat, threatening to cut off her air supply as he pulled her across the crowded room. Kierin nearly cried out from the bruising pressure of his fingers on her upper arm. She bumped along behind him like a shadow, all but invisible to the grinning patrons of the Independence.

Pompous pop-in-jay! she thought as she watched the tall man receive winking grins, slaps on the back, and bawdy words of encouragement from the drunken men who lined their path to the back of the saloon. Only Jeb, whose eyes she met briefly, seemed bothered by

18

the outcome of the game. He shook his head sadly as she passed him, but soon disappeared from her line of vision.

Stopping in front of the long polished bar, Holt pulled a shining twenty-dollar gold piece from his pocket and flipped it onto the bar.

"A bottle for me and the lady here," he requested loudly, "and drinks all around!"

Malone, the bartender, made a grand show of testing the gold piece first with his teeth before smiling and swinging a bottle of whiskey down on the bar with two glasses.

A whoop went up from the men nearby as he crowed, "You heard him, me boys. The next round is on this lad here."

The crowd pressed close to the bar, awaiting their share of the spoils. Holt grabbed his bottle and the glasses one-handed and pushed his way back toward the stairway, dragging Kierin behind him.

His eyes scanned the exits. He was not surprised to find that Talbot's men had placed themselves strategically at each one. To his left he noticed Kyle Jessup leaning against the wall, grinning at him through tobacco-stained teeth like the cat who had just caught the canary. Jessup touched the brim of the hat that was slung low over his brow in a silent challenge.

There's your first mistake, Jessup. Never let them know what you're thinking. Holt smiled back at the man pleasantly. *With luck, this canary will come out of this with all his feathers.*

Together, Holt and the girl climbed the stairs. He pulled. She resisted. He could see her eyes frantically searching for someone in the crowded room below, but didn't have the time to dwell on who it might be.

"Which one?" he demanded when they reached the landing. He glanced back over his shoulder at the room below them.

"Please, Mr. —"

19

"Look, don't play games with me here." He glared at her menacingly. Jessup was no longer in sight. "Show me your room. Now!"

Kierin jumped at his words and moved quickly to her door. Taking a deep breath, she turned the handle. She was shoved from behind as he pushed his way into the room, closing the door firmly behind them.

He slid the bolt home with a loud click and the girl's head turned sharply at the sound. Through the moon-lit darkness in her room, Holt could see the fear in her eyes. Damn. That's all he needed. He rubbed a hand slowly across his face — a gesture that spoke as much of his frustration as his anger.

Setting the bottle and glasses down on the small washstand beside the door, Holt moved to the window at the far side of the small room. He pulled the filmy lace curtains aside and surveyed the street below. He could spot no one watching her room and was relieved to see the narrow balcony that ran the length of the false-fronted building just below her window. Holt knew he would have no trouble making the drop of some eight feet to the street below, but he wondered if he could expect the same of her.

"Are you up to climbing out a window?" Holt asked suddenly.

Whatever Kierin had imagined him to say next, it had not been that. She pressed herself closer to the wall behind her.

"A—am I . . . what?"

"Are you any good at jumping?"

"Jumping?" She was completely at a loss.

"Look," he explained more patiently in a low, controlled voice, "judging from Talbot's mood when he left the table and the fact that at this very moment he has men positioned at every door waiting for us to leave, I'd say the only sure way of getting out of this mess in one piece is to hightail it out your bedroom window here, before Talbot's men know we've gone."

"I—I don't understand," Kierin whispered, trying to grasp what he was saying. She stared at the man before her as if seeing him for the first time. What he said didn't make any sense. "I thought . . . I thought you won my contract in that game."

"I did. Unfortunately, your friend Talbot is a man who doesn't take his losses well. Especially when it involves a piece of property that he had no intention of losing."

The fire he had seen in her eyes earlier rekindled and she shot him a scorching look. "Just what makes you so sure that John Talbot has any intention of going back on his word, Mr. Holt? He signed the paper in front of dozens of witnesses deeding his . . . *property,* as you so aptly put it, to you."

He looked at her with a directness that made her distinctly uncomfortable—as if he was weighing her ability to see the reasonableness of his argument. Apparently, he decided she was both dim-witted and troublesome.

"You'll just have to trust me on this," he said. "I've met men like Talbot before." Holt lowered his eyes and frowned. "Let's leave it at that."

Kierin had no reason to trust this man or any other man for that matter. Men had done nothing in her life but betray her. Why should this one be any different? Her best instincts told her to put as much distance as she could between herself and this man named Holt. For now, however, she knew that there was no choice but to go along with him. Grudgingly, she admitted he was right.

John Talbot was one of the most powerful men in this town. Who would ask questions if she suddenly became his property again or if this man mysteriously disappeared? Talbot was undoubtedly capable of that and worse. She shuddered as she remembered the threat he'd snarled in her ear as he left the table. No. At least the stranger was right about this. She would go along with him for now and take her chance when it came.

"What do you think he'll do if he . . . catches us?"

Holt looked back to the street. It was a prospect he didn't intend to waste time considering. "Get a few things together. Just what you'll need. Keep it light. We'll have to move fast," he ordered. "If we don't get out of here soon, we won't have to wonder, will we?"

The amber moonlight spilled lanternlike onto the street below, mingling eerily with the fingers of misty air rolling in from the river. Holt and Kierin scanned the scene from their vantage point on the balcony below her window, and she pulled her thin wrap more tightly against the chill that clung to the damp night air. She wished now that she'd taken the time to put on something warmer, but Holt had only allowed her to stuff a few dresses and some other bare necessities into the bag before hauling her out the window. She pulled her small tapestry bag into the crook of her arm, and pressed it against her for the small amount of warmth it would provide.

Holt was crouched beside her with his back against the wall. He leaned deeper into the dappled shadow cast by the giant poplar that grew in front of the Independence. The tightly coiled muscles of his right arm pressed unavoidably against hers. Kierin felt her heart race unexpectedly at his closeness and she chanced a covert glance in his direction.

The soft shadowed moonlight played across the planes of his chiseled features as his eyes searched the darkness. He was a handsome man, she realized, taking in the near perfection of his profile. His angular cheekbones emphasized the strong masculine line of his jaw and the shadowed hollow of his cheeks. Lips, full and sensuous, curled slightly upward at the corners, giving him a look of boyish mischievousness that belied the grim concentration etched there. She could just make out a thin white scar that ran nearly the length of his jawline—the only flaw on an otherwise flawless face.

Kierin looked away, scolding herself for admiring him as she had. He was a man like any other man. She had learned from Talbot that external beauty could be cruelly deceiving. She dared not allow her guard down with this man, she told herself, no matter how he affected her.

"Let's go," Holt whispered, breaking into her reverie. He uncoiled lithely from his place at her side and vaulted over the banistered railing onto the exposed part of the balcony. He perched there on the edge of the roof, looking back at her expectantly.

"Well, come on," he encouraged. "I'll go down first and help you down. It's not a long drop."

"You needn't worry about me, Mr. Holt," she whispered back defensively, meeting him at the railing. "If you can do it, I can do it. I don't need anything from you."

He shrugged. "Suit yourself. I was only trying to be a gentleman." At that, he dropped with a graceful thud to the soft dirt below.

"Ha!" she scoffed from above. "That's a good one. If you were a gentleman, you would have walked away from that game like Calvin Bennett did." She threw her leg over the balcony and wavered there, gripping the rail in one hand and her bag in the other.

Holt's brows furrowed together and he placed his hands on his hips in aggravation, craning his neck up to see her.

"This is hardly the time to be discussing the finer points of etiquette, lady. Let's go!"

She let the tapestry bag fly and missed hitting his shoulder by mere inches. He caught it one-handed and set it down soundlessly on the street. He glared back up at her.

"You missed."

"That's a shame. I didn't mean to." She glared back at him.

She had climbed trees a thousand times with her younger brother Matthew and she was good at it, too. Balconies, however, were another matter altogether. She climbed down as far as she could, gripping the banistered railing, but as soon as she let go with one hand, she lost her grip with the other, bandaged one and, with a small cry, plummeted like a broken sparrow to the ground. She dropped, humiliatingly, into Holt's waiting arms.

Had it been any other time, any other man, she would have gracefully admitted that he had been right and thanked him for catching her. But it was *this* man with his arms around her and a silly grin on his face. She twisted free from his grip, still feeling the heat of his touch where his hands had circled her waist. With fists clenched, she glared at him.

"I *told* you I didn't need your help. I could have done it by myself."

He stared at her for a moment, utterly dumbfounded.

"Pardon me, *Princess*," he returned finally in a disgusted whisper, "but if it's all the same to you, I'd rather not have to carry you out of town with a sprained ankle or worse because you were too bullheaded to ask for my help." He slapped irritably at his buckskin leggings, sending up a small cloud of dust. "So, let's get moving, shall we?"

Without waiting for an answer, Holt turned and stormed off into the darkness, muttering something about ungrateful wenches.

Kierin narrowed her eyes and set her jaw against the anger that welled in her. He had been right about her bullheadedness and she even grudgingly admitted to herself that she would have certainly hurt herself if not for him. But she would be damned if she would thank him for it.

Ungrateful! Ha!

As if she should be grateful that he had won the next few years of her life in a game of cards! The man had nerve. If she hadn't been sure that she had no chance of escaping Talbot on her own, she would have turned and run in the opposite direction. But they were still close enough to the saloon to hear the music and laughter spilling from the open doors.

Shivering at the thought of being found, she hurried to follow Holt's long-legged strides. The tapestry bag, which he had pointedly left behind for her to carry, bumped along uncomfortably against her leg and she cursed him silently.

Princess, indeed. Damn you, Clay Holt!

She didn't know how, or when, but she'd find a way to get away from him. She silently vowed she would never be his, or any other man's, slave again.

Chapter Two

John Talbot leaned back in his tufted leather chair and slugged a double shot of fine Irish whiskey down his throat. He grimaced as it burned him, closing his eyes with relief. Whiskey seemed to be the only thing that brought him relief these days.

He got up from his desk and paced, silently cursing the turn of the evening's events. Women! The truth was he had no use for any of them, but for what they could give him in bed. He snorted derisively, pouring himself another drink. Lately, even the bottle gave him considerably more pleasure than that. That damn little McKendry bitch would have gotten what was coming to her tonight if only he'd won that hand. With Lily out of the way—

Talbot slumped into his chair again. He thought of the woman he'd taken on as a partner two years ago when he had first moved into this town. He'd had a small stake—enough to start a modest saloon which would have, in time, grown in reputation to what the Independence was now. But Lily—a madam with a reputation already built on first rate clientele and enough money to give him the edge over the competition—had offered to throw in with him.

It was a decision he had never regretted, because the success of the saloon had given him the power he had always craved. He was, without a doubt, one of the richest citizens of Independence now and owned a good portion of its real estate and commerce.

No, taking Lily on as a partner had been smart business. But when it came to the girl, Kierin, he and Lily butted heads. For as fine a businesswoman as Lily was, something about the McKendry girl brought out the mother hen in her. She had taken Kierin under her protective wing as soon as Talbot had brought the girl to work here for him. And despite Talbot's objections, Lily had made sure that Kierin's bed was off-limits not only to the customers, but to him as well.

Well, Lily was gone for a few days to St. Louis. It had been the perfect opportunity for him to teach Asa McKendry's brat a lesson. Somehow, he thought angrily, it had all gone awry.

And Clay Holt! Right under his goddamned nose and he hadn't even known it! Talbot's thoughts skipped erratically as he paced the room again, becoming more and more agitated.

A knock interrupted his pacing and he shot to the door, swinging it open wide.

"Well?" he demanded of Kyle Jessup, who stood with his hand still poised over the frame.

"They're still up there, Mr. Talbot. I've got two men watching the door."

"Damn." Talbot stalked across the room again and slammed his empty glass down on the desk. "What the hell are they doing up there?"

Jessup shrugged and stuffed his hands in his pockets. His look indicated that the answer to that was only too obvious to him, yet he wisely kept his mouth shut about it.

"Did Holt know you were watching him?"

"No sir," Jessup answered too quickly. He straightened up and slicked his greasy hair back with one hand. "He made a big deal about buying up drinks for the house and takin' a bottle up for him and the girl."

"Sonofabitch."

Talbot's choler rose at the mere thought of the two of

them together, but he had to be smart about this. He couldn't risk gunplay in the saloon. Nor could he take the chance that Holt would survive long enough to finger Talbot for his past transgressions. Holt hadn't spent the last three years chasing Talbot's shadow for nothing. He was a dangerous adversary and Talbot wasn't about to underestimate him again.

"I want him, Kyle," Talbot said finally. "He's not going to get away from me this time. Now that we've finally met face to face, there's nowhere he can go."

"It's too bad those hired guns—Sands and Wilkerson—weren't in the saloon tonight," Jessup said, leaning against the splendid mahogany desk and eyeing the crystal decanter of brandy there. "They would'a known Holt right off."

Talbot sneered. "Those two idiots wouldn't know a snake if it came up and bit them on the ass. They told me this morning that they'd lost him in St. Louis. The bastards didn't even realize that he was right under their noses here in Independence!"

"Do you think he followed them here?" Kyle asked.

"I don't know. I may be wrong but I still don't think he knows who *I* am. But that just puts the odds a little more in my favor. Kierin overheard me talking to Sands and Wilkerson this morning. I can't take the chance now that she'll tell someone." He paused, then added, "We'll have to kill them both."

Talbot eyed Jessup, trying to gauge his reaction to the order. Jessup was not much more than a hired gun himself and had killed his share of men for Talbot and others. Still, he knew some men had qualms about killing a woman. He wondered if Jessup fit into that category.

Jessup puckered up and let fly a long stream of tobacco juice, which hit, more or less, the center of the brass spittoon beside Talbot's desk.

He rearranged the wad in his mouth and then nodded at Talbot, a slow grin spreading across his face.

The office door burst open and another of Talbot's men, Gunther Hallas, rushed into the room.

"Sorry, boss, but . . . we lost them."

"You *what!*" Talbot fairly shrieked. "I thought they were upstairs in the girl's room!"

Hallas swallowed hard. "So did we, Mr. Talbot, but it got mighty quiet in there, and we figured to take us a look. They uh . . . they went out through the window."

"*The window?* How long ago?"

"Couldn't be too long," he answered hopefully. "I'd say they've only got ten minutes on us. I've already got the others out lookin'."

Cursing foully, Talbot strapped on his gun belt and checked the knife he kept sheathed inside his boot. There wasn't time to waste berating the morons who had let the two of them escape. If he wanted this job done right, he'd have to do it himself. Talbot turned to the first man.

"Jessup, you stay with me. Gunther, you take the others and fan out." He jammed his hat down on his head and headed for the door.

"When you find them—nobody touches the girl until I'm done with her. Is that clear?"

Hallas and Jessup nodded.

"What about Holt?" Hallas asked.

"Kill the son of a bitch."

Kierin drew a jagged breath and leaned against the splintery weather-worn wall of Connelly's Feed and Seed. She closed her eyes and swallowed down the panic rising in her throat. They had been running for nearly five minutes, but to Kierin it seemed more like hours. Her legs ached from trying to keep up with Holt's long-legged strides, for she had to take two steps for each one of his. Yet he stood beside her now, annoyingly unaffected by the run. He had slipped deftly

29

in between the shadows of buildings, keeping the two of them hidden all the way to the west end of town until they were fairly certain no one had followed them.

"Where are you taking me?" Kierin demanded when she caught her breath.

Holt spared her a quick glance. "To get my horse. I left him at the farrier to be shod this afternoon."

"Oh, *that* was good planning."

"Keep your voice down," he told her in a hoarse, irritated whisper. "Besides, when I left him I wasn't planning on having *your* charming company or half the town chasing me on the way back."

Kierin sniffed unsympathetically. "You have only yourself to blame for that, Mr. Holt."

"Yeah, well, remind me of that fact the next time I'm about to do something stupid, will you?"

Kierin's gaze followed him as he edged out of the shadows to get a better view of the shops between them and the river. She didn't plan on being with him long enough to remind him about anything. But she wouldn't tell him that.

Grudgingly, she joined him at the corner of the building and tried to make out the darkened street ahead. They were near the edge of town. The moonlight danced on the newly paved cobbled road that led to the waterfront wharfs and slivered through the wavering shadows cast by the rows of poplars which lined the main street.

Holt pushed away from the wall and slipped cautiously down the row of shops, with Kierin close behind. They stopped alongside the newly constructed Beaudry's Livery. Its raw, unpainted siding was still fragrant with resinous pitch. The woodsy scent drifted to them with each breath as Holt and Kierin pressed deeper into the barn's shadows. A bone-chilling cold settled upon her as soon as she stopped moving, but Kierin stubbornly resisted the temptation to press against Holt's warm bulk. The damp river mist slithered between the thin wrap and her nearly bare shoulders and she pulled the shawl more tightly around her, pressing her fists to her face.

A screech owl's cry pierced the night's quiet. Kierin ducked her head as the huge bird swooped down close by to scoop up an unsuspecting mouse who had ventured into a moonlit patch of street. She let out a small horrified gasp as she watched the tiny mouse dangle helplessly from the talons of the night creature who disappeared beyond the trees.

She stood very still, eyes fixed on the darkness, unable to control the tremors that gripped her body. Unwelcome tears burned the backs of her eyes and she swiped at them with her shawl-entangled fist. She felt at that moment as out of control of her own destiny as that tiny mouse certainly was. The currents of the night's events had swept her into dark and unfamiliar territory with a man she did not know.

Get a hold of yourself, Kierin! she scolded herself silently, taking a deep calming breath. It was then that she became aware that Holt was staring at her through the darkness. Her eyes were drawn to his as if by a will of their own. Though the moonlight robbed his eyes of their vivid blue color, it did nothing to lessen the unexpected intensity of his gaze. After a long moment she looked away—fearful that he might, somehow, look right into her.

"You cold, Princess?" His voice was surprisingly gentle.

There was that name again, but this time the mocking tone was gone. Kierin bit her lip and refused to look back at him. She shook her head no, but couldn't stop shivering.

He sighed and looked down the street toward the river. "Have you got anything . . . more appropriate for night travel in that bag of yours?" he asked, gesturing to the tapestry bag at her feet. His breath formed a

31

little white cloud as he spoke and he fingered the thin silk fabric of her dress. "You're going to freeze your little fanny off in that thing."

"This is hardly the time or place to be thinking about changing, Mr. H—" she began, but he silenced her with a hand on her arm and a warning finger to his lips.

"Sh-hh," he whispered, drawing her back farther into the shadow of the livery. The dark figure of a man on horseback passed them on the opposite side of the street. His horse plodded along slowly and the man twisted in his saddle, peering down a dark alleyway between two buildings.

Holt pulled her closer against his chest. She could feel the ragged pounding of his heart against her back in an odd echo of her own and she heard his gun leave the sheath of its leather holster just below her arm. They stood perfectly still that way, not daring to breathe, until the rider moved out of sight and into the enveloping darkness.

Holt sheathed his Walker Colt and slowly, almost reluctantly, loosened his grip on her. It wasn't until that moment that he became aware of the sweet womanly scent of her, or how she had fit against him the way fine glove leather fit his hand.

He raked his fingers through his dark hair, sweeping it out of his eyes. *You've been too long without a woman, Holt. Face it—any woman would feel good to you right now. But this one's on the next stage to St. Louis and the sooner the better,* he reminded himself. *Get your mind back on getting the hell out of here.*

"Do you think he saw us?" The tremor in her voice was more pronounced, from fear or cold he couldn't be sure.

"No, but it's only a matter of time if Talbot's men are all mounted."

He pulled on the wooden-handled livery door and found it locked. The soft nickers of the horses within

32

carried on the still night air, and Holt gave a useless tug on the door in frustration. One horse! One damned horse was all they needed and they'd be well out of this.

His gaze moved down the row of closed shops to a window that spilled soft yellow light onto the street and he heard the faint clanking of a smithy's hammer. It was the farrier's shop.

Holt motioned the girl to follow him. They made their way past hogsheads and stacked crates piled on the planked walkways in front of the mercantile and cooper shops, but kept within the shadows of the shops' overhangs.

He stopped beneath the glowing window and peered cautiously inside. Through the paned glass, Holt could see the huge man he'd done business with earlier in the day. Sweat and grime clung to the dark hair that covered his chest and arms. The top half of him was naked but for the heavy leather apron that moved with him as he worked the billows above him up and down with his muscular arm. Though his main business was horses, Holt knew that Brown kept busy late into the night with the heavy demand for smithed iron rims for the emigrant trains. He and Jacob had used the smithy's services not two days ago themselves and he had done a fair job for them, too. Now, with any luck, Taeva would be shod, saddled up, and ready to go.

Kierin reached the window just seconds after Holt and looked longingly at the fire. She rubbed her arms beneath the shawl, alternately breathing into her stiff hands in the vain search for warmth. She turned away, unable to look any longer, and leaned back against the cool brick wall.

"Do you know him?" Holt whispered.

Kierin nodded. "Scudder Brown? I've known him for most of my life."

"Can he be trusted?"

Kierin looked back into the grimy smith shop. She

shook her head after considering it for a moment. "No. Talbot is part owner in this shop, just as he is for many of the businesses in this part of town. Scudder would be a fool to cross him." She looked up at Holt, wondering if he knew just how foolish *he* had been to go up against a man like John Talbot. She doubted that the stranger had any idea how dangerous Talbot was.

"We haven't much farther to go. Can you make it without warming up?"

"You needn't worry about me, Mr. Holt. I am q-quite capable of a great many things that might surprise you."

Holt found himself amused by the girl's bravado, transparent as it was. It was refreshing after knowing so many women hardened by the life in brothels. And though at first, he had been taken aback by her obvious youth, he knew that, too, was not all that unusual for the times. Especially in a town like Independence, which sat on the edge of the frontier, peopled by thousands of would-be emigrants on their way to a new life. The trains moved out of this teeming outpost regularly, with as many stories of hardship to be told. Holt wondered briefly what hers was and how she had wound up becoming involved with a snake like Talbot.

Dismissing the thought, he quickly stripped his buckskin shirt off over his head and handed it to her. She stared at him in wide-eyed disbelief.

"That you're capable, I have no doubts, Princess," Holt told her, removing the money pouch from around his neck and tucking it into the waistband of his smooth elkskin leggings. "But I know gooseflesh when I see it, and whatever else you're capable of, hiding your discomfort is not one of your best talents."

"But . . . wh—what will you wear? Won't you be cold too?"

"I'm used to the night air. Once we're moving again, I won't notice the cold at all. Put it on."

Kierin slipped the shirt over her head and felt instant relief from the warmth that still clung to it. It hung ridiculously down to her knees, and her hands were lost in the long sleeves, but it felt deliciously warm.

"Thank you."

Holt grinned that charming grin and nodded. "I think we'd better slip around back and get my horse. I'll leave some money for Brown at the back of his shop. Let's go."

Turning the corner of the smith shop, Holt caught the glint of moonlight off a steel blade, just before he felt the searing pain it wielded. He ducked instinctively, but the blade slid smoothly into the firm muscle of his shoulder, far from where its original aim intended.

The force of the blow nearly knocked him off his feet and he slammed back against the wall behind him with a groan. He sucked a deep hissing breath between clenched teeth and squeezed his eyes shut against the white-hot intensity of the pain as his assailant withdrew the blade.

John Talbot smiled in victory as the pain registered across Holt's sculpted features.

"I'm disappointed in you, Mr. Holt," Talbot sneered. He pressed the blade cruelly against Holt's throat and drew a fine bead of blood from beneath its razor-sharp edge. "Somehow I hoped there would be more sport in it for me. Though I must admit, your escape through the window did delay me for a bit." Talbot chuckled derisively as he slipped Clay's gun out of its holster, and cocked it menacingly close to the taller man's ear.

"Bring the girl, Kyle," he ordered, motioning toward the smith shop.

Holt clutched his throbbing shoulder and, for the first time, noticed that Kyle Jessup held Kierin with one hand over her mouth and the other pinning her arms behind her back.

Damn! How could he have been so careless? He'd

35

walked right into it. Holt felt the cold steel barrel of his own gun pressed against his back as Talbot urged him forward.

The sticky warmth spreading beneath Holt's fingers felt strangely incongruous to the numbing chill that now seeped into his body. He stumbled forward on legs which were oddly slow to respond to his command, toward the doorway of the smith shop. It wouldn't do, he thought grimly, to have one of the town's upstanding citizens caught in the act of murdering someone in the street.

With renewed certainty, he knew that Talbot meant to kill them both. He could feel the strength draining from him as the crimson stain of his blood spread down his chest. Steeling his mind against the pain, Clay struggled to keep a clear head.

The pungent smell of heated iron assaulted him as they moved into the warmth of the dimly lit shop. Scudder Brown's mouth gaped open in surprise as Holt was shoved inside, stumbling to the hard-packed dirt floor at the burly man's feet.

"Mr. Talbot! What the hell—w-what's going on?" Brown looked anxiously at the bloody man lying on the ground.

"Nothing that concerns you, Brown," Talbot told him, tucking Holt's gun into the back waistband of his pants. "And if you know what's good for you, you'll forget this ever happened." Talbot glared menacingly at Brown who, despite his size, seemed to shrink under Talbot's scowling countenance.

Brown backed up a step as he looked again at Holt, who was slowly getting to his feet. The frightened blacksmith shifted from one foot to the other and glanced uncertainly at Kierin.

"Mr. Talbot, th-this ain't right," the huge man began bravely. "Whatever's goin' on here, I'm sure Sheriff Barker could straighten it all out. Why don't you let the girl go with me and we'll get the sheriff and bring

36

him back here directly. He'll see that this fella's taken care of legal-like."

John Talbot's face clouded dangerously and he took a step toward the blacksmith with fists clenched.

"Have you forgotten, Brown," Talbot snarled, "that I *own* this shop? That without me, you and your family would have been out on the street!" Talbot moved one step at a time closer to Brown's flushed face as he spoke, until Talbot's face was only inches from the other man's.

"Don't you know I own *you?*" he ranted, grabbing a fistful of Brown's leather apron. Talbot's voice held the brittle edge of a man on the brink of losing control. Suddenly, he released Brown and took a step back. The saloon owner shrugged his fine wool coat back into place and yanked irritably at his cuffs.

"Now," he continued more calmly, "I suggest you mosey on down to the bar . . . have yourself a drink or two—oh, that's right. You've given all that up, haven't you? Well, why don't you just go on home to your family. And while you're there, consider what kind of a life they would have if you weren't here to provide for them. I don't need to tell you that you won't get another warning from me."

Talbot stepped aside with a sweep of his arm toward the door. Brown hesitated for only a moment, glanced apologetically at Kierin, then turned and left the shop.

Kierin watched the scene with the creeping conviction that Talbot meant to kill both her and Holt. Her arms still pinioned in Jessup's grasp, Kierin's heart thudded furiously against her breast as she searched for a way to help Holt. He stood swaying unsteadily against the far wall. Yet as weak as she knew he must be, she saw a strength in his eyes which she doubted Talbot would perceive. It sent an unexpected shiver of hope down her spine. She hadn't expected that kind of a show of character from a gambler like Holt, but there it was. His fierce look told her that they were not going to give up without a fight.

Beads of moisture clung to Holt's brow, and his lips were etched in a grim slash across his pale face. His gaze captured her own for a moment, then he looked deliberately at the hard-packed earthen floor and back up to her again.

Kierin wasn't sure she understood what he was trying to tell her, but guessed he meant to make a move and wanted her out of the way. She nodded to him very slightly and readied herself for what was to come.

With the blacksmith out of the way, Talbot turned confidently to Holt and smiled. "There'll be no help coming from that quarter, I'm afraid, if that was your hope." Talbot fairly swaggered as he continued, "Now, down to the business at hand. I feel you cheated me tonight, Mr. Holt, and *that* I simply can't abide."

"Why don't you just admit you can't abide losing a fair game of cards, Talbot?" Holt gritted out.

"Fair?" Talbot snorted. "Well, fair or not, I have no intention of losing a nice piece like Kierin to a yokel like you."

Kierin twisted angrily in Jessup's grip, but he wrenched her arm up painfully behind her, making her cry out in pain.

"You bastard!" Holt shouted at Jessup, his eyes darkened with fury. "This is between you and me, Talbot. Tell your lackey to leave her out of this."

"She's right where you put her, Mr. Holt," Talbot answered evenly.

"You won't get away with this, you low-life snake!" Kierin spat at Talbot.

Talbot shot Kierin an icy look.

"Shut up, you bitch!" he swore, and took a step toward her.

It was the opening Holt had waited for. With an effort, he bent and pulled a knife from inside his boot. Kierin yanked herself from the arms of Jessup as Holt's knife whizzed through the air. Kyle Jessup could do little more than gasp before the blade embedded itself to the hilt in his chest. The man crumpled to the ground. Talbot wheeled around to face Holt, a look of disbelief on his face.

"No!" Talbot bellowed, rushing headlong at Holt.

Holt swayed and managed to evade the deadly swipe of Talbot's extended knife, sending Talbot crashing into the wall of iron tools behind Holt. The tools clattered noisily to the floor around Talbot, but he struggled to his feet. He rose like an angry bull, punishing Holt's injured shoulder with a brutal blow which sent Holt crashing against the cluttered workbench. Before Talbot could hit him again, Holt grabbed an iron rod and brought it down hard against Talbot's upper arm.

Talbot moaned in pain, clutched his arm, and staggered backward against the handle of the bellows.

In the shadows against the far wall, Kierin had wasted precious moments trying desperately to pry Kyle Jessup's gun from beneath him, but he was far too heavy for her to move. Her eyes searched the darkened room frantically for a weapon as Holt and Talbot fought. Suddenly, she spotted the end of an iron poker sticking out of the glowing fire. If she could only get to it . . .

Holt leaned against the wall, his face the color of chalk. The room swayed and darkened in crazy patches as he fought the blackness closing in on him. He stumbled toward the girl in a last-ditch effort to protect her; his last conscious thought was that he had failed her.

Horrified, Kierin watched him sway on his feet and stumble toward her, then pitch forward, landing face-down on the floor in the center of the small room.

"Oh, no . . ." Kierin breathed. "No."

John Talbot grinned and pushed away from the fire pit, crossing the distance to Holt's body in three easy strides. He knelt beside Holt and pushed the unconscious man over on his back.

"All these years . . ." Talbot murmured with a satisfied look on his face. "All for nothing now, Holt. You lose." Talbot raised his knife high in the air over Holt, his features twisted with rage. But just as he began his downward thrust, he heard Kierin scream and caught her movement out of his left eye. She flung herself at him, brandishing the red-hot-tipped iron, and before he could protect himself, she swung the hot metal at his face, striking it with violent force. A single cry escaped his lips as his cheekbone shattered beneath the impact of the blow which sent him crashing like a toppled tree to the floor.

The odor of his burned flesh assailed Kierin and her stomach roiled as she looked at Talbot's ruined, bloodied face. There had been no choice, she told herself. No choice at all between his life and Holt's. An odd sensation formed like a knot in her chest as she remembered how Holt had fought for her.

Holt!

Kierin knelt beside him and desperately searched for a heartbeat at the side of his throat. She was rewarded with a weak pulse, and she let out a long sigh of relief. He was alive. His wound was still bleeding and his skin felt cool and clammy to the touch. Her limited knowledge of medicine told her that he would die of shock if she couldn't stop the bleeding and get him warm. Ripping the red silk of her dress, she tore a strip and pressed the cloth against his wound firmly to stanch the flow. With her free hand she rubbed vigorously up and down his arm, trying desperately to warm him.

Holt's eyes flickered open at her touch and she could see that he was struggling to focus on her face. His eyes rolled closed again momentarily as he fought the pain that engulfed him.

"Holt?" she whispered, touching his face, willing him to stay conscious.

"Where — where's Talbot?" His voice was a croaking

whisper.

"I think I killed him," she answered, looking back at Talbot's still form. "We've got to get out of here. Can you help me? I can't get you up alone."

Holt blinked his eyes, fighting the blackness that threatened to descend again. "I don't know," he admitted. "I'll try."

Kierin helped him sit up, supporting him with her arm behind his back. He stopped there for a moment, waiting for the room to stop spinning.

"Can you make it?" she asked, unable to hide the fear in her voice.

"Listen to me," Holt said, his words slurring slightly as he spoke. "If I can't, you get yourself out of here—"

"No—"

"Go *without* me," he told her. "Go to the wagon train camped just outside of town. . . . It's the Kelly train." He paused, catching his breath. "Find a man named Jacob. He's a friend of mine. He'll help you."

Kierin wrapped his good arm around her neck and stubbornly pulled him to his feet.

"I . . . won't . . . leave you here to . . . die, Mr. Holt," she told him, struggling to balance beneath his weight. "But don't you go falling on me. I don't think I could get you up again."

"Wait." Holt stopped her as they started across the small room. "My gun. Where's my gun?"

Kierin's eyes frantically searched the room until she found the weapon near Talbot's body.

"It's there," she told him. "Can you stand by yourself?"

He nodded. "Get it," he told her. A tremor passed through him as she released her hold on him, but he didn't fall.

Kierin retrieved the gun quickly and returned to him. She slipped her arm around Holt and held the heavy gun up with a trembling hand.

Holt shook his head. "Can you shoot a gun?"

Kierin hesitated. She had never shot one in her life. The most she'd ever done was hold her father's old hunting rifle. "No."

Holt blew out a shaky breath and closed his eyes. "Can you hold the damn thing straight?"

Kierin swallowed hard and nodded. "I think so. But what if—"

"Bluff."

Heaven help us both, she thought, pulling him upright.

The pair struggled to the door and Kierin fought back the tears that threatened to blur her vision. Truly, she didn't know if she could simply leave him if he fell again to die of his own wounds, or worse, at the end of a hangman's noose. He had tried to save her life and nearly given his own in doing so. No. She knew she would not leave him to die alone.

Holt and Kierin staggered out onto the darkened street, moving slowly and trying to stay in the sheltering shadows of the poplars. His weight was almost too much for her small frame, but she stubbornly refused to give in to her need to rest. He leaned more heavily against her with each passing moment.

From behind them, the sound of hoofbeats on the dusty street stopped Kierin's heart cold. She was afraid to look; afraid to move. Her heart sank along with her hopes of escape. Talbot's men had found them.

Beside her she heard Holt's soft curse as he turned to look back at the shadowed rider who slid from his horse and hurried toward them. Fear like she'd never known welled in her throat, choking back the knot of tears that formed there. It couldn't end like this! Not after all they'd already been through!

Kierin raised the gun with a wobbly hand and pointed it at the approaching man.

"Don't come any closer!" she warned in a low, shaky voice. "I'll shoot!"

Chapter Three

"Miss Kierin?"

The deep, gentle voice came from the shadowy figure approaching them. Hope surged through Kierin. That voice . . . she knew it.

"It's all right, ma'am," the man told her, moonlight finally touching his craggy features. "It's me . . . Scudder Brown." Kierin didn't know whether to laugh or cry, for the urge to do both was equally strong. Trembling with relief, she lowered the gun.

"Mr. Brown!" Her words came out with a rush of air. "Thank God, it's you! I was sure you were one of Talbot's men."

Brown dropped the reins of his two horses and caught Holt as he slumped toward Kierin. She staggered when Holt's weight was lifted from her. The blacksmith slung Holt easily over his beefy shoulders.

"But — why? Why would you risk coming back?" she asked as Brown pulled her down an alleyway beside the Mercantile, out of sight from the street.

"I don't reckon I could'a lived with myself if I hadn't come back for the two of ya. There's some things a man has to do so's he can wake up and live with himself in the mornin'," Brown explained simply. "Where's Talbot?"

Kierin swallowed the lump that formed in her throat at the memory. "He's dead, I think."

"You *think?*"

43

"There wasn't time to be certain. We left him in your shop."

Brown nodded. "Let's get out of here. Can you sit a horse? This one here is your friend's." He patted the neck of the Appaloosa stallion.

"Yes. I'm a good rider," she answered truthfully. She quickly explained about the Kelly train and Holt's friend Jacob. "Holt needs a doctor, but it's too dangerous to try to get him to Doc Taylor's."

Brown agreed and shifted Holt's weight across his shoulder. He stripped a rolled blanket from behind his saddle, then tossed it over Holt's naked back.

"I know the wagon. I'll take you there. I just hope your friend is still alive when we get there."

Brown's words sent a chill through her, though she knew there was every chance he was right. Holt's color had worsened and he was shivering uncontrollably. If only they could make it to the wagon, maybe there was a chance.

"You're gonna have to ride with him, ma'am. We'll make better time that way."

The blacksmith slid the semiconscious man onto one of the horses, propping him up until Kierin had mounted behind him. She wrapped one arm around Holt's chest, tightening the blanket around him, then grabbed the reins with the other hand. Brown mounted his own horse and spurred him forward. Kierin did the same, and though she kept a watchful eye on the street behind them, no one followed.

In minutes, they reached the sheltering cover of the tall cottonwoods that lined the banks of the sprawling Missouri River. Holt's head fell against her shoulder as he slipped in and out of consciousness. His soft moans told her the jostling ride was causing him a good deal of pain, but there was no help for it. They would have to move fast to escape the ever-widening arc of Talbot's men searching the town for them.

The April moon hung high in the cloud-swept sky

by the time they reached the wagon train encampment, little more than a mile from town. The canvas-topped wagons sprouted like giant mushrooms in the darkness along the lush banks of the great river. Kierin's arms ached with her effort to hold the tall man upright.

The encampment was quiet. Only the snapping of an occasional burning twig in a campfire or the gentle lapping of the water intruded the night's stillness. Brown slowed his horse as they approached a wagon standing slightly off by itself, parked beneath a huge cottonwood. Brown nodded toward it.

"This here is the wagon," he told her quietly, dismounting. He helped Kierin down and then balanced Holt across his shoulder again.

A knot of fear twisted her stomach as she approached the wagon. How would she ever explain what had happened to Holt? What if he died? Would Jacob blame her? Certainly, he could blame her no less than she already did herself. Though logic told her that she could not have changed what happened tonight, she could not help feeling partly responsible for Holt's condition. Now two men were dead and Holt was barely alive — all because of some ridiculous bet over her. Kierin swallowed hard and straightened her shoulders with resolve. There was nothing to be done for it now. All she could do was try to get Holt help as quickly as possible and put the consequences out of her mind.

She stepped out of the shadows and lifted her fist to rap on the side of the planked wagon, but the sound of a cocking gun stilled her movement. She froze with her hand still poised above the wood. In the darkness beneath the wagon, she caught the glint of steel and knew the barrel of a gun was pointed directly at her. Behind that she could see the whites of a man's eyes, but no more. She opened her mouth to speak, but her traitorous voice failed her.

"What you be wantin' here 'round my wagon?" came

a deep voice from the shadows.

"A—are you . . . Jacob?"

"That be the name my mama give me. Who's axin'?"

She glanced back nervously at Brown. "My name is Kierin McKendry. It's about your friend, Mr. Holt."

"Clay?" A burly black man rolled out from beneath the wagon, his face etched with concern.

"Yes, he—he's been hurt—"

"What! Where is he?" Jacob demanded. He followed her gaze back to Brown and rushed to Holt's side. Laying a hand almost tenderly on Holt's back, he lifted the blanket to get a better look at him. Then, he wheeled angrily on Brown and Kierin.

"What *happened* to him?"

Brown spoke first. "He was knifed by a low-down snake named John Talbot back in Independence. The girl 'n' me was only tryin' to help him. But your friend here ain't got the time for us to worry about who did what to who. He's lost a lot of blood and he's losin' more as we're sittin' here jawin'." Brown's gaze was steady on the black man and Jacob's anger seemed to dissipate with the blacksmith's explanation.

"Sorry," Jacob replied, running his fingers over his short-cropped hair. "It's just—can you help me git him into the wagon? I can tend him better in there."

Jacob lowered the tailgate on the wagon and swept back the canvas flap. Together, the men lifted Holt onto the thin straw-filled mattress that filled one side of the narrow wagon's dark interior. Jacob struck a match and lit the oil lamp which hung from one of the hickory bows supporting the canvas cover. A soft, yellow light filled the enclosure.

As the men worked over Holt, Kierin stood outside and tried to collect her thoughts. A powerful tremor coursed through her body, not from the cold but from the tumultuous emotions that battled within her. For reasons that she couldn't explain—even to herself—she wanted Holt to live. He was a complete stranger to

46

her; a gambler who considered her his property! By rights, she should hate him.

But she didn't.

Tonight they had depended on each other for their very lives and Holt had nearly lost his — and still might — protecting her. Kierin let out a long sigh. It had been a long time since she'd allowed herself to care about anyone. A long time since anyone had cared about her.

Her head hurt and she was weary beyond words. Tears welled behind her tired burning eyes, but she refused to cry, refused herself the relief tears would bring her. Instead she reached for the pile of neatly stacked kindling and began to build up the banked fire. After it sputtered back to life, she fetched an iron pot that hung nearby and filled it with water from the large barrel lashed to the side of the wagon. She set it over the fire to heat, knowing that Jacob would have need of it soon.

The blaze was warm and soothing and she stared at the flames, willing them to heat the water quickly. For the first time she looked at her hands. They were covered with blood, as was the front of the shirt Holt had given her to wear.

She stood stiffly and walked to the river's edge. The narrow path twined through hedges of wild grapes, heavy with the promise of a summer harvest. Moonlight spilled across the water, mixing eerily with the tendrils of fog that lay like a winter's breath upon the river. Kierin bent and washed her hands and face in the frigid water. Shivering, she hurried back up the path to the campsite.

Brown met her at the fire when she returned.

"How is he?" she asked.

"Still unconscious. But that feller's got the constitution of an ox. If anybody can pull through somethin' like this, I reckon it'll be him. You known him long?"

Kierin was struck by the irony of his question.

Long? She'd only known the man for a few hours, but right now it felt more like years.

"No. Not long."

Scudder nodded, scooting his eyes away from hers. "Jacob asked me to get some water boilin' but I see you already got that taken care of."

"Yes, it's nearly hot enough," she replied, trying to fill the uncomfortable silence.

"Well, I reckon I better get a'goin', ma'am. You be all right here?" he asked.

"Yes, I—I'll be fine," she told him with more conviction than she felt. "Mr. Brown, I want you to know how much I—that is, we both appreciate your help. If you hadn't come back—"

"Like I said before, it was somethin' I had to do."

"But what if there's trouble? I mean, it all happened in your shop . . ."

"If Talbot's dead, like ya say, there ain't gonna be no more trouble than I can handle. If not . . . well, Talbot'll never have ta know it was me that helped you." Brown looked thoughtful for a moment and then continued. "And the law'll never hear about you two from me. Be sure on *that* account. I reckon my family an' me may just pull up stakes one of these days an' head west. Independence is gettin' a might too crowded fer my tastes anyway. I reckon there'd be a call fer a good smithy out West, too."

Kierin smiled at him. "I'm sure there'll be a place for you wherever you choose to go, Mr. Brown. You're a good man."

Brown lowered his gaze from hers and twirled the brim of his hat in his big hands.

"Good luck to ya, ma'am."

"And you, Mr. Brown."

He gathered the reins of his sorrel gelding and swung easily up into the saddle. Brown turned one last time and nodded to Kierin before nudging his horse into an easy lope in the direction of town.

Kierin watched until she could see him no longer and then turned back to the fire. Steam rose from the hanging pot. Wrapping her hand in the long sleeve of Holt's buckskin shirt she lifted the pot from its hook.

Jacob was bent over Holt, pressing a white cloth against his shoulder, when she stepped up into the wagon. She set the pot down and moved closer. In the light, Holt looked deathly pale and still. His dark curls clung damply to his face.

"Git me that bag over on top of that crate," Jacob commanded suddenly, startling her.

She reached for the squat leather bag and handed it to Jacob. Still holding the cloth to Holt's shoulder, Jacob reached into the bag with his free hand and pulled a small corked vial from it.

"Mix some o' this with that warm water. Mix it up good—like you was makin' soup," he ordered.

Kierin looked at the vial curiously. "What is it?"

"Marigold powder. Stops the bleedin' an' holds down infection."

"I never heard of that before."

Ignoring her comment, he handed her a small metal bowl, and focused on Holt's wound again. Kierin poured some water into the bowl and added the powder, mixing it with her hands; the pungent odor filled the wagon's interior. When the mixture reached a consistency that seemed to please Jacob, she handed him the bowl.

Jacob quickly tore another piece of sheeting and dipped it into the marigold decoction. He wrung it out slightly and laid it gently upon the wound, pressing it firmly.

"That ought'a do it," he mumbled to himself. He laid a work-roughened hand on Clay's forehead. His ebony skin made a startling contrast to Holt's whiteness.

"Come on, Clay boy . . ." he urged. "You gots to fight this, now. Don't you go givin' up on me here. We gots a long way to go."

49

There was a softness to his voice that touched Kierin. She looked away, feeling suddenly like an intruder on the two friends.

Jacob reached for his bag again, and pulled out a pouch filled with dried herbs. "If he wakes up, give him some tea out'a these rosehips. Keep the pressure on that bleedin' 'til it stops and change that dressin' every half hour or so 'til I gets back."

"Back?" she stammered in bewilderment, "Where are you going?" *Surely he didn't intend to leave her alone with Holt!*

"Clay left a trail of blood I reckon a blind man could follow. I jist aim to backtrack a little sos they don't trail him back to this wagon."

"Oh, of course . . ." A wave of apprehension swept through her. What if it was too late for that already? "Be careful, Jacob."

He nodded. Unfolding a spare blanket, he wrapped it around her shoulders. "I'm much obliged to you for bringin' Clay back," he said with grudging gentleness, a hint of a smile touching his full lips. Then he turned and left the wagon.

First one, then two hours passed as Kierin watched over Holt, changing the poultice on his shoulder and keeping cool cloths on his forehead. He rested fitfully. He seemed to be fighting the fever that now warmed his body and she forced sips of tea down him when he roused enough to drink it. Kierin held the blankets on him when he fought to kick them off and added her own when he shivered uncontrollably under the pile that covered him.

All the while her concern for Jacob's safety grew. Had he been caught covering their trail? What could be keeping him so long? She looked out the half-opened flap. It was close to dawn and the sky was turning a deep, cobalt blue. The subtle change of light filtered through the white canvas of the wagon top. She pressed a hand against the ache in the small of her back; a symptom of the weariness that vibrated throughout her body.

She returned to Holt and mechanically renewed the poultice, wringing it out in the warm water. His fever was worse, she realized, when her hand brushed his hot skin.

"Come on, Holt," she urged him, "don't give up. You can *fight* this."

Automatically, she wrung out another cool cloth for his head. She was startled when his long, slender fingers closed around her wrist, stopping her. She found him staring at her. His sky blue eyes were glazed and overly bright with fever and he frowned as if trying to focus on her face.

"Amanda?" The word was little more than a whisper.

"What?" Kierin leaned closer to his face.

Holt's fingers tightened around her wrist. "Sorry . . . so sorry . . . forgive me."

"Shh-h, she soothed, "don't try to talk."

"No . . . I didn't know, Amanda . . . God! If I'd known . . ."

"No, it's all right . . . Mr. Holt." Kierin tried to make her voice calm, but his growing restlessness alarmed her. Clearly, he had mistaken her for someone named Amanda in his delirium. For the first time, it occurred to her that he might be married. Could Amanda be his wife? Lover? Whoever she was, it was plain Holt cared very deeply for her.

He struggled to sit up, but she held him down firmly.

"I'll *kill* them . . ." he said suddenly, his voice a harsh, rasping whisper. "Bastards . . . my gun."

His cold, hollow tone sent a chill through her.

"Mr. Holt—Clay, please," Kierin begged, "stay . . . still." She struggled to keep him flat, but his wound

51

began to bleed again.

"Oh, no . . ." she sighed, and wrung out another cloth in the marigold solution. She pressed it against him and Holt began to shiver again.

"C-cold . . . I'm . . . so cold. Hold me, Mandy . . . the snow is so c-cold."

"Shh-hh." Kierin brushed his dark brown hair back from his forehead. She could see no other remedy. There were no more blankets to pile on him and still he trembled. Quickly, she lifted the covers and slid in beside him, nestling against the damp heat of his body. She kept one hand on the poultice, draping her arm across his bare muscled chest, and leaned her head tentatively against his other shoulder.

With his good arm, Holt drew her closer still, tightening his grip on her almost fiercely. Minutes passed—her body entwined intimately with his—and his shivering began to subside. Slowly, gratefully, she felt his breathing become deep and regular with sleep.

How long she lay like that, listening to the lulling sound of his breathing—afraid to move for fear of waking him—she didn't know. Her sense of time was framed solely by the rhythmic rise and fall of Holt's chest beneath her arm. Her body molded to the lean, male contours of his, fitting together like two pieces of a puzzle. She watched his face in the lamp glow. The fine even features were shadowed by a dark growth of stubble and his long, dark lashes lay still in dreamless sleep. Her breathing became attuned to his and soon, despite her best efforts to stay awake, her eyes drifted shut. She had never felt so exhausted as she did now. Sleep took her gently, but insistently, as the morning sun lit the eastern horizon.

The rich deep scent of coffee found its way beyond the haze of sleep which had encompassed Kierin and brought her slowly to an unwilling consciousness. Her uncooperative eyes refused to open as if she were lost somewhere, deep in a dream from which she had no desire to escape. She curled toward the warmth beside her, her arm still comfortably draped across Holt's chest. Her fingers tightened around the almost dry poultice lying against his wounded shoulder.

Kierin's eyes flew open. She sat bolt upright on the straw mattress, letting the bloodstained cloth slip from her fingers. The oil lamp had somehow gone out and she blinked in the half-light, trying to focus on the man beside her. A wave of panic swept her as she realized she had fallen asleep, leaving him completely unattended. Silently, she cursed her carelessness and leaned close to the still man to check his breathing. Relief flooded through her when she found that he was breathing with the slow, easy rhythm of sleep.

She touched his brow lightly and found that the searing fever had subsided somewhat. Kierin sank back on her heels with a sigh of relief. She dipped the cloth in the now cooled marigold concoction and wrung it out slightly. As she placed it gently on his shoulder, her gaze traveled unbidden down the expanse of his darkly furred chest. A disturbing ripple of excitement stirred within her at the memory of lying beside him, caught in his embrace.

Silly! she scolded herself. *He was delirious. He thought you were someone else.* Someone, she reminded herself, named Amanda who was probably his *wife*. Did gamblers like him keep wives somewhere? she wondered. Holt hadn't struck her as the kind of man to settle down with any one woman. Kierin shook her head. What *did* she really know about this man?

Her fingers reached out and brushed a silken strand of dark brown hair from his forehead. She only knew that she cared for him in a way she couldn't yet fully understand. A bond had formed between them in that transient moment between life and death. Her mind burned with the memory of the pain he had unwit-

53

tingly shared with her last night and the warmth their bodies had imparted to each other.

All of that didn't matter now, Kierin sighed, pulling the quilts up under Holt's chin. All that mattered was that he survive. She eased herself up off the mattress, careful not to disturb him. Wrapping a blanket around her shoulders, she stepped out of the wagon into the dazzlingly bright morning sun.

"Mornin', ma'am," Jacob called to her from the campfire as casually as if he said those words to her every day. With a cigarette dangling from his mouth, he was lifting a coffeepot from the fire. He pointed a cup in her direction. "Coffee?"

"Jacob!" she cried, "I was so worried about you. Where did you go? I thought you'd be back hours ago! I was afraid they had—"

I'm fine," he told her, pouring her a cup anyway. "It just took me a might longer than I expected to do what needed doin', is all."

"Thank God, you're all right! Did anyone see you?"

"I don't reckon I was see'd or we'da heard from them by now," he drawled. He handed her the coffee. "I been back since nigh on sunup.

"Sunup—" Kierin's faced flushed with the knowledge that Jacob must have seen her sleeping with Holt. "Oh, I . . . I'm sorry I fell asleep. Holt was so cold. It was the only thing I could think of to warm him . . . and I—"

Jacob waved his hand as if to dismiss her apology. "Probably the best medicine you could 'a give him. Sometimes a man . . ." He hesitated and looked back at the fire before continuing. "Sometimes a man gots ta have a reason ta fight his way back from somethin' like that. Someone ta hold him gentle—like a woman can. I 'spect that done as much for him as that powder I give ya." Jacob looked at Kierin sideways and smiled.

There was no malice in it. No judgment. Kierin met his smile and returned it. She found that she liked Ja-

54

cob. But she couldn't let him think there was more between her and Holt than there really was. She
wrapped her hands around the cup and took a sip. A
small sip. *Strong* hardly described the taste. "Jacob," she
began uneasily, "it's not what you think between Holt
and me."

Jacob nodded his head, seemingly not surprised by
that bit of information. "Brown told me what happened. I seen the papers in Holt's pouch. And a good-
size stake to boot."

"If Holt had only known what kind of a man John
Talbot was, he wouldn't have stayed in that game to
bid on my papers and none of this would have happened."

"Don't you go blamin' yo'self for that," Jacob told her
sternly. "Clay's the kinda man likes a challenge. Fact is,
sometime he ain't as careful as he oughta be. That boy
gots a wild streak in him." Jacob took a drag on his
cigarette, then looked up at the wagon. "A good challenge draws him like a honeybee to a flower. Got hisself
stung this time though. Stung good."

Kierin watched the pain flit across the black man's
features before he reined in his emotions. It was obvious that he cared deeply about the man in the wagon.
She wondered what type of man earned that kind of
loyalty from his friends.

Jacob's voice broke into her thoughts.

"This yours?" He handed her the tapestry bag she
had dropped behind Brown's shop.

"Yes! Oh, Jacob. You took a big risk going back
there. Did you find out anything?"

"Only that there's a posse formin' ta look for the two
of you."

"A posse," Kierin breathed.

"Me an' Clay planned to pull out with the wagons
this mornin'. I reckon as how we ain't got no choice
but to stick with that."

"This morning?" A new kind of fear sliced through

55

her. "I'm not sure Holt can take the jolting of a ride like that. It could kill him."

Jacob stirred the fire with a stick. "It be risky. But Clay's a strong man. I don't see how we can wait."

"His fever *is* down a bit this morning," she said, hoping to convince herself that Jacob's words were true.

"I know, I checked him when I got back from town."

"Oh, yes . . . of course," she murmured dumbly. "I guess I'd better go back and look in on him." Kierin rose, picked up her bag, and started to walk toward the wagon. Jacob's worried voice stopped her.

"Uh-oh."

"What is it?" she asked, turning back to him.

"Pull that blanket around you an' let me do the talkin'." He discarded his cigarette and crunched it beneath his boot. Jacob turned to the small weasel-faced man who had stepped up to their campfire.

"Reverend Beaker." Jacob's greeting was cool and blunt.

The man nodded curtly, but refused to actually acknowledge the black man with words.

Kierin could almost feel the thickness in the air between the two men. Jacob's face was a study in control. The weasel—dressed entirely in black, save his white clerical collar—peered at Kierin through narrowed eyes, his mouth set in a sour expression. She flushed deeply under his scrutiny and she looked back at Jacob.

"Somethin' I can do for you this mornin', Reverend?" Jacob asked in a tight voice.

Beaker gestured at Kierin several times with his bony finger as if he were pointing at a piece of dust that had been missed in a cleaning.

"You and Holt know the rules on my train about . . . camp followers." The words slid out of his mouth with distaste. "This is a family train, boy. We don't tolerate . . . single women.

A muscle twitched in Jacob's jaw, though he managed to keep an even expression on his face.

"I don't reckon Mr. Holt would take too kindly to you callin' his new bride a camp-follower, Reverend Beaker," Jacob said with quiet control.

Kierin's eyes flew to Jacob in disbelief! Did he say *bride?* She tried to breathe normally, knowing Beaker was watching her reaction.

Beaker pursed his thin lips. "Are you telling me that Holt has taken a wife since I saw him yesterday?"

A smile curved Jacob's lips. "Love works in strange ways, Reverend. You ought'a know that. Besides, I reckon he couldn't face my cookin' all the way to Oregon. Mrs. Clay Holt, meet the Reverend Josiah Beaker, the spiritual leader of this here wagon train."

Kierin clutched the blankets more tightly around her and nodded to Beaker, who stood looking down his thin nose at her. Lifting her chin, she tried her best to look self-assured.

"Mrs. Holt," he said finally, touching the brim of his fat-crowned black hat. "I beg your pardon for the misunderstanding, ma'am." The apology came grudgingly. "Where is your husband this morning, by the way? I have yet to see him. I should offer him my congratulations."

"He's sleepin', Reverend," Jacob said. "You know how it is with newlyweds. A little too much celebratin' last night." Jacob winked at Kierin.

"I see. . . . Well, I'll be on my way then," Beaker said. "We'll be pulling out within the hour. Perhaps Mr. Holt will see his way clear to join us by then. Good day, ma'am." Beaker turned and strode out of the campsite.

The sound of voices penetrated Holt's senses slowly, as if the darkness that surrounded him was wrapped in thick cotton, unwinding layer by layer until the muffled sound became the familiar deep voice he recognized as Jacob's. The other voice had a higher pitch to it and he knew it was a woman's, but for the life of him he couldn't remember where he'd heard it before. She sounded downright irritated though.

His eyes ground open as if they'd had a fistful of sand thrown into them. He blinked at the sunlight streaming through the canvas cover and wondered briefly what he was doing lying in the wagon in the middle of the day.

His first movement answered all of his questions and then some. A blinding pain shot up his arm and through his chest and he squeezed his eyes shut tightly. When the throbbing subsided, the memory of last night came flooding back to him.

He fixed his stare on the dust motes churning through the morning sunlight filtering into the wagon and tried to remember how it had all turned out—how he had gotten here. But that part of it flitted teasingly on the edge of his memory, out of reach. The image of the woman—her delicately drawn face and her green eyes, the color of a stormy sea and the way they had flashed at him, first in anger, then in fear—leapt to his mind.

In truth, he hadn't expected either one of them to get out of that situation alive. But somehow they had. The pain in his shoulder confirmed that for him. He lay quietly, recovering his senses one by one.

There was the smell of Jacob's coffee brewing on the fire. It was always strong enough to knock a man on his ass, he mused, but it was infinitely better than his own, so he never complained. Mingled with the coffee smell was the scent of something else that touched off a growling deep in the pit of his stomach. It was broth, whose beefy aroma drifted up tantalizingly into his senses—as readily as did the memories of the woman who had once cooked it for him.

That thought caused him nearly as much pain as his shoulder did and he struggled to put it out of his mind.

But the memory of holding Amanda last night came unbidden. He could still almost feel her warmth against him. He knew he must have dreamed it, but it had seemed oddly real. Holt clenched the fingers on his good hand into a fist in frustration. His brain must be as muddled as the rest of him, he reasoned. Either that or he had finally gone over the edge. Amanda was dead. Dead along with their unborn child. Dead for years.

His grief over their deaths had consumed much of the past three years, but he thought he had gotten beyond that; left it behind him. Why then did he still imagine her touch or her voice encouraging him to fight against the death he would have once welcomed?

A new, hot wave of pain stabbed at his shoulder and he sighed deeply, allowing the pain to take him back to the dark, comfortable place where he had been. To the place without memories.

He woke again as the wagon tilted with the weight of someone's step, though he had no way of knowing if his eyes had been closed moments or hours. The girl moved into his line of vision, and Holt watched her through half-closed eyes, taking in the tiredness of her movements; the worn expression on her face when she leaned over him. Her eyes opened wide as she realized he was conscious.

"Mr. Holt! You're awake! I—I'm so glad."

She seemed truly pleased. He opened his mouth to try to respond, but it was as if someone had stuffed it full of feather ticking and he could not manage more than a muffled grunt.

"Don't try to talk," Kierin admonished. "I've brought you some water. Do you think you can manage some?"

His eyes followed her as she reached over to feel his forehead. The smooth leather of his familiar buckskin shirt molded to the soft curves of her breasts as she pressed her hand to him. Her touch—gentle and blessedly cool—left him wishing she would not move her

59

hand. But in the end she did, seemingly satisfied.

Holt nodded toward the water and tried to ease himself up on his good elbow, but a crashing pain set him flat again.

"Here, let me help you." She lifted his head ever so carefully and he fought down the wave of nausea that swept over him as he gulped down the water greedily.

Finally, she pulled the cup from his lips. "Not too much. You have to take it slowly at first."

Cautiously, he licked his parched lips with a wet tongue and found that he had gained use of it again.

"What . . . happened back there?"

Kierin lowered her eyes and picked at some invisible thread on his quilt. "I killed John Talbot."

"Y-you what!" he rasped, astonished. But somewhere in the back of his mind, the dim memory of what she was telling him rang true.

"At least I think I did," she added. "He would have killed you."

Clay rolled his eyes. *Sweet Jesus! What had he dragged this girl into?* He cursed his impulsiveness once again, sure now that she would have been better off working for Talbot than wanted for murder.

"He . . . Talbot didn't . . . hurt you, did he?" he asked finally.

"No," she answered simply, understanding his unspoken question.

"How did you get me back here? I don't remember any of it. Did anyone see us?"

"Only Scudder Brown. He came back to help us. He was the one who brought you here. I'm sure I'd never have gotten you back by myself."

I'll be damned, Holt thought. He never expected that of Brown, considering his family and all.

"Jacob says there's a posse forming in town. We'll have to pull out with the train this morning. Do you think you're up to it?"

"I'm up to it," he answered, though he didn't feel up

to it at all. "Where's Jacob?"

"He's hitching up the team."

"Get me my gun," he told her.

"Y-your gun? But why?"

Clay let out a long sigh, too tired to make long explanations.

"Just *do* it," he told her irritably. At the surprised flush that leapt to her cheeks, he added more gently, "I feel naked without it."

Kierin slid the heavy revolver from its place atop a box at the foot of the wagon.

"Here—if it makes you feel better," she said, holding the weighty gun out to him with a steady, even hand.

"Thanks." He slid the gun under the quilts next to him then sank back, tilting his head toward his injured shoulder in a vain effort to ease the burning ache there.

"You should eat something," she told him. "I made some broth."

He nodded, feeling suddenly tired beyond words. Kierin slid several sips of the broth between his lips before he sank back into the mattress, unable to take more. He stiffened as she changed the dressing on his shoulder. His limbs felt weighted down; flushed with an abnormal, achy heat. The gentle touch of her hands on him sparked a fleeting memory of something more and his eyes fastened, with a fevered man's fascination, on the sweet curve of her breasts again. No matter that he was in no position to act on the urges those breasts inspired, or that her sweet scent drifted down to him— some heady combination of summer wind and the honeysuckle bushes he'd hidden under as a boy. His eyes feasted on her like a starving man clinging to his last crumb of food, then slid shut with the weight of uninvited sleep.

Kierin sat watching Holt long after he had fallen asleep. That he was a strong man, Kierin had no doubt, for she had only to remember the feel of his powerful body against her own to remind her of that. But looking at him now, vulnerable and unguarded with sleep, she realized that his ability to survive an injury like this required another kind of strength, one which ran deeper than what she could see

His desperate plea for Amanda's forgiveness still haunted her and she wondered what personal demons he battled from his past. Whatever had happened between Holt and this woman remained a powerful force in his life. Powerful enough, she wondered, to give him the will to live? Although her usual level-headed reason told her that it was none of her affair, she found herself curious about the woman he'd called for. What was she like? Was she beautiful? Did they love each other?

Wearily, Kierin dropped her face into her hands and rubbed her eyes. She was right the first time. It *was* none of her affair. It was best for all concerned if she kept it that way.

Kierin quickly changed into a rumpled green calico dress from her bag, and put Holt's buckskin shirt aside until she could wash the blood from it. She looked at her red dress one last time before stuffing it into a corner. With a disgusted frown, she decided to dispose of it as soon as she could.

Outside the wagon, she found Jacob backing a pair of yoked oxen up to the wagon.

"How is he?" Jacob asked from his place between the two animals.

"Better. He woke up and took some broth. That's a good sign, I think."

Jacob nodded silently with a relieved grin on his face and ran the back of his hand across his sweaty brow.

"Don't 'spect I could'a done any better by him myself. I'm obliged to you for stayin' with him last night — not runnin' off when ya had the chance."

Strangely, Kierin realized that the thought of leaving Holt alone last night had been the farthest thing from her mind. In fact, it hadn't even occurred to her. Jacob's words simply served to remind her of the harsh reality of her situation—that Holt owned her. Once they left Independence, she faced the prospect of years of indenture to him. That fact was now hopelessly entangled with the ragged emotions that warred within her—the ones she had never meant to let loose, the ones that had allowed her to come to care for him.

Kierin laid a hand on the oxen's smooth meaty haunch and bent to thread the trace through the yoke as Jacob was doing on the other side. She kept her gaze directed down at her work, but could feel Jacob's eyes on her. Finally, she looked up to find that he had stopped his task and leaned one arm across the animal's rump. With the other, he was wiping the back of his neck with a bandanna. But his eyes were no longer on her. They were fixed on some distant point behind her and he straightened suddenly as if he'd been burned.

"Oh Lord," he murmured, climbing up behind the team onto the wagon's tongue. He reached into the jockey box below the benched wooden seat and pulled out his rifle.

Her heart jumped to her throat. "What is it, Jacob? What's wrong?"

Jacob's fluid motion never stopped as he jumped down from the wagon, catching her arm and propelling her to the back of the wagon before she could protest.

"Posse," was the only word he uttered before he pushed her toward the tailgate and left her there.

Kierin heard the thundering of hoofbeats before she spotted the cloud of dust kicked up by their horses as the sheriff and his posse galloped up to the train's encampment.

Chapter Four

Kierin's heartbeat echoed the thunderous rumble of hoofbeats as the posse approached the lead wagon. She'd recognized the sheriff and at least two of Talbot's men before she had scrambled up into the safety of Holt's wagon. She cautiously lifted the canvas cover and peeked out as the cloud of dust settled around the riders, whose horses pranced nervously at the abrupt stop.

From her hiding place, Kierin watched as a tall, strongly built man stepped out from behind the team of oxen at the lead wagon and spoke to the sheriff. The tall man swept his hat casually from his head, swiped at his brow with the back of his sleeve, and replaced the hat again, covering his sun-bleached hair. His stance gave him an air of authority and Kierin guessed he must be the train's leader. A chill ran through her as she waited for him to turn and point in her direction, knowing full well the sheriff had secured Holt's name from Talbot's men.

Seconds ticked by. The ebb and flow of air through her lungs was heedlessly forgotten as she clutched the smooth planked side of the wagon. Her heart pounded raggedly against the wall of her chest and her pulse surged in her ears. The men were too far away for Kierin to hear the words that passed between them, but after interminable moments, the blond man finally shook his head, turned, and pointed downriver.

The sheriff yanked his mount around and galloped away from the encampment with the others. The clods of dirt kicked up from beneath the hooves of the posse's horses pelted the standing wagons and scattered the curious onlookers who had ventured from their own work to see what had caused the stir. Had she looked away, Kierin might have missed the glance the blond man stole back at Holt's wagon before ducking back between the harnessed team of oxen.

Kierin sagged against the crate she was leaning on, confused and shaken by what she'd just witnessed. Why had that man sent the posse off in another direction when he had most certainly known Holt was part of this train? The man's look toward their wagon had confirmed that for her. His complicity in hiding Holt was surely enough to jeopardize his position with the train if he were found out. It didn't make sense.

Beside her, Kierin heard the click of a gun's hammer being carefully uncocked and she spun around to see Holt, his face pale and tight, slide the revolver beneath the covers. Though she hadn't known he was awake, it didn't surprise her to learn he'd had been prepared to fight even when they both knew the absurd odds they would have faced. His azure eyes glittered again with fever as he stared at her.

"Are they gone?"

She nodded. "The man in the lead wagon sent them downriver, toward Westport."

"Blond guy? Tall?"

"That's him," she answered. "Who is he and why did he send them away? He looked directly at your wagon after the posse rode off. He must know who you are."

Holt's eyes slid shut again. "He knows."

Before she could get any more out of him, he was asleep. With an impatient sigh, she tugged the quilts up under Holt's chin.

His persistent fever worried her. Unchecked, it

alone could kill him and the ride ahead of them could only serve to worsen it.

Kierin wrung out a wet cloth and sponged Holt's damp face. She pulled aside the covers, and trailed the cloth down his neck and across the broad expanse of his chest. How odd, she thought, that in such a short time, she had become so intimate with a strange man's body. In fact, she knew *it* far better than she knew the man himself. The well-muscled contours and the firm leanness of his limbs spoke of a life lived hard and unsparingly.

What made a man become so reckless with his own life, she wondered, as Jacob's words suddenly echoed in her ears. *Sometimes, Clay ain't as careful as he oughta be. That boy's got a wild streak in him.*

What Holt had done last night *was* reckless and, no doubt, impulsive. It was probably only one in a long string of gambles that he had entered into on a whim, she realized, swallowing back the anger that rose at the thought. But this time Holt's gamble had cost *her* dearly; she had been forced to kill a man and now had a posse scouring the countryside for her. And though she fought to save his life, Holt would *own* hers if he lived.

She glanced down at the sleeping man, her hands clenched into fists. "You'll live, Mr. Holt. You're probably too stubborn to die. Besides, I won't let you. God knows, I owe you that much. But I swear you won't hold me to those papers. No man ever will again."

Outside the wagon, she heard the preparations for leaving being made. Children laughed and squealed with excitement and oxen bellowed in complaint as they were hitched to wagons. She knew the train would move out soon—leaving behind the only life she had ever known. She didn't regret leaving any of it; there was no one left here for her.

Kierin tugged the blankets up around Holt, pushing aside her thoughts. She would go and find Jacob.

Maybe he could answer the questions that had nagged her since the posse had ridden away.

"His name's Kelly. Jim Kelly," Jacob told her. "Beaker hired him on as wagonmaster 'cause he be the best one for the job. Been criss-crossin' this here country since 'forty-five, an' knows more 'bout the land 'tween here an California than most folks ever will." Jacob bent again to finish greasing the wheel's axle with the tar and tallow mixture from his bucket.

Kierin's brows drew together in a puzzled frown. "But why would he send the posse away?" she pressed.

Jacob reached toward an awkward spot under the wagon. "Clay an' Jim have know'd each other since Churubusco, in 'forty-seven."

"Churubusco? You mean the war with Mexico?" She didn't try to hide the surprise in her voice.

"Yes'm. I reckon as how Clay's saved Jim's skin once or twice over the years. It was Jim asked Clay an' me to hook up with this train full o' greenhorns. Don't reckon as how Clay would'a done it for nobody else."

"Is Mr. Holt working for Kelly then?"

Jacob appeared thoughtful for a moment. "No, but with all the Indian troubles brewin' in the Plains tribes, I guess Jim figured it made sense to travel with somebody who knows his way around a hostile campfire."

"And Holt does?"

Jacob swung the grease bucket back up on its hook beneath the wagon. "I 'spect he does at that, ma'am."

It seemed the more she found out about Clay Holt, the more the mystery around him deepened. She was beginning to see that he was a complex man — much more than simply the gambler she had thought him to be at first.

Kierin had lived long enough on the edge of the frontier to guess what Jacob had left unsaid about Jim

67

Kelly's actions this morning. In the wilderness, lives often depended on the unquestioning trust of one's friends. Kelly hadn't doubted Holt's innocence when the posse came for him and that spoke of the respect he had for the man and Kelly's unflagging belief in Holt's integrity.

She thought back to Holt's reaction when she had told him that Kelly had sent the posse away. She remembered he hadn't been surprised by it at all. It was no less than he expected from Kelly. She guessed if the situation were reversed, he would have done the same.

The shimmering mist which had earlier blanketed the Missouri River lifted, giving way to the spectacle of a perfect spring morning as the train lumbered out of Independence. More than fifty wagons of emigrants made up this westward-bound caravan. A fair share of wagons were aimed at the thinning California gold fields, she guessed, but from the OREGON OR BUST banners that draped many of the vehicles, most seemed headed there. The Willamette Valley, nestled in the heart of the Oregon territory, held some of the most fertile farmland known to man. It was a place rich not only in soil, but in timber and game too, she had heard. The promise it held drew Easterners like steel to a magnet. They were headed there, Jacob told her, to a place called Willamette Falls, which had recently been given the grander name of Oregon City.

"Pull up those oxen!" shouted a voice from ahead of them, interrupting her thoughts. "Keep 'em tight back there!"

Kierin saw Jim Kelly galloping up and down the lines of the strung-out train, shouting orders at the inexperienced wagoners. He cracked a bullwhip near the ear of a particularly stubborn ox whose lagging pace was holding up the whole line of wagons. From her perch on the bench seat beside Jacob, Kierin couldn't help admiring the way Kelly handled himself on the piebald gelding. He looked as if he'd been born to ride a horse and the two moved fluidly together across the trampled meadow that ran alongside the Missouri. After tightening the ranks of the train, Kelly rode up alongside their wagon and nodded a greeting to her.

Silvery-blond hair peeked out from under the brim of his worn leather hat. The battered brim shaded the crinkling crow's feet around his blue-gray eyes. She guessed his age to be around thirty-two or three, though his deeply tanned skin aged his boyish features slightly.

"Jacob?" Jim Kelly turned a serious look on the black man. "I suppose you know what that posse was all about this morning?"

"Obliged to you for sendin' them on their way, Jim," Jacob answered. "Clay had a mite o' trouble back there. Got hisself cut up pretty bad." Jacob hitched a thumb toward the interior of the wagon.

Kelly's glance shot to the canvas opening. "You mean, he's in the wagon? I hadn't seen him and I thought . . . well, damn! How is he?"

"Middlin'. Jim, this here is Kierin—" He stopped there, hesitating between truth and the lie they'd concocted. "Clay's wife."

Jim Kelly reined in his horse with a jerk and fell behind a step before nudging his horse back up even with the wagon. His lips were parted in surprise as he eyed Kierin with renewed interest, his gaze flicking down the length of her in unconscious appraisal.

"I'll be damned—" he muttered under his breath, then chagrined by his rudeness, Kelly reddened. "Beg your pardon ma'am. It . . . uh . . . it just caught me by surprise is all. I'm real pleased to make your acquaintance."

Kierin felt her heated blush travel all the way up to her ears. Nodding politely to him, she couldn't help wondering why Jacob had chosen to tell Holt's good friend the lie they used. And even more curious was the fact that Kelly didn't mention Holt's "other wife." Surely he must have known about her, as long as the two have been friends. Kierin sighed, and decided to save those questions for later. A safer route, she decided, was to steer the conversation completely away from the subject of her "marriage" to Holt.

"I thank you for what you did this morning, Mr. Kelly. I don't want to think about what would have happened if you hadn't helped us."

Kelly seemed unable to draw his gaze from her. "It's Jim, ma'am." He smiled with a flash of even white teeth. "And just what did happen back there? The sheriff did make mention of murder."

"Seems the two of 'em ran into a fella named Talbot back at the Independence who didn't cotton to Clay beatin' him at cards," Jacob told him.

A hard look crossed Kelly's face. He shook his head, and turned questioning eyes on Jacob. "It's not like Clay to let himself get caught off guard like that."

Kierin's mind flew to the moment when Holt had offered her his shirt last night, dropping his guard momentarily. She looked off into the distant horizon, glad to have something other than Kelly's questioning gaze to focus on.

Why should *she* feel guilty? After all, Holt had dragged *her* into this, not the other way around. So why couldn't she shake the miserable feeling that she was responsible for the condition of the man lying in the back of the wagon?

"Done is done," Jacob concluded with eloquent simplicity. "Ain't no help for it now but the healin'." Jacob flicked his whip near the ears of the lead pair of oxen and added, "That, an' avoidin' these blasted ruts!"

Kierin glanced anxiously back into the dim interior of the wagon as it lurched over a deep furrow. "It's not going to do him any good to be traveling like this. I'd better go back and check on him." She stood and balanced precariously in the rocking wagon.

Kelly touched the brim of his hat again as his horse danced sideways, anxious to move at a faster pace. "We got a late start today. That'll cut our traveling time down some. You just do what you can for him. I'll take care of the rest."

"Thank you, Mr. Ke—" She stopped herself. "Jim."

He turned a grateful smile on her. "It's a pure pleasure, ma'am. If I know Clay, that pretty face of yours will be all the inspiration he needs to get him up and on his feet again." Kelly nudged his horse and sprinted away up the line, leaving her blushing in the wake of his unexpected compliment.

Jacob eyed her with a sideways grin and then clucked to the team and flicked the long bullwhip above their backs. "H'yaw!" he called, with a grin tugging at the corners of his mouth.

Kierin pretended not to notice and climbed ungracefully over the benched seat, then over the crated supplies in the front part of the wagon. It was fortunate that their wagon was not loaded down with heavy furniture and heirlooms which weighed down many of the pioneers' conveyances. Holt and Jacob had packed only the necessities: primarily staples such as flour, salt pork, coffee, and dried beans and fruit.

Earlier, she had also discovered eggs—ingeniously suspended in the flour sacks—molasses for sweetening, tinned milk, along with sugar, rice, and salt. There were other crates she had yet to explore, but they seemed well equipped for the long journey ahead of them.

Kierin climbed over the last gunnysack of flour and knelt down next to Holt. The fever was still stubbornly there and she turned to wring out the cloth in the tepid water. When she turned back to him, she found his blue eyes watching her.

"How are you feeling?" she asked, laying the cloth across his brow.

"You really need to ask?" His voice was roughened by sleep and fever.

"No," she answered, "I'm just trying to keep you awake long enough to take some water. It'll help bring that fever down."

His gaze traveled across the fine, ivory planes of her face to the long wisps of auburn hair that had escaped the knot at the back of her head. He watched her fill a tin cup with fresh water, wondering if the coppery highlights in her hair were only a trick of lighting in the dim wagon. Without thinking, he reached up and caught a strand, rolling it gently between his fingers, savoring its feel at last. Kierin jumped back at his unexpected touch, pulling her hair from his grasp.

Holt swallowed, his arm poised in midair for a moment before he let it drop back tiredly to the blanket. Kierin sat on her heels, inches from his reach, yet very aware of the safety in that span of space.

"I've been wanting to do that since the first time I saw you," he told her as they sat sharing the stuffy, sun-warmed air. "I didn't . . . mean to scare you."

"You didn't. Just . . . startled me, is all."

"Ah-h . . ." he murmured as if he didn't believe her. "You have beautiful hair, you know."

Her fingers leapt unconsciously to her hair, trying to smooth the unruly wisps into submission. "You must be feeling better than you look," she said, gracing him with a shy smile.

His breath caught at that smile; the first he had seen from her. It changed her face entirely and revealed a small, appealing dimple in her left cheek. A shiver ran through him and he couldn't be sure if it was the fever or her nearness that made him tremble.

"Actually . . . I doubt that." His weak grin belied the burning ache which seemed to have settled permanently in the upper left side of his body. He shifted his weight on the pallet, but comfort was a useless pursuit. With a whispered curse, Holt turned finally onto his good side, facing her. He closed his eyes, tired from even that small effort. It was a defeating weakness that assaulted his usually strong body. Invasively hot, it compelled him to sleep. The sound of her voice called him back from that alluring threshold.

"Drink this before you fall asleep again," she insisted, sliding a cool hand beneath his head and guiding the cup to his mouth. Holt complied and drank greedily, heedless of the tiny rivulets from the overflow tracing a path down his chin. She released him and he sank back, swiping carelessly at the moisture with the back of his hand.

The blatant maleness of his gesture unsettled her and dampness sprung to the palms of her hands. She turned away from him, busying herself with some unnecessary tidying.

"Kierin." His hoarse voice cut through the steady creak and groan of the wagon's movement. She turned to find him watching her again. A crooked smile curved his lips.

"That's your name, isn't it? Kierin." He slurred the word slightly as he said it, rolling it off his tongue as if tasting the sound of it.

"Yes," she answered, though for a moment, she forgot that he had asked her a question.

"Must be the fever. . . . I've been lying here trying to remember what it was. But . . . I kept thinking . . . it was Princess. Isn't that odd?"

She stiffened ever so slightly at the name. "I think it's odd you would call me that, considering—"

"What?" he interrupted with a wary grin. "That my knight-in-shining-armor act was a bit tarnished?"

"Oh, is *that* what it was?" Her voice tinged with sarcasm. "I thought it was a simple wager."

Her cutting reply silenced him as surely as if she'd struck him. He'd deserved that, he knew, but somehow he hadn't been prepared to hear her say the words. He closed his eyes and took a deep, strained breath.

"Not a simple wager," he answered finally. A muscle jumped in the hardened set of his jaw. "Not simple at all."

The wagon lurched just then, jarring Clay on the thin pallet. He gasped from the sudden stab of pain and clutched his injured shoulder. A low groan escaped his lips and he swallowed convulsively, fighting for control over the nausea that rippled through him.

"Christ Almighty!" The hissing oath was torn from between his clenched teeth with a rush of air, like steam rising off a hot griddle. Pain, hot and overpowering, shot through his chest. It was through that haze that he felt Kierin lay her hand tentatively, soothingly on the tight corded muscles of his arm. Waves of heat mingled with the softness of her touch, making it difficult to discern one from the other.

When the pain eased finally, he opened his eyes. She sat watching him, her expression a curious mixture of fear and concern. He wondered then why she had saved him. Why she hadn't just left him back on the floor of the smith shop and taken her chance at freedom. He wouldn't have blamed her if she had. God knew, he had tempted fate often enough to deserve such an end — even welcome it. He had considered his own death many times in the past, embracing the idea as a drowning man finally would the cold water as it swept over him.

But as he looked up at her now, he was unreasonably glad she hadn't left him there . . . glad for her touch on his arm; glad he was still alive enough to feel it.

"I think I saw some laudanum in Jacob's medicine kit." She moved to turn from him but he caught her hand before it could completely leave his arm.

"No." The word held an urgency which, even to his own ears, had a pleading, desperate quality. He'd seen dozens of men become hopelessly addicted to the drug after Churubusco and he'd sworn never to use it. Still,

74

he knew it had as much to do with his fear of that mind-deadening drug as with the fear of being alone right now. Bereft of her touch.

Chagrined, he let go of her arm as she turned a surprised look his way. His hand fell back against his shoulder. *What the hell's the matter with you, Holt?* he chided himself silently, rolling his head away from her questioning stare. *Get a grip, man!* warned the inner voice that had kept him aloof, protected all these years. Aloof, protected, and safely alone.

"My . . . brain is already muddled enough with this damn fever." He muttered the half-truth, disgusted not only with his traitorous body, but with the need he knew she had heard in his voice. The need for company. Comfort. The word itself had lost its meaning over the last few years. It was strange, he thought, pondering it. Until now, he hadn't felt the lack. Not for years. Aside from the decidedly carnal touches he'd received from whores he'd bedded, no woman since Amanda had touched him the way Kierin just had. Freely — without strings.

The sound of her voice brought his gaze back to her face and he realized his mind had been wandering.

". . . traveling's not going to get any smoother today, Mr. Holt," she was saying. "If Jacob doesn't have any, I'm sure someone . . ."

Her voice drifted away from him again as he wiped at the sweat that trickled into his eyes. It was damned hard to concentrate on what she was saying when it took so much effort simply to lie still. His stomach rebelled at the thought of another five hours in this wagon. As if to prove Kierin's argument, the wagon rumbled across another series of small ruts.

". . . and you *need* to sleep," she concluded, with a frown that puckered her eyebrows. Her voice had taken on a no-nonsense edge and held the hint of a challenge.

He fixed a bleary gaze on her which he hoped would

make it perfectly clear these were his last words on the subject.

"No laudanum."

"All right, Mr. Holt," she said, backing down. "If that's the way you want it. But I—"

"It is."

"Are you sure you're all right then?"

He nodded, eyes closed, not at all sure that he was. Holt pressed back against the pallet, fighting the wave of nausea that swept over him again. *Oh God, don't let me be sick now!* he prayed fervently to the same God he had earlier blasphemed. His hand moved from his shoulder to his gut, in an effort to contain the roiling there. Maybe if he could just lie perfectly still for a moment—

"Oh! Mr. Holt," Kierin gasped, drawing his startled glance. "You're bleeding again!"

A quick look at his shoulder revealed a bright red stain of blood seeping through the bandage there. The wagon rocked like a ship at sea with the steady gait of the oxen. Not jarringly—just with a sickening persistence. He pushed her hand away as she started to inspect the bandage.

"I'm afraid that's not the worst of it," he told her weakly, suddenly certain his prayers would not be answered. "Get me a bucket—I'm gonna be sick."

Kierin sat frozen for a moment, her lips drawn apart in surprise. She blinked—her huge green eyes finally registering what her mind had been slow to grasp.

"Oh! Oh, dear!" She flew into action, searching the barrel behind her for an appropriate container.

Holt groaned and she snatched a pot noisily from beneath a muffin form. She slid it in front of him just as he lurched forward and retched, emptying the contents of his stomach into the receptacle. All the while, he felt the soothing touch of her hand touching the back of his neck. He repeated the process several more times before he slumped back, exhausted, to the bed.

He lay panting, with one arm flung over his eyes, feeling as if the wagon had just rolled over him. He heard her slosh some water into the pot and spill the contents out the back of the wagon.

"The nausea will pass," she told him, wiping a cool damp cloth over his face. "You lost quite a lot of blood last night, you know. That's why you're so weak. Are . . . are you feeling any better now?"

Holt just groaned in return. He had never felt so god-awful in his life. His shoulder throbbed and he could feel the warmth of his own blood as it trickled down past the bandage toward his armpit.

Without asking his permission this time, Kierin started to work on his shoulder, easing the bandage off and pressing a clean cloth to the jagged, oozing wound. He gritted his teeth until she finished, glad for even that distraction from the wretched feeling in the pit of his stomach.

Kierin sat back on her heels, eyeing her handiwork.

"There," she said. "I've got the bleeding stopped but what you really need is a bed that stays still long enough to give that shoulder a chance to heal. When we stop for the nooning, I'll make you some camomile tea from Jacob's herb bag to settle your stomach."

"I'm sorry you had to see that," Holt told her. Hell. It laid a man's pride nearly flat to have a woman hold his head while he puked his guts out. He couldn't remember ever having another woman do that for him since his mother, when he was a boy.

"It's nothing," Kierin told him gently, dismissing his apology with a tug on the quilts beneath his arms. "You need to rest now."

As if what had just happened was the most natural thing in the world for a woman like her, he thought. One minute slicing him up with her tongue and the next soothing him with a touch.

"I'll stay with you until you fall asleep," she contin-

77

ued without pause as he watched her, heavy-lidded.

Sleep? Yes, sleep, he agreed mutely, unable to find cause to argue against it any longer. *Get your mind off her, Holt. It's just the fever making something out of nothing.* But as his eyes slid shut, his last thought was of the feel of her fingers on his neck. Touching him.

"Clay?"

The familiar male voice broke into that part of Holt's consciousness which hovered somewhere between sleep and wakefulness. The sudden stilling of the wagon's motion had roused him sometime before. Becalmed and adrift, he resisted the voice and lay savoring the quiet with his eyes closed.

There was a woman with him in his half-dream. She hovered over him silhouetted by the halo of sunlight behind her. Her gentle fingers brushed his face, beckoning him to come with her. Her loose, flowing hair glimmered like spun fire in the sun as she backed away from him. He rose to follow still unable to make out her features. Reaching out, he caught her by the waist and drew her to him. She laughed and pressed herself tantalizingly against his taut body. Cupping the siren's breast in the palm of his hand, Clay drew her closer still. She was soft and pliant beneath his touch, offering herself to him wordlessly. Her sweet, familiar scent pulsed through him, filling his senses.

"Amanda?" he whispered against her silken hair, already knowing — as one does in the certainty of dreams — that it wasn't her.

"Clay, are you awake?"

Wrenched again from his dream by the persistent voice, Clay grudgingly opened his eyes and blinked in the half-light. He bit back the curse he was about to hurl at the source of his irritation when he realized who it was.

"I am *now*," Clay answered in a voice roughened with sleep.

Jim Kelly smiled crookedly at him in the dim light.

A swatch of blond hair fell across Kelly's brow and he swept it back with his hand.

"Sorry, Clay . . . Jacob told me you'd be awake. He said you'd had a rough time of it this morning. How are you doing?"

"Better—I think," Clay answered groggily, still disturbed by his dream. "Where are we?"

"Near the junction of the Kansas," Kelly replied. "We've covered about eight miles since this morning. We're pulled up for the nooning, but the train'll be moving out again soon."

"No sign of the posse?"

Kelly shook his head with a laugh. "Hell no. They're probably halfway to the Arkansas border by now."

"Thanks for that, Jim," Clay said. "I owe you one."

"Yeah. Don't worry, I'll collect. You just concentrate on getting better," Kelly told him. "You feel like talking about it now?"

"The truth?" Clay asked. "No."

"All right," Kelly conceded, accepting the delay. "But we *will* talk."

Clay took a deep breath and nodded to his old friend. He'd have a *lot* of explaining to do, but right now he was too tired. He knew his mind was too fuzzy to get all the facts straight. He hadn't even straightened them out for himself yet. Sleep beckoned him again as Kelly rose and stood in the cramped wagon.

"By the way, Clay," Kelly added before turning to leave, "you can tell me it's none of my business, but if she were my wife, I'd be thinking about putting down roots, raising a family. Not dragging her into the middle of some gunfight. She deserves better than that, you lucky son of a bitch."

Kelly swung out of the wagon, leaving Clay staring after him, in slack-jawed bewilderment. What the hell was he talking about? *Wife? Roots?* Had he missed something in that conversation, Clay wondered, or had Jim Kelly lost his marbles?

79

Clay frowned as his thoughts turned of their own accord to Kierin. Smudged and tired as she had looked earlier, her face still captured his imagination—delicate, wary, but somehow achingly vulnerable. He closed his eyes, trying to shut her out of his heart, to keep her at a safe distance. But in the recesses of his mind as he fell back asleep, her image mingled unsettlingly with the red-headed temptress of his dreams.

Chapter Five

"Darn it all," Kierin muttered when the evening breeze snuffed out the flame of yet another sulphur-tipped match. She tossed the cursed thing into the neatly arranged firewood and pulled a fourth match from the oilcloth pouch. She wet her index finger and stuck it up in the air to test the fickle current of air that seemed to move wherever she did. Angling her body against the breeze once more, she struck another match. The flame flickered threateningly, but caught at last on a bit of dry tinder beneath her carefully stacked cook fire.

She blew on her tiny fire and waved her hand furiously. She knew she must look ridiculous — on her hands and knees, breathing life into an obstinate tongue of flame which seemed to have a contrary mind of its own. She was covered with dirt smudges and her hair had escaped all its confines save a pin or two. But frankly, she was too tired to care.

The train had traveled some fifteen miles before Jim Kelly had called for the wagons to circle up for the night. Except when she had been in the wagon checking on Holt's condition, she had covered most of that distance on foot. In fact, only the small children were allowed to ride in the wagons for any amount of time. To save the ox teams the added strain of unnecessary weight, the rest of the people walked. And walked.

Kierin sat back on her bare heels and winced. Her

feet were blistered and sore. She had slipped her shoes off at the river and soaked her feet in the cool water for a few minutes, which had helped some. But now, they were too tender to even consider putting her shoes back on. She tucked her toes under the hem of her dress and decided to ask Jacob for some salve to put on them when he got back from unharnessing the team.

Kierin gathered up a handful of tinder and fed it — one stick at a time — to the growing fire. The breeze worked *for* her now that the flame had caught. She turned in time to see Jacob and Jim Kelly walk into the campsite together. In Jacob's hands were two buckets of fresh water from the river.

An appreciative smile tipped the corners of Jacob's mouth as he set the buckets down. "Ain't as easy as it looks, is it?" He gestured at the fire.

Kierin laughed softly. "I don't think I've ever tackled anything more frustrating in my life."

"Clay awake?" Jim asked.

"He was asleep last time I checked. I don't know how, but he managed to sleep most of the day."

"Best thing for him," Jacob said, setting the black iron tripod over the fire for her. "I got's to go settle the stock in for the night. Be back directly."

"Jim, won't you stay for supper?" Kierin asked before he turned to go. "I can't guarantee how it will turn out, but you're welcome to share it with us."

A smile crossed the wagonmaster's face. "I doubt you could do to a stew what I do to a stew, Mrs. Holt. It's not pretty. I'd be obliged to share supper with you. I've got to see to the wagons before it gets dark, but I'll be back by the time it's ready, ma'am."

Kierin smiled. "See you then."

Jacob and Jim headed out toward the center of the circled wagons while Kierin fixed the supper. She hummed as she set to work hanging the pot over the fire and plopped chunks of carrots and potatoes from their store of fresh vegetables into the soup. She added a hunk of salted beef and some leftover navy beans from their noon dinner and stirred it up with seasonings she had found packed in among the dry goods. After she had mixed the biscuits and settled them in the Dutch oven over the glowing coals, Kierin sat back and savored the bubbling aroma of the meal, her mouth watering in anticipation. The day's walk not only had given her blisters, she thought, touching her tender heels, but had stirred up a growling appetite.

Kierin stoked the fire with more kindling and was lifting the pot lid to stir the stew when she heard the creak of the wagon springs. With her back to the wagon, she assumed that Jacob had returned from tending the animals.

"Dinner will be ready soon, Jacob," she told him without turning.

"Am I invited?" asked a voice that was definitely not Jacob's.

Kierin spun around to see Holt standing—or rather, swaying—beside the wagon, looking very pale and weak, but wearing the lopsided grin she remembered from the night before. He had pulled on a clean pair of Levi's and a light blue denim shirt. Unbuttoned, it only partially concealed his bandaged shoulder and did little to hide the muscular physique she had been trying to put out of her mind all day.

"Mr. Holt! What are you doing up? You should be in—" The scolding died on her lips when she saw him trying to blink back the dizziness that threatened to topple him. He listed perilously to one side, clutching the wagon for support. She jumped to her feet and caught him around the waist before he could fall. Her face pressed unavoidably against his broad chest and she felt the ragged pounding of his heartbeat against her ear. The flush of fever was still on him, but he was considerably cooler than he'd been earlier.

Holt leaned on her, silently cursing his weakness. The fever had claimed more from him than he had imagined. He dragged a hand across his face to clear the black spots from his vision. He felt Kierin push him back against the wagon, and hold him there, bracing both palms firmly against his chest.

"Are you all right?" she asked, searching his eyes.

All right? Hell no, Holt thought, looking into the depths of her sea green eyes as he tried to sweep the dizziness from his brain. He swallowed hard. *Eyes like that could make a man forget himself,* he mused in silent warning. He was reminded of all the times in the past twenty-four hours she'd saved his neck—all the times he'd wondered if he had merely conjured up what he had glimpsed again in her eyes just now.

"Mr. Holt?"

Holt blinked and released his hold on her shoulder.

"I'm okay, now," he answered, rubbing a hand across his stubbled face. "I . . . just need to get my legs under me again is all. It's a wonder what a day in bed can do to your stamina."

"Stamina? Well, for heaven's sake, you nearly *died* last night!"

"Well, thanks to you, I didn't."

"And if you have anything to say about it, you'll try your best to undo everything I did. Is that it?" Kierin glared stubbornly at him, arms akimbo.

"If you really must know," he answered, not sure quite how to put the issue to her delicately, "with all the liquids you've been pumping into me for the past twenty-four hours, I felt the sudden urge to pay a visit to the bushes down by the river."

Abashed, Kierin's face suffused with color and she mouthed the word "oh," but no sound accompanied it. She cleared her throat and tried again.

"I'm—I'm sorry I didn't think of that. But still, you shouldn't go alone. I'll go get Jacob to help y—"

"Don't bother him," Holt told her, pushing off from the wagon. "I can manage. I'd be obliged, though, if you'd fix me a plate of whatever you're cooking there, when I get back. It smells good."

Kierin softened at the compliment, and suppressed the urge to warn him about the possibility of scorched stew and biscuits with soggy centers. She nodded with a tentative smile and turned to the fire to give the pot a stir.

"And by the way," he added, turning once more before he headed to the river, "you have lovely toes."

Kierin shot a mortified glance at her bare feet and then toward his retreating back. She curled her toes into the soft dirt.

She narrowed her eyes and let out an indignant huff. "He might have had the decency to pretend not to notice," she said under her breath. Turning back to the bubbling kettle, she stirred the stew with more vigor than was wise. The fire hissed and spat as the hot liquid slopped over the sides of the blackened pot.

She replaced the lid and sat down on a nearby rock to tug on her shoes. And oh, how it hurt. Her heels were twice as sore now that they'd had a few minutes of freedom. She was limping back to the fire when Jacob sauntered back to the campsite, depositing his hat and damp leather gloves on the rim of a wheel.

"Somethin' smells good."

He rolled up his sleeves, poured bucketful of water into a basin, and splashed his face with the cool liquid. "Ah-h," he sighed, swiping the water from his face with one hand. "Been wantin' to do that all day. Supper almost ready, ma'am?"

Ma'am. Now there's a word I'll never hear leaving Clay Holt's lips. She gave Jacob a grateful smile. "It's ready, I think. Just sit down, Jacob. I'll serve some up for you."

Kierin wrapped a towel around her hand and lifted the three-legged Dutch oven from the coals. The biscuits, much to her consternation, were indeed scorched on the bottom and, in weight, more closely resembled the stones she'd been kicking all day than the biscuits she used to cook for her family. Kierin sighed and dropped one onto Jacob's plate with a clunk. Luckily for them all, the stew had fared better.

Jacob sank down near the fire with the plate Kierin had fixed for him. The firelight gleamed off his face, highlighting his strong features: a broad, handsome face; skin the color of rich coffee; black hair, already peppered with gray, though she guessed he was not much over thirty.

It was his arms that drew her gaze away from his face. Long, sweeping scars, which she judged could only have come from a lash, snaked around his forearms and beyond. She stared at them, horrified, unable to pull her gaze away.

Jacob looked up from his food and followed her gaze. He sighed and set his plate on the rock in front of him, then rolled his shirtsleeves down to his wrists.

Heat stole to her cheeks. "Forgive me, Jacob. I didn't mean to stare."

"It's natural," he told her kindly. "Most folks do. That's why I keep 'em covered most times so's nobody gots to look at 'em. They ain't a pretty sight and that's a plain fact. Ain't for no lady like you to be seein'."

Kierin released a breath. "It's been a while since someone has called me that."

"What?"

"A lady."

Jacob shook his head and retrieved his plate. "You's as much a lady as I come across in quite a while, ma'am. Quite a while indeed." He smiled at her across the firelight and the tension between them melted.

"Jacob," Kierin began, not sure how to continue, "can I ask you something?"

Jacob nodded, waiting.

"Do you know who Amanda is?"

A deep furrow appeared between Jacob's eyes as he considered her question. "Yes'm. What about her?"

She had a thousand questions she wanted to ask. Why isn't she here with Clay? Does he love her and why does she haunt his dreams? But Kierin couldn't bring herself to ask him any of those questions. Instead she asked, "Is she Clay's wife?"

Jacob rubbed at his nose evasively. "Clay talk to you about her?"

"Not exactly," she admitted. "When he was delirious with fever, he called out her name. He thought I was her."

"I think it be best if Clay be the one tells you about her."

"Jacob," Kierin sighed, "please."

Jacob lowered his head and stared into the flickering amber fire. "Clay don't talk about it to nobody. Hardly even me. It happened a long time ago."

"I see." She had no choice but to respect the loyalty Jacob felt toward Clay. "I'm sorry. I didn't mean to pry."

"How is he, anyway?" Jacob asked, deftly changing the subject. "Still asleep?"

"No, you old rooster," Holt answered as he appeared out of the darkness, startling them both. "I'm up. I think I've seen my fair share of that canvas roof, don't you?"

Jacob rose and clasped Holt's hand. "Clay." The emotion behind the word spoke volumes. "For a while there, I—I was worried you was fixin' to weasel your way out'a this trip."

Holt eased himself down to the fire next to Kierin, cradling his left arm with his good one. "You ought to know I'm too ornery to let a man like John Talbot be the end of me."

Jacob chuckled and shook his head. "Yeah, I 'spect I should'a know'd that. From what I hear, Talbot got the short end of the stick in that fight anyway."

"I guess I had some help there," he admitted, glancing up at Kierin as she handed him a plate of food.

"How's the shoulder?" Jacob asked.

"It's felt better, but it'll heal." Holt took a mouthful of

food just as the Reverend Beaker and his wife and daughter strolled into the campsite. Clay paused in mid-chew and gave Jacob a heavenward roll of his eyes.

"Oh, now you see, Josiah," the plump woman on Beaker's arm exclaimed as they neared the fire, "we're interrupting their supper. Mr. Holt, I told Josiah we should wait 'til later to come over to meet your new wife."

Holt nearly choked on his food and shot a disbelieving look at Kierin. "My . . . my—"

"My, my," Kierin finished, standing and offering the woman her hand. "How good it is to meet you, Mrs. Beaker. Of course, it's no inconvenience at all. I'm sure that's what my *husband* was trying to say." Kierin aimed a warning look at Holt. He glared back at her.

"Well, mercy! It's so good to have another young woman on the train my daughter's age . . ." The Reverend's wife spoke rapidly, waving a delicate, lace-edged hanky to emphasize her words. Her voice burbled on, but Holt didn't catch the words. He was too busy trying to grasp the bombshell she had just dropped in his lap.

He narrowed his eyes and cast a suspicious frown at Jacob, who merely shrugged and tossed him back a halfhearted yet hopeful smile. Holt rose, set his plate down deliberately on the rock beside him, and crossed to stand next to Kierin.

Clara Beaker was too involved with introductions to notice the dark clouds that had gathered behind Clay Holt's sky blue eyes, but Kierin could scarcely have missed them. She knew she should have told him about this sooner, but he had been too ill to broach the subject. Now, any opportunity she might have had to break it to him gently had just vanished. She cast a fearful, sideways glance at him and was not surprised to see that he was furious.

". . . and this is my daughter, Rachael," Clara effused, introducing the beautiful, willowy blonde standing beside her. "Rachael, I'd like you to meet Mrs. Holt."

"Please, call me Kierin," Kierin told the younger woman.

Rachael Beaker smiled back at Kierin with an all-too-practiced smile—one that sent a cold shiver up Kierin's spine.

"Kierin," Rachael repeated, fluttering her eyelashes becomingly in Holt's direction. "What a quaint little name. Really, Clay, you should have given us all some warning. My father could have done a proper ceremony for you and your wife *here,* instead of some secret affair back in Independence."

Clara Beaker fluttered her hanky around her face and flushed a bright pink at her daughter's bold words. "Rachael dear," she said, taking a conciliatory tone, "I'm sure Mr. and Mrs. Holt had a perfectly lovely ceremony in—"

"Now wait just a minute," Holt blurted hotly, "she's not—" he began, but the words died on his lips. Kierin's desperate, imploring look stopped him just short of saying that she wasn't his wife, that he hadn't the foggiest idea what was going on here. It took only that fraction of a second for his denial to flounder and become lost in the green depths of her eyes.

At his outburst, all heads turned in Clay's direction. "She's not . . . what, Mr. Holt?" Josiah Beaker asked, puzzled.

Clay hesitated, feeling slightly sick. God Almighty! Nothing in his life had gone smoothly since he'd met this blasted woman! Now she had him hog-tied and married, for Christ's sake! And as he opened his mouth to speak, he had the sinking feeling that it was about to get worse. "Well . . . I just meant to say—she's . . . uh . . . not upset that she missed a big wedding. Are you, *darlin'?*" Holt slipped his good arm around Kierin's shoulder and pulled her close to him.

Two can play this game, he thought as he splayed his fingers beneath her arm and brushed her firm breast with his thumb. It gave him a measure of satisfaction to feel her sharp intake of breath at his touch and see the confused expression in her eyes.

"N-no," Kierin answered finally, forcing her gaze back to the Beakers. "No, not at all." She patted Holt's arm with mock affection, shrugging his arm discreetly off her shoulder. "Of course, he *did* promise me a proper ceremony once we reach the West . . . i-in a church . . ." she added for good measure.

Holt had to restrain the urge to roll his eyes.

"Oh," Clara cried happily, pressing the hanky to her cheek, "Two weddings! Isn't that just the most romantic thing you've ever heard?"

"Well, *I* think so . . ." Jacob mumbled at Holt's shoulder, smiling broadly, then shrinking back at Holt's withering stare.

"Yes, Clay," Rachael crooned, "who *knew* you were such a romantic?"

Kierin felt a curious rush of jealousy at the look that Holt exchanged with Rachael and her familiar use of his given name. Unconsciously, she moved closer to Holt.

"Indeed," Holt muttered, "who knew?"

"Well, dear," Clara Beaker said to Kierin, "it's a lucky woman who marries a man with a little romance in him." She smiled up wistfully at her husband and patted the coarse black sleeve of his clerical jacket. "Come along, Josiah. Let's leave these two lovebirds to their supper. We've kept them from it long enough."

"You're right, Mother," Josiah Beaker said. He held his hand out to Holt and shook it with bone-jarring vigor. "Mind you, be true to your word, boy, and find a House of God in the West. The Lord blesses those who seek him. Congratulations, Holt," Beaker told him briskly, then clapped Holt hard on his injured shoulder.

Beaker failed to see Holt's reaction as he turned back to his wife, but Kierin didn't. She watched the color drain from Holt's face as he struggled to maintain control over the pain from the unexpected blow. She moved close to him and allowed him to lean on her. *Oh, if only he'd stayed in bed where he belonged! If Beaker discovered that Holt was injured . . .*

"It was so nice to meet you, Mrs. Beaker, Rachael," Kierin said, hurrying them on their way. "We'll see you again soon, I'm sure."

"What else have we in this desolate country but each other for solace and company?" Clara Beaker called over her shoulder. "Good night, my dear!"

"Good night," Kierin answered halfheartedly, her attention already focused on Holt. She steered him toward the wagonbed.

"Are you all right?" she asked when the Beakers were out of sight.

Holt reached out and braced a hand against the smooth, planked wood and leaned into it, closing his eyes. "Yeah," he said curtly, swallowing hard.

"I *told* you, you should have stayed in bed," Kierin scolded gently while she inspected the fresh blood on the bandages. "You're—you're bleeding again."

Holt brushed her hand away angrily. "Leave it. It'll be all right."

"But—"

"I *said* leave it." His voice was brittle, angry.

Jim Kelly strode into the encampment just then, doffing his hat and shaking off the trail dust. "Holt! You're up! Hey, I was just asking your wife about you and she—"

"Christ! You too?" Holt snarled, turning on his old friend, whose mouth dropped open in surprise.

A knot formed in Kierin's throat as she watched Holt push away from the wagon and disappear into the darkness outside the circled camp. She couldn't leave it like this. She had to explain . . . .

91

Kierin turned to Jacob and an astonished Jim Kelly. "Excuse me, will you?" She followed Holt into the darkness. Spotting him stalking to the river, she ran to catch up with him.

"Mr. Holt!" Her call fell on deaf ears. He kept moving toward the water. "Clay, stop—will you? Please, I need to talk to you!"

Chapter Six

Holt turned just as Kierin caught up to him. They nearly collided there, beneath the spreading branches of an ancient elm that stood alone at the edge of the Kansas. She regained her balance, taking great care not to touch him. He pointedly made no effort to help her.

"Just tell me this," Holt demanded, leaning one hand imperiously against the trunk of the giant tree which stood like a sentinel between them. "Was it your bright idea to tell the whole goddamned train we were married—"

"No—I—"

"—and just who the hell do you think you are saying something like that?" he continued, ignoring her denial.

Kierin drew back, stung by the contempt she heard in his voice.

"I—I'll thank you not to swear at me, Mr. Holt," she said at last, swallowing back the knot of tears in her throat.

"I'll say anything I damn well please, *Miss* McKendry," he told her, his blue eyes blazing with anger. "Or should I call you *Mrs.* Holt, since you seem to have so handily arranged our marriage! I should have guessed how skilled you were at deceit, madam, considering your particular field of expertise!"

His words were aimed to wound and they found their mark with deadly accuracy. Her hand slashed out at his face, but he caught her wrist in his viselike grip before she could connect with a stinging slap.

"Ah, the cat has claws!"

Her eyes narrowed with anger. "You're wrong about me, *Mister* Holt."

"Am I?" he scoffed. He pulled her roughly against him and wound his fingers in her hair, forcing her head back so she'd have to look at him. "I don't think so."

Kierin's eyes widened at the dangerous glint in his dark blue ones. A current of fear swept through her like an icy blast of air. He had never given her cause to fear him before, but now she knew it had been foolish to come out here to talk with him alone. Would anyone hear her if she screamed? She tried to twist free of his ironlike grip, but he was too strong.

"Let . . . go of me! Don't you touch me!"

A hard-bitten smile crossed his face. "Don't *touch* you?" he asked incredulously. He pulled her closer still, drawing her tighter against his lean, hard body. "Surely you can't mean to refuse you own *husband?*"

Before she could answer, Holt's mouth slammed down on hers in a punishing kiss. It was a kiss born of anger, not passion, and his lips ground against hers, bruising her and devouring her muffled cry of fear. The harsh stubble on his face burned her tender skin, but he seemed not to notice. With her fists, she pushed against his chest. The heel of one hand slid over his bandaged shoulder and she heard his grunt of pain but it didn't stop him.

She felt herself being pushed back hard against the trunk of the elm behind her. Holt trapped her there with the weight of his own body. His mouth clung possessively to hers, leaving her only for the second it took to change its slashing diagonal attack.

Kierin fought him and struggled for breath, but her

resistance only seemed to make him more insistent. Finally, she forced herself to go limp in his arms, knowing that it was useless to pit herself against his sinewy strength.

She could feel the pounding of his heart against her chest, the hardness of his arousal that pressed against the soft curve of her belly, and finally, she heard the moan that escaped him as his kiss deepened, gentled, changing from fury to need.

In spite of her anger, something deep within her was stirred awake by the fiery touch of his lips on hers. A tremor passed through her when his hand slid up the side of her ribs and closed over her breast, caressing and claiming it at once. She stiffened, hating herself for responding to him, for allowing him to have any effect on her at all.

Kierin gasped when he wrenched his mouth abruptly from hers. She took small comfort in the fact that his breathing was as ragged and uneven as her own. His chiseled face remained only inches from hers, while his steely eyes probed the shadowed depths of hers.

"Are you quite through?" she choked indignantly.

Holt's eyes remained locked with hers and he blew out a harsh breath. "Do you want me to be?"

"You arrogant—there's n-nothing I want more in this world!" Tears of humiliation stung her eyes and she ran the back of her hand angrily across her cheek where his beard had burned her. She could still feel the heat of his kiss on her lips but she would never admit what that kiss had done to her.

He traced a calloused finger down the hollow of her reddened cheek. "Next time, I'll be sure to shave first," he murmured close to her ear in a voice that reflected no regret for what had just happened.

"There won't be a next time if I can help it." She shrank back from his unexpectedly gentle touch.

Holt watched her, a mixture of heated passion and

95

anger still burning in his loins. He was still trying to come to terms with the effect she had just had on him. He *had* meant to hurt her, humiliate her.

But he'd found the sensation of her soft breasts crushed against him—the smooth sweetness of her skin next to his—dangerous in a way that startled him, made him pull away from her before he did something he'd regret. Still, he wouldn't—couldn't—release her.

"I wouldn't bet on that," he replied in answer to her retort. His heated gaze took in the way the silver moonlight played across her cheek. His fingers still bit into the soft flesh of her upper arms.

"Oh, that's right," Kierin returned venomously, "when you're not attacking women, you're betting on them."

Holt laughed. "You alone have that dubious distinction, Princess."

"Stop calling me that!"

"What?"

"Princess. My name is—"

"Kierin . . ." he finished, "Kierin Holt. Which brings me back to my original question."

Kierin looked away from him and worried the edge of her lip. "You'll pardon me if I've forgotten what that was," she lied.

"Shall I prod your memory?" With an ingenuous smile, he fitted his hips suggestively against hers.

"No." She pushed him away with her hand. "That won't be necessary. Please let me go. I can't think when you're standing so close."

My thoughts exactly, Holt mused as she squirmed in his embrace, but he didn't release her.

Her chin came up stubbornly. "I won't say another word until you let me go."

"All right then," he agreed, reluctantly loosening his hold on her. Holt stepped back, ignoring the painful messages his shoulder was sending him. Right now, he wanted answers. And one way or the other, he meant to get them.

Kierin took a deep breath and pressed a hand to her throat to still the pounding of her heart. She eyed him warily, afraid that any moment he might spring again. Her glance darted furtively, searching for an escape route, but she sighed, knowing there was none.

"I'm waiting," he said impatiently.

In an unconscious gesture, she moistened her bruised upper lip with the tip of her tongue. She flinched when Holt straightened, but he made no advance toward her. "I told Jacob it was a bad idea," she began. "I would have—"

"Jacob! What the hell has Jacob got to do with this?" he demanded, clearly miffed that she would try to involve his old friend in this.

"Nothing! And everything. It was my fault for going along with it in the first place."

"Will you stop talking in circles, woman! Look, I may still be a little confused about last night, but I sure as hell would have remembered exchanging 'I do's' with you—" Holt stopped, a worried frown creasing his brow. "I think . . ." The possibility that he might have no memory of exactly that seemed not to have occurred to him until this very moment. "Christ! We're not, are we?"

"Not . . . what?" Kierin asked, wanting suddenly to prolong his obvious discomfort.

Holt took a threatening step closer to her. "Blast it, you know *what*," he nearly shouted. Then, at her stubborn, closed expression, he lowered his voice. "Not *married*, damn it all."

"I asked you before not to swear at me, Mr. Holt." She knew she was pressing her luck, but she found that she couldn't help herself. "If you can't keep a civil tongue—"

Holt's eyes narrowed dangerously and he took another step toward her.

She threw her hands up to stop him. "All right—in

answer to your question—no, we're not married." She lowered her eyes, reluctant to see the relief wash over his expression. Defiantly, she skewered him with a glare of her own. "Did you honestly think I could have done the deed while you were unconscious? Nearly dead? No. It was a lie Jacob was forced to make to Beaker."

"Go on," Clay said impatiently.

"Before the train pulled out of Independence this morning," she continued, "the good Reverend kindly reminded Jacob that he doesn't allow 'camp followers'—I believe those were the words he used—to travel with his faithful flock." Kierin didn't attempt to hide the bitterness in her voice. "So Jacob told him that I . . . that I was your new wife."

Holt raked his long fingers through his thick, dark hair with a groan. "Kierin—"

"No—" she stopped him in a choked half-whisper, "let me finish. Granted, I should have told you earlier, but the time never seemed right. Seeing your anger now, I doubt there would have been a 'right time' to tell you something like this. You were ill and I thought I *would* have time to . . . to break it to you gently. I can see now that I was wrong."

Ignoring his surprising look of protest, she continued, "I assure you, I find this arrangement as disagreeable as you do. I am grateful to Jacob for trying to help me, but I know now that it was . . . a mistake. I should never have gone along with it and I—I'm . . . sorry."

Holt was shaken—not only by her words, but by the pain he saw in her eyes. Hell, he deserved her contempt! He was suddenly angry—not with her, but with himself. He'd been wrong. What had happened hadn't been her fault. And, he admitted, if he'd been in Jacob's place, he would have done exactly the same thing himself. After all, didn't he owe her that much? She had saved his life more than once. And, God knows, she didn't ask to be dragged along on this trip. He'd given her no choice. He had an obligation to protect her now. Didn't he?

He frowned. It was a question that didn't bear repeating, Holt thought as his chest tightened with an old, unfamiliar ache. He already knew the answer.

"No . . . look," he said, shaking his head, "I shouldn't have . . . I mean . . . it took me by surprise is all. I thought . . ." Oh, hell! It didn't matter now *what* he thought. He'd been wrong about her and he couldn't remember ever feeling like such a heel. "I'm grateful to you for saving my neck back there—"

"I don't *need* your gratitude," she shot back in a cool, tempered voice. "In fact, I don't need anything from you except—it would seem—your name." She looked at him finally, her chin tilted up in defiance. "You own my papers, Mr. Holt, and I intend to pay you back in full measure for your wager. But I won't be treated like dirt under your feet, or like your backdoor whore either."

He made no move to stop her as she determinedly sidestepped the sprawling elm trunk and found herself suddenly free from his unwanted closeness.

"Unless you're prepared to take me back to Independence tonight, I'm afraid we'll have to live with this arrangement until others can be made." She hesitated only briefly, taking in his bewildered expression before setting the terms. "Our marriage will be in name only, for the benefit of the others on the train, and when the trip has ended, so will our so-called 'marriage.' Is that agreeable to you?"

He searched her eyes for a moment before answering, knowing that he was responsible for the pain he saw there. "Yes," he answered finally. "But you don't—"

"Fine," she told him abruptly. "It's settled then. Good night, Mr. Holt." She started to go, but turned back to him one last time.

"If your shoulder should need attention again, I'm

sure Jacob will be only too happy to change your dressing. He is, after all, much better versed in medicine than I."

She waited for a moment, as if expecting him to answer, but when he gave her none, she disappeared back in the direction of the wagons.

Holt watched her go and then slammed his good fist into the trunk of the elm in frustration, sending a jolt of pain to his already aching shoulder. He clutched it absently and threw his head back, staring blankly at the mauve-tinged evening sky. He deserved that and worse for what he had just done. He muttered a curse that echoed hollowly on the still night air.

"Hello, Clay," came a woman's voice from behind him.

Clay jerked his head up to see Rachael Beaker strolling toward him.

"Rachael."

The moonlight shimmered off her honey-blond hair. Her walk was seductive, utterly predatory. And he was definitely not in the mood for it tonight.

They'd met on the steamboat between St. Louis and Independence several weeks ago. Rachael had been charming, available, and hungry — a combination especially appealing to him after what he'd just been through in St. Louis. They'd shared a few kisses in darkened corridors, but nothing more. It hadn't taken him long to discover that she wasn't just looking for a man — though, happily that came in the bargain — she was looking for husband material. And that, he would never be.

"What are you doing down here? You should be up near camp."

"Just taking a walk. Why? Aren't I safe here with you. Clay?"

"Perfectly."

She clucked her tongue. "Too bad." She moved closer. "You know, you didn't tell me you had a fiancée waiting for you in Independence."

"Life is full of little surprises," he returned with a shrug. He started up the hill that led back to the train. Rachael followed him.

"Yes, isn't it? I must say, she doesn't look like your type," Rachael observed.

"Really?" he remarked dryly, still walking, "Just what *is* my type?"

She looked up at him through a fringe of lashes. "Me, I suppose," she answered with a small laugh.

"I thought we'd settled that, Rachael," he said, not looking at her.

"And I thought you weren't the marrying type."

He wasn't, damn it, but he couldn't tell her that. "Things change."

"I couldn't help but notice your new wife stalking back to the wagon a few minutes ago," she went on. "She seemed upset. Honeymoon over so soon?"

Clay turned, his expression tight. "That's none of your business, Rachael. Leave it alone."

"It or you?"

"Both."

"I'm worried about you, is all. You don't look well, Clay. I wonder if this marriage agrees with you?"

His shoulder throbbed, but he resisted the urge to clamp a hand over it. His patience was wearing thin. "Look Rachael, I'm married now. Let's just leave it at that, okay? There are plenty of single men on this train who would fall all over themselves to have your attention."

She put a slender hand on his arm. "But I don't want any of them."

Even a week ago, her clinging had put him off. Now it simply angered him. "Leave me alone, Rachael. Leave my wife alone. Understand?" He didn't wait for her reply but turned and quickly put distance between them as he headed back to camp.

Bed was what he really wanted. Sleep. But as he

walked toward camp, he decided he didn't want to face Kierin just yet. Abruptly changing course, he headed toward Jim Kelly's wagon. He had a few misunderstandings to clear up.

Long after the evening winds had scoured the stygian sky free of clouds, and the stars appeared as pinpricks of light on the velvety half-dome above her, Kierin sat in the back of the wagon staring out into the darkness. Sleep proved maddeningly elusive. Holt had not come back since their standoff at the river, but she wouldn't allow herself to worry about him. The insufferable mule could *stay* there for all she cared!

The stars occupied her attention now, and she focused her thoughts on trying to pick out a constellation that always gave her trouble — Aquila, the Eagle, and its brightest star, Altair. Watching the night sky was something she had learned to do long ago when she was troubled. She and her brother, Matthew, would sit for hours on the roof of their small cabin outside of Independence, huddled beneath a blanket, taking turns pointing out the constellations and pouring over astronomy charts by lantern light.

Matthew had been as eager a student of the heavens as Kierin had been when their mother had taught her. In the years Sarah McKendry had been well, she had woven wonderful stories around her love of the stars — mythical tales of heroes and maidens, dragons and swans. They were the bedtime stories Kierin was raised on. She had passed them along to her brother, who embellished the yarns with fanciful escapades of his own. And how he'd loved to embellish.

The memory of him brought a smile to her lips and she hugged her knees tightly to her, missing him immensely.

"A penny for your thoughts," came a deep voice out of the darkness beyond the fire.

Kierin was jolted out of her reverie by Holt's words and she tensed as he crossed to the wagon and rested a hand tiredly on the tailgate. A nasty scrape on the knuckles of his right hand caught her eye, but she bit back the questions it brought to mind.

"I'm afraid they're more precious than a penny," she answered coolly, forcing her gaze back up at the heavens.

Holt traced the path of her look with his own. "I didn't mean to put a price on them," he answered with a wan smile.

"Only on me then?"

Holt slowly shifted his gaze to her. Fatigue embraced his movements like a heavy cloak. "It was just an expression, Kierin. Look, it's late. I need to sleep. Can we talk about this in the morning?"

"I don't suppose there's much point in talking about it at all." Warding off the chill, Kierin pulled the patchwork quilt more tightly around her high-necked cotton nightgown, though she knew it was him and not the night air that sent a shiver through her.

"We *will* talk," he told her, weariness etching deep lines around his mouth, "but not now." Before she could stop him, Holt braced a hand on a hickory bow support and, with an effort, hauled himself up into the dark interior of the wagon.

"Wh-what do you think you're doing?" Kierin stammered. "You don't mean to sleep in here again tonight, do you?"

Holt shot her an indulgent look and laughed. "Damn right I do." He struck a match on the sole of his boot and lit the lantern that hung from the bow. The soft, yellow glow filled the wagon.

"But . . . but I left a stack of blankets for you outside. Jacob said . . . I thought . . . you'd sleep under the wagon."

"Under the wagon?" he echoed incredulously. "When there's a perfectly good bed in here? Now why

103

would I want to do that?" He peeled off his shirt, grimacing as he eased it off his left shoulder.

Kierin's mind raced frantically with alternatives. He *couldn't* sleep here. Or she *wouldn't*. How could she after what had happened between them tonight? The memory of his kiss still burned on her lips.

"Well then, you could . . . share the tent with Jacob." Even as she said it, though, the thought of the two big men sharing the small canvas tent Jacob had pitched outside the wagon seemed ridiculous.

"The hell I will!" Holt growled. "Look, lady, this is *my* wagon, *my* bed. My shoulder hurts, I'm more than a little cranky, and right now, I can barely see straight I'm so tired. So let's quit arguing and go to bed!"

"Fine," she said petulantly, gathering up her oversized quilt. "If you're taking the bed, *I'll* sleep under the wagon." She started to climb out, but his hand stopped her.

"No you won't."

She tried to shake his hand free, but he held her fast.

"What do you mean I —"

"I mean you're sleeping in here with me." His tone was unequivocal.

"I will not!" She yanked the quilt from his steely grasp. To her chagrin, she heard the delicate stitchery tear.

"You *will*, by God, if you want the rest of this train to think we're husband and wife."

His words hit her like a fist and let all the air out of her argument. She gulped back the few chosen words she had readied for him and brushed back a strand of auburn hair that had come loose from the thick braid that fell over her shoulder.

He was right. How would it look for a newlywed couple to sleep apart? At the very least, it would raise unwanted questions, and at worst, she and Holt would become the objects of meddlesome gossip which *could* get her thrown right off the train. She saw then that she really had no choice. No choice at all.

"I hadn't . . . You're right, of course," she admitted reluctantly. "But . . ."

"Right. Subject closed. Give me a hand with my boot, will you?" Perched on a crate, Holt proffered a booted foot for assistance.

Kierin stared at him as if he had just asked her to stand on her head. "You—you mean to disrobe?"

He lowered his foot. "That's what I usually do before I sleep, yes."

"Oh." Kierin swallowed hard. Of course she'd seen him nearly naked when he had been injured, but that—that had been different. He'd been unconscious, for heaven's sake. He was a far cry from that now.

He raised his foot again. "My boot?"

Kierin nodded halfheartedly and tugged at his boot. It came off in her hand and she let it drop to the wagon bed with a thud. It seemed an intimate act—one, she imagined, performed unthinkingly between a husband and wife. Probably as commonplace as a man's fingers unlacing his wife's corset, or hers darning his socks.

But she and Holt weren't married. They were strangers. When she looked up at him, he was leaning back against a crate with his eyes closed and a hand pressed to his bandaged shoulder. The man was practically asleep on his feet, she thought, watching him covertly. Where had he been in the two hours since she'd left him at the river?

"Could you get the other one? Please?" He cracked one blue eye open in supplication.

Silently, she tugged his other boot off as well, setting it aside with its mate. When she had finished, Holt mumbled his thanks and eased himself carefully down onto the narrow mattress, covering himself with the heavy woolen blanket there. A small wave of relief washed over her when she realized he was too tired to doff his pants.

Kierin stood with her arms tightly crossed in front of her, unsure of what to do next. The thought of stretching out next to him, in *their* bed, sent a shiver up her spine. The memory of the kiss by the river and the unexpected sensations it had stirred inside her sent color flooding to her cheeks. What if he tried to kiss her again tonight? Another, equally disturbing thought struck her. What if he didn't?

"Kierin, come and lie down," Holt said, almost as if he had heard her innermost thoughts. "You have my word, I won't touch you." He paused, pulling aside the blanket in silent invitation. "Come on."

She'd have been a liar to deny the ridiculous twinge of disappointment she felt at his pledge, yet she teetered on the reckless edge of accepting his proposal. She *could* sit up all night, make a nest for herself in the corner of the wagon out of harm's reach. But the next logical question reared its ugly head: What about the hundred or more nights that would follow this one?

In the end, exhaustion overcame hesitation, and after turning down the wick on the lamp, she crawled in beside him on the narrow pallet, careful not to touch him. She pulled her side of the blanket around her, clutching it under her chin

"G'night." His voice came softly from the darkness beside her. The word hovered between them like a white flag, fluttering on the still night air.

It would be childish, she reasoned, to snub him now when they lay only inches apart, the heat from his body warming her skin. Childish and pointless. No matter what they thought of each other, they were destined to spend the next few months in close quarters together. It would serve little purpose to let the animosity between them fester and grow.

"Good night," she whispered back, but the steady deep rhythm of his breathing told her that sleep had already claimed him. Kierin sighed, staring up into the blackness above her, and her mind still whirled with unanswered questions.

The man beside her remained as much a mystery as he'd been twenty-four hours ago, except that he'd apparently decided to go along with their farcical marriage. But the question that really nagged at her had less to do with him than with the woman he'd called for in his sleep. The woman named Amanda.

Kierin tried to picture her, conjure up an image of her there in the darkness of the wagon, but she couldn't. To her discredit, she'd had been tempted, so tempted, to throw the woman's name up to Holt earlier in her anger, but some sixth sense had warned her not to. Whoever Amanda was — wife? lover? — she possessed a part of Holt which Kierin doubted anyone else ever would. If Amanda was his wife, what would she think of the charade the two of them were playing out now?

Soon, despite her conviction that she would not sleep a wink all night with him beside her, Kierin fell into a deep, much-needed slumber, which didn't release its hold on her until the sun broke the horizon the next morning.

Chapter Seven

Holt flexed the stiff muscles of his shoulder with a circular motion, wincing as he did it. He was bone-tired. He'd pushed himself hard today. Maybe too hard, he admitted reluctantly, shifting his backside on the tooled leather cradle of his saddle. The high-strung black Appaloosa beneath him pranced nervously, nose to the pungent rain-scented air and Holt patted the stallion's sleek neck to soothe him.

"Easy, Taeva," he murmured. "We'll be home soon." Holt scanned the prairie ahead, hoping to spot the canvas wagon tops over the next rise, but he knew he'd traveled miles farther than he'd intended tracking the herd of buffalo. A weary sigh escaped his lips. After nearly two weeks on the trail spent regaining his strength, Holt had grown impatient with his recovery. It irked him to be less than a hundred percent. He'd grown used to doing everything for himself in the last few years. It didn't sit well with him to be dependent on others. Especially on a woman. And not just any woman, he thought irritably. That one.

Holt's lips quirked up in a half-smile. It wasn't the first time she'd crossed his mind today. Not by a long shot. In fact, Kierin hadn't been far from his thoughts since he'd laid eyes on her in Independence. Not that it mattered. He hadn't gotten so much as a how-do-you-do from her since their little misunderstanding by the river the first night out.

She'd done her part, just as she'd promised him she would. Cooking, washing, even milking the damn cow. She'd been pleasant as you please to Jacob and everyone else on the goddamned train, he thought with a flash of irritation. Everyone but him. To him, she was about as warm as the Missouri River in January.

Holt muttered a curse and stood in the stirrups to lengthen his view of the darkening prairie. *Where the hell are the wagons?* Holt turned his collar up to the brisk chill that suddenly stirred the air and he shivered. The stallion blew out a quivering snort in reply, and gave a jangling shake to its bridle. Rain clouds, dark and heavy, massed in the distance, coming fast from the direction in which he was headed. Only minutes ago the late afternoon sky had been clear, but he knew that was often the way with prairie storms. They were unpredictable at best and downright dangerous at their worst. He'd heard of men freezing to death in the middle of summer in a prairie blizzard. This one, thankfully, smelled of rain, not snow.

Holt shifted the two bags of fresh meat slung over the pommel of his saddle and wedged his knees around them in search of a more comfortable position. Reaching back, he untied the thong that held his rolled up India rubber slicker in place behind the saddle and slipped it over his head. A clap of thunder in the distance echoed warningly over the landscape and Holt nudged Taeva forward into an easy lope, anxious to be home.

Home. To his *wife.*

Holt blew out a harsh puff of laughter and tried not to think of the cold shoulder she'd likely turn on him when he got back. Christ! A man could only take so much of that. Sleeping beside her night after night had become torture for him. What sleep he got was hot, achy, and restless. When he'd awaken in the darkness, with her next to him, he'd find his good intentions bathed in a sheen of longing sweat. He'd lay awake for hours listen-

109

ing to the sounds of her breathing, imagining her soft and willing beneath him. Her sweet-scented hair would be scattered enticingly across the pillow like a whisper of flame, crossing the invisible line she'd drawn down the center of their bed. Sometimes as she slept, he would touch it — roll it between his fingers as if that alone could satisfy the ache she stirred up in him.

Not likely.

Hell, he admitted grimly, she had every reason to detest him . . . dragging her into that mess back in Independence then attacking her down at the river like some kind of low-life bully. What did he expect? The truth was, as the days passed, he was finding it harder and harder to think of her as just another of Talbot's strumpets. She was different from other whores he'd known. In fact, she was different from any woman he'd ever met — full of pride, yet fragile — strong, yet achingly vulnerable. It struck him that those very qualities were what had enticed him to bid on her in that poker game back in Independence and, likewise, stirred a feeling of protectiveness in him now.

A fat droplet of rain splattered upon the brim of his battered hat, dousing his thoughts and focusing his attention back onto the situation at hand. He didn't particularly relish the idea of being the tallest object on this godforsaken prairie in the middle of a thunderstorm. Standing in his stirrups again, he peered through the gloom of the sheeting rain ahead and cursed.

Where the hell is that train?

The wagons had circled up early on Jim Kelly's direction. With the wind whipping at her hair, Kierin fought the canvas cover flat and lashed it securely at the front of the wagon. She hoped to fend off the inevitable seepage of rainwater, but by the looks of the storm coming, she had little hope of keeping the contents completely dry. The cover flapped noisily in the rising wind, rocking the wagon on squeaky springs. She removed the cover from the water barrel, hoping to collect some rainwater. At least the storm wouldn't be a total loss, she thought resignedly.

Jacob was pounding in the last of the stakes on his small tent when she finished.

"Are you sure you'll be all right out here in this tonight, Jacob?" Kierin eyed the sorry-looking tent doubtfully.

"Don't go worryin' about me none, ma'am." Jacob swiped at his forehead with the back of his sleeve. "I seen worse. Much worse in my day. I be fine here."

She nodded, unconvinced. "I'm afraid we'll have to settle for a cold supper tonight. There isn't time for a fire."

"No, ma'am. That be just fine." Jacob unfurled the rubber ground cloth into his tent and spread it out carefully.

Kierin climbed up onto the wagon but didn't go in. Instead, she scanned the eastern horizon for signs of a rider, but for the umpteenth time today, she was disappointed. *Where could he be?* she wondered, trying to keep the worry which seemed lodged in her throat in check. Holt had left her before sunup, and almost against her will, she had found herself watching for his return ever since. Jacob had told her Holt had gone hunting. Alone.

An uncomfortable silence had shrouded their days since the argument that night by the river. The night he'd—

Kierin clamped her eyes shut at the memory. She had pointedly avoided discussing it with him as he had promised her they would. *What point is there?* she thought miserably. It was clear he thought her a fallen woman, a strumpet like all the others at Talbot's. What else *could* he think after seeing her in a whore's dress, dallying drinks in a saloon? No, she knew what she'd see in his eyes if she looked at him squarely. And lately, he didn't even try to hide his contempt. He'd made it plain he found it dis-

111

tasteful to share a bed with her. He climbed into the wagon long after she had retired and was gone in the morning before she awoke. That seemed to suit him just fine, she mused, considering that he had ceased all attempts at communication days ago. Well, it suited her just fine, too.

"Stock's hobbled for the night," Jacob said, breaking into her inner dialogue. She jumped a little, embarrassed he had caught her looking for Holt.

He rested one hand tiredly on the wagon side. "Any sign of him yet?"

She shook her head and gave him a half-smile. Jacob wasn't easily fooled she thought, climbing down beside the wagon again. "No. Do you think he's all right?"

"Clay?" he asked, looking off at the looming storm. "He be fine, ma'am. I 'spect he'll be along. If 'n it gets too bad, he can bivouac out there for the night."

Jim Kelly's deep voice came from a few feet away. "He'd better damn well get back here tonight." Kelly wore a scowl as Kierin and Jacob turned to greet him. "Sorry ma'am, but I told that mule-headed fool not to go out on his own today. He still isn't running on a full head of steam."

Jacob slid his hat off his head and rubbed his forehead with the back of his sleeve. "You know Clay once't he gets his mind set on somethin'."

"Well, I don't like people bein' separated from the train in one of these storms," Kelly grumbled to no one in particular. "Taylor would'a gone with him, or Mel Watkins . . . they've both been itchin' to get a hunting party together. But we've been crossin' too much Indian sign lately for my taste."

"Indians?" Kierin looked anxiously at both men. Jacob had made her fears of the storm seem groundless, but Jim Kelly was being anything but reassuring.

Kelly seemed to realize his mistake at mentioning the Indians. He shuffled his feet and tried to soften his words. "Now don't you worry yourself about that, ma'am. They won't bother a train as big as this one. They'd be fools to try it."

"I wasn't concerned with the train, Mr. Kelly, and you needn't try to protect me from the facts just because I'm a woman," she told him coolly. "My concern is for the safety of one man out there alone on the prairie who's too stubborn to admit he might need someone other than himself." She stared at the wagonmaster, waiting for a reply.

Kelly shifted uncomfortably, looking to Jacob for help and finding none. Jacob was busy hiding a grin behind his weathered hand. "I . . . do apologize for talkin' down to you, ma'am. It's just . . . most women faint at the mention of those savages."

"Well, I'm not most women, Mr. Kelly, and you'll not likely see me faint at the sight of an Indian or two. I lived in Independence all of my life and saw more than my share of Indians there."

"I don't mean to argue with you, ma'am, but there's a big difference between town Indians and the wild ones you'll see out here on the plains. I've no doubt you're a brave woman, but you'd be smart not to stray far from the wagons or go off on your own in these parts."

"I'll remember your warning, Mr. Kelly."

"I thought we agreed you'd call me Jim," he said with a quirked smile.

"Jim," she acknowledged with a tilt of her head. "But about . . . my husband. Will you send someone to look for him?"

Jim Kelly shook his head. "We can't spare any men now. The stocks likely to get spooked by the storm and I've got men posted to watch them. If he's not back by morning, we'll talk about it then."

Kierin looked at Jacob, who was studying the toes of his boots. His silence acknowledged his concern. "Thank you, Jim," she said, with as close to a smile as she could manage. She climbed up into the wagon and then leaned back out again. "Jacob, supper will be ready

113

when you are."

The black man nodded. "Be in directly."

The men moved out of hearing range, though Kierin knew they were discussing the oncoming storm. To distract herself, she clattered noisily through the pantry box of pans as she prepared their cold supper, then spooned the sticky clump of cold beans onto two plates. She wrinkled her nose.

Beans again and hard tack.

The only palatable part of this meal would be the sweet butter she'd skimmed off the top of the milk in the butter churn they'd lashed to the side of the wagon. She still marveled at the way the butter appeared at the end of the day, churned by the action of the wagon. Churning was certainly one chore she could do without, Kierin thought, pouring two cups of milk from the tin container. A crash of thunder nearly made her spill the lot.

Redolent with the heavy scent of damp earth, the air thickened around her. She set the cups down and pulled her sticky blouse away from her damp skin. The sound, when she first became aware of it, came from far off, like a steady drumbeat.

Rain.

It engulfed the wagon in seconds until all she could hear was the sound of its steady pounding against the sturdy oiled-canvas cover. It drowned out all other sounds, including the pounding of her own heartbeat as it clattered in her ears.

Like a gust of wind, Jacob leaped into the wagon, already drenched to the bone.

"Whoo-ee!" he cried, wiping a hand down his rainslicked face. He stood like some kind of drenched scarecrow, his expression somewhere between amusement and shock.

"Jacob!" she cried over another clap of thunder. "You're soaked through!"

"Yes, ma'am!" he shouted. "Mercy, Lord, yes I am."

She couldn't help laughing at the comical sight he pre-

114

sented, and he laughed along with her. Both of them were glad to be rid of the tension which had been there only minutes before. Jacob changed while Kierin turned the other way and finished preparing their meal.

The food did little to warm the chill that had settled in the air. When they finished their meager meal, they wrapped themselves in blankets and sat for a long time, listening to the storm outside.

"Can I ask you something, Jacob?" Her question broke the long comfortable silence that had settled between them.

"You kin ask."

"Well, I was just wondering how the two of you — you and Holt, I mean — came to be traveling together. How did you first meet?"

Jacob sighed heavily as if the question had opened a long-closed door. Kierin was immediately sorry she'd asked.

"It's really none of my business, Jacob. I'm sorry," she told him.

"No," he countered, "s'all right. It be somethin' I don't think on much. But I 'spect it bears tellin' seein's how you and me gots a lot in common when it comes to Clay."

Kierin wasn't sure she'd heard him right. *"We* do?"

A sad smile tipped the corners of Jacob's mouth and he bent his head, staring at his laced fingers. "First time I laid eyes on Clay was two years ago. I was standin' on a auction block in Mississippi, wid chains on my wrists and ankles, an' just enough strength to stand up an' face the bastard that was sellin' me." Kierin's jade eyes widened as he paused there, gaining control over the painful memory.

"Bein' a slave was somethin' I was born to but I 'spect it ain't in me to be a slave to any man. I grow'd up on a plantation just south o' Natchez under a master name o' Carstairs, Nathan Carstairs." The name spilled like poison from his lips and it was all Kierin could do to keep from shuddering at the hatred she heard in his voice.

115

"Nastier man never lived," he continued. "Beat a man . . . for jist lookin' his way. I had me a wife. Bess." A sparkle glistened in Jacob's eye as he remembered. "Fine woman. Prettier than a black-eyed Susan in a meadow o' grass. Worked hard, same as all the rest. Didn't give nobody trouble. Her way . . . her way was to smooth things over. Not make a fuss.

"Carstairs, he took a fancy to her. Come around the kitchen where she worked, botherin' her. Come special when he know'd she be alone—me off on some job he'd come up wid for me. Bess, she don't tell me about it right off, cuz she figures I kill that white man if'n I know'd.

"But one night," Jacob continued, a catch in his voice, "I comes back an finds her covered with bruises an' bleedin' from the beatin' he give her. She tol' me he done it when she try to fight him off—but he got mad an' beat her for bein'—uppity." He took a shaky breath. "I never kilt a man before, but I had it in my heart to murder that man."

The rain splattered hard on the canvas roof, insulating Jacob's deep voice. "My Bess . . . she say no. She tells me we never be free if we kills him." He lowered his head. "She was right, but I shouldn'ta listened. Instead, we make a plan to escape.

"The night we run, Carstairs be waitin' for us. Somehow he found out and he had him a whole passel o' white men from down by the river to make sure we don't get away. Took ten of 'em to hold me down whilst they string up my Bess to a tree. They . . . beat her—beat her bloody, an' all the time me screamin' for them to stop."

"My God—" Kierin whispered, stricken with the horror of it.

Jacob ran a hand over the back of his neck then clasped his fingers tightly in front of him as if trying to hold back the pain of the memory. "Then," he continued, "he turned the lash on me. Near kilt both of us that night. Only thing stopped him was knowin' the plantation owners association come down hard on any slave

116

owner who kilt a slave." Jacob snorted derisively. "In Natchez you kin beat a slave bloody, but if you kills him, you gots to answer to them."

"After we heals enough to walk, Carstairs decides to sell us off—for bein' unmanageable, he says. Looks bad for the other slaves havin' us think we can run off. But I seen the look in his eyes. He be afraid I'm gonna kill him when I gets the chance.

"He took Bess, my Bess, an' sold her from me. Sold her so's I wouldn't know where she be. Then he takes me up to Natchez an' stood me on the block and sold me. To Clay."

Kierin's mouth dropped open. She tried to speak but couldn't make a sound.

"Paid hard cash for me," Jacob went on. "Told Carstairs to let me loose of the irons. The old man just laughs and tells Clay he be a fool to let me loose 'fore I be seasoned some in my new place.

"Clay, he just stares at that old sonofabitch with them cool blue eyes of his an' says, 'Do it!' Then Clay, he puts his arm around me an' helps me onto a horse. Before we goes, he rides up to Carstairs an' tears up my paper an' throws it at the bastard's feet. The whole mess of them owners just stood there gapin' as we rides off."

"He—he just tore up your papers? He freed you?" Kierin repeated, trying to convince herself that she'd heard him right.

Jacob nodded and wiped at the moisture in his eyes. "I never axed him why he done it and he never tol' me. He give me free papers an' said I was welcome to ride wid him if I was a mind to. When I tol' him I had to find my Bess, he helped me."

"Did you find her?" Kierin asked.

Jacob cleared his throat and nodded again. "Clay an' me, we finally tracked her down to a rice plantation in Georgia. She done took a fever down there and died 'fore I could reach her.

"If somebody hadn't beat me to it, I'd a kilt the bastard who sent her there. But Carstairs wasn't so lucky with the next slave he tried to beat . . ."

"Oh. Jacob," Kierin whispered. "I'm so sorry. About Bess, everything."

Jacob looked into her eyes. "I ain't never told nobody that story 'cept'n Clay, and now you. I want you to know the kinda man you's dealin' with in Clay. He be a good man. Best I knows. He be madder'n a hornet if he know'd I talked to you about this, but I think you owe him the chance to work out whatever's got the two of you acting like a pair o' ornery mules — no offense, ma'am."

Kierin worried the edge of her lip between her teeth, suddenly sure he was right. While the past few days had been almost unbearably tense for her and Holt, she knew now they'd been a strain on Jacob as well. "No offense taken, Jacob. And you're right," she admitted. "I do owe it to him to try and make this trip as pleasant as possible. I'll talk to him . . . I will."

"Just hear him out," Jacob told her, unwinding his long legs and standing in the cramped wagon. "I guess I'll turn in."

"Goodnight, Jacob. And . . . thank you."

"Night, ma'am." Jacob turned and stepped out into the driving rain. She heard him splash through the soggy ground to the small tent nearby, but soon all sound was absorbed again by the rain. A bolt of lightning illuminated the wagon, followed closely by a clap of reverberating thunder. It pounded across the prairie like a giant fist. She hugged the blanket tighter around her and shivered in the dim light. Her thoughts returned to Holt. He was out there in that storm somewhere, alone. Had she been wrong about him? Her mind raced over all that Jacob had told her. Was it possible that he didn't mean to hold her to the papers he'd won from Talbot? Had she completely misread his intentions?

Kierin felt a flush of heat creep up her neck as she remembered the searing kiss he'd forced on her the other night, his own heart beating hard against her fin-

118

gertips. She remembered the look in his eyes when he had pulled away from her. For the first time in days, she allowed the feelings she'd been fighting to surface—the feelings she'd been trying so hard to deny.

The sound of the rain on the canvas lulled her and she leaned back against the sacks of flour behind her. When she closed her eyes, she tried not to think of him lying hurt somewhere in the rain. After all, didn't Jacob say that Holt knew the country around here better than most?

"Mercy—" she said aloud. "Why does the darkness always make my mind race so? After all, he *is* a grown man."

She jumped as another streak of lightning lit the sky. Suddenly, she wished he were there, holding her against him again, making her feel safe.

Safe? The thought struck her oddly. No, his touch made her feel anything but safe. It made her feel wanton, reckless. It made her feel as she never had before.

The image of his face rose up in her mind: his cheeks, covered with stubble of a day's growth, dark against his skin. His eyes, steely blue with tiny flecks of gold, rimmed by dark thick lashes. Dark tousled hair which defied control, spilling carelessly onto his forehead.

Handsome. In a dangerous way, handsome.

"Lord help me," she sighed, listening to the lonely sounds of the rain. "Where is he?"

Chapter Eight

Holt shivered beneath the thin slicker, his buckskin shirt and leggings damp and clinging despite the covering. The cold air fingered through to his skin and he reached into his saddlebag for a piece of dried jerky, hoping to generate some warmth by eating. He chewed it slowly, thinking what he'd give for a hot cup of Jacob's strong coffee.

The sting of the pelting rain and icy blasts of wind numbed his hands, making his grip on both reins and food tenuous at best. He peered into the sheeting gloom. If he got as far as the river and still hadn't found the train, he decided he'd have to hole up until daybreak. If he kept searching in this soup, he could end up miles downstream from them, depending on how far they'd gotten today. Hell, he could pass right by a herd of elephants in this weather and never even see them.

Another jagged streak of lightning peeled back the darkness momentarily, followed closely by the hollow swell of thunder. Ahead of him lay only naked prairie. Treeless. Empty.

His mind wandered back to the first time he'd seen it, crossing its vastness on the heels of his wife's death in pursuit of her murderers. The land's emptiness had been a comfort to him then — in harmony with the void that had cradled him since her death.

The wide-open prairie had freed him from reminders of his ranch in the Oregon Territory, dense with towering, ancient trees. The loneliness of the rolling plain had soothed his grief and given him time to sort out the guilt that had settled like an albatross around his neck after Mandy's death.

Eventually, he'd made a kind of hollow peace with himself and learned to live with the knowledge that he'd been partly to blame for her death. How many times had he wondered how different his life would be now if he'd stayed home with her that day instead of leaving her to attend to ranch business in Oregon City? But as she did so often, Mandy had waved away his concern about her and told him to go.

When he'd returned, she was dead and the ranch lay in ashes before him.

Until now, nothing had upset the delicate balance he had maintained between mere existence and the wish to join her. Yet now, when he tried to picture Mandy's face, her smile — it was Kierin's he saw. *Her hair,* wild as a fanned flame setting off eyes that reminded him of the turbulent Pacific after a storm. *Her lips,* beckoning him and kindling a spark long dead inside him.

Her face. Not Mandy's.

Taeva's shrill whinny pulled his thoughts back to the inky landscape ahead. The horse's ears were pricked up and he snorted impatiently at something in the darkness Holt could not yet see. Slowly, as they moved closer, the dark shapes of the circled wagons appeared like ghostly shapes nestled in a hillock. A mare's answering whinny came from within it.

"You've got eyes like a cat, Taeva. Or was it that mare's scent you were following?" Holt asked, slapping the horse's rain-slick flank.

He dismounted, threw the reins over the horse's neck, and led him to the barricaded opening between the first and last wagons. Surprised by Holt's appearance, the man standing sentry pointed an anxious rifle in his direction.

121

"Hold there!"

"Whoa!" Holt shouted, throwing his hands up protectively. "It's me, Daniel. Clay Holt."

The man, Daniel Thorp, sagged with relief and lowered the gun. Rain dripped off the brim of his hat in a steady stream. "God damnit, Holt! You just took a year off my life. Where the hell have you been? Jim Kelly told me to look out for ya, but ya nearly got yer head shot off, sneakin' in here like some damned redskin!"

"Yeah," Holt answered over the downpour, leading his horse into the circle, "It's easy to miss someone on a night like this."

"Yer tellin' me!" Thorp blinked back the rain that splattered in his eyes as he scanned the gloomy sky. "Wilkerson's got the next shift. One more hour and I'll be snug and cozy next to my Susan." He shrugged back an involuntary shiver beneath his slicker. "But then," he added, nudging Holt with an elbow, "I don't reckon you'll be cold fer long either, eh, Clay? That's a fine-lookin' bride you found yerself there. Fine-lookin'." Thorp's mouth twitched in a mischievous smile.

Holt stared back at him impassively, lost in his own thoughts.

"Yes sir," Daniel rambled on, trying to keep up his end of a one-way conversation, "a man needs a little comfort on a night like this. We're lucky men, Holt. Plain lucky."

"Yeah, lucky." *I'll be lucky if she shares the damn blankets with me tonight,* Holt thought glumly. A bone-rattling tremor raced through him as the damp chill seeped beneath Holt's wet clothing. His shoulder throbbed and all he could think of was getting dry and warm again. "See you later, Daniel," he said, and moved off before the other man could buttonhole him further.

He made his way to the wagon and unsaddled Taeva. He ground-staked the horse, gave him a ration of oats from his saddlebag, and watered him. Passing Jacob's small tent, he carefully eased his tack into the front of the wagon along with the bundle of meat and covered them with a tarp Jacob had left for him.

Like a beacon, a dim light glowed from the interior of the wagon. Was she still awake? he wondered as he slogged across the muddy ground to the back of the wagon. It baffled him to think she might have waited up for him. Biting back that small seed of hope, he clenched his jaw and pulled aside the canvas cover.

What he saw there made him catch his breath in wonder. Kierin lay against the pile of grain sacks, her hair spread out upon them like an auburn cloud. She was fully dressed . . . and asleep. One slender hand, relaxed with slumber, lay curled close to her face and seemed to beckon him in. Her expression, guileless and unguarded in sleep, was free of the strain he'd seen there for the past days. He released a shaky breath as the rain continued to fall, but he found he was unable to move—forward, backward—he stood rooted to the spot. God in heaven but she was beautiful!

"Wha—?" Kierin sat bolt upright, awakened by something she couldn't identify. Her eyes were clouded by sleep and she blinked to clear them.

The figure of a man just outside the wagon stood out in shadowed relief against the storm. Silhouetted in the darkness, rain spilling from the brim of his hat, she knew that he'd come back. "Clay."

He cleared his throat and she felt the weight of his step on the wagon. "Yeah. It's me."

Relief swept through her like a gust of warm wind. *Thank God!* she wanted to cry. *I was so worried something had happened to you!* But as he moved toward the light, his clouded expression forced those words back in her throat. She swept her hair back from her eyes. "Are you all right?"

Holt didn't answer as he climbed into the wagon and peeled off his wet rain slicker and hat. His clothes were, indeed, soaked through, and another involuntary shiver rattled through him.

"You must be half-frozen." Kierin reached for a dry blanket.

"I am," he agreed, blowing into his stiff hands. "You think you could scare up a few dry clothes for me to change into while I get out of these?"

"Oh—of course." Her heart did a little dance in her throat. She turned her back on him and dug through his small trunk of clothes. When she turned around with his things, he had already peeled his wet buckskin shirt over his head and was pressing a hand to his tender shoulder. He stopped self-consciously when he found her watching him.

She lowered the bundle deliberately to her lap. "If you're going to pretend you didn't hurt yourself today, you needn't bother."

He stared at her for a long moment. "No?"

She shook her head.

"I guess there wouldn't be much point, would there?" He squeezed his eyes shut and reached up again to his shoulder, kneading the cramping muscles. "You're right. It hurts like hell."

"You'd better get out of those wet things," she told him. "I'll take a look at it." Turning her back on him while he undressed, Kierin swallowed hard and pulled her blanket more tightly around her. A thousand thoughts flitted through her mind, but none told her how to approach the taciturn man standing behind her. Almost overwhelming was her need to resolve the bad feelings between them. But how?

She rummaged through Jacob's medicinal bag for something to soothe his shoulder. Her search produced a bottle of witch hazel. The strong-smelling stuff served double-duty as both astringent and liniment. It would do.

Behind her, she heard his soft curse as he struggled out of the sodden buckskins and dropped them to the floor. Kierin resisted the ridiculous urge to turn around and admire him. She didn't have to look to recall the powerful contours of his body, his broad shoulders, the whip cord strength in his arms, even the feel of the dark silky hair on his chest.

She remembered it all. Unbidden came the memory of holding him through that long night when he'd been so ill. Entwined in his arms, the struggle she'd faced with him had been so simple: life or death, survival or defeat. There was no middle ground in that battle just as there seemed to be nothing but this yawning distance between them now.

Now she had to deal with him as a man. A complex, living, breathing man. A man she'd never be able to trust.

She heard his weary sigh as he sank down onto the pallet and she turned around. He'd pulled on a dry pair of denim pants. A blanket hung loosely around his shoulders and he leaned wearily against a crate. The hair on his chest, still damp from the rain, glistened like jet in the lampglow.

Kierin swallowed back the lump that formed in her throat as she knelt beside him. Gently, she pushed aside the blanket that covered his injured shoulder. His wound had healed well, despite the punishment he'd given it. Only a slight discoloration surrounded the jagged reddish scar now. But the newly mended muscles in his shoulder jumped with fatigue.

"It's late," he said. "Why aren't you in bed, asleep?"

Kierin's eyes met his. "I *was* asleep."

His gaze raked slowly down the length of her rumpled gown. "You're still dressed."

It was no use denying the obvious. "I fell asleep waiting for you to get back," she admitted.

He frowned at her with something akin to disbelief.

She sat back on her heels and shook her head. "You were gone longer than anyone expected. Do you really find it so hard to imagine that I'd be worried about you, alone out there in this . . . ?" She gestured at the clatter of the pounding rain outside.

125

Hell yes, he wanted to say, but couldn't. "There was no need for you to worry," he told her evenly. "I asked Jacob to tell you where I was going. Didn't he?"

"He told me. But I wish *you* had."

Holt ran a hand tiredly across the stubble on his cheeks. "To be honest, I didn't think it would matter to you one way or the other."

Kierin sighed. "Do you really believe that?"

His eyes darkened. "I don't know," he answered slowly. "Are you trying to tell me otherwise?"

"I—" Kierin looked down at her hands, unable to meet his gaze. "Well . . . yes."

Holt's lips parted in surprise as he watched her. *I'll be damned,* he thought, straightening slightly. "I'm . . . glad to hear that."

As her eyes met his again, his gaze traced a path down her face to her full lower lip. A warning tremor of desire tore through him like a low rumble of thunder.

Kierin's gaze skittered away from him and then back as she screwed up her courage. "I don't want us to go on the way we have the past few days," she told him without preamble. "We have a long trip ahead of us. I've been stubborn and willful and—"

"No—" he interrupted. "The truth is that I behaved badly the other day and whatever's gone on between us is more my fault than yours." He reached out and touched her fingertips.

A hot electric shock traveled up her arm at his touch but she allowed it. It was as much of an apology as she guessed she'd ever get from him and more than she'd expected. As she searched for something to say in return, the rain beat a tattoo on the canvas roof, insulating them and giving her the sense that they were completely alone. "Mr. Holt—"

"Clay. You called me Clay before."

"I did?"

He nodded slowly. "When I came in." His steely blue eyes searched hers. "I can't remember you calling me

126

that before."

"Oh. I . . ." His gaze seemed to caress her face and she nearly forgot to breathe.

"I liked it."

She swallowed, eyes wide. His closeness made her feel light-headed and off balance.

He reached up with one hand and brushed her cheek gently with the backs of his fingers. "Look, I know I've given you reason to be afraid of me, Kierin, but I don't want that between us."

Afraid? A moment ago she might have attributed the churning sensation within her to fear. Now she hesitated, mesmerized by his eyes, held motionless by his voice. He reminded her of a hunting animal and she, the stalked prey. His gaze moved from her eyes down to her mouth and back up again. God help her, he was giving her a way out. Waiting for her to tell him no. But she didn't. She couldn't.

His fingers curled into the fine, coppery hair at the nape of her neck and he drew her to him. His mouth covered hers gently.

Tasting. Sipping.

His lips slanted across hers, first one way, then the other. With maddening deliberateness, his tongue traced the inside edge of her lower lip.

Open to me Kierin, his mouth invited. *Let me taste all of you.*

His kiss awakened a yearning deeper than any she'd known and stronger than her will to fight against it. Lips parted, she leaned into him. He cupped her face with his other hand and pulled her closer still, plundering her trembling mouth.

His kiss tasted of rain. His lips, still cool with the night's chill, warmed as they took possession of hers. She wanted this — needed it as much as the thirsty grasses of the prairie did the storm raging outside. She'd even dreamed of it in the nights since he kissed her by the river.

Instinctively, she flattened her hands against him and felt the taut muscles of his abdomen quiver and his heart thud in the same erratic rhythm as her own. His hand slid to the small of her back, and he pulled her across his chest, drawing her fully against him.

His hips tilted up reflexively against hers and she felt the undeniable evidence of his passion, hard and warm between them. Rational thought returned to her with a jolt.

"Oh, God — stop," she moaned, tearing herself abruptly from his arms. He made a noise deep in his throat and released her without argument as if he'd half expected her to leap away from him that way.

Kierin pressed the back of her hand to her lips. "Oh, God," she whispered again, knowing that kiss had been as much her fault as his. What must he think of her now? Maybe she *was* like the others at Talbot's. Maybe that's what she'd become.

He raked a hand through his damp hair. *It's better this way,* he thought. He knew from the look on her face that their kiss had affected her as much as it had him. He took a deep steadying breath and leaned against the crate — head tilted back, eyes slammed shut. What had flared between them just now crossed dangerously beyond the realm of simple lust and into a place he wasn't ready to explore again. He had no intention of allowing himself to fall in love with another woman only to risk losing her. And something told him there would be no going back for him with a woman like Kierin — no matter who or what she'd been before.

Kierin scooted away from him to the other side of the narrow wagon, taking small comfort in that space. Thunder rumbled in the distance, but the steady thrum of rain was gentler now.

"Tell me something," she asked in a voice that betrayed her fear, "Why did you take me in that game? Was it for *this?*" She was afraid of his answer but she had to know.

"No."

"Then why?"

"I don't know." He paused, as if mulling over his own confusion, and rubbed a hand across the dark stubble on his cheeks again. "I sure as hell didn't intend to drag you into any of this."

She looked at him incredulously. "Just what *did* you intend?"

Holt returned her look. "As you might recall, Talbot didn't leave us a lot of time to make any plans." Frustrated, he plucked out a long piece of straw that had worked its way out of the mattress beneath him. "If things had been different . . . I probably would have put you on the first stage out of there. St. Louis, maybe."

"But what about my contract? What about the money you risked?"

"What about it? I won. Your contract never entered into it," he told her matter-of-factly, clamping the straw between his teeth. "I never meant to hold you to those papers, Kierin, and if you'd let me get a word in edgewise that night by the river, I would have told you that."

Her stunning sense of freedom was tempered only by an inexplicable pang of disappointment. "And once you'd unchained me, what then?" she asked. "Just send me off without a thought as to where I would go, or how I would get by?"

A single line of consternation bisected his dark eyebrows. "Well, it sounds pretty damn awful when you put it that way, but at the time it seemed like a good idea. Hell! I don't know what I thought. I guess I *didn't*. Sometimes I just follow my gut feelings, and that night they were telling me not to let that bastard Talbot treat you that way. But to be honest, Princess, I don't think you would've gone anywhere with me without a fight. You tell me. What *should* I have done?" he asked, bracing his elbows on his knees and flinging the straw negligently in the air. "Left you there to be picked over like

129

some old ham bone by Talbot and that simpleton Thrumball?"

"No." She squeezed her eyes shut at the thought "No. I'm grateful you stayed, that you got me out of the Independence," she admitted impetuously. Her eyes glittered in the lamp glow. "I hated John Talbot and I was afraid of him. I don't even know why he bid me in that game. Just out of pure meanness, I suppose. I don't think he had any intention of losing the hand to you. He rarely lost at poker because he cheated."

"I know."

Kierin's eyebrows shot up in surprise. "You do? I mean, you did? But how did you — ? A-Are you saying you cheated to win that hand?"

He grinned noncommittally. "I never said that."

She let out a short laugh and shook her head. "No, you didn't."

They both leaned back, appraising each other silently — she, with her arms folded protectively against her chest; he, with his wrists draped indolently across the tops of his bent knees.

The rain had stopped. The only sound was the occasional rhythmic *plink-plink* of raindrops as they slid from the oiled canvas into the open rain barrel outside.

Holt toyed with a question of his own, dismissed it, and called it back again. "While we're on the subject of *why*s," he said at last, "suppose you tell me why, when you could easily have left me back there to die, you didn't."

She lowered her eyes and stared at her hands. "I should have an answer for that, but I don't," she admitted. "I just couldn't leave you there."

"Well, I'm glad as hell you didn't. I guess I haven't really thanked you for pulling me through it, have I?"

A tentative smile teased the corner of her lips. "Is that a thank-you?"

"I guess it is," he said with a laugh.

"You're welcome, then. It was really Jacob though.

He's a wonder with herbal remedies. I didn't do much."

"That's not the way he tells it."

She wondered just how much Jacob had told him and how much he himself remembered of that first night. "About that night . . . there's something I need to ask you."

"Ask away."

She hesitated. "Who's Amanda?"

Holt paled and rocked back as if he'd been struck. *"What?"*

"Is she your wife?"

A combination of pain and anger flitted across his sculpted features. "How the hell — ? Did Jacob — "

"No," she assured him. "Jacob didn't say anything. You called her name when you were out of your mind with fever. You thought . . . I was her." Kierin watched his eyes shutter like curtains drawn across a painful scene. She half wished now she hadn't asked him. But she had to know.

"Mandy was my wife. She died three years ago."

Relief and sorrow warred inside her. "I'm sorry, Clay. You must have loved her very much."

His long silence spoke more eloquently than words. "It was a long time ago," he said finally. He eased away from the crate and stretched himself out on his side of the pallet. "We'd better get some sleep. Morning'll be here soon enough."

Helplessly, she watched him close off from her again. It didn't matter now. She had her answer. He was still in love with a ghost.

"What about your shoulder?" she asked.

"Never mind," he told her. "It'll be fine tomorrow. I just need to get some sleep."

She nodded and slowly reached up to turn down the wick on the kerosine lantern.

Holt closed his eyes, fighting the emotions doing battle within him. He'd thought it was a dream that night, holding Mandy in his arms, but it was Kierin who'd

131

wrapped her warmth around him, soothed the fear and cold from him; encouraged him to fight, to live. He should have known. He flung an arm silently over his eyes. *Let it be. She's not for you, Clay.*

Still he found himself listening to the sounds of Kierin undressing in the darkness. He heard the small metallic clicks of hooks and eyes releasing, the sound of cotton skirts rustling, like wind hissing through a crowded stand of aspen. He imagined what he'd see if he turned to look when the last of her garments was shed, before she pulled the white cotton gown over her head.

She slid in beside him and curled with her back to him.

"Clay?"

"Hm-m?"

"Did you mean what you said about the papers?"

"Yeah." In the darkness, he turned to look at her.

"Then . . . when we get West," she told him, "I'll be heading for California."

His chest tightened with an old familiar feeling. "California?"

"I have a brother out there and I mean to find him."

Clay pressed his head back into the ticking of the pillow. *It's better this way.* "If that's what you want."

"It is." The silence stretched between them, thick with unsaid words. "Clay?"

"Yeah?"

"Thank you."

"Yeah, sure. Go to sleep now." He closed his eyes again and swallowed back the inexplicable lump of disappointment that formed in his throat. *It's better this way,* he repeated to himself. And he tried to believe it was true.

Chapter Nine

The wagons pushed on, following the course of the Blue Earth River north across rolling plains of emerald green grass. The sporadic rain brought with it a new profusion of spring wildflowers. White pasqueflower, tiny bird-foot violets and golden black-eyed Susan rode the crests of waving grass. The riotous colors served to break the sheer monotony of the endless rolling prairie.

Kierin and the other women and children would stray far afield in search of the most beautiful flower. Often as not, it turned into a game of hide and seek for the children, who constantly disappeared in the waist-high grass near the trail.

Still, it was a rare night in Kierin's camp that didn't find a bucket or container straining with armloads of fresh-picked wildflowers from the long day's walk.

Daily, they saw evidence of those who had come this way before. Hardly a mile went by now when they didn't pass a broken-down piece of a wagon or a treasured heirloom. Hand-carved wardrobes, grass-choked cast-iron stoves, orange with rust, even fine cherry-wood dining tables littered the edges of the trail. To carry such luxuries, many had discovered, was to put an unnecessary added strain on teams already taxed by this, the easiest part of their long journey.

More disturbing than these were the graves that lined the rutted trail. Hundreds and hundreds of graves, some with crosses of wood and some distinguished only by river stones, lined the pathway like gruesome trail markers.

Most, Kierin simply passed by. It was harder to ignore the smaller graves of the children without thinking of Matthew. Even though she'd never gotten the letter her father had promised to send when they reached California, she never doubted they'd arrived. There were a hundred reasons, she told herself, why she'd never received word — the first, and most likely, being that Asa McKendry rarely concerned himself with the banalities of correspondence, except when there was a profit to be made.

It was possible, too, that the letter might have been sent, but had gotten lost or ruined on the trip back to Independence. That was the excuse she preferred to believe. Nevertheless, she found herself studying the small graves as she passed them, each one reassuring her that Matthew was still alive and well.

That was how Clay found her one afternoon as he rode up behind her on his Appaloosa.

"That's a cheery way to pass the time," he remarked, pulling Taeva up short beside her.

Kierin straightened abruptly, surprised by the sound of his voice. A flush crept up to her cheeks and she prepared for their usual crossing of swords. But when she turned to him, his easy smile forced the contentious words back in her throat.

Clay's body cast a shadow over her, blocking the sun. He was nearly silhouetted against the late afternoon glare. He held the reins loosely in one hand and leaned a forearm against the saddlehorn.

He doffed his sweat-soaked hat and swiped at his glistening forehead with the back of his sleeve. "Looking for someone you know?"

"Not really," she answered truthfully, looking back down at the small grave at her feet. "It's just that someone planted a wild rosebush by this little girl's grave."

Her fingers brushed the petals of the pink blossom. "I was thinking how dear she must have been to her parents."

Clay settled his hat back on his head. "It's easy to get caught up with the tragedy of the trail, Kierin. There are a thousand graves like it ahead of us and almost as many behind," he said. "It's best if you try not to think about it."

He couldn't have known how close he'd come to the truth. With an effort, Kierin pushed back her fears about Matthew and forced a smile. "Where have you been all afternoon?"

He smiled and untied a pair of prairie hens from around his saddle horn. "Looking for dinner." He nudged Taeva forward, and tossed the game into the front of their wagon. Then, he came back and extended his hand down to her.

"Come on."

"What—up there?" Her disbelieving gaze traveled back and forth between his appealing grin and the powerful callused palm of his hand.

"I want to show you something and it's a hell of a walk. Come on," he encouraged, beckoning her with the waggle of fingertips.

She hesitated, eyeing him suspiciously. "Where are you taking me?"

"What, and spoil the surprise?" he asked in a wounded voice. "Never."

Her smile reflected the mischief in his eyes. "All right," she told him dubiously, slipping her hand into his and stepping up onto his flexed foot. "But this had better be good."

Clay lifted her smoothly onto the saddle in front of him and settled her sideways across his lap. "Have I ever steered you wrong?"

Kierin gave him an astonished look. "As a matter of fact—"

"Don't answer that," he interrupted with a laugh and

135

kicked Taeva into an easy lope.

The wind licked at her hair, whipping unruly auburn strands loose from the bun at the back of her head, and she smiled in spite of the misgivings she'd had only a moment ago. She'd forgotten how much she loved to ride.

Clay's arms, in the same moment gentle and steely, circled her. Even through her layers of clothing, she could feel the sinewy muscles in his thighs working as he guided the horse up a gentle swell. She wondered if he could feel her heart pound against his arm.

For a time, she tried to keep a modicum of space between them but, in the end, gave it up and relaxed against him. She'd never seen this playful side of him before and she wanted to enjoy it, even if it lasted for only a few minutes.

The train disappeared behind a rise, but Clay pushed the Appaloosa on, heading north into the endless span of grass. The verdant sameness of the tallgrass prairie made it appear from a distance as flat and monotonous as the sea, but in fact, the land was filled with dips and gentle hills. The green flower stalks of the big bluestem grass were so tall, they brushed their knees as they rode through it.

"Are you sure you know where you're going?" Kierin asked Clay when he'd slowed the horse to an easy trot.

"It's not much further," he told her, "What's wrong? Don't you trust me?"

She let out a throaty laugh, catching his playful mood. "That's a dangerous question, Mr. Holt. But frankly," she admitted, throwing her head back, "I don't care if we *are* lost. It's so beautiful out here without the dust and the cattle and all the noise . . ." She filled her lungs with the sweet-scented air. "You may have to drag me back to civilization."

Clay's dark eyebrows arched with feigned surprise. "Civilization?" His blue eyes made a cursory scan of the empty grasslands. "Did I miss it somewhere?"

136

Kierin laughed in reply.

Clay tightened his arms around her slightly and flicked the reins. "I like it out here, too," he admitted, gazing out across the plain. "I never tire of it."

They headed for a lone bur oak tree which sat at the knoll of a hill. Beneath its spreading limbs, Clay dismounted, then reached up to help her down. She braced her hands atop his broad shoulders while his fingers circled her waist. He lowered her slowly to the ground.

Holding her closer than was purely necessary, Clay's thumbs traced the boning beneath the front of her blue gingham dress, stalling for time. He was reluctant to release her even while he reminded himself that wasn't the reason he'd brought her out here. He swallowed hard and stepped away.

The air crackled between them and Kierin pushed away from the horse's flank. She scanned the shiny-leafed branches above them. "Is . . . this what you wanted me to see?" she asked.

"No." He resisted the urge to touch her again and motioned silently for her to follow him. At the top of the rise, he lowered himself to the ground and gestured for her to do the same. She flattened herself to the earth beside him with a perplexed expression.

Without speaking, he pointed below to a sparsely covered meadow of short grass which was scattered with countless little mounds of dirt. It was a hundred acres wide and startlingly alive with thousands upon thousands of prairie dogs.

"Oh!" Kierin breathed, trying to take it all in. "Oh, it's—it's wonderful—enormous. I've never—" Words utterly failed her at the sight. From their position on the crest of the hill, she and Clay were only thirty feet from the closest burrows, but the breeze favored them and carried their scent away from the dog town.

Clay rested his chin on the backs of his hands and watched her with unconcealed pleasure. Somehow, he'd known she'd enjoy this as much as he had the first time he'd seen it. Her green eyes sparkled with childlike fascination. With her fingertips pressed delightedly against her lips, her smile reminded him of a child who'd tasted her first peppermint.

"How did you know it was here?" she asked, without pulling her gaze from the sprawling meadow.

"I found it this afternoon while I was hunting," he explained. "Used to be able to see towns like this from the trail, but you rarely see one this big anywhere near it now."

For a long time, they silently watched a family of prairie dogs on one of the mounds closest to them. The male stood several inches taller than the others, his shiny black eyes darting back and forth, ever alert to danger. Around him, the pinkish-brown females and young groomed each other with their little paws, then affectionately touched noses.

"Look, they're kissing," Kierin whispered.

Clay nodded. His mouth curved into an unconscious smile. "I don't know what else you could call it. They seem almost human, don't they?"

Kierin tipped her head in Clay's direction. "Mm-m, in a way. It would be nice if our lives were that simple, wouldn't it?" she mused. "We could spend our days preening in the sun, loving our families, undistracted by the worries of the world."

He chuckled. "Their worries are a little more immediate, I guess. Simple things like chasing the owls out of their burrows, keeping grass on the table, that kind of thing."

He was teasing her and Kierin returned his smile. "I guess what I mean," she said after considering her words carefully, "is they don't allow survival to come between them — to break apart their families — like we do."

Clay rolled onto his side and propped a hand at the back of his head. His dark brows lifted inquiringly.

"Are we speaking from personal experience?"

She propped herself up on her elbows and deftly avoided both his stare and his question. "Observation," she answered. "Everyone suffers losses. I doubt I'm any special case."

His hand reached out and stroked her shoulder with a whispering touch. "I'm afraid I'd have to argue with that," he told her. Gently, he brushed a strand of her hair from her face and tucked it behind her ear. "You're very special, Kierin."

A rush of heat swept up her spine at his words.

"Clay . . ."

His hand lingered near her cheek. "Hasn't anyone ever told you that before?"

She edged away from him slightly. "No. I mean— well, only Lily."

Clay's eyebrows tipped downward. "Lily?"

"She . . . worked at the Independence." Kierin hesitated. "She . . . ran the upstairs."

"A *madam?*" Clay's eyes narrowed fractionally and his lips parted in a silent curse. Rolling onto his back, he glared into the perfect blue dome above them. "Christ! Kierin, that's hardly what I meant."

She bristled like a bad-tempered cat at his tone and her voice became flat with anger. "Lily was my friend."

Clay glared back at her. Seeing her here, with the afternoon sun playing in her hair and the prairie reflected in her eyes, it had been easy to forget what she'd been before he'd met her. That, he knew, wasn't even the issue for him anymore. It was all the other men who'd had her before—the way *he* ached to now. And *couldn't.* That unreasonable jealousy made him deliberately cruel.

"You sell yourself short, Princess." His jaw was set in a firm, angry line. "Madams don't have friends. They have business investments."

Kierin sat up abruptly, propelled by her anger. Hundreds of prairie dogs scattered for their lives in the meadow below, dashing down to the safety of their holes, but neither Kierin nor Clay noticed.

"It wasn't like that," she snapped, angry at having to defend her relationship with Lily and determined not to. "What would you know about it, anyway?" she demanded. "When was the last time you had to live in a brothel? When did you ever look at one of the women you wrestled under the sheets as something besides chattel, designed to fit neatly into the back corner of your mind where you wouldn't have to ever think of her as a person?"

Clay propped himself up on one elbow and glared at her. "I don't seem to recall hearing any complaints on that account. In fact," he continued, with uncharacteristic disregard for his hard-and-fast rule never to discuss one woman while in the company of another, "strange as it may seem to you, not a single one cowered before me like a goddamned virgin, afraid that I would hurt her or leave her less than completely satisfied."

Her eyes narrowed and she tipped her chin up haughtily. "I suppose, by that, you're referring to *me?*"

He leveled an insolent "you said it, I didn't" look at her with his steely blue eyes.

Infuriated, Kierin snatched up a handful of grass and flung it at his face. Clay feinted to the right, dodging the sudden and unexpected attack. His brows arched with surprise as if he were looking into the eyes of a crazy woman.

"Ooh-h! Damn you, Clay Holt!" Kierin's voice was shrill and barely controlled. "Why did you even bring me out here? Just to pick a fight?" She pushed herself up to her knees, hampered by the tangle of her cotton skirts. "You know what your problem is?" she spat, tugging irritably at the troublesome fabric around her legs.

"No," came his equally testy reply. "Why don't you enlighten m—?"

"You're so damn busy being mad at me and the rest

140

of the world, you've forgotten how nice it can be to just enjoy the simple pleasures in life—like . . . like this perfectly beautiful day," she ranted, "without dredging up the past and arguing about things that don't even matter anymore!"

She stood, gesturing angrily with her arms. "What's past is past, for God's sake! Can't you—" The toe of her boot caught in her hem. "—just . . . oh-hh-h!"

Balance lost, momentum gained, she pitched forward, her lecture ending abruptly in a tangle of cotton gingham. Arms flailing, she fell smack on top of the scowling object of her anger, flattening him to the ground.

"Oof—"

"Agh!"

"Oh!" Kierin gasped, irritated beyond endurance to find herself in his arms. "Let me up, you—you—"

Her elbow dug him painfully in the ribs. "Ow! Simmer down, will you?" Clay yelled, clamping his steely hands around her wrists. He rolled over on top of her and shifted his weight, pinning her completely to the ground.

"Get . . . off . . . of me," she panted. "What do you think you're—"

He wrestled her still. "Did anyone ever tell you that you're breathtakingly beautiful when you're clumsy?"

"Ooo-hh! You are the most impossible man I've ever met!"

"So," he replied mildly, pinning her arms above her head, "now you've added *impossible* to my long list of faults?"

His amused expression sent her temper flaring. "Yes!" Her heart was knocking against her ribs so hard it shook her whole body, "And irritating and closedmouthed. And let's not forget bullheaded!" she added for good measure. She squirmed underneath him, but she felt about as puissant as a trussed-up squirrel.

He lowered a quelling amount of weight against her.

"What was that you said?" he asked. His mouth tipped up at the corners with mischief. "Simple pleasures?" With its flash of white teeth, his grin was as dangerous as it was seductive.

She nearly stopped breathing. "That wasn't what I meant."

Nose to nose, they glared at one another. His lean body pressed against hers with the unyielding rigidity of iron. He'd trapped her wrists up by her ears and her breasts were flattened against the lean-muscled wall of his chest. If he'd wanted to crush her, she knew it would have been a simple matter of shifting his substantial weight off his elbows.

"Perhaps you should show me what you *did* mean," he taunted, rocking his hips against hers until she could feel his arousal hard against her.

Her breath returned in short, angry puffs. "You're a bully, Clay Holt. Let me up," she demanded, but had little hope of his compliance.

His stormy eyes explored the jade depths of hers as if truly seeing them for the first time. His heated lips caressed her cheek. "I don't think so," he murmured in a voice that was almost a whisper and nearly lost to the vibrant hum of the prairie.

Her lips parted—with the vague awareness that he intended to kiss her—and unconsciously, she moistened them with the tip of her tongue. She felt him quicken against her belly. A shock raced through her at the foreign sensation and her nerves stretched taut as a fiddle string.

His head dipped with calculated slowness to her ear, where his tongue traced little circles against the sensitive lobe and then he nipped it playfully.

"Is this what you meant?" he murmured in a low, breathy hiss.

"No." The word was little more than a whisper.

His open mouth descended to the hollow dip in her shoulder. "Or . . . this?"

Her head rocked slightly back and forth in a useless denial of the inevitable.

"No?" Clay's eyes, raised now to hers, had darkened to the color of thunderheads. His mouth hovered a heartbeat away from hers. "What about this?"

"Don't—" Her lips formed the word, but no sound accompanied the protest, for at that moment, his mouth swooped down on hers. It took complete possession of hers in a kiss so like the man who gave it—passionate and disturbing. Her mouth yielded to his in the space of a breath and her lips, newly tutored by him, opened to the insistence of his tongue.

The passion exploded between them with such unexpected intensity it left them both gasping. His open palm made a slow, maddening descent down the length of her arm and closed over the full swell of her breast. His fingertips caressed the hardened peak that rose beneath the fabric of her dress, sending exquisite ripples of heat through her limbs.

Relinquishing her mouth momentarily, he burned fiery, open-mouthed kisses down the length of her slender neck. She thought to protest, but her brain seemed to be working too slowly to form the words. An involuntary shudder raced through her.

"Ah . . . perhaps this . . . was what you meant." His mouth hovered over her, barely touching her neck with butterfly touches of his lips.

Kierin tilted her head back against the ground, wantonly exposing more of her throat to him, and she pushed her fingers into the dark curls at his temples. Was it what she'd meant? She couldn't remember. More accurately, she couldn't think. Not when his mouth was doing such wonderful things to her.

His lips sought hers again. "Kierin . . ." he whispered against her mouth, the raw hunger roughening his voice. "God . . . you make me—"

The prairie had swallowed the sound of the approaching horse until it was almost upon them. Instincts dulled by languid passion surged through him with a rush of adrenaline.

"Bloody hell!" Clay rolled off her, his Colt already clearing the leather strapped to his thigh. His vision was momentarily impaired by the glare of the late afternoon sun, but he saw the dark shape of a rider haul back on the reins some twenty feet away.

"Holy hell! — don't shoot!" a familiar voice cried. The man wheeled his mount as if ready to flee.

Clay squinted into the blinding glare. Relief swamped him. It was Mel Watkins on his dun horse, looking, at the moment, as if he'd rather be anywhere else in the world but where he was.

Clay lowered the pistol, but his heart thudded heavily in his chest. He looked back at Kierin, who was sitting up now, arms splayed at her sides against the ground. Her cheeks were flushed a bright pink — from passion or embarrassment he couldn't be sure — and her teeth toyed worriedly with the edge of her bottom lip.

It wasn't like him to let his guard down like that. With a shudder, he realized it could have easily been an unfriendly Indian hunting party as the harmless man mounted before them. A bead of sweat tricked down his back between his shoulder blades. What if his carelessness had gotten her killed?

Watkin's horse pranced nervously in a circle. Its rider, dark-haired and with the solid build of a farmer, fought to keep his seat. "Hey, remind me not to come at you from the blind side again, huh?"

"Sorry, Mel," Clay answered with a singular lack of candor. "What do you want?"

Mel raised an amused eyebrow at the blunt dismissal in Clay's voice and eyed the beautiful, somewhat rumpled woman beside him. "Mrs. Holt." He touched the brim of his hat to her and returned his gaze to Holt. "Jacob asked me to come out and find you. Says he needs a hand with the stock when we make the crossing."

"Crossing?" Clay replied, straightening. "I thought we weren't supposed to make the ford until tomorrow."

"Yeah. But Kelly found a promising spot a day closer and he's already moving some of the wagons across."

Clay holstered his gun and sighed. "Thanks, Mel. Tell Jacob we're right behind you."

Mel tossed him a knowing smile. "Will do. And my apologies for the . . . interruption," he added as tactfully as possible. He nodded to Kierin. "Afternoon, ma'am."

Kierin blushed deeper in reply and forced a small, tight smile. "Mr. Watkins."

Watkins laid a spur to his horse's flank and soon disappeared over the rise.

Kierin flopped back with a dramatic moan to the ground, arms flung wide, eyes clamped shut. "Oh God!"

"It's all right," he told her, getting to his feet. He knew exactly what she was feeling.

"All right?" She nearly laughed. She *would* have laughed if it hadn't all been so humiliating. "Did you see the look on his face?"

"Yeah," Clay answered, his grin returning at the memory of Watkin's expression. "Sheer terror."

Kierin ignored his optimism and groaned. "I give him all of ten minutes before the whole train knows what we were doing out here."

He leaned down and reached a slender hand down to her. "If he says anything," Clay responded gently, "it'll be that I was having a hell of a time controlling myself around my beautiful 'wife.' " His gaze swept over her face. "And who would blame me?"

She was caught off guard by the sudden tenderness in his voice. It was the nicest thing he'd ever said to her. Kierin lifted her gaze slowly to meet his, fearful that he was merely teasing her again. But one look told her he wasn't. The candor in his eyes startled her, sending currents of warmth flooding through her.

"Come on," he repeated, taking her hand. "We'd better get back." He helped her up and whistled for Taeva, who'd been grazing not far away.

He pulled her up behind him this time after he'd mounted. Her arms circled his tapered waist and she clung to him, cheek pressed against his back as the prairie sped by them.

Her mind was a jumble of emotions. Clay was as unpredictable as the wind that buffeted the plain, as mysterious as its secrets. But in spite of his hostility and all the other things she'd accused him of earlier, she was suddenly and unalterably aware of a new truth.

She was falling in love with him.

"H'yaw!"

Jacob's voice rang out above the rush of the Big Blue's current. His bullwhip cracked sharply, then landed with an ineffectual splat in the water a few feet away from the lead team of oxen. "Git up there, you miserable lame-brained tubs a' gleet . . ."

Mose and Tulip, the two oxen in the lead, bellowed stubbornly in complaint as the rain-swollen river eddied around their flanks, but refused to budge. They'd planted themselves squarely at the midpoint of the fifty-yard span of water, apparently oblivious to the string of blue oaths Jacob flung at them. The second team shifted restlessly in their wooden yokes, grinding the wagon's wheels deeper into the muddy bottom.

Waist-deep in water, Jacob snatched his hat off in frustration and slapped it across the wooden oxbow. "I never see'd no animals as ornery as you, you mule-headed piece o' fish bait! Git up there. H'yaw!"

Kierin tightened her grip on the rocking bench seat at the front of the wagon and tried to keep from smiling. Jacob's temper didn't flare often, but when it did, it was truly something to behold.

"We takin' in water yet?" he shouted, ignoring her amused expression.

Kierin shook her head. "The blocks you and Clay put above the axles seem to be doing the trick, but not if it gets much deeper."

"Ain't gonna *get* no deeper . . . less 'n we sink," Jacob muttered irritably.

"Hey, Jacob. Got trouble?" Mel Watkins called from his wagon as they forded past. Beside him on the seat, his young wife, Elizabeth, held two of their four small children on her lap. She smiled and waved at Kierin. The two older boys, eyes shining with curiosity, peeped out around the canvas cover in the front.

Jacob waved him on. "Nah, just an ornery team, I reckon."

"Where's Clay?" Mel asked, leaning back out as they passed.

"Takin' the rest of the stock across," Jacob answered.

"When I see him at the other side, I'll send him on back for ya."

"Be obliged," Jacob called after him. He waded back against the current to the wagon front, the late afternoon sun sparkling off the moisture in his wiry black hair.

Tulip bellowed again.

"What do you think's wrong with them?" Kierin asked.

Jacob reached into the jockey box and pulled out a long-handled crowbar. "They's fractious critters," he muttered with a growl. "But maybe we's hung up on somethin' down below. Gonna have me a look at the wheels."

"Is there anything I can do?"

"You 'member how to use this?" He held out the bullwhip to her, then stripped his dark cotton shirt over his head and tossed it into the wagon.

Kierin smiled. "Do bees buzz? Flies fly?" she teased. Jacob had spent hours on the trail patiently teaching her to use the lead-weighted whip made of braided raw-hide and she could finally muster a respectable crack out of it. "You just tell me when."

"Yes, ma'am," he acknowledged with a grin and he waded back to inspect the rear axle.

Kierin watched Jacob go, grateful that things were so easy between them. Since the night in the wagon, their friendship had blossomed as naturally as the carpet of spring wildflowers amid the long prairie grasses. Some days they'd walk along in companionable silence, admiring the ever-widening landscape of the plains and other days he'd spend hours teaching her something useful like, how to crack a whip or cleat an ox shoe.

He'd told her, without a trace of self-pity, about growing up on the plantation in Mississippi, about the cotton and the endless work and bloodied fingers he'd had from the picking. Sometimes he talked of Bess and he'd get that faraway look in his eyes as he had that night in the wagon.

In her turn, she'd told Jacob about raising her brother, Matthew—being more mother than sister to him and about the terrible void he'd left in her life when her pa had taken him West. She'd even spoken to him of Lilly—without, she mused, so much as a blink from him—and her regret over not having said good-bye. It seemed a natural consequence of their friendship to share these things with Jacob.

If only it could be that simple with Clay, she thought. Kierin's gaze was pulled to the far bank in search of his familiar shape atop the tall Appaloosa stallion. Her heart constricted when she spotted him coming back toward the wagon. Head bent in concentration, he guided his horse across the rocky river bottom near the shore.

The afternoon breeze ruffled through his thick dark hair. It had grown longer since the trail's start and brushed the tops of his shoulders in back. The wildness of it suited him, just as the freedom of the trail seemed

148

to. He rode with the ease of a man at home in the wilderness, in complete harmony with the animal beneath him.

It made her stomach flip-flop to see him approach. The memory of his kiss made her press her lips together in silent warning. She could still taste his kiss and remember how his arms felt around her. Desire ebbed through her again, making her pulse thud in her ears.

At that moment, Clay looked up and his eyes found hers. He urged the black horse forward with his knees and held her with his smoky gaze. His expression betrayed nothing of what he might be thinking as he approached, but his steely eyes met hers squarely, almost arrogantly, as if challenging her to be the first to look away. When she didn't, an appealing smile crept to the corners of his mouth.

"What's the problem? We stuck?" he asked over the noise of the bawling animals.

"Jacob's gone to check," she told him. "Mose and Tulip refuse to move and the others seem a little spooked, too."

Clay gave an understanding nod. "Water's pretty high and running fast," he said, unfastening the leather thong on his gunbelt where it spanned his muscular thigh. "Almost lost the cow driving her across." He handed her the weighty holster, then stripped off his shirt. "You okay here?"

Kierin's eyes fell of their own accord to the sweat-sheened contours of his chest. He swiped the wadded shirt across his face and across the back of his neck, brushing away the beads of moisture there. The gesture made her mouth go suddenly dry.

"Kierin?" he asked again, tying the horse's reins to the brake handle.

Her head snapped up guiltily. "Huh? What?"

A smile tipped one corner of his mouth. "I asked if you were all right here."

"Oh, yes. Perfectly fine." She swallowed back the

lump of humiliation in her throat. *Lord, she couldn't even look at him anymore without making an utter fool of herself.*

"Good girl." He eased down off the horse and lowered himself gingerly into the chilly river. "Waugh-hh!" he gasped. "By damn, that's cold!"

"Clay," Jacob shouted from the other side of the wagon, "We got us a hunk of dead wood wedged in the spokes o' the right front wheel. Stuck tight. We gots to back the team up to git it outta there."

"All right. I'll get up by Tulip and see what I can do." Clay braced himself against the flanks of the animals as he maneuvered himself to the head of the team.

The oxen both bawled and shifted uneasily in the water. "Back, shh-h-h," Clay told Tulip. "Back up, girl."

The wagon moved almost imperceptibly backward and Jacob braced his shoulder against the wheel, reaching below the level of the water to the snag. "Not yet."

"Shh-h-h, back, Tulip."

Kierin watched Jacob try again, the muscles in his shoulder straining against the wheel. Out of the corner of her eye, Kierin saw a flash of movement in the water. Her eyes darted upstream and caught the zigzag motion of a huge dark snake headed directly for Jacob.

"J-Jacob! Behind you!" she screamed. "Snake!"

150

Chapter Ten

Jacob whirled around, flattening himself against the wagon with a look of stark terror on his face. A strangled sound escaped him that was not quite a word, not quite a scream.

"Jacob! Get up! Get up in the wagon!" she begged, reaching out to him with her hand.

He couldn't move. Paralyzed with fear, Jacob pressed himself against the wagon, black eyes riveted to the oncoming devil.

"Clay!" Kierin's voice was hoarse with fright. Awkwardly, she tugged the heavy pistol from the holster in her lap. Clay struggled against the current, frantically trying to reach Jacob. The oxen rolled their eyes in panic when they spotted the snake, heaving in all directions in their yokes. As the wagon lurched and bucked sideways, Kierin was thrown painfully against the hickory bow. Clay's gun flew out of her hand and fell with a hollow clatter to the planked floor at her feet.

The black serpent was coming fast, carried by the swift-moving water — unerring in its deadly aim.

Fifteen feet. Kierin fumbled for the fallen gun.

Ten feet. Oh, God, where is it? she screamed silently. Her fingers closed around the stock.

Five feet. She yanked the gun up, but the tip flailed wildly as she tried to balance its weight.

151

Two feet. The water exploded and blew the black serpent apart in two pieces, raining blood and bits of flesh down on the wagon. Kierin stared down at the cold gun in her hand in disbelief, then up at Jacob.

His eyes were closed and his throat worked up and down convulsively. Shock had turned his dark skin to pasty gray and she knew it mattered not a wit to him *who* had fired that shot.

Clay reached them as she lowered the pistol. "By God, what a shot!" he shouted. Gingerly, he inspected the severed head of the snake and let out a low whistle. "Cottonmouth," he said, revealing the starkly white interior of the snake's mouth. He gave her a puzzled frown. "I thought you said you couldn't shoot a gun."

"I can't . . ." she murmured, confusion etched on her face. "I didn't—I mean I was going to but—"

"Haw, haw, haw!"

Kierin's head snapped around at the sound of the raucous laughter from the eastern shore, audible even over the rush of the river. On the far bank, she saw a tall, gray-bearded trapper slapping his knee in a fit of glee. Beside him stood a two-wheeled cart hitched to two pairs of mules, half in and half out of the river. Perched on the seat of that rickety vehicle was a young Indian woman who held a smoking rifle in her hands. She was ripe with child and her quilled doeskin dress was pulled tightly across her swollen belly.

"Ain't she a caution?" the trapper shouted in a deep baritone voice that rivaled the volume of his laugh. "I'll be ding-dong damned if she cain't shoot the ear off a fly!"

While Kierin and Jacob exchanged astonished looks, Clay squinted across the glare of the sun-flecked water.

"*Ben?*" Clay called. "Ben Crowley?"

The old man shaded his eyes with a bear paw-sized hand and let out a whoop. "Well, if that don't beat all! 'Zat you, Sprout?"

Clay's face brightened like a candle-lit birthday cake. "It sure as hell is, you old grizzly eater. What're you doing so far east?"

The old man let out another sharp laugh. "Remindin' myself why I left!" Crowley hopped aboard his cart and slapped the traces across the backs of the mules. The Indian woman beside him stowed the rifle beneath their feet.

When Crowley's wagon pulled up alongside theirs, the old trapper reached down and seized Clay's hand in a bone-crushing squeeze and the two men slapped each other hard on the shoulder.

"God, it's good to see you again, Ben," said Clay. "How long has it been?"

Ben ran his fingers thoughtfully through his scraggly beard. "Five winters, near as I can figure." Eyeing Clay speculatively, he added, "You filled out some since then, boy."

Clay smiled broadly and slapped him on the arm again.

"Oh, Ben, I'd like you to meet Jacob, the man whose neck your friend here just saved. Jacob—Ben Crowley."

Jacob, who was still recovering from the shock, extended a hand to the older man. "Pleasure's mine, suh."

"Ben. Just Ben," Crowley corrected, pumping Jacob's hand. "An this here's Wakinyela." He cupped a hand on her shoulder. "That's her Sioux name, but she answers to Dove."

Dove was even younger than she'd looked from a distance, and Kierin doubted she was over twenty. Her features, strong yet utterly feminine, were marred only by the thin slash of a scar that ran across the length of her cheek. Her straight black hair, neatly plaited and tied with leather thongs, rode along the top of her swollen belly. They were an odd pair, the trapper and the girl, Kierin thought.

153

Ben's gaze fell on her. "An' who's this pretty thing?"

"This is . . . Kierin, Ben," Clay told him. He couldn't bring himself to tell the old man the lie.

If Ben caught the hesitation in Clay's voice, he didn't mention it, but nodded approvingly. "You always was one with an eye for beauty, boy."

Kierin's cheeks flushed pink and she smiled back at the grizzled old trapper. She prepared herself for his bone-crunching handshake, but when his hand swallowed hers, it was met with surprising tenderness.

"Ma'am, it's a downright pleasure," he said.

"Mine too," she agreed. "If you and Dove hadn't happened along when you did . . ."

"Fair shot, ain't she? Taught her everthin' she knows," Ben bragged. "Well, ain't we a sight, jawin' in the middle o' the river. Let's get over to dry land an' we'll do us some serious palaverin'."

The offending deadwood had worked itself free during the fracas, but not before damaging several spokes on the wheel. Clay mounted Taeva and led the still-nervous team of oxen slowly across the span of water, and Jacob rode with Kierin in the wagon.

By the time they reached the shore, the decision to stop for the day had already been made. Theirs wasn't the only wagon suffering damage from the crossing. The Tolefson wagon had broken a hound, while two other rigs had taken on water and their supplies had to be dried out.

Ben and Dove set up camp beside Clay's wagon, and while the light was good, the men worked on repairing the wheel. Dove helped Kierin prepare the evening meal, contributing freshly picked wild onions and Lamb's Tongue to the common stew pot. Kierin was glad for the company, but she wondered about Dove's curious silence. She had yet to hear the girl utter a word, either in her own tongue or in English, though she understood everything that was being said to her. She seemed to communicate through those expressive eyes of hers—bright, inquisitive, and brown as ripe buckeyes.

Kierin ladled helpings of the savory-smelling stew onto the sturdy tin plates, absently wondering if the baby Dove carried belonged to Ben. The spark of affection between the two was unmistakable, just as it was between Ben and Clay.

Clay.

She smiled, remembering the look that had transformed his face when he'd recognized Ben at the river. The change had taken her breath away. Free for that moment from the ghosts of his past, Kierin glimpsed the man Clay *could* be if only he would allow it.

She released a long breath. Providence, she decided, had seen fit to put Ben in their path. For that she was grateful. Who knew what would come of it?

Ben Crowley was a man who enjoyed his food. His manner of eating was at once artless and fascinating. He used the spoon he'd been given, but Kierin supposed that the lack of one would prove no obstacle to him. With each savored bite, he hummed a little tuneless melody which clearly held a note of appreciation. Already on his third helping of stew, he mopped the last spot of gravy from his plate with the remains of his biscuit and popped it into his mouth, relishing the taste. He patted his belly and waggled his shaggy eyebrows at Kierin.

"A man can forget a lot of things about civilization," he said, "but good food ain't one of 'em. You think you kin teach Dove to make biscuits like these?"

Dove and Kierin exchanged conspiratorial smiles. "I already did," she told him with a laugh. "Not bad for a first attempt, mm-m?"

A look of awe crossed Ben's face and he let out a bark of laughter. "Wal, I'll be cornswaggled. You made these, Dove?" The girl hid her shy smile behind her hand. "By jingo, girl, I knew you had possibilities. I reckon I'll have to lay us in a supply o' wheat flour at Kearny in that case."

Clay set his empty plate down close to the flickering fire of buffalo chips. "Does that mean you'll be traveling with us for a while, Ben?" he asked hopefully.

"Can't find much argument agin' it," Ben answered. "Me an' Dove's headed back to the Absarokas. Got me a trap line up there and a cabin big enough fer two." He glanced at Dove's ripe belly. "Or three."

"You said Dove was Sioux?" asked Kierin.

The old trapper nodded, fishing an intricately carved bone pipe out of a small beaded deer-skin bag tied to his waist. "Dove's folks was Lakota — all killed by the same Pawnee raiders that took her for a slave. Now that she's marked," Ben's explained, indicating the slash on her cheek, "she ain't of a mind to go back to the Sioux. I bought her from a lickered up Pawnee named Coyote Runs back in Council Bluffs four months ago."

Ben poked a thin stem of stiff grass into the blackened bowl of his pipe and scooped out the old, spent ashes. "And if yer tryin' to reckon if it's my babe a-growing in there, I'll save ya the trouble," he told them matter-of-factly. "It ain't. The rest is Dove's business an' none'a mine. I'm long past my prime mating years anyway," he said with the characteristic bluntness Clay remembered. "She says she wants to go with me and I'm glad fer the company." He rubbed his gnarled fingers across the smooth stem of his pipe and smiled at Dove.

Clay frowned slightly, regarding the old trapper in a new light. It hadn't occurred to him before this moment that Ben might have regrets about the solitary life he'd chosen. Oddly, Clay mused, it was the path he seemed destined to follow as well.

He looked up and found Kierin studying Ben and Dove with an almost wistful expression. The firelight played across her delicate features and her hair took on the brilliant color of the flame. A wave of desire shot through him so strong it made his breath catch. *God, she's a beautiful woman,* he thought, unable to drag his eyes from the sight of her. The image of her struggling to save Jacob from that snake rose in his mind. Her feisty spirit and her sense of loyalty surprised him again, and again. She deserved more than she'd been handed in life—more than he would ever be able to give her.

Ben tamped a good-sized pinch of tobacco into his pipe then lit the pipe with the glowing end of a piece of dead grass. "Sprout, you still remember the old place we had up in the Bitterroot Range?"

The Bitterroots. The name sent memories rushing back to Clay. It had been home—as much of a home as he'd known for years. Ben had found him in '42—young, green, and stubbornly alone in the foothills of those mountains, trying to eke out a living as a trapper. The old man, who would become more of a father to Clay than his own had ever been, gathered Clay under his wing and taught him his trade. Ben took him into his world, explained the ins and outs of fur trading, and instilled in Clay a deep and abiding respect for the Indians who shared the land with them.

The place they'd called home wasn't much, but even now, if he closed his eyes, he could almost smell the earthy blend of wood smoke and tanned hides which were as much a part of the small cabin they shared as the rough-hewn timbers that supported it.

"How could I forget that little hole we called home?" he asked, pulling himself from the self-indulgent memory. "Those were good times, Ben."

Ben made a sound deep in his throat as if the memory gave him as much pleasure as it did Clay. He took a few long draws on the stem of his pipe and leaned forward. His fringed elbows dangled over his knees. "I was right sorry to hear about your troubles a few years back, Clay."

Clay's back straightened and his gaze flicked up involuntarily to Kierin. She was clearing the dishes with Dove. For a fraction of a second, she looked up to search his face and the tenderness in her eyes sent an unexpected shock rippling through him. He glanced away quickly, afraid to ponder what was behind that tenderness.

It shouldn't have surprised him that word of what had happened on his ranch had gotten around to Ben. Still, it did. "How'd you hear?"

"Old Tom Fitzpatrick. Said he'd run into you at the Fort Laramie powwow a couple years back. Said you was after the bastards that done it." He paused, waiting for Clay to respond.

Silence.

"You ever get 'em, son?" Ben prodded gently.

The familiar mask descended over Clay's face, but this time the look was couched in pain. "Two of 'em," he admitted. "Never did find the other one. He was hiding behind the name of some company that was trying to buy up the land north of Oregon City for the timber. After the fire, near as I could figure, the third man sold out and moved back East. That's where I've been for the better part of three years."

Ben crossed his moccasined feet, pulling them close to his body, and wrapped his arms around his knees Indian-style. "Dammed shame," he said with a regretful shake of his head. "You headed back there now? To Oregon?"

"Yeah. The trail is cold behind me now. If I go back to where I began, maybe . . ." His voice drifted off, his thought left unspoken. The fire hissed in the silence that fell. Across the encampment someone was playing a wistful tune on a mouth harp.

"Maybe it's time to let it go, son," Ben suggested gently.

The flare of anger in Clay's eyes was brief and, out

158

of respect for Ben, disappeared almost as fast as it came.

Let it go, Clay repeated silently. It was a litany that had crossed his own mind many times in the past few years though the very idea seemed a betrayal. Until now, no one had dared to say it to him, but it was a sentiment he'd read often in Jacob's eyes.

In his heart, he knew they were both right. Killing those two men hadn't brought back Amanda or their child. Instinctively, he'd known from the start that she wouldn't have wanted it. That wasn't her way.

None of that had mattered to him three years ago, so blinded was he by anger and hatred. It had simply become, over the years, a personal vendetta for him — a temporary if fleeting balm for the pain of his loss. Revenge, he'd discovered, wasn't sweet and it hadn't changed anything.

Except him.

"About Tom Fitzpatrick, Ben," Clay began, wanting to change the subject but reluctant to embark on an equally painful one.

Ben quickly came to his old friend's defense. "Aw, he didn't mean no harm, tellin' me about your troubles, Clay. He was worried about you is all."

"I know. It's not that." He hesitated again, knowing what good friends the two men had been in the old days. "I saw Tom this winter, in Washington."

"Hell's bells! Washington? Ain't he come up in the world!" Ben chucked a sound through his teeth. "Washington. Well, he makes a damn good Indian agent and that's a fact. How the hell is he?"

"He . . . died this past winter, Ben," Clay answered slowly. "Pneumonia."

Ben was quick to hide the stricken look that leaped to his eyes. Clay knew Fitz had been a good friend and a dependable trapping partner to Ben in years gone by. He was a man you could count on in a squeeze. He watched as the trapper mechanically tamped another wad of tobacco into the bowl of his long-stemmed pipe.

"When he heard I was heading West again," Clay continued, "he asked me to deliver his last report to the new commander at Fort Laramie. Some green first lieutenant named Randall."

"A first lieutenant!" Ben nearly choked on the smoke from his pipe. "What the hell are they trying to do? Start a goddamn war? Them West Point Willies is so wet behind the ears they don't know their asses from a hole in the ground, much less a hostile Indian from a friendly one."

Clay shrugged in silent agreement.

"Why you?" Kierin asked, wiping her damp hands on the towel she'd pinned around her dress as an apron. "Surely they've appointed a new agent for the Plains tribes by now."

Clay looked up at her. "By now I'm sure they have. But Tom asked me to do this as a personal favor to him, partly because I was there with him in 'fifty-one when the treaty was negotiated and I know the terms. He told me the Sioux were pretty hot last year over a long list of grievances, including cuts in their annuities."

"Annuities?" Kierin asked.

"The U.S. government promised to pay the Plains tribes in goods each year for the right to move the wagons through their territory safely."

Ben shook his head sadly. "Ain't no stoppin' it now," he predicted as much to himself as to the others sitting around the fire. "Annuities or no, the day's coming when the Indians is gonna run outta fuse with the *wasikun*, the white man. There won't be no place safe out here for us to be."

Dove touched Ben's sleeve and, for the first time since Kierin had met her, spoke in remarkably good English. "You are brother to the Sioux, *Mato*," she told him proudly. "Many have smoked your pipe of friendship. No Sioux brave will harm you."

The old man's face crinkled in a sad but affectionate smile. "There's truth in your words, Wakinyela. But there'll come a time, mark my word, when no *wasikun's* hair'll be safe on the prairie, because the Indians doin' the scalpin' won't bother with all them pleasantries like introductions."

"Then," she answered, "you must wear a fine tunic. I will quill it for you as I did once for my brother. Then all will know you are Sioux—here." She tapped a closed fist over her heart.

Ben's expression had turned solemn. "You do me honor, Dove." Dove fell silent again, but sat back on her heels with a satisfied smile.

Jacob tossed the stick he'd been stirring the fire with into the blaze and stood up. "Jim gave me first watch tonight, so I best be on my way." He turned to Dove. "I ain't thanked you proper for savin' my life today, Wakin-yela," he told her, stumbling over her proper name. "I . . . I'm beholden to you."

Dove didn't answer but searched Jacob's dark eyes for a long moment. Kierin watched something elusive spark between them before Dove nodded and lowered her eyes. Almost reluctantly it seemed, Jacob pulled his gaze from her, bid them all good night, and walked off into the darkness.

Ben rubbed the stem of his pipe for a moment thoughtfully. "Well," he said, slapping his thigh, "I'm plumb tuckered out. Think I'll hit the hay. You comin', Dove?"

The Indian woman cast a furtive glance into the darkness after Jacob. Then, in spite of her condition, she rose gracefully from her knees and took her place beside Ben.

"G'night, Dove, Ben," Clay said, standing to clasp the old trapper's hand once more. "It's damn good to see you again."

"You too, boy," Ben answered, taking Clay's hand in both of his in a warm handshake.

Long after they'd gone, Clay stood staring off into the darkness, lost in thought. Watching him, Kierin realized no one would be privy to the memories he grappled with. *He's such a solitary man,* she thought. He kept his thoughts and emotions bottled up within him like fine whiskey. Were they too precious to share, she wondered, or too painful?

"Well, I think I'll take a walk," Clay told her finally, shoving his hands into the pockets of his denims. "I'll be back . . . later."

Disappointment stung her as she watched him walk away. It had become his habit to take a walk at night, giving her time to prepare for bed in private. It was a consideration that she'd always been grateful for.

Until tonight.

She didn't feel like going to sleep and she was much too wound up to be tired. Before she could stop herself, she called after him. "Do you want some company?" Her courage nearly faltered as he turned to face her with that inscrutable expression of his. "I'm . . . not really sleepy yet," she added with a hopeful smile.

He pulled his hands slowly out of his pockets. "Sure. I just thought . . ."

Ignoring him, Kierin took a deep breath of the crisp evening air. "It's a beautiful night, isn't it?" she asked, taking his arm.

Clay nearly jumped at the contact. He released a shaky breath. "Mm-hm," he agreed, letting his eyes roam over the deep auburn color of her hair in the moonlight. "Beautiful."

The obsidian sky above her glittered with a million pinpricks of light, scattered like so many seeds in the wind. Wildflowers scented the gentle breeze. Across the encampment, a fiddle and melodian had joined the harmonica and a crowd had gathered around the fire to listen.

Clay and Kierin strolled slowly toward the group.

"It's on nights like this," Kierin said, breaking their comfortable silence, "that I miss Matthew the most."

"Matthew. Is that your brother?"

Kierin nodded. "We used to study the stars when the sky was clear like this. He was quite accomplished for a ten-year-old."

Clay stopped walking. "Your brother's only ten?"

"He was a year ago. He's nearly eleven now. Why?"

"I don't know," he answered. "I thought . . . when you said you had a brother in California, it was an older brother. Your whole family out there?"

Her expression changed subtly. "Just my father and Matthew. My mother died soon after Matthew was born."

"How did you happen to stay behind in Independence?" he asked, suddenly wanting to know.

Kierin looked away uncomfortably. She didn't want to talk about this; it was too painful. But it needed saying. "Didn't you even look at those papers you signed back there?"

Her answer threw him off balance. "What are you talking about?"

She sighed into the night air, emotion burning the backs of her eyes. "It was my father who left me with John Talbot to work off his gambling debt. He . . . took my brother and went to California to find gold."

"He *what?*"

Kierin didn't raise her head. It shamed her to think of what had been done to her. "He said he'd come back for me when he struck it rich."

"Christ!" he swore. "Your own father? Why didn't you tell me any of this before?"

Kierin's eyes met his on common ground. "Would it have changed anything if I had?"

His eyebrows went up fractionally. "I . . . I don't know. You could have told me anyway."

"Why? Like you've told me about yourself? About your wife or Ben?"

His expression stilled and grew serious. "That's different," he replied.

"Is it?" She stopped and faced him. "You know, I found out more about you today from that old trapper than I have from you in a whole month."

"That's just who I am, Kierin," he told her without apology. "Don't expect things from me I can't give you."

She laid a hand tentatively on his arm and tipped her chin up to look at him. "It doesn't have to be that way between us, you know."

Clay searched her eyes for a truth he knew he'd find there. It would be so easy to trust her. Easy to share the burden he'd been carrying for so long with a woman like her. But it was an old habit, long ingrained and hard to break. Even if he did tell her about the ghosts that haunted his sleep, it would serve no purpose. He had his devils to chase and she had hers.

Impulsively, he pulled her close to him in the darkness. "It's better if you don't get to know me too well, Princess," he told her, splaying his fingers across her back. "You might not like what you find."

For a long moment, she allowed his arms to enfold her in his embrace. She pressed her cheek against the hard wall of his chest. It felt good just to stand there and let him hold her like this.

"Is that really what you're afraid of, Clay?" she asked against his sleeve. "Or are you simply afraid to let anyone that close to you again?" She untangled herself from his arms and shrugged her loose-woven shawl around her shoulders. Not wanting to hear his answer, she walked on ahead of him into the circle of music and light, leaving him behind to ponder her words.

Chapter Eleven

Fort Kearny sat on a low sandy bluff overlooking the Platte River. Originally called the Post at Grand Island, both for its lack of fortification and its view of the large, tree studded sandbar on the Platte, Kearny was not much more than an unimpressive collection of buildings strung out around a rectangular parade ground.

The fort was, nonetheless, a bustling center of activity on the Oregon Trail. As the only munitions and supply depot between Forts Leavenworth and Laramie, Kearny served as a hub in the spokes of the army's Western deployment and as protection for the California- and Oregon-bound emigrants.

Kierin's disappointment with Kearny's lackluster appearance was short-lived. The fort was humming with the sounds of civilization—something she hadn't realized she'd missed until now. Everywhere she looked, there were people. Blue-uniformed troops drilled in the central square under the noonday sun, while others lounged near the soldiers' barracks watching the wagons roll into the fort. Civilians peppered the walkways in street clothing.

A two-column formation of mounted cavalry troops stirred up a cloud of dust as they rode by the wagons on their way to patrol. They galloped past a small ragged contingent of tepees camped near the entrance. The Indians were Pawnee for the most part and a few Ponca. Kierin eyed them nervously as Jim Kelly called a halt to the wagons.

Clay, who was riding alongside the wagon, reined in Taeva and dismounted. Kierin started to climb down from her perch on the wagon seat, but suddenly felt Clay's strong hands around her waist. His touch sent shock waves up her spine. Effortlessly, he lifted her down and set her on the ground. His hands lingered at her waist, and a half-smile crossed his face.

"Jim's giving us an hour or so to buy what provisions we need before we make camp," he said. A teasing look lit his eyes. "I don't suppose you're interested in accompanying me to the sutler's store, are you?"

After more than a month in the wilderness, the idea of browsing through a shop surrounded by four solid walls sounded like heaven. She lifted an eyebrow in mock warning. "Just try to leave me behind, Clay Holt . . ."

He chuckled in response. "Jacob? You want to come along?"

Jacob untied the neckerchief at his throat and wiped his dark face with it. "Naw," he drawled. "I reckon I'll head over to the ordnance depot." With a nod of his head, he indicated the thick-walled earthen building at the north end of the fort. "We's running low on balls and powder. I'll meet you back here if you needs a hand." Jacob started to saunter off, but turned around, walking backward a few steps. "Be obliged if you'd pick up some more tobacco an' papers for me," he called. "Oh, and if they got a peppermint stick or two . . ."

Clay grinned at Jacob, well aware of his innocuous vices. "You sure you don't want to come with us . . . ?"

Jacob waved him off good-naturedly and headed

166

across the parade grounds.

Ben appeared at Clay's shoulder with Dove. "You reckon DuBecque still runs the sutler's store here?" the old trapper asked, massaging his fingers through his thinning hair before replacing the knit cap that almost always covered his head.

"Probably," Clay replied with an offhanded grin as they started toward the store. At Kierin's questioning look, he explained. "DuBecque was trading with the Ponca and Pawnee in these parts before the fort was even here. That rascal could fleece a bear out of his winter coat and then convince the poor animal that he'd done him a favor. If the old fella's got a breath in him, you can bet he's still at it."

Ben threw his head back and let out a booming hoot of concurring laughter. "Don't let DuBecque hear ya talkin' that way. He'll have you horse-tradin' fer feather pillows without the stuffin'."

The small, but bustling sutler's shop was tucked between the quartermaster's store and the officers' quarters. The first thing that caught Kierin's eye as she walked in were the rich pelts of beaver, fox, and wolverine that decorated the rough-hewn walls. Racks of antlers and antelope prongs hung over the windows and doorway. Shelves stocked with tinned goods and other paraphernalia laddered up two sides of the room.

At the opposite end of the room, a long double-planked bar rested atop two oak barrels. Several men lounged nearby nursing whiskeys while a middle-aged woman dressed in baggy trousers and a loose-fitting flannel shirt poured drinks for others. Her gray-streaked hair frizzled around her face like a halo, seemingly immune to all attempts at controlling it. She was laughing at something one of the men said.

Ben smiled and walked past the hogsheads of apples and the fragrant pickle barrels to where the woman

167

stood. "Still got a steady hand on the pour, I see."

The woman's head snapped around in instant recognition of the voice. Her dark brown eyes widened
with surprise. "As I live and breathe!" she gasped.
"Ben! Ben Crowley!" She fairly leaped from behind
the bar to give him an enormous bear hug, which he
returned with equal enthusiasm. His eyes squeezed
shut as if he were trying to carve the moment of holding her in his memory as a keepsake.

"Joey . . ." Ben murmured against her hair. "You're
lookin' fine as rain." He took a deep breath, untangled
his arms from hers, and held her away from him so he
could look at her.

She cuffed him affectionately on the shoulder, but
blushed like a schoolgirl at his compliment. "You old
flirt," she scolded. "You're a sight for sore eyes, Ben."
Her gaze took in the others standing beside him now.
"And Clay, too!" She crossed the space between them
and gave him a quick affectionate squeeze. "Where in
tarnation you been fer the past few years?" she asked,
turning to Ben. "We missed ya."

"Here and there," Ben answered noncommitally,
surveying the dimly lit store. "DuBecque still around?"

At that moment, a heavyset man carrying an arm-
load of boxes appeared at the door.

Joey tipped her head in his direction. "In the flesh.
Henri," she called, "look who we got here!"

Henri DuBecque, six feet two inches of brawn and
silver-tipped black hair, unloaded his burden and
straightened. "*Sacre Bleu!*" he cried, seeing his old adversary. "Ben, *mon ami* . . ." He extended his hand and
clasped Ben's firmly. "It has been too long, no?"

"I reckon so," Ben answered with a smile.

"You have been well?"

"Life's been good to me," Ben admitted.

"Ah," DuBecque answered warmly, "and to us." He
looked with affection at Joey. "But still we struggle,

eh? *C'est la vie.*" He shrugged, looking around at his shop. "*Mieux vaut sagesse que richesse.* Wisdom is worth more zan money, no? Are we wise yet, my friend?"

"Wiser than we were twenty years ago, I hope."

"*Oui,*" DuBecque chuckled in agreement. "One can only hope." With a warm handshake, he greeted Clay and was introduced to Kierin and Dove. He turned back to Ben, his expression suddenly puzzled. "You are not wiz ze train, yes?"

Ben guffawed loudly. "I see you still ain't learnt English, Henri. I *am* with the train—yes," he answered with a broad smile. "Hard to believe, ain't it? But me and Dove here run into Clay and his friends a ways back on our way to the Abrasokas. We decided to hitch up with 'em fer a spell."

DuBecque eyed the pregnant Indian girl with a sly smile. "Oh-ho, I see ze old grizzly bear still growls."

A quick look passed between Ben and Joey, but it was gone as soon as it came.

"Henri," Ben said, good-naturedly, neither acknowledging DuBecque's implication nor denying it, "are ya of a mind to do some serious dickerin' here or do ya plan to flap that jaw of yours all afternoon?"

DuBecque hadn't stayed in business all these years by being dense. He was quick to pick up on Ben's reticence to discuss the girl and he promptly dropped the subject. "Ah, *oui, mon ami.* My humble store eez at your disposal."

Ben and Clay gave DuBecque their lists, which included additional supplies of flour, sugar, and coffee and Jacob's requests as well. Joey helped another customer in the busy store, but Kierin noticed the woman's eyes strayed often to Ben. *Were they in love once?* she wondered. It would explain the bittersweet look she'd glimpsed in both of their expressions.

While Dove examined the bolts of yard goods, Kierin's fingers trailed enviously over the fine-textured

169

spools of satin ribbon on the table. Her hurried departure from Independence had precluded bringing along such small luxuries as hairpins and ribbons. Most days, she simply tied her unruly tresses back with a rough leather thong.

She glanced up to find Clay's eyes on her from across the room. The unfathomable expression in his smokey eyes caused her heart to caroom, and suddenly trembling, she forced herself to turn away. She let out a small cry of surprise when she ran smack into the solid bulk of a man.

"Whoa, little lady!" a voice said just above her ear.

A man's hands caught her by the shoulders and steadied her. The rank odor of his unwashed body and the stale smell of chewing tobacco assailed her before she even got a look at his face. She swallowed back the bile that rose in her throat.

"Excuse me," she said, glancing up at him. A chill went through her and she shrugged off his hands. He wasn't a tall man, but he was built like a bull. No shirt covered his dirt-stained long johns and the placket lay open, exposing a mat of hair the same reddish color as that of his scruffy beard and thinning hair.

His sharp blue eyes narrowed fractionally when he caught sight of her face, and he made a quick assessing perusal down the rest of her. Absently, he touched the brim of his battered hat to her.

"Ma'am."

Kierin breathed a sigh of relief as she edged by him. Something about the way the man looked at her made her uneasy. She could still feel his eyes on her back.

Kierin shook off the feeling. It was probably just her imagination. Still, she decided to put as much distance as she could between them. On the opposite side of the store, she stopped at a glass case near the front of the shop to admire the trinkets there. Silver-edged hand mirrors, fine-cut crystal bottles of perfume, and trinkets of jewelry lay against a green felt cloth, looking utterly out of place in a post so far from civilization. Her gaze roamed over the fine things slowly, like a child examining a forbidden plateful of cookies.

"Like 'em?" Joey asked at her shoulder.

Startled by her voice, Kierin jumped then laughed at her foolishness. "They're beautiful."

"Got more if you're interested. I keep 'em under the counter," she said, already reaching for them.

"Oh, no." Kierin put a hand up to stop her. "I couldn't possibly buy any of them."

"Who says you gotta buy? Lookin' can be almost as much fun." She set a tray on the counter and pulled away the cloth cover. "Henri scolds me fer tradin' fer these things 'cause we hardly ever sell 'em. I tell him that bein' a woman gives me the right to do foolish things now an' then."

Kierin smiled and looked down at the delicate pieces on the tray. There were gold rings with precious stones, silver-filigree pendants, and even a few plain wedding bands which had been parted with, she guessed, at great sacrifice.

Suddenly, her breath caught in her throat. Her gaze fell on a gold locket on a thinly braided gold chain. With trembling fingers, she reached out to touch it.

"Like that?" Joey asked. "Me, too. Simple but elegant, ain't it?"

Kierin nodded, unable to speak for a moment. She looked up at the older woman. "I . . . I know this locket."

Joey's face flattened with surprise. "You do?"

"It used to be my mother's . . . before it was mine," she murmured, fingering the piece.

Joey had a doubtful look on her face. "You sure, honey? Yer a long way from home."

Kierin looked up at the older woman. "I gave it to my brother before he left for California. It has a picture of me in it."

"You don't say? If that ain't the dangdest thing . . ."

Clay walked up beside Kierin. "See something you like?"

Joey pried the locket apart. Inside were two tiny photographs: one was of a young boy whose expression spelled mischief, and the other was of Kierin.

"That looks like you," Clay announced redundantly, a perplexed frown drawing his brows together.

"Where did you get this, Joey?" Kierin asked with a note of quiet desperation. "Do you remember?"

Joey scratched her wild gray hair. "Well, now lemme think. I've had it a spell. Least a year."

"Kierin, *is* that you?" Clay persisted.

Both women ignored him. "Did you buy it from the boy in the picture?" Kierin asked.

Joey was thoughtful for a moment. "No . . . I seem to recall it was an older feller who sold it to me, but now that I look at the picture, I do remember there bein' a boy with him."

"You do?"

"Yep. Dark-haired lad? Freckles? Yea high?" She angled a flat hand across her throat to approximate his height.

"Yes!" Kierin clasped her hands together under her chin. "That's him. That's Matthew! Oh, Joey—was he all right when you saw him? Did he look well? Was he—"

"Whoa . . ." Joey laughed. "Near as I kin recall, the boy was just fine. Healthy and cute as a button."

Kierin pressed the locket to her heart. "Thank God. For a minute, I thought . . ." She pushed the worry from her mind. "I gave that locket to Matthew so he would have something to remember me by. Why would my father sell it?"

Joey shrugged. "Same reason as most folks, I expect. Need food more'n they need trinkets."

172

"Of course." Slowly, Kierin untangled her fingers from the chain and replaced it on the tray. Though it broke her heart to return it, she had no money to buy it back from Joey.

Clay rested a hand on Kierin's shoulder and squeezed it gently. "Joey, tell me how much you want for it." Kierin's eyes darted to his in surprise.

Joey shook her head with a warm smile. "Some things oughtn't to have a price on 'em." She pressed the locket into Kierin's palm. "You take it, dearie. Let's just say I was holdin' it for ya."

Tears stung the backs of her eyes and she squeezed Joey's hand in thanks. "I don't know what to say . . ."

The gray-haired woman waved away Kierin's thanks. "Nothin' needs sayin'. Now" — she caught Clay's eye — "are you gonna hook that thing around this pretty little lady's neck or am I?"

Clay responded with a laugh. "You're a peach, Joey." He leaned down and kissed her on the cheek and took the locket from Kierin.

His fingers brushing her skin, Clay fastened the necklace around Kierin's throat in one deft movement. She felt her heart skip a beat at his closeness. He stayed behind her, hands bracketing her shoulders while she gazed at her reflection in the small hand mirror Joey held up. The locket settled against the cotton fabric of her dress like an old friend. Wearing it, she felt suddenly whole again, as if a piece of what had been torn away from her had been restored. *Matthew had made it this far and a little part of him was back with her again.*

Having concluded his business with another customer, Henri walked over to admire her selection. "Ah, *tres belle!* A wise choice, madam." He gave Joey a quick wink for her salesmanship. Joey's self-satisfied expression gave away nothing of her secret. She passed the wink on to Kierin when Henri turned away.

173

"You will come to the fandango at the fort tonight, *mes amis?* The young lady needs a place to wear such a trinket, no?"

"Fandango?" Clay echoed.

"It's Saturday," Joey offered in explanation. "We have a dance every Saturday night as long as there's trains comin' through. Keeps all these blue boys on their toes—if you know what I mean."

"What time?"

"Sundown, or thereabouts." Joey tucked a stray piece of hair behind her ear. "There's two other trains camped up on the river. Mormons in one—don't expect we'll be seeing much of them. The others will be here, though. Pass the word among your folks, will ya? The more the merrier."

Clay hefted a crateful of supplies into his arms and glanced at Kierin. "We'll do that. I think we can all use a break from trail dust for an evening."

"Should we bring something?" Kierin asked Joey.

A lively smile touched her lips. "You won't see any of them soldiers turnin' away home-cooked sweets," Joey hinted, "but for their part, I can pretty much guarantee you won't be dancin' with a dry throat neither."

Evening's long shadows slanted across the camp by the time they heard the first strains of music coming from the fort across the meadow. Jacob, Ben, and Dove walked on ahead, leaving Clay to pace near the fire, waiting for Kierin to finish dressing. He slid an index finger along the inside of the collar of his white chamois shirt, then straightened his black string tie. He felt vaguely uncomfortable in such trappings of civility, but then it had been a long time since he'd bothered with them.

"Kierin?"

A long pause. "Mm-hmm?"

"Are you, ah . . . almost ready?"

174

"Mm-hmm," came the muted reply.

He nodded silently to himself, absently twirling his flat-crowned hat between his fingertips. "Ben, Dove, and Jacob already went on ahead . . ." He heard her murmured response and cast a furtive glance back at the wagon. Bending low over the sweet fragrance of the dried-apple cobbler Kierin had made this afternoon, he inhaled deeply and closed his eyes. With mischievous resolve, he poked a surreptitious finger into a vent at the top of the crust, then popped the sweet-tipped digit into his mouth. Clay let out a sigh of pure pleasure.

"Perhaps I should have made two cobblers. One for the party and one for you."

Clay straightened guiltily at her words, let out a little laugh, and turned to meet the smile he heard in her voice. "I think that would have been a good i—" He stopped as he caught sight of her. His teasing words gathered at the back of his throat in a lump.

As he had hoped, she wore her green calico dress—the one the color of newborn leaves. The drop-shouldered sleeves were gathered at her slender wrists with the same tiny seed pearl buttons that ran down the front of her gown. The gold locket caressed the hollow between her breasts and caught the bronzed glimmer of the fireglow. In her loose auburn hair was the emerald satin ribbon he'd bought earlier from DuBecque and left in the wagon for her to find.

"You look . . . beautiful, Kierin." Clay tightened his fingers around the brim of his hat. It was an effort not to cross the short distance between them and gather her up in his arms.

Two telltale splotches of color rose in her cheeks at the look of undisguised hunger in his eyes. Her dark lashes fluttered down, casting long shadows across the delicate planes of her face. "Thank you," she said. Smoothing the bodice of her dress with the palm of her hand, she let her eyes stray back up to his. "And thank you for this, too." She touched the satin ribbon she'd threaded through her hair. "You didn't have to do that."

Seeing the smile it brought to her lips, he was suddenly very glad he had. "I wanted to. Besides, how could I resist?" One corner of his mouth quirked up as he slung a narrow parfleche over his shoulder. "The color matches your eyes." Picking up the warm cobbler, he offered her his arm. "Shall we?"

Kierin nodded, but her hand trembled as she placed it in the crook of his arm. His gift had touched her more than she could say. It was so unlike the other men she'd known to think of such small things. She couldn't remember her father ever giving her a gift or putting her needs before his own. She'd come to accept such insensitivity from men, even learned to expect it. But the protective barriers she'd erected against the inevitable hurt it caused were being steadily chipped away by Clay Holt's small kindnesses. The ribbon was only a tangible display of the thoughtfulness he'd shown her all along.

She remembered all the times he'd relieved her of the water-hauling chores when she was so tired from a long day's walk she could barely put one foot in front of the other; all the times he'd let her sleep a few extra minutes and started the morning fire for her. She thought of the small silly things, like the time he'd shown her the prairie dogs and his unexpected laughter when he'd pointed out the artful theatrics of a nesting killdeer.

She glanced up at him as they walked toward the fort in the twilight, and felt her heart swell with love for him. She was as helpless to contain the powerful emotion as she was to deny it. She would just allow herself to enjoy this one evening with him. What could it hurt to put aside their differences for one

176

night? She tightened her hand around the taut muscle of his arm and leaned fractionally against him.

"Cold?" he asked.

"No. Just excited," she answered, drawing in a lungful of the blossom-scented evening air. She watched a red-wing blackbird skim the surface of the grassy sea in pursuit of a fat evening moth. "I think it's only fair to warn you though, I'm . . . not much of a dancer."

"No?" His face registered his surprise. "Well, that's not a problem," he told her with a cocky grin.

Her expression was doubtful "It isn't?"

"Nope."

"Why?"

He shrugged. "Because I am."

Chapter Twelve

Clay's boast was not an empty one, she discovered minutes later. Pole-hung lanterns defined the impromptu dance floor, which was simply a collection of canvas tarps spread across the fort's central parade ground. After depositing the cobbler on the groaning dessert table at the north end of the circle, and dispensing with perfunctory greetings to friends, he swept her onto the crowded dance floor.

The musicians played a lively rendition of "Turkey in the Straw." Kierin stumbled several times at first, but as she grew more comfortable in Clay's arms, she forgot to worry about stepping on his toes. He pulled her close, resting his left hand against the small of her back. The fingers of his other hand intertwined with hers. He guided her expertly through the lively two-step, compensating for her lack of expertise with his own skill. His ability on the dance floor shouldn't have surprised her, but it did. He danced the way he did everything else — with an easy, self-assured grace.

Kierin and Clay nodded their hellos to Mel and Elizabeth Watkins as they whirled by and then nearly collided with Daniel Thorp and his young wife, Susan. Daniel kicked his heels up with hilarious gusto, careening across the floor with all the finesse of a runaway freight train. Susan's dark blond hair flew around her face and she let out an unladylike whoop of raucous laughter as she clung to the whipcord-thin shoulders of her husband.

The crowd was quick to pick up on Daniel's enthusiasm and soon even some of the reluctant dancers were out on the floor. Clay spotted Ben and Dove near the refreshment table. Ben wore a happy grin and Dove's moccasined foot tapped out the rhythm of the music against the canvas floor.

Clay shouted to them. "What're you two waiting for? The first snow? Come on out here and dust some canvas."

Ben answered with a booming laugh. "I'm willin'," he called. "It's my bones that ain't." They laughed and Clay spun Kierin away toward the center of the circle.

The song ended a minute later, but they barely had time to catch their breath before the small band struck up a new tune. Jim Kelly, holding a battered old banjo, and Jacob with his mouth harp, had joined the musicians up on the wood-planked platform, prompting whistles and catcalls from Clay and some of the others from their train. The song was "Camptown Races," and Deemer Penry belted out the catchy lyrics as the crowd fell into step.

"Having fun?" Clay shouted to Kierin above the music, his arms holding her firmly in his embrace.

Her eyes sparkled with laughter and she nodded. "Where did you learn to dance like this? You're very good, Mr. Holt."

"Why, thank you, *Mrs. Holt,*" he retorted, and with a comical dip of his knees, twirled her off again.

She giggled at his loose-limbed playfulness and allowed him to pull her closer. Her feet kept time with his and their bodies moved as one across the floor.

"No, really," she insisted. "You are. You make it easy for me."

"Ah," he argued, "I must return the compliment. A man is only as good as his partner."

One fine eyebrow arched suspiciously. "That's not

what you said before. You said it didn't matter if I could—"

"That," he silenced her before she could finish, "was before I saw what a quick study you were. Confidence," he stated unequivocally. "That's the key."

"And . . . if I hadn't caught on. . . ?"

Clay gave her a little squeeze. "That possibility never crossed my mind." He dipped his head down against her hair, letting its softness caress his cheek. She'd washed and given it a vinegar rinse earlier and he'd watched her dry it by the fire. Then, as now, his fingers had itched to touch it. He liked it when she wore her hair down like this—loose and flowing like a molten cascade. He reminded himself to tell her that.

Someday.

The music stopped and he released her reluctantly. He instantly regretted it. A scrawny-necked soldier with muddy blown hair and a smitten look in his eye tapped him on the shoulder, requesting the next dance with her. Clay lifted his eyebrows inquiringly at her, hoping she'd say no. But she smiled at the young soldier and gave him her hand. The kid tossed Clay a cocky chipped-toothed grin over his shoulder as he guided Kierin toward the center of the floor.

Clay watched them go as the music began, and combed his fingers through his long dark hair. Shoving his hands in his back pockets, he ambled over to the refreshment table, ignoring the invitation in the eyes of several single women he passed.

He told himself he needed a drink. But what he really wanted was to throttle that little whelp for putting his skinny hands on her. He suddenly hoped there was something in those punch bowls with more kick than punch.

He was watching her dance, already on his third cup of a homemade brew from the men's punch bowl when Jacob found him.

"Troubles?" Jacob asked, seeing the expression on

Clay's face.

Clay looked at his old friend with a wary smile. "Why do you ask?"

" 'Cause," Jacob chuckled, "you gots the look of an animal wid his leg caught in a trap."

Clay snorted disdainfully. "Funny you should put it that way . . ."

Jacob shook his head and slid his mouth harp into his pocket. "My mama used to say traps o' the heart— they's the most dangerous kind."

For all the time they'd known each other, Jacob's uncanny perception still surprised Clay. "Your mama was a smart woman."

"She done her share o' trap settin', I expect. Take my Bess. She had me snared 'fore I know'd what she be up to." Jacob's dark eyes took on a faraway look. "But then, she be the right woman, wid the right trap." He paused, glancing at Clay. "See what I mean?"

Clay tossed back another gulp of the fiery punch. "I guess I do." His eyes scanned the crowd for Kierin but he couldn't spot her. Ben and Dove walked up behind them. She shadowed the trapper, looking as if she'd rather be anywhere else but at a shindig full of white folks. Though none of the white women on the train had been overtly unkind to Dove, all but Kierin had kept their distance from her.

Clay saw Dove wince and rest her palm over the buff-colored deer-hide dress where it pulled tight across her stomach.

Beside Clay, Jacob stiffened and asked, "You all right, Dove?"

Her dark eyes met his with a wry smile and she patted her taut belly. "The young one will be a strong runner."

Jacob's eyes searched hers. "Maybe he wants to dance. You dance, Dove?"

She tipped her head proudly. "The women of the Sioux are all dancers, Jay-cob, but I do not know the dance of the wasicun."

A smile played at the edge of Jacob's generous mouth. "Care to try?"

Tempted, Dove swallowed and looked briefly at Ben. He nodded his encouragement to her. "Go on," he said. "Give that young'un somethin' to kick about."

Jacob's hand rested lightly on the small of her back as he led her to the dance floor. Ben watched them go, with the resigned look of a man who had suddenly glimpsed the future. He gave himself a shake and clapped Clay on the back. "What're you doing over here, boy? You should be out there with that pretty little gal."

"Yeah." Clay mused grumpily, scanning the crowd. "If I could get near her."

Ben raised a bushy eyebrow. "I ain't so old I don't remember what it was like, ya know."

Clay slid a glance toward the old man. "What *what's* like?"

Ben chuckled. "You two are like a couple of lovesick buffalo, dancin' around the bold-face truth."

Clay rubbed his face hard. He'd told Ben everything about Kierin and her brother, about his need to find Amanda's killers. Stated unemotionally, his reasons for staying uninvolved had made perfect sense. But Ben was right about one thing. It was becoming harder and harder to separate that logic from the gut-twisting sensations he felt every time he got near her.

Ben's gaze settled on Henri and Joey, dancing out on the floor near them. "The Clay I know never waited around fer somethin' to be give to him. That's a quality I always admired about you, boy. You always took what you wanted out of life."

Clay met Ben's steady gaze with his own. "It's knowing what you want . . ." Clay absently squeezed the empty tin cup in his hands. "That's the problem."

Ben's fingers tightened for a moment on Clay's shoulder—his tone suddenly serious. "Ya know, it's possible fer a man to think his way plumb outta happiness, son," he said. "It's my fondest hope that don't happen to you."

Ben smoothed both hands down the front of his buckskin shirt. "I'm gonna go find Joey and snag her fer a dance. I don't think Henri will mind . . ." Then he added with a wink, "Too much."

Twilight had given way to darkness. Ben's dark shape disappeared along the shadowy edge of the circle. Clay retrieved his parfleche and replaced his cup inside. The warm glow of the bourbon-spiked punch lingered in his bloodstream, mellowing the hard edges off his restlessness.

At the far end of the circle, he caught a glimpse of Kierin's red hair as she turned on the arm of tall, blond officer. He felt his heart trip at the sight of her and he frowned. When, he wondered with sudden bewilderment, had he begun to think of her as his? From the moment he'd set eyes on her in Independence? Or was it the first time she'd smiled at him?

It was a moot point, he decided with unsettling certainty. Kierin was as much a part of him now as waking and sleeping. She dogged his thoughts whether he was feeding the stock or curled up beside her at night in a hot sweat.

Tossing the parfleche under the table, he started to shoulder his way through the crowds toward her. He suddenly wasn't in the mood to share her anymore.

A delicate hand on his arm stopped him.

"I was wondering if I'd ever get a chance to dance with you, Clay." Rachael Beaker cocked her head prettily, offering him her best angle. Her silvery-blond hair shimmered in the lantern glow like fool's gold. It was, Clay observed with detachment, her most compelling feature.

"Hello, Rachael."

"Hello, Rachael? Is that all you're going to say?" Her expression grew petulant. "Aren't you going to ask me to dance?"

Clay sighed, tossing a glance back in Kierin's direction. He knew he was trapped. "Would you care to dance, Rachael?"

"I'd love to." She plucked up the skirt of her yellow silk dress and offered him her hand.

The tempo of the music had changed from a lively Virginia reel to a waltz, and Clay cursed the timing. Rachael pressed herself close. Though her neckline was necessarily modest, the silk fabric did nothing to conceal the full swell of her breasts. Her chin nearly reached his shoulder, and he found himself comparing her statuesque height unfavorably with Kierin's petite figure.

"All this time, Clay, and you've hardly given me so much as a how-do-you-do."

He could hear the pout in her voice.

She looked up at him, flashing her large brown eyes. "I really shouldn't be speaking to you at all."

"I'm a married man now, Rachael. Or weren't you listening the last time we had this conversation?"

"Oh, I heard all right. But I've been a minister's daughter long enough to know that all marriages aren't made in heaven. You see, there's married, and then there's *married*. I wonder which of those you are, Clay?"

He impaled her with a steely-eyed warning as they moved across the floor. "Don't go sniffing for trouble, Rachael. You're likely to find it where you least expect it."

She threw back her head and laughed. "Did I strike a nerve, darling? Actually," she replied in a low voice, "all I'm offering is an alternative to cold dips in the river."

Clay's eyes narrowed and he stopped dancing. "What?"

"You didn't know I saw you the other night, did you?"

"Christ, Rachael—"

She gave him a cajoling smile. "Don't stop dancing, Clay. People might think we're having a lover's quarrel."

Clay jerked her back in his arms but his movements were angry and without gentleness. Had he ever found her attractive?

"My guess is," Rachael continued, unperturbed by his rough treatment, "that it wasn't the first time she's turned you away, is it?"

His answering laughter was hollow and cold. "What's the matter, Rachael? All those lost lambs in your father's flock and you can't get a single one to take a tumble with you in the bushes?"

She tipped her chin up sharply at his remark then tossed her hair with a little shake of her head. "I've always enjoyed a challenge. That's what I find so attractive about you, Clay. Those other men are mice. Like that little wife of yours —"

"Leave Kierin out of this," he told her in a tone that erased the smile from her face. "She's way out of your league. Why don't you find a willing victim among these lonely calvarymen? I'm certain one of them would be happy to oblige you. And just think. For once you wouldn't have to worry about the man spilling the beans to your father in confession."

If looks were lethal, he would have been bleeding all over the ground. Mercifully, the music stopped and the crowd mingled noisily around them. "Thank you for the dance, my dear," he said with a mock half-bow. "It's been" — he searched for the right word — "unpleasant."

Kierin felt a stab of disappointment as the musicians struck up a slow, romantic waltz and Clay had still not come back to claim her. It wasn't that she'd lacked for partners. She'd danced with four different men in the space of as many songs. But she didn't care about dancing with any of them.

She glanced up at her latest partner: a tall, sandy-haired lieutenant. His fine features were burnished by the prairie sun, his body muscled and firm. In another time, she would have appreciated his startling good looks. But she realized her notions of handsome had been forever altered by the dark intensity of Clay Holt.

The lieutenant seemed oblivious to her inner turmoil and smiled down at her, his hand pressing lightly against her back. "Are you enjoying our fandango, Miss—?"

"Mrs.—" she corrected quickly, returning his smile. "Mrs. Holt. And yes, thank you. I am."

"Ah," he sighed with a wistful smile, "my luck. Find a pretty girl and she's already taken." With a flourish, he twirled her past several couples and she followed his graceful movements with surprising ease. "Are you and your husband headed for the Oregon Territory?"

"Yes." The lie came so easily. "To the Willamette Valley, in fact." Askance, she caught sight of Clay's familiar silhouette across the way. Her head snapped around to get a better look at the blond woman on his arm. Her heart sank like a stone.

It was Rachael.

Her perfect blond head was thrown back in laughter at something Clay had said and he held her scandalously close. Something crumbled inside Kierin as she stared at them. She closed her eyes and looked away, unable to watch him make a fool of himself over Rachael's beauty.

"Lots of opportunity there, I hear," the lieutenant offered, breaking into her miserable thoughts.

"What? Oh, in Oregon?" She felt as if she'd swallowed a thistle, whole. "I suppose so." She stopped dancing and pressed a hand to her temple. "Uh, would you excuse me, Lieutenant? I suddenly have an awful headache. I think I'd like to sit down for a while."

A look of disappointment clouded his eyes. "What a shame," he said taking her arm. "Here, let me help you."

Somehow, his solicitousness made everything worse. "Please . . ." She stopped him with her hand. "You're very kind, but I'll be fine." She left him staring after her as she made her way through the crowds to the edge of the dance floor.

Stalking beyond the circle of light with her fists clenched at her sides, Kierin took a deep draught of air into her lungs and kept moving, heedless of the shadowy darkness ahead of her. It was one thing to dance with that . . . that *woman,* Kierin thought. She could have accepted that. It was another thing altogether for him to ply her with that fatal charm of his and to hold her so tightly they looked joined at the seams!

"So, we meet again, little lady."

Kierin spun at the sound of the voice in the darkness beside her. She knew immediately who it was even though the shadows cloaked his features. It was the man she'd bumped into at Henri's store.

She took several steps backward. "I . . . I was j-just going to find the refreshment table," she lied. "Isn't that silly? I guess I got turned around. If you'll excu—"

"Not so fast, little lady." He grabbed her by the upper arm. His broken teeth leered at her in the moonlight. "Ain't no need to rush off. I got me a bottle of refreshments right here in my pocket." The flask made a little chinking sound as he patted it. "I'm more than willin' to share."

"No. I mean—I don't want—"

"Seein's how you wouldn't give me the time of day last time we met, I figure you owe me."

She shook her head in alarmed confusion. "What are you talking about? I've never seen you before today."

"Took me a while to place ya," he said, cutting her off, "but I don't never forget a face. 'Specially one as purty as yours."

Kierin pulled against his hand, but he only tightened his grip. "I've never seen you before today. Now please, let me go!"

"Oh, now that hurts—your not rememberin' me. Luther Bledsoe's the name, though I reckon we wasn't

187

formally introduced." He trailed a dirt-encrusted finger down the front of her dress. "Just tell me one thing, missy. How'd a purty little whore like you find yer way outta that saloon and headin' fer Californee?"

Chapter Thirteen

His words made Kierin dizzy and she took a faltering step backward. A sick sense of dread crept over her as she remembered where she'd seen him before. Of course it had been at Talbot's—his face, one of the thousands she'd seen there. Had it been only weeks since she'd been serving whiskey and beer to the likes of him? Out on the dance floor with Clay, it had seemed like another lifetime ago, a past she could leave behind. How foolish she'd been to let herself believe that.

"You're mistaken, Mr. Bledsoe," she said with all the conviction she could muster. "Y-you must have me confused with someone else . . ."

"Oh no I don't. It's Karen, ain't it?"

Her eyes widened.

"No . . ." His smile broadened. "It's *Kierin.* I remember now. Unusual ring to it. Had every head turnin' yer way in that waterin' hole. All woman, you was, in that little red thing you was wearin'."

Kierin was stunned into a hopeless, forbidding silence.

"Got you a sweet setup here, ain't ya?" His pale eyes lingered on her bosom. "All these God-fearin' men an' their dried-up wives, just waitin' fer you to scratch their itch."

Her voice returned in a rush. "No, you're wrong—get away from me."

189

"Why, I'll bet yer servicin' every buck on this train from here to—" His eyes suddenly narrowed. "What— you think I ain't got money like anybody else? Well, I do." He reached into his pocket and pulled out some jingling silver.

She blindly knocked the money from his hand. "I don't want your money. Take your hands off me or I'll scream."

An angry look clouded his face and he crossed his forearm brutally against her throat, pushing her up hard against the rough-hewn wall behind her. "Fine," he spat. "We'll do it without money, then. Makes no never-mind to me." He spit a stream of tobacco juice at her feet. "You whores are all alike. Always thinkin' yer too good fer the likes o' men like me."

She tipped her chin up and gritted her teeth. "I'm not . . . a whore . . . at all."

He gave her a mean little shake, banging her head against the hard wall behind her. A pain shot through her temples.

"The hell you say, girl! I know what I know." His squinty eyes narrowed further and an evil gleam came into them. "But I'm gettin' the notion the good folks on this here train maybe don't know what you was back there."

Kierin's chest rose and fell rapidly against the grimy sleeve of his long johns.

He let out a little laugh. "I'm right, ain't I? Well, you kin play yer little game with the rest of these green-horns, but you ain't foolin' me none. I reckon as how that little secret's worth somethin' to ya, ain't it, little lady?" He glanced back at the circle of dancers. The music was still loud enough to drown out their conversation. "I don't reckon I'll have to think too hard on how you can get me to keep it."

His mouth came down hard on hers and his tongue impaled her. Her futile scream was absorbed by his mouth. She felt his hands bracket her hips, pulling her fully against his arousal. She pushed futilely against his chest with her hands but she was no match for his strength.

Without warning, Bledsoe was spun around. Kierin heard his grunt of surprise as he released her. In the darkness, she recognized Clay's silhouette just as his fist caught Bledsoe hard in the stomach. The man gasped and doubled over in pain, but Clay sent his knee crashing into Bledsoe's chin. He flew backward like a launched egg and landed with a groan in the dirt, sprawled near Clay's feet.

Bledsoe's mouth was bleeding and he hauled himself up on one elbow, shaking his head back and forth to clear his vision. He tested his jaw with his hand, then staggered up from the ground, ready to take his assailant on. Clay's hard-bitten words stopped him.

"Get near my wife again, you bastard, and I'll kill you." Clay's voice was low and deadly.

Kierin sucked in a breath. He'd called her his wife!

Luther staggered unsteadily, and touched his thumb to the corner of his bleeding mouth. His gaze traveled back and forth between Clay and Kierin. "Wife?" he said in a low mean voice. "She didn't mention no husband to me, mister."

Clay's eyes flashed for a split second to Kierin's. She didn't miss the uncertainty she saw there.

Nor did Luther. A small victorious smile curved his bloodied lips. Foolishness made him carry it one step too far. "You better keep a better eye on this one. She was askin' me fer i—"

Clay's knife flashed from its sheath and its tip was at Luther's throat before he could finish the word.

"I could kill you now for saying that, you stupid son of a bitch," Clay ground out, his face only inches from Bledsoe's.

For a moment, Kierin thought he would. She'd never seen him so close to losing control. "Clay," she warned, "don't—"

191

"It would give me a lot of pleasure," he went on, ignoring her, "to serve you up in little pieces to the fort's commander for attempted rape."

Sweat broke out on Bledsoe's forehead and his eyes widened with fear. His Adam's apple bobbed in his throat.

"Do you have something to say to my *wife,* you bastard? Or," he asked, twisting the knife under his chin, drawing a bead of blood, "shall I show you how the Cheyenne deal with men who rape women?"

"Ow! No—" Bledsoe squirmed, with his head tipped back. "I—I'm sorry, miss. I m-mean, ma'am. I didn't mean you no harm."

Clay's knife point lingered at the man's throat. "Good. Consider yourself warned. Get near her again and you're dead." He lowered the blade and stepped back away from the bleeding man.

Bledsoe swiped angrily at his mouth with his hand, slid one last glare at Kierin, and turned, disappearing into the darkness.

Only after he'd gone did Clay sheathe his knife and turn back to her. She wasn't prepared for the anger she saw in his eyes. He grabbed her arm roughly, pulling her back between the buildings, away from the music and dancing.

"Clay, you're hurting me," she cried as he pushed her up roughly against a wall. She could smell the bourbon on his breath and wondered briefly if he was drunk.

"Damnit, Kierin—" His face reflected his frustration. He spun around and paced a few steps away, then turned on her. "What the hell do you think you were doing back there? Do you have any idea how dangerous a man like that could be?"

Affronted, her lips drew into a thin line. "Of course, I do. I didn't—"

"You sure as hell didn't," he said, picking up his pacing again. "This isn't the Independence, Kierin. You don't have your *friend* Lily here to protect you from men like that. He could have killed you without blinking an eye."

"Damn you," she whispered, too choked with anger to scream at him.

His temper flared unchecked. He swung around on her again with an angry laugh. "Damn me? Oh, that's a good one. I'm afraid it's too late for that, Princess. This farce of a marriage wasn't my idea in the first place. But you seem to remember it only when it's convenient for you. Did you plan a quick roll in the hay with that bastard before—"

She slapped his face hard, catching him off guard. He staggered back a step in shock. His hand went to the stinging red welt coming up on his jaw.

Tears burned the backs of Kierin's eyes and threatened to spill down her cheeks, but she held them back. "I've had it up to here with your accusations"—she slashed an angry palm across her forehead—"and your sanctimonious self-righteousness! Just who the *hell* do you think you are?"

Clay stared at her—silent, grim-faced.

"Nothing I could ever say would change your mind about me, would it?" she accused. "Well, here's a piece of news for you—I don't care anymore. I don't give a damn what you think of me. Why don't you just go back and let Rachael Beaker hang all over you again! Perhaps a minister's daughter is *virtuous* enough for you. J—just leave me alone." Her throat was clogged with captured sobs. "Do you hear me? Leave me alone!" She turned and ran off into the darkness before he could see the torrents of tears she was about to shed over him.

"Oh, hell." Clay slammed an open palm against the wall of the building. *You bastard. Now look what you've done.*

"Kierin—wait!" He started after her.

She ignored him and kept up her angry pace through the tangle of long grass. The hem of her dress twisted

193

between her legs and threatened to trip her. She gathered up her skirt on her arm, ripping it from the long spiked thistles that lay hidden in the darkness. She had no idea where she was going. Only that she couldn't bear to be around him any longer. She heard his footsteps behind her and she started to run, but tears blurred her vision.

"Kierin, stop. Don't run away from me."

His voice was suddenly close. She felt his hand close around her arm and he spun her around.

"Where do you think you're going?"

She struggled to get loose of him. "Anywhere!" she screamed, "Away from *you*—let go of me!"

His breath was coming hard and fast. "If you think I'm going to let you go running off into the darkness in the middle of the prairie, you're crazy. Now, just . . . just calm down and let's talk this out."

"I have nothing to say to you," she gritted out. "And I think you made yourself perfectly clear back there."

"No I didn't." He swallowed hard. "I—I shouldn't have said any of it."

"But you did, didn't you? You said it and you *meant* it."

"No," he repeated, realizing it was true. "I was angry. Damn it, Kierin, when I saw you with him I—"

"I don't want to hear this," she warned, pressing her hands to her ears.

"—I wanted to kill him," Clay finished, capturing her wrists. He pulled her clenched fists against his chest, forcing her to hear him. "I wanted to kill that bastard for touching you."

She tugged futilely against his hands. "At least I knew what *he* wanted from me," she cried. Tears streamed unfettered down her cheeks. "What do *you* want from me, Clay?" she sobbed. "W-why are you d-doing this? Why c-can't you just—"

"Ah-h, God, Kierin. I'm sorry . . ." he murmured, tipping his forehead miserably against hers. "So sorry.

Forgive me. I don't know what I'm doing around you half the time. I do crazy things. Christ! Maybe I *am* crazy. I don't know anymore." He stroked her cheek with his thumb, wiping at her tears. "Don't cry," he whispered. "Please, don't cry."

But she did. Pushing futilely against him with her clenched fists, she turned her face away, ashamed and miserable in his arms. Surrounded by the vacant prairie, he held her that way, allowing her to vent her grief. Her body convulsed with sobs while his hand stroked her hair. He pressed his cheek tightly against it. What was he supposed to do with this woman who made him crazy and utterly alive in the same moment?

"Sh-hh," he soothed. His heated breath warmed her as he pressed his lips against her hair. "It's all right now . . ."

Her hands flattened against his chest, half clinging to him, half pushing him away. She felt the uneven rise and fall of his chest beneath her fingertips, the steady thudding of his heart. Clay's hands moved along either side of her face, and his mouth dipped to vanquish the salty tears on her cheeks. "We can't go on this way . . ." he whispered hopelessly against her skin. "It's . . . going to kill us both."

Kierin squeezed her reddened eyes shut. "I know."

He felt, more than heard her words against his cheek. "Do you have any idea," he murmured with his mouth against her skin, "what you do to me?"

How can I hate him and love him so in the same moment? "Heaven help me . . . I do," she answered, wrapping her arms around his back and drawing him close.

With a hand on either side of her face, he tipped her head back. His eyes searched hers in the darkness; his catching the silver reflection of the crescent moon. She knew suddenly that he wouldn't seek her permission this time. It was a simple gesture of confirmation. It was, she knew suddenly, a truth they couldn't deny.

His lips stalked her, brushing the fullness of hers

195

twice before claiming them fully. His kiss — penetrating and insistent — slashed diagonally across hers with an ardor wrought by weeks of denial. She opened to him, meeting his passion with an urgency of her own.

Clay's tongue traced the inside edge of her lower lip, then invaded her mouth. Kierin's senses were on fire, ignited by the molten flame that leapt between them. She knew he'd felt it, too. He groaned against her mouth and pulled her closer, as if any space between them was too much.

His hands slid down to her buttocks and he drew her hips up against his, so she could feel his need for her. His arousal pressed against her belly, hard and warm and wanting.

"I didn't want to share you with anyone else tonight," he whispered. Cradling the back of her head in his hand, his tongue caressed the outer edge of her ear, then wandered with a tantalizing languor across the sensitive lobe.

She felt a tremor rock her and she swayed against him, suddenly weak-kneed. "I didn't want you to," she answered.

His hand moved deliberately to her breast, cupping the fullness she offered up. He felt her nipple pucker under the thin cotton gown as his thumb traced its circumference and his mouth captured hers in a fierce kiss.

In one swift movement, he reached down and swept her up in his arms. "I want you — now," he told her unequivocally.

She answered him in a fervent kiss that stirred his heart in the same undeniable way she did the rest of him. Carrying her to the base of a gentle swell in the prairie, hidden from view of both the fort and the trains camped downriver, he lowered her to the ground.

She pulled him down to her and he covered her with his weight. Their bodies carved a shallow nest in the soft prairie grass. Kierin trembled in his arms. Fear and need warred for control within her and she wondered if he could hear her heart pounding. The time for thinking was gone. She wanted him as much as he did her. She would meet him as a woman, not as a frightened girl.

"Show me what you want," she whispered against his hair, while her hands roved across his back and the taut muscles of his shoulders.

Her words fired his blood, making him tremble with his need for her. She moved beneath him and the peaks of her nipples brushed against his chest through his chamois shirt. He wanted to feel her silken skin against his own. His fingers fumbled with his buttons.

"Let me . . ." she offered, nudging his hand away. Her request was, at the same time, artless and enticingly accomplished. He closed his eyes, willing himself to be patient, letting the sensations drift over him. One by one, the buttons released from the straining fabric and he felt her warm hands slip beneath it to his bare chest.

His skin was hot to Kierin's touch. A cloud passed in front of the moon and he became only a pale outline in the darkness. She suddenly wished she could see all of him as she'd longed to do. Her hands became her eyes then, exploring the lean, elegant contours of him.

Shrugging out of his shirt, he shifted his weight over her from one arm to the other, then discarded it in the knee-high grass beside them. With a low growl, Clay caught her beneath her arms and rolled with her onto his back. He settled her atop him, astride his hips.

Her eyes widened momentarily and she let out a small gasp at the intimate sensation of feeling him hard and hot at the vortex of her legs. A dash of fear flickered through her body, but she pushed it away.

"Take off your dress," he ordered softly. His hands circled her waist and his hips tilted up reflexively to meet her softness.

She smiled and watched his face as her fingers

worked the tiny buttons at the bodice of her dress.

Flick. The first pearly fastener eased out of its home. With instincts ancient and primal, she moved her hips against his and heard him moan.

Flick. His eyes drifted shut and he clamped down on her waist, pulling her against him more fully. *Oh, God, what you do to me, woman!*

Flick. Flick. His fingers moved up impatiently to help her. The tapered bodice of her dress fell away from her shoulders. His flattened palms slid up over the whale-bone stays of her corset and across the curve of her camisole-covered breasts.

"Now, the rest," he told her, skimming a finger across the scalloped edge of her camisole, teasing the fullness of her breast.

Her skin quivered in response. She raised her arms obligingly and he drew the camisole over her head. He dispatched the fasteners on the front of her corset with the same unhurried expectancy. As the constraint slipped away, Clay's heated gaze fell on her breasts. They were round and youthfully pert and fit the curve of his palm as if they were designed for that purpose.

She drew in a breath when he touched her, stunned by the exquisite sensations his caress evoked. A spiraling ache spread upward from her thighs to the center of her womanhood. *What we're doing must be wrong,* she thought abstractly. *But could something so wrong feel this wonderful?* Regrets be dammed, she thought, closing her eyes to the thoughts as if she could chase them back with utter darkness. His fiery touch burned away all rational thought once more and she tipped her head back, arching into his hands

"You're so beautiful . . ." His voice was low and intimate, roughened with desire. His thumb drew tiny arcs around the crest of her nipple. Dropping his hands to the waistband of her dress and petticoat, he swept them over her head. They spread like a billowing sail, over the grass beside them. ". . . but you're too far away." He rolled her onto her back again, capturing her beneath him.

His mouth found hers again before she'd fully reached the ground. His tongue impaled her, exploring the smooth surface of her teeth, before leaving her lips to trail moist circles down the length of her throat.

"Shall I taste you here, now?" he asked, devilishly fingering one dusky-crested nipple.

She wasn't sure what the etiquette was in matters such as these, but her entire body throbbed with wanting and his tone seemed to require an answer.

"Yes . . . please."

His eyebrows went up fractionally in amusement. Yes, please? Was she always so polite in bed? he wondered. There was something so deliciously innocent in her hushed reply, it made him hesitate for a moment before dipping his head in compliance. A hint of vanilla lingered enticingly on her skin. Her taste filled his senses as he took the fullness of her nipple into his mouth, stoking it with his tongue. She cried out softly and plunged her fingers through the dark waves of his hair, pulling him closer.

Any wishful thoughts he might have had about taking her leisurely disappeared with that cry. She was like a fever in his blood. His need for her was hot, compelling, and raw with unsated hunger, like a man who'd gone too long without food to ever again believe excess was possible.

Kierin was lost in a haze of sensation and was only vaguely aware when he caught the drawstring at her waist and slipped her pantalettes down her thighs. Realizing only that they impeded her movement, she kicked them off and wrapped her bare legs around him. His mouth continued to tease her breasts with soft, sucking bites, spinning her headlong into a blissful daze. For the first time in her life, she felt reckless. Free. She didn't want to question what was happening. She simply allowed it to be.

Every muscle in her body quivered as his fingers made the long, delicious descent to the soft V of curls at the apex of her thighs. But as his fingers slid against the slick warmth there, she gasped and reached down, stopping him with her hand. It was all so intimate, so unfamiliar. She just needed a moment to . . .

Clay turned a heavy-lidded look of inquiry on her and smiled. He recognized that hesitation for what it was, but he was in no mood for delays. He quickly dispatched the row of buttons on his trousers and slid them down his legs. Taking her trembling hand in his, he guided it against his hot length, and released a shuddering breath. It had been too long. He felt his control slipping, and having no desire to embarrass himself, he forced himself to go perfectly still when her fingers curled around him.

Experimentally, Kierin slid her fingers up and down, exploring the turgid length of him; its velvety texture was an intoxicating surprise. She heard him groan against her shoulder.

His fingers caressed her satiny warmth, and this time, with her hand still closed around him, she arched into his palm like a cat being stroked. He felt the whispering heat of her breath as she sighed into his ear, an acquiescent purr.

He slipped out of the rest of his clothes without ever completely leaving her. Then, he lowered his primed body over hers, nudging her thighs apart with his knee. His blood pounded in his ears as he guided himself into her. Kierin's arms tightened around him as he surged forward. He heard her cry out when his first thrust met with an unexpected barrier.

Impossible.

Stunned and too aroused to believe the indisputable evidence of her virginity, he rocked against her again. Her cry this time was muffled against his straining shoulder.

"Oh, God," he groaned, slumping against her. "It

200

can't be."

"It doesn't matter," she urged, begging him with her hands to go on. She needed him desperately, wanted him in ways she'd never even imagined before. "Please . . ."

He raised his head and searched her eyes in the darkness. All the denials and words flung, all the angry bitterness—it had never occurred to him that she could have escaped that brothel unscathed. He shook his head in disbelief. "Doesn't mat—?"

"Clay—I'm asking you . . ." She tilted her hips up wantonly against his. Her eyes met uncertainly with his. She was willing to risk everything—her pride, even her dignity, to have him. "Make love to me. Don't make me beg."

If his passion had waned momentarily with discovery, her pleading words restored it. "Oh God, Kierin," he murmured. His lips claimed her half-opened mouth with a desperate urgency, suddenly undisposed to deny himself or her.

The delicate membrane broke with his next movement and he held himself still for a moment inside her. She answered his silence with a gentle rotating of her hips. "Clay . . ." she whispered.

Flames shot through her limbs as Clay buried himself deep inside her. Her breathing became as erratic as her pounding pulse. He tucked his arms around her, his body fastened by invisible bindings to hers. His rhythms became her own as he moved inside her.

Clay held himself in check and took his time—holding sway the fever pitch of passion that threatened to strip away his last remnant of control. Her hips arched up to his as his deliberate thrusts filled her, then slowly withdrew. By degrees, his tempo increased as he heard her breathing become as ragged and uneven as his own.

Kierin's arms tightened convulsively around him. Her body arched and strained under him as he brought her ever closer to the brink of rapture. Splintering halos of light pricked the darkness above her, and with a cry, she relinquished her last fraying thread of control.

He poured his own hot release into her only a fraction of a second after he knew she'd found hers. As the waves of passion subsided, they clung to each other while their breathing slowly returned to normal.

A fine sheen of sweat coated Clay's skin. He slid his weight off her, but held her still. His arm lay heavily across her stomach. One thumb absently stroked her ribs. Kierin felt whole, utterly sated—as if a part of her she'd never known was missing had been suddenly found. He was the answer to her unasked question, the fulfillment of a destiny, the ending of an unfinished dream.

"Why didn't you tell me?" His soft-spoken question startled her out of her romantic fantasies.

"Tell you?"

"That you were a virgin." His caress had stilled upon her abdomen.

She turned her head to look at him in the moonlight. "I tried. Quite often, as I recall."

Their numerous arguments eddied in his memory like troublesome current. "But you never said it."

"Would you have believed me if I had?" she asked. "It doesn't matter now. I'm not a virgin anymore." It gave her an ironic thrill to voice that thought. She thought she would feel some kind of loss when it happened, but she felt just the opposite.

"No," he agreed with a long sigh. "You're definitely not." He rolled onto his back and stared silently up into the night sky. "I'm sorry," was all he could say.

A chill sliced into her at his words and she watched him wedge that familiar distance between them again. Her joy died abruptly in her throat. *Sorry?* her mind echoed hollowly. *Was he sorry that they'd made love, or regretful, perhaps, that he'd made her what he thought she'd been all along?*

"Don't be," she told him coolly, sitting up to search in the dark for her camisole.

Her indifference first surprised, then irritated him. He'd just seduced a virgin, damn it all, she ought to at least be gracious enough to let him apologize. He sat up abruptly. "Kierin . . ." He searched for the words to tell her how he felt. "What I'm trying to say is—"

It was a mistake. She heard the words pounding in her ears before he spoke them. "I *know* what it was," she interrupted before he could trample the shattering pieces of her heart. "Lust." When his eyes narrowed, she blundered ahead. "D-do you think I'm such an innocent I don't recognize simple lust when I see it?" Finding the thin camisole, she shrugged it over her nakedness and turned her back on him. "But please, don't let it bother your conscience. I mean, you hardly forced me. After all, I asked you to."

"Lust?" he repeated incredulously. If it had been about simple lust, he could have satisfied himself with that bitch Rachael Beaker. Kierin's sudden change of attitude rankled him. He felt an uncharacteristic warmth rush to his face as he watched her pull on her clothes. "Is that what it was for you?"

Kierin slipped her pantalettes over her bare thighs, glad for the darkness so he couldn't see the tears threatening her eyes. "Of course. What else would it be?" He'd offered up no endearments, no words of love to make her think it was otherwise. *Please, don't let him see me cry.*

"You got me, Princess. Why don't you tell me?" came his sardonic reply. He shot her a smoldering look.

Flustered, she continued. "I'm sure y-you'll agree, now that our curiosity has been . . . satisfied, it's best for both of us if this never happens again."

Her words stuck like a knife blade between his ribs.

"How fortunate you're so easily satisfied, my dear," he told her with an ironic twist to his mouth.

The bitterness of his comment startled her, but she

wouldn't allow it to affect her. She tugged on the dress that lay beneath him. "Excuse me, may I have my dress back?"

He lifted his hips and slid it out from under him, handing it to her with an angry glare. "Absolutely."

"Thank you." She slipped it on over her head and fumbled with the buttons, wondering how to escape from this horrible situation gracefully. He didn't help, sitting there, singularly unconcerned with his nakedness. He stared off into the darkened prairie, arms folded tightly across his bent knees.

"You don't need to walk me back," she told him when she'd finished. "I'm going to the wagon." He didn't answer her. Didn't even look at her. "Well . . . good night then."

"Yeah." He watched her disappear toward the wagons, with a welling ache in his chest, feeling as if he'd been sucker-punched.

Slowly, he pulled on his clothes again and headed back to the crowded dance. He needed a drink. And this time, by God, he wouldn't stop at three.

Chapter Fourteen

Long after she heard the others return from the fandango, Kierin lay awake waiting to feel the wagon tilt with Clay's step. But he didn't come. With eyes red and swollen from crying, Kierin buried her face in the pillow and cried some more. A deep grieving pain clawed at her heart. After what they'd done tonight, she wondered how she could bear being near him in the days to come. She'd been a fool to trust him with her heart. More foolish to imagine that he could love her in return.

Sometime, during the early hours of the morning, she fell into a fitful sleep. It was punctuated by nightmarish dreams of falling out of control down a steep canyon wall. Her body bounced painfully against the sharp, jutting rocks, and as she spun ever downward, she glimpsed Clay and Rachael standing together at the top of the cliff—laughing. She awoke with a start as the first light of dawn crept over the sky. Her nightgown clung to her sweat-drenched body. Kierin lay back with a shudder and cursed the weakness that assailed her mind and body.

Clay appeared at breakfast. His jaw was dark with unshaven stubble and his eyes, when they flashed to hers, were bloodshot and sullen. He refused the bowl of porridge she offered him, and drank only a cup of Jacob's tarlike coffee.

There was, for Kierin, a certain satisfaction in

knowledge that Clay had obviously gotten no more sleep than she. His movements were slow and she couldn't help noticing he winced when spoken to. His answers were curt and intended to discourage idle chit-chat.

He didn't speak to Kierin at all.

They all said their bittersweet good-byes to Joey and Henri, who'd come out to see them off. Joey kissed Kierin on the cheek and gave Dove a bracing hug.

"You take care of him, mind you," she told Dove firmly. Her luminous brown eyes were suspiciously damp. "He's a rare one, Ben is. And"—she glanced at Dove's stomach—"mind that little feller of yours too," she added, helping Dove into the two-wheeled cart. "Let us know what ya have." Dove squeezed Joey's hand in promise.

"Bon chance, mes amis!" Henri called as they left.

Ben shouted back, "I'll be back next fall with so many pelts you'll have to add another room to that little post of yours just to hold 'em." And to Joey, "You keep them dancin' feet limber, darlin' Joey, and that Frenchman off 'n yer toes." With their arms around each other, Joey and Henri both laughed and waved good-bye.

The animals were rested and content after the brief layover at Kearny and the train made good time for the next few days. The countryside changed noticeably as they moved into the corridor between Cheyenne territory to the south and west and the Pawnees' to the north. The land grew steadily more arid, though the supply of sun-ripened grass was still plentiful. They passed under the shadows of the celebrated Courthouse Rock—which climbed some two hundred feet straight up and reminded all of a ruined cathedral— and the smaller Jailhouse Rock. Beyond these, and visible for days, was Chimney Rock, a slim stone tower in the shape of an inverted funnel. Its height was estimated at five hundred feet, though no one dared climb it to be sure.

Several times they encountered small parties of Indians along the trail who traded food for safe passage. The Pawnee looked ragged and hungry, and had little patience with offers to trade for trinkets such as mirrors and ornaments. For this purpose, the wagons each carried an extra supply of sugar and molasses, and occasionally offered freshly killed meat.

Dove traded a pair of finely beaded moccasins she'd made to an Indian woman for a fresh supply of pony beads and porcupine quills. With these, she began work on Ben's elk-skin shirt. Using dyes made from dried red buffalo berries and wild sunflowers boiled with the roots of cattails for yellow, Dove created a brilliant color scheme. The design she embroidered on the shirt back was a sixteen-point star-shaped shield with a red dot in the center. It was, Dove told Kierin, a Sioux sign of protection for any warrior wearing it. She covered the shoulder and sleeve seams with strips of beading in a diamond-shaped pattern, denoting power. She wouldn't allow Ben to see it until it was finished, in spite of his impish efforts to get a peek at it sooner.

On the fifth day, they made the crossing of the South Fork of the Platte. The muddy river stretched here to nearly a mile and a half. Rumors of treacherous pockets of quicksand in the river set everyone's nerves on edge, but the crossing was remarkably smooth.

Two days later, camped for the Sabbath beneath the mammoth cliffs of Scott's Bluff, Kierin was finishing the milking chores while Dove started the morning meal. The sun was barely up, yet the air held the promise of heat.

With her forehead pressed against the warm, fragrant flank of the milch cow, Kierin was lulled by the steady rhythm of the milk hitting the bucket.

Tsst-tsst. Tsst-tsst.

Her arms had grown accustomed to this chore and no longer required her full concentration. She allowed her mind to drift — as it often did since leaving the fort — to Clay.

Clay had moved out of the wagon entirely since that night at Kearny. Disregarding the propriety of their situation, he started sharing the small tent with Jacob. She didn't argue as to the sensibleness of his decision. In fact, they never discussed it. Kierin told herself it was for the best. But in spite of her resolution to put him completely out of her heart, she found herself missing his company terribly.

Tsst-tsst. Tsst-tsst. Absently she watched the fragrant milk spurt little craters in the half-filled bucket. She closed her eyes. Her brow prickled against the sweaty flank of the cow, but she ignored it — her thoughts were on Clay.

He wasn't openly hostile. On the contrary, he was exceedingly polite, which made his withdrawal from her seem all the worse. For her part, she avoided being alone with him whenever she could. Each day apart seemed worse than the last, and even though they were both careful not to let their personal tensions spill out over the others, everyone felt the strain.

In the distance, she heard the men's voices returning from unhobbling the stock and she lifted her gaze in search of them.

"Will you join us on the hunt today?"

Kierin turned sharply at the sound of Dove's voice. "Hunt?" she asked dumbly.

"Tatánka. Buffalo," Dove replied. "The men have seen a herd to the north and today they will fill our drying racks with meat."

Kierin had heard the grumblings of several men in the camp about going on a hunt as a group. Whatever meat was taken would be distributed equally among the wagons. Clay had expressed reservations about a green party of men attempting such a large-scale hunt.

Antelope and rabbits were safer and more easily obtainable game.

"Surely *you're* not going, Dove?" Kierin asked in a voice that betrayed her disapproval. She lifted the heavy bucket full of milk from underneath the cow and set it down near the wagon. Dove couldn't be more than a month away from delivering.

"Yes," Dove answered. "But only for the butchering. Will you not come and share the *tapi* with us?"

"*Tapi?*" Kierin echoed, almost afraid to hear the answer.

Dove frowned, mentally searching her store of English words for the proper one. Rewarded at last, she replied, "Li-ver."

Kierin made a face that didn't begin to express what she thought of the idea, but the sound of the men returning stayed her answer. Ben was bending Jacob's ear with one of his trapping stories and their laughter rang out in the thin morning air.

Kierin's gaze went automatically to Clay, who followed some twenty feet behind them — head down, deep in thought. He'd bathed in the river. His dark hair was wet and slicked back from his face and his shirt clung to his broad chest. Unbidden came the memory of holding him in her arms — feeling his slick, damp warmth against her. The unwanted wave of desire fanned her blood like a hot, buffeting wind. Kierin hugged her arms tightly across her chest, as if that could make her immune to him.

He glanced up at her and for a moment his expression was unguarded, vulnerable — and as wretched as her own. But the look vanished almost as soon as it appeared. Clay's jaw tightened and he turned abruptly, heading off toward the remuda of saddle horses. She was tempted to follow him, desperate to ease the ache between them, but Jacob's voice stopped her.

"Mmm-mm. Dat biscuits I smell, Miss Kierin?" he called, patting his stomach. "I hope you made lots cuz

209

I's hungry enough to eat a whole panful by myself."

"Dove made them this morning, Jacob, not me, and yes, there's enough to satisfy even an appetite like yours."

"Good." Jacob grinned and unfastened the butter churn from the side of the wagon. Since the wagon's were laying over today, it was a job that needed tending by hand. He poured her bucket of fresh milk into the churn, reserving some for the nooning.

As they ate the biscuits and salt pork, Ben and Jacob talked animatedly about the coming hunt. Ben regaled them with stories about hunting buffalo with the Sioux in the Black Hills years ago. Jacob was as anxious as any first-time hunter and listened to Ben's stories with rapt awe. Kierin tried to be attentive, but her mind kept straying to the one man absent from their circle.

Clay pulled the curry brush through Taeva's white streaked tail, working out the barbed cordgrass flowerheads entangled there. The mindless work soothed him, settled him. And it gave him an excuse to get out of camp for a while.

Any excuse in a storm, he thought gloomily.

He smoothed a hand over the stallion's rump and gave him a pat, sending up a small cloud of dust. "Where have you been anyway, boy, hm-mm? Romping with some mare down by the river? So much for hobbles, huh?" He dragged the brush over the sleek black coat. "Well . . . can't say I care for 'em much myself, buddy," he said, thinking of the woman who had captured his heart as easily as she had his name.

The horse nickered softly and pricked up his ears. Attuned to the stallion's signals, Clay pivoted to find Kierin standing behind him. He felt the ground shift under him and he lay a steadying hand on Taeva's rump. The morning sunlight limned Kierin's fiery hair with gold where it strayed out of the confines of the ribbon at the nape of her neck. She held a towel-covered packet in front of her.

"I thought you might be hungry," she said, offering it to him. "You shouldn't ride out on an empty stomach."

He remembered the first time he'd seen her in Talbot's looking like a deer poised for flight. That look was back in her eyes again. He hesitated only for a moment before accepting her peace offering.

"Thanks." He folded back the towel and picked up a bacon-filled biscuit. The smokey aroma made his stomach growl and he realized he was hungry. He took a bite and rolled his eyes shut with pleasure. "They're good."

Kierin clasped her hands behind her back and walked around to Taeva's head. The horse nuzzled her shoulder and she petted his velvety muzzle. Clay's eyebrow went up. She even had a way with his horse, the witch.

"He's beautiful, you know," she said, stroking the stallion. "What does his name mean?"

"In Cheyenne, it's pronounced *Taa'eva hotóhke,* which—loosely translated—means Nighttime Star."

"He's an Indian pony?"

"Born and bred. He was given to me a few years ago by a chief named Many Horses in return for a favor."

Her curiosity peaked, she remarked, "It must have been quite a favor for him to part with such a fine animal."

"I guess Many Horses thought it was enough."

Kierin stroked the stallion's muzzle, her eyes still on Clay. "But you're not going to tell me what it was, are you?"

Clay studied the brush in his hands, sensing the conversation had taken a sudden turn. "You want to know? It's not a secret. Just something I don't talk about."

Resignation shadowed her eyes and she turned away.

"Add that to the list."

"What's that supposed to mean?"

"It's not important. Never mind."

"Isn't it?" He grabbed her arm. "Okay, I killed a marauding grizzly that was attacking Many Horses' son. Practically got myself killed in the bargain. You probably saw the scars when you doctored me."

Her wide eyes strayed to his chest, remembering the marks vividly.

"Anything else you want to know? Just ask," he said acerbically. She could get under his skin faster than any woman he'd ever known. "Want to know about this one—?" he asked, pointing a finger at the thin white line on his jawline.

She swallowed hard and looked away, avoiding his eyes.

"A saber at Churrubusco."

"Stop it—"

"What's this all about, Kierin? Not about my scars or the time I spent with the Cheyenne."

"I didn't come out here to fight with you, Clay," she told him, prying his fingers from her arm. "Let's just forget it, all right?"

"No. Not this time, darlin'. I'm getting tired of shoving everything under the carpet and pretending nothing's happened between us." He let go of her and raked his fingers through his damp hair. "Something did happen back there and I'll be damned if I understand what it was. You came out here and started this. Okay. Finish it. What's on your mind?"

"All right. Yes. Something happened. We can hardly deny it. But as you said, it was a mistake."

Clay put a hand up. "Don't put words in my mouth. You were the one to draw that conclusion, not me."

Was she? she wondered. She couldn't remember. *It doesn't matter. A mistake is a mistake.* "Well, it was and there's no getting around it."

"Suppose you tell me why?" he demanded. "Why

212

was it a mistake? I liked it, and you sure as hell seemed to. If two people—"

"Because you don't love me—" she blurted.

Denial sprang to his lips, but she cut him off.

"—and I don't love you." She lowered her eyes so he wouldn't see the lie.

Her statement silenced him as surely as a slap. He blinked and looked away with a grim set to his jaw.

"And if we weren't out here," she continued, "in the middle of nowhere, it would be easy to walk away. We could just . . . say good-bye. Go our separate ways. But we *are* here. And it won't do either of us any good to go on the way we have." She wrung her slender hands together unconsciously. "I came out here hoping we could work things out, maybe even be friends again."

"Friends?" he repeated woodenly. The word stuck like a fish bone in his throat.

She lowered her head. "Yes. But if you'd rather not . . ."

He rocked his head back, tipping his face up to the morning sky and let out a long breath. "You ask a lot of a man, Kierin," he replied, thinking of the months ahead—of being near her without touching her. To her silence, he replied, "All right. If that's my only choice."

"It has to be," Kierin answered, and then turned before her eyes could betray her.

Ben spotted the herd first as the six men and Dove approached the crest of a hill. He raised his hand to signal the others to stop behind him. Like an enormous ink stain on a green felt blotter, the bison spread across the shallow valley before them. Thousands of the shaggy beasts grazed there, leaving the bluestem grass and thistles cropped short in their wake. An occasional buff-colored pronghorn mingled companionably with the herd.

Ben dismounted silently and crouched down at the top of the hill, testing the direction of the wind with the moistened tip of his finger. The sun-warmed breeze favored them, keeping their scent from the herd, but they were still too far away for a shot.

"Hellfire. Just outta range," he told Clay, who'd crouched beside him.

"Yeah, and no cover between us and them," Clay added with a frown. The day had started out bad and only seemed to be getting worse. He had a bad feeling about this.

"Once they get a look at us, they'll tear outta here like they was burned with the business end of a stove poker."

"What's the hold-up?" asked Daniel who, along with Jim Kelly, joined them at the knoll. Catching sight of the herd, Jim let out a low whistle.

"We're too far away," Clay answered, "and we'll spook 'em if we try to just ride in there."

Daniel studied the herd below. "Maybe we can wait 'em until they drift this way, then take our shots from here."

Ben shook his head and pointed out the thinly stubbled ground directly before them. "They've already covered this patch of graze. They're headin' north." He rubbed an anxious hand across his silvery beard. "We could try a good old-fashioned surround, but it's risky with these tinhorns."

"Too risky," Jim agreed.

"Then we got only one other choice," Ben said with a shrug. "And just pray the wind don't change."

Leaving Dove on the grassy knoll alone with the improvised travois and the mule, the men began a painstakingly slow descent down the gently sloped hill. Ben had cautioned each of them not to make a sound and to hang low over their horses' necks to disguise their silhouettes. They spread out across the hill: Daniel rode beside Billy Lovell, a fair-haired nineteen-year-old whose lanky frame belied his solid strength. Clay and Ben veered off to the right to get behind the herd while Mel Watkins took the left. Jim Kelly angled off toward the center of the herd.

With a perverseness Clay had grown accustomed to, Kierin's face invaded his mind as he rode toward the herd. Why would he think of her now, when his mind should only be on the job at hand? Lately, he seemed to have little control over her comings and goings inside his head. At the strangest times, he'd imagine he could smell her sweet scent or remember how she'd felt under him—impossibly soft and willing.

He cursed, remembering their conversation this morning. Friends, she'd said. As if they could ever be only that after what had happened between them. He took a deep breath and he pushed the vision aside, willing her out of his consciousness.

They were nearly in range when the first shaggy head came up in sudden startled awareness. Another looked up and the herd began to move restlessly. The animals' tension was a palpable thing. Fear thickened the air. A cloud of dust stirred at the center of the herd and they collided against each other, sensing the unknown danger.

Clay tightened his knees and ankles around his stallion and fingered the trigger of the rifle in his hand. Sweat prickled his skin and trickled down past his ear. Beside him, Ben crouched low over the sorrel's neck, his weathered face a study of control and determination. Slowly, he shouldered his Hawken, giving the others the signal to fire. "Now!" he shouted.

The first crack of gunfire rent the air like the roar of cannon. As one, the massive herd thundered into motion, stumbling over one another to escape. The riders gave chase, firing into the melee of bellowing animals. Ben's first shot dropped a huge cow in its tracks. Taeva hit a dip as Clay squeezed off his first round and he missed his target completely. Cursing, he one-handed

215

his horn of powder and pulled the plug out with his teeth. As he reloaded, he caught sight of Billy and Daniel riding hellbent behind the stampeding herd, their rifles leveled.

Billy Lovell's shot hit an enormous bull in the shoulder, wounding him, but not stopping him. Youth and inexperience failed to warn him of the dangers of a wounded animal and he bowed his head to reload. In a frothing rage, the bull turned and charged Billy's horse.

"Lovell!" Clay screamed over the thunderous noise. "Watch out!"

The boy's head came up with a snap, but it was too late. His horse screamed and reared as the bull neared, dumping his rider to the ground. Blindly, the bison kept coming at horse and man, bellowing its rage. Billy scrabbled backward furiously, unable to get his legs under him.

There was no time to reload the rifle, so Clay tossed aside his powder horn and reached frantically for the pistol strapped to his hip. Taking aim, he fired at the wooly back, but the small-caliber bullet barely made the beast flinch. The bull careened into Billy's terror-stricken horse, tossing it sideways like a rag doll.

"God in heaven!" Billy screamed, getting to his feet. "Somebody help me!"

Clay's heart pounded in his chest as he headed for the fallen man but before he could cross the distance between them, Ben intervened, placing his horse between the beast and Billy. The younger man scrambled to get up behind Ben while the older man shoved the ramrod down the barrel of his Hawken.

"Come on, you devil!" Ben shouted wildly over the cloud of dust between them. "I'll blast ya to hell and back."

"Ben! Get out of there, for God's sake!" Clay warned.

Ben shouldered the gun to fire as the pain-crazed

animal bore down on them. The sorrel horse, wild-eyed with fear, shrieked and stumbled backward with Lovell dangling across its hindquarters. Ben's Hawken exploded with a flash of fire. The charging bull stumbled but, incredibly, kept coming like some kind of four-legged demon.

A scream tore from Ben's throat as the huge bull sank a horn into the old man's abdomen in a final desperate plunge, then collapsed to the ground, dead.

Clay let out an anguished cry. "Ben! Oh, God—"

The trapper's panicked horse lunged away from the lifeless animal. Ben hung on, doubled over in the saddle, clutching his blood-soaked belly.

Spurring Taeva, Clay raced alongside Ben's horse and grabbed the loose reins, slowing it to a stop. He leapt to the ground, catching Ben as he slipped, unconscious, from the saddle toward the unyielding earth below.

Clay cradled the older man in his arms and sank with him to the ground. Tears blurred his vision and he blinked rapidly trying to clear them. "Don't die, Ben, please, don't die," he whispered, but Ben's hardy body seemed suddenly frail in his arms. Thick crimson blood seeped from his gaping wound and Clay tore the shirt from his own back to try and stanch the flow.

Billy Lovell dropped to his knees beside the old man. His gaze traveled across Ben's ruined body with eyes that bespoke the misery he felt. "Sweet Jesus—it's m-my fault . . ."

Clay glanced up at the boy, whose face was stricken with guilt. A part of him wanted to pin the blame on Billy, wanted to thrash him good for being so goddammed careless and inexperienced. He wanted someone to be responsible for this terrible mistake. But he knew there was no one.

"It could have happened to any one of us, Billy," he said at last. "Ben knew the risks."

"He . . . s-saved . . . my life," Billy replied haltingly,

shaking his head.

The trembling roar of hoofbeats faded in the distance. Billy's horse lay dead in closely cropped weeds beside the carcasses of the slaughtered buffalo. The pungent tang of blood and death and the rank scent of Clay's own fear burned his nostrils. Only the sibilant rush of wind over the arid plain and Ben's labored breathing stirred the eerie silence now.

"Billy," Clay said gently, "go fetch Dove. Take my horse. And bring back the travois. We'll need it."

Chapter Fifteen

Ben moaned as he came around. His features were pinched and shadowed with pain.

"Ah, Ben," Clay whispered, cradling the old man's head. "Ben."

"I reckon I . . . misjudged that devil . . . didn't I?" Ben's voice was rasping and thin.

"We're gonna get you back to camp," Clay told him. "Fix you up. You'll be—"

Ben raised a hand weakly to silence him. "No. We both know that ain't so. Let's not . . . waste our time lyin' to each other. Not . . . now."

Damnit. Damnit to hell. Clay wasn't ready to let him go yet. Not yet. He nodded silently, unable to hold back the tears that spilled down his cheeks.

"None a' that now," Ben admonished gently. "It's a good day to die." He coughed and Clay felt Ben's body go stiff from the pain. Finally, it passed. "I ain't got much time . . . so I want ya to . . . hear me, boy." Clay leaned closer to the older man.

"Yer the closest thing to a son I ever had, boy . . . couldn'ta asked fer better. I'm proud of the way you turned out." He sighed and shook his head. "A feller shouldn't wait . . . til he's a' goin' out to say them things. He's liable to . . . come up short."

Clay squeezed Ben's shoulder. "You taught me everything I know about being a man, Ben. You're more a

219

father to me than my own ever was. I'll never forget that."

Ben nodded and swallowed hard. Emotion roughened his voice. "Somethin' I been meanin' to say to ya, boy. Ya ain't . . . cut out to be a loner like me. I know'd that since that first day . . . in Wind River."

Clay closed his eyes. He'd believed that about himself once, too. Now, thinking of the woman who'd turned him away, he didn't know. *Time has a way of changing things.* Ben coughed again, and Clay tightened his arms around him.

"Bendin' never come easy to me . . ." Ben said, gripping Clay's arm. "An' I lost her . . . was too stubborn . . ."

"Lost—? You mean Joey?" Years ago, Ben had mentioned a woman. Said he'd lost her to another man. A steadier man. He'd never told him the woman's name. All the times he'd met Joey over the years he and Ben had been trapping together, he'd been too young or stupid to notice. But back at the fort, only a blind man could have missed how much they still cared for each other.

Ben smiled and his eyes slid shut. "My only regret. But you . . . you ain't made of hickory, like me. Take yer chance. Bend a little. She'll come to ya."

Clay's brows drew together in a frown. Ben was talking about Kierin. Clay sighed, knowing Ben was wrong about her. But this was no time to argue. "All right, Ben. Don't worry."

Ben's breath rattled in his chest like seeds in a dried locust pod. The sound of pounding hoofbeats sliding to a stop made Clay look up. Jacob, Jim, and Daniel were already off their mounts and hurrying toward the fallen man. Clay and Jacob exchanged bleak looks.

Ben blinked slowly, trying to focus on Clay. His voice was a whisper. "Dove . . ."

Clay ran his hand across Ben's damp brow. "She can stay with us for as long as she wants. We'll all watch out

220

for her."

Too weak to respond, he managed a smile that tipped the corner of his mouth. Ben took one last shuddering breath, then was gone.

With a heavy heart, Clay pounded the marker into the ground at the head of Ben's freshly covered grave. They'd buried him at the foot of the bluffs where the soil was still soft enough to take the blade of a shovel. The fine, reddish dirt accepted the wooden stake as generously as it had the body of his old friend. The others had gone, leaving him alone with the grave. Clay sat back on his heels and stared vacantly at the rough placard he'd carved.

> *Ben Crowley*
> *Voyager & Friend*
> *Died: June 16, 1854*
> *By the horn of a buffalo*
> *Rest in peace*

Damn few words to sum up a man's life, Clay mused bitterly, tossing the fist-sized rock aside. Above him, a red-tailed hawk circled in the mauve-tinged evening sky, sailing on the fickle currents of air below the bluff. Clay tipped his head back to watch it dip and soar. If his friend, Many Horses, were here, he would call the hawk a sign from the All Father that Ben's spirit had begun its journey heavenward. Clay wasn't sure he believed in any god that could have stripped him of so many of the people he loved. So many.

He knew, however, that Ben believed in the great circle of life as the Cheyenne did. His gaze followed the ascending hawk. *"Wakantanka opa, tsehe-heto,"* Clay whispered in Cheyenne. Go with the Great Spirit, my father.

He stood and slapped the brim of his hat against the

knees of his trousers, sending up little clouds of dust into the air. It wasn't until he turned around that he saw her. Kierin was standing back some twenty feet away, holding the wilted bouquet of wildflowers she'd picked for Ben's grave. His gut tightened at the sight of her. He thought she'd gone back with the others.

Their eyes met over the freshly turned mound—hers filled with pain, his, hardened against it. Weighing his options and finding them seriously lacking, he nodded curtly to her and started toward the wagon.

"Clay . . ." Kierin called as he passed, halting him midstride.

He stood with his back to her, silent.

"Clay," she said again. "I'll miss him, too."

"I know," he answered, not turning around. He held himself stiffly, turning his hat between his fingers, staring out across the deepening sunset.

She walked toward him and rested a hand on his arm. "We're friends, aren't we?" Her voice was gentle and pleading. "Will you just walk away from me, and not let me comfort you?"

Ben's last words rang in his ears—*Bend a little,* he'd said, *she'll come to you.* Clay let out an audible breath. Here she was, offering him the very thing he craved. Why was it so goddammed hard to accept it? For so long, he'd depended on no one to comfort him, share his thoughts or his pain. Now . . .

Bend a little, the voice persisted.

Kierin's heart fluttered like a caged bird in her chest as he turned toward her, letting her glimpse the grief in his eyes.

Wordlessly, he pulled her into the circle of his arms and pressed his face against her hair. With her cheek against his shoulder she felt him give in to the pain he'd been holding inside.

"God, Kierin, it all happened so fast," he told her in a choked whisper.

"I know," she soothed. "There was nothing you could

have done. Billy told me what happened."

Clay nodded against her hair. "One minute he was there and the next he was gone. It just doesn't seem possible."

"He loved you, Clay," she whispered. She felt his fingers splay across her back in answer.

"I know. I guess I've always known it." Clay pulled back, resting his forearms on Kierin's shoulder, and his forehead on hers. "He was a wise man. Wiser than I ever knew."

Kierin nodded against the warmth of Clay's skin. Would she ever be able to forget the feel of his body against hers?

"Did you know he was in love with Joey?" he asked.

"I guessed as much."

"He told me she was his one regret."

Kierin drew back, her gaze meeting the sudden intensity of his. "I—I think Joey loved him too."

"I think you're right. I think all these years he regretted not settling down and marrying her before Henri beat him to it." Clay looked down at the mound of earth at their feet and back into her eyes. He swallowed hard before he spoke again. "Is that what's going to become of us, Kierin?"

Her pulse leaped, sending a rush of color to her cheeks. "Us?"

His fingers caressed the back of her neck. "Yeah." Then he repeated, softer this time, "Us."

Confused, Kierin searched the gold-flecked blue of his eyes. "I—I thought . . . we decided—"

"No, *you* decided. I conceded."

Fearful of being swayed again, she dropped her chin to her chest and looked at the tops of his boots. "And I was right. Under the circumstances . . . it's the best thing."

He tipped two fingers under her chin and brought it up to meet his gaze. "For who?" he asked in frustration. "You? Me? Hell, for us?"

"Wh—what are you saying?" Entreaty darkened her eyes. "That we should go on as we were? Fighting each other at every turn? Making ourselves miserable over—"

"Wanting each other?" he finished.

"Yes," she blurted, but horrified by the bald-faced truth of it, she took it back. "No." A chorus of striped frogs chirped on the riverbank, mocking her denial. "Oh, I don't know anymore."

He bracketed her shoulders with his hands. "I do. I want you. I admit it. But it's gone way beyond that for me." He paused, and his Adam's apple bobbed like a cork in a stream. "And no matter what you say, I think it has for you, too. Look me in the eye, Kierin, and tell me I'm wrong."

"I—" Denial caught like a burr in her throat when she saw the earnest expression in his eyes. Was it possible? Could he care about her after all? "You're not wrong," she admitted after a long pause. "But—"

His mouth dropped to cover hers in joyous censure, chasing away her arguments. A muffled groan came from deep in his throat when she relaxed almost instantly against him, reaching up to meet his kiss with an urgency of her own. The bouquet slipped, forgotten, from her fingers.

With his open mouth on hers she breathed deeply of his scent; the masculine smell of his skin; his hair, where it fell against her cheek. She committed it all to memory in case this was all just a dream.

He lifted his head reluctantly, his breathing harsh and fast. He pulled back so he could see her. "I love you, Kierin. Hell, it took Ben's dyin' to make me realize it, but I do. Life is too short and precarious to let this get by us. I love you," he repeated, slower this time.

Shock raced through her, churning her thoughts and emotions like a wind eddy. "Oh, Clay—"

"I never thought I'd hear myself saying those words to anyone again," he said, throwing his head back with

224

relief. "I was a walking dead man before I met you, honey. Now I can't imagine my life without you in it. I don't want to imagine it anymore." He paused, searching her eyes. "Marry me."

She stared at him in astonishment, unable to speak.

"Marry me, Kierin," he repeated.

His thumb ran across her cheek with such tenderness it made her heart swell with love.

"We can make each other happy," he said. "I know we can. I don't have much to offer you. Just a burned-out piece of land, but it's got possibilities. We can build a life together there. What do you say?"

She pulled him closer, hugging him tightly to her. She wanted to tell him yes. She wished life were as simple as that. But it wasn't.

"Oh, Clay—I love you too. I've never felt this way about anyone before. But don't you see? I . . . I can't marry you."

The smile slipped from his face like a sunset stripped of its color. "Why not?"

"Because I've made a promise to myself and to my brother that I'd find him." Miserable, she looked down at her hands. "I have to go to California when we reach the West."

"I'll come with you."

"What?" Her heart staggered a beat.

"I'll come with you—help you find him. With two looking, it's bound to go faster," he told her. "Anyway, you have no idea what it's like down there in the gold country. It's no place for a woman alone."

She shook her head. "I . . . couldn't ask that of you."

"You didn't ask. I'm volunteering. As soon as we reach Oregon and get Jacob and Dove settled, we'll take a packet down the coast. We'll find him."

"But . . . your ranch . . ."

A hopeful smile eased the lines of concern on his face. "It's survived without me this long. I guess it can stand a few more months."

Kierin lowered her eyes from his gaze and flattened her palms over the firm muscles of his chest. She didn't want to consider the possibility that all this was simply his overwrought emotions speaking, but she had no choice. She couldn't bear it if he took it all back later after thinking it through.

"Are you . . . sure all this is what you want?" she asked. "Ben's death has been a shock. Maybe it's made you say things . . ."

He pulled her close to him again. "No," he said, silencing her question. "Ben's death has just reminded me how little time we all have here and how important it is not to waste it. I know what I want and it's you. Time won't change the way I feel right now."

His ardent expression pulled at her heart. "Are you sure?"

He took her face between his large hands and forced her to look at him. "I've never been more sure of anything in my life."

"Oh, Clay!" she cried, and hugged him tightly. "Then yes! I'll marry you. I will."

She felt the smile on his lips as he kissed her again, this time gently, almost gratefully. She ran her fingers through his hair, taking a moment to envision herself doing this for the rest of her life with him.

He blew out a shaky breath as he freed her mouth and leaned his chin against the top of her head. "We're only a few days out of Fort Laramie. I'll make arrangements with the fort's chaplain to marry us in a private ceremony—away from prying eyes." His lips brushed her hair again as if they couldn't be coaxed away from it. "But in every way that counts, Kierin, you're my wife already."

Nothing he could have said would have touched her as those words did. "I love you Clay. With all my heart."

They held each other while the sun settled below the far bluffs. The sky to the west of them was deepening to the cobalt blue of dusk and the first glittering stars appeared above them. They started back toward the wagon, arms wrapped around each other, when Jacob's dark figure approached them at a run. He was out of breath.

Clay put his hand on Jacob's arm. "What is it, Jacob?"

"It's Dove." Fear tinged his deep baritone voice. "She be in pain somethin' awful. Her child's coming. She be askin' fo you, Miss Kierin."

"Oh, no," Kierin whispered. "It's too soon."

"Yes'm. That's what Dove say." Jacob's worried eyes probed hers intently. "She say the pains started on the hunt, right after—" He didn't need to finish his thought. They all knew what had brought Dove's labor on.

Kierin lifted her gaze to Clay's for one brief moment and he squeezed her hand in encouragement. Without another word, Kierin ran ahead of them toward the camp.

First one, then two hours went by. Night settled over the camp with its blanket of stars. In the distance, a wolf howled to its mate. Hundreds of striped chorus frogs warmed to their tasks, covering any telltale sounds from within Dove's tent. Daniel's wife, Susan, had brought a stew over for their dinner, but neither of them had much appetite. The pot sat warming by the edge of the cook fire, untouched. The Reverend Beaker and his wife, Clara, had delivered a pie along with their condolences. It, too, was untouched.

Clay and Jacob sat near the fire, periodically adding more water to the pot heating over the flame.

Waiting.

They'd boiled the knife that would be used to cut the baby's cord, warmed water, and provided Kierin with the clean bedding and blankets she'd requested. Jacob had stayed busy for a while brewing a mixture of raspberry leaf tea and tincture of squaw root from his herbal bag—a remedy his mother had imparted to him—to help Dove's labor. Clay was bent over a haunch of buffalo meat, paring thin slices from it with a small-bladed knife, keeping his hands and his mind occupied.

With a cigarette dangling from his lips, hands thrust into his pockets, Jacob got to his feet for the hundredth time and paced outside of the lamp-lit tent where Dove and Kierin were.

"Jacob," Clay called to him across the fire. "You're making me nervous. Is all that pacing helping?"

Jacob took a final drag on his cigarette and dropped it to the ground, grinding it cold with the toe of his boot. "No. But neither is sittin' on my hands." He looked at the tent again and ran a hand over the back of his neck. "It's taken' a long time, ain't it?"

Clay spread the strip of meat he'd just cut across the drying rack, then added fuel to the ebbing fire, producing a shower of colorful sparks. He glanced up at Jacob's back. "You got special feelings for her, Jacob?"

He hesitated for a moment before answering, but didn't turn around. "I reckon so." He turned to face Clay. "That sit all right with you?"

Clay looked back down at his work. "If you mean because of Ben—"

"I do."

Clay nodded, guessing as much. It hurt just to talk about the old man, but he did for Jacob's sake. "If you're of a mind to take care of her, I'd say Ben couldn't have made a better choice himself."

"I thank you fer that," Jacob replied. "Means a lot to me. But I wants you to know, I never meant to do nothin' 'bout it. If Ben'd lived . . ."

Clay sent him a reassuring look. "Jacob, we both know it wasn't that way with Ben and Dove. He was like a father to her. A friend. Ben was in love with Joey. Always was, always would be, I suppose. He would have wanted Dove to be happy."

Jacob nodded thoughtfully, then cleared his throat and looked intently at the ground. "You reckon she be wantin' a colored man like me?" His black eyes flicked up to Clay's briefly, then down again.

In all the time he'd known Jacob, Clay had never heard him refer to his color disparagingly before. "It's only whites who tend to see your color as a problem, Jacob. The People have a more generous nature than that. They look to a man's honor to judge his worth. Not the color of his skin. I think when Dove looks at you, she only sees a man. A good man."

At that moment, the small mewling wail of an infant came from within the white canvas tent. An astonished smile spread across Jacob's face like the sun peeling back the clouds "Whoo-ee!" he exclaimed, clapping Clay on the back. "You hear that?"

Clay returned his smile. "Why don't you take that bucket of warm water into them, my friend. I think they'll be needing it now."

When Jacob had disappeared into the tent, Clay wrapped the remaining meat and had washed up by the time Kierin found him sitting cross-legged by the fire. She sank down beside him with a sigh of exhaustion, but a smile on her face.

"How is she?" Clay asked.

"Oh, Clay . . ." Awe tinged her voice. "She's just fine. I wish you could have seen it. It was . . . wonderful. I held him in my arms. He's small, but perfect . . ."

Clay's gaze took in every nuance of her joy as she prattled on like a proud aunt about the birth. Her face was flushed with excitement and her hands fluttered descriptively like the wings of a bird. He loved seeing her like this, so alive and vibrant. Just being close to her made him feel alive too. She was what he needed—her joy in living, her healing touch.

". . . and he's a little miniature of Dove. He's going to be handsome when he—" She stopped, taking in Clay's amused smile. "Oh, listen to me go on. I guess I got caught up."

"It's all right. I was enjoying it," he told her honestly. "A boy, huh?"

She nodded, slipping her slender hand into his callused one. "Dove wants to name him . . . Ben."

Clay's throat constricted suddenly with the raw emotions still swirling around him. He tightened his fingers around hers and was silent for the moment it took to rein in the feeling. "Ben would've liked that," he murmured.

"I'm sure he would have." Kierin cast a sideways glance at him. Blue smudges of fatigue showed beneath his eyes when he met her look.

"Tired?" he asked, as if reading her thoughts.

"Mm-hmm. Exhausted, really. You?"

He sighed in affirmation. Tentatively, she rested her cheek against his shoulder, and closed her eyes when she felt his arm curl around her back. His fingers splayed at her waist, drawing her closer. Relief flooded her as she allowed him to draw her into his arms.

"Susan Thorp made some stew and the Beakers brought a pie. You hungry?" he murmured against her hair.

"Not really." She glanced up, studying the angular planes of his face, made more distinct by the shadows of the fire. It was the face that haunted her dreams, both waking and sleeping—more ruggedly handsome than any man's had a right to be. There was a desperate vulnerability in his expression tonight she'd never seen before. It made her love him all the more.

No longer the innocent she'd once been, he'd taught her how she could comfort him and sensed that he needed that comfort desperately now. Trailing her fingers along his back in silent invitation, she stood beside him. "I think it's time for bed."

Clay's gaze followed her up. He hesitated, hoping to God he wasn't misunderstanding her. He needed her tonight more than he could ever tell her. So much so, it frightened him. His body trembled with the power of it.

"Come on," Kierin said, extending a hand down to him. "I need you beside me tonight, Clay."

He released the breath he'd been holding and stood up beside her. His shadow obscured her when he towered over her. "Kierin," he breathed, taking her into his arms, with all the restraint he could muster. "You have no idea how glad I am to hear you say that."

"I've missed you, Clay," she admitted, twining her arms around his neck. She covered his cheek with small moist kisses. "It's been . . . so miserable . . . without you."

Clay's body quaked at her touch. He savored the feel of her lips against his skin until he could stand it no longer, then he claimed her mouth with his. She returned the urgency of his kiss in kind, molding her body to his. Their tongues danced the dance of lovers— exploring and entreating at once.

When the kiss ended, she took his hand and led him to the wagon. They undressed in the dark, shedding their garments one at a time, until they stood naked together. Clay knelt in front of her and wrapped his arms around her slender hips. With a sigh, he nestled his face against her stomach. With Ben's death so fresh in his mind, he needed her to remind him that he was still alive. He wanted to bury himself inside her until the pain went away.

"It scares me how much I want you," he admitted, clinging to her. "I don't want to . . ."

"What?" she prodded gently.

"Hurt you."

Kierin knelt down beside him, understanding suddenly. "Clay, you could never hurt me that way." She ran her fingers through the unruly waves of his thick, dark hair. "Come and lie down with me."

With his hand behind her back, he lowered her to the

bed. He covered her body with his, flesh against flesh, and soon, his driving need became hers. What had been a smoldering ember burst into flame between them, and beneath the sheltering canvas they spent their grief on each other. Then, having cast it aside, they gloried in their union.

Exhausted but not sated, Clay lay with his arms around her, thanking whatever god was responsible for sending her to him. The more he had of her, the more he wanted. She was like a thirst that could never be quenched. She was his destiny, his woman. His mate.

Fear crept into his thoughts, remembering the last woman he'd loved and lost, and he tightened his arms around the sleeping woman beside him.

"I won't let anything happen to you," he whispered. "I swear it." He kissed the top of her head and she curled against him like a sleeping cat. "I swear it," he repeated to the still night air.

Chapter Sixteen

A twenty-nine-man detachment of infantry soldiers marched past the stockaded gates of Fort Laramie just as Clay and Kierin rode in astride his black Appaloosa. Several mounted officers and civilians accompanied the troops, followed by two mule-drawn limbers burdened with a twelve-pound field howitzer and a smaller mountain howitzer. While Kierin batted at the cloud of dust they stirred, Clay stared after the departing men, a frown creasing his brow.

Troubled by his look, Kierin's own gaze went back to the disappearing soldiers. "Where do you think they're going?"

Clay shook his head. "With that firepower in tow, it'd be an unlikely bet they're off to tend the fort's vegetable garden." Clay dismounted, lacing the reins around the smooth rail of the hitching post before reaching up to help Kierin down.

"They did look menacing, didn't they?" she admitted. She braced her hands against Clay's shoulders and he set her lightly on the ground. Her fingers lingered on the soft deerskin of his shirt for a moment longer than absolutely necessary, then she brushed off an imaginary piece of lint.

The fort was noisy and crowded with people. Trappers, decked out in skins and an array of weaponry, dickered with traders who'd set up stalls to sell their

233

wares. Friendly Sioux moved freely, both in and out of the fort. Soldiers, Kierin observed, were notably scarce.

Clay caught the arm of a passing blue-uniformed enlisted man and stopped him. "Where's that detachment headed, soldier?"

The ruddy-complexioned young man looked Clay up and down before answering. Puffing up his ample chest, he said, "I reckon that's army business, mister."

Thwarted, but not stymied, Clay released his arm. "Then tell me where to find First Lieutenant Randall's office."

"Randall? He ain't been in command here since the middle of last month. Second Lieutenant Fleming's in charge now."

Clay shook his head in disbelief. A second lieutenant, in charge of a whole post? It was getting worse all the time. "And where will I find *him?*" Clay returned with a patient look.

"Have a look-see in his office down yonder," he answered, pointing at the small room which housed the army headquarters. It was tucked under the catwalk that circled the inside walls of the fort. "If he ain't there, try over at Old Bedlam."

"Old Bedlam?" Kierin echoed. "What in the world is that?"

The soldier's eyes widened appreciatively at the sight of Kierin stepping out from behind Clay. He doffed his cap and gave her a gap-toothed smile. "How do, ma'am."

Kierin dipped her head. "Corporal? You were saying?"

It took him a moment to remember what he had been saying. "Oh, yeah. Old Bedlam. Officers' quarters. Well," he corrected himself, "it ain't strictly for officers any more, 'cause the truth is there ain't many here. No calvary stationed here neither. Anyway, check over there if you don't find Fleming in his office."

Kierin smiled engagingly, hoping to pry more information from him. "Are you sure he's not among those men who just left the fort?"

"Fleming? No, ma'am. He'd a been a fool to go with that hothead Grattan."

Clay's arm tensed beneath her hand and she glanced obliquely at him. A narrow-eyed frown tugged at his expression. She gave the soldier her full attention again. "Why's that, Corporal?" she prodded.

The soldier evidently caught Clay's expression and stopped himself before he overstepped his bounds. Licking his lips, he answered, "Well . . . it ain't purely for me to say, ma'am." He glanced at Clay again. "You'll have to ask Lieutenant Fleming about it yourself." He touched two fingers to the bill of his cap, excusing himself. "Ma'am."

"What do you think he meant?" Kierin asked, when the soldier was out of earshot.

"I don't know," Clay answered, "but I'm going to find out." He turned to her, a smile softening the lines on his face. Sliding his hands up her arms, he held her shoulders and asked, "Think you can entertain yourself, while I talk to Fleming?"

"Oh, I'm sure I can find something to do," she said with a teasing grin.

"Good." He bent down, planted a kiss on the tip of her nose, and gave her shoulders a squeeze. "I shouldn't be long."

His touch sent a current of warmth through her and made her heart hurry its pace. As he turned to go, she put a hand on his arm. "Clay, you won't forget to ask him about marrying us, will you?"

A playfully wolfish look came into his eyes. "Not a chance, Miss McKendry," he told her, capturing her mouth in a brief but fervent kiss. "I'll be right back."

Kierin's cheeks were warm with color as she watched him go. A shiver of pure happiness ran down her spine. Had it been only two days since he'd asked her to marry him? she wondered with a contented sigh. Two days since he'd told her he loved her? It had been the most wonderful two days of her life.

She brushed her fingers against her lips. She could still taste his kiss there—warm and fresh with a hint of the wild mint they'd collected earlier that morning.

A woman with a young boy by her side smiled at Kierin as she brushed past her on the narrow boarded walkway. Kierin's gaze followed them as they passed. Her thoughts turned naturally to Matthew.

He'd be bigger than that now, she mused, looking after the boy, who nearly reached his mother's chin. He always sprouted like a joe-pye weed in the summers. She smiled, remembering how she'd barely get his pants let out before she'd have to turn around and do it again. She sighed. Everything would be perfect if only Matthew were here to share her joy. Scanning the fort, her eyes came to rest on a small sign over a doorway opposite the sutler's store. It read: RECORDS OFFICE. There was only a slim chance that she'd find out anything about her father and Matthew, but she decided to try it.

A bell jangled from the door jamb as she entered the dimly lit office. An immaculate polished-oak counter bisected the smallish room. Behind this, at an equally orderly desk, sat a thin, bespeckled man wearing sergeant's stripes, scratching entries into an oversized ledger book. He looked up at the sound of the bell. His spectacles slipped down to the tip of his nose when he stood to greet her and he pushed them back with a practiced forefinger.

"How do, miss. What can I do for you?"

"My name is Kierin McKendry, Sergeant. I'm looking for my father and brother, who passed through here last year. Would you keep records on that?"

"Yes, ma'am. Best we can. Any idea what month they may've come through?" he asked.

"August, I imagine," she answered. "They didn't

leave from Independence until the end of June."

The clerk frowned. "That's a mighty late start. With a train, were they?"

"Yes. A small one. Maybe fifteen wagons. But more might have joined them on the way." She explained about the locket she'd found at Kearny and showed him the pictures inside.

He shook his head. "I'm not too good at remembering faces," he admitted. "Names. Now that's another matter." He hauled out a large ledger from beneath the counter and laid it open in front of him. "McKendry, you say?"

"Asa and Matthew."

He flipped through the pages, reciting the names of the months until he came to August. "Ah, here we are. Now let's see." His thin finger indexed down several pages. "McKendry . . . McKendry . . . Last year we had a lot of trains slowed by the cholera," he said absently. "Epidemic. Might have put them in here as late as September."

Kierin chewed on her lip, disheartened by the news.

"Some folks didn't bother to register their names," he went on. "Could your pa write his — ah, wait . . . here it is. Asa McKendry and son, Matthew. Tenth of September, 1853. With the . . . ah, Hadley train."

Relief poured through her and she rolled her eyes shut for a moment. "Thank God. Their names were both there?"

"Yes, ma'am." He stared at the book, scratching his thinning hair as if searching his memory for an out-of-place fact.

Kierin folded her hands tightly in front of her. "Is something wrong?"

He cleared his throat. "Like I said, names have a way of sticking in my head. The Hadley train was one of the last trains through here last year. In fact, they were so late, half the families decided to stay on here for the winter. The others decided to chance the weather over the pass." He pulled another ledger from beneath the counter and leafed through it.

"You mean it was dangerous to go on then?"

He glanced up at her briefly. "Winter comes early that high up."

A cold knot formed in her stomach. Her father was a gambler. He loved taking chances. He would have gone over the pass and taken her brother with him, in spite of the dangers.

The clerk's finger stopped at the bottom of the page he was scanning while he read the entry. He cleared his throat, then slipped the spectacles off his nose with deliberate slowness.

"What?" she asked in a small, frightened voice. Somehow, she knew she wouldn't want to hear his answer.

"Your pa's wagon *was* among those that went on," the sergeant replied slowly. "It was a small party, only seven wagons. They were warned before they left the fort about traveling in such small numbers . . ."

In agonized silence, she waited for him to go on.

His expression was pained, reluctant. "We . . . had no way of knowing until this spring. . . . It appears by the markings on the arrows, they were hit by a band of Crow up near the South Pass." He hesitated before going on, avoiding her stricken eyes. "They found no survivors."

A snot-nosed private who appeared decidedly underage answered Clay's knock on Fleming's door and showed him into the office.

"A Mr. Holt to see you, Lieutenant," the private announced in a voice that hadn't yet made a decision on octave.

The officer behind the desk looked up at his visitor from behind a clutter of paperwork. Darkly tanned by the prairie sun, the young sandy-haired lieutenant shuffled the papers he was holding into a chaotic pile and rose to greet Clay. "Holt, you say?" Fleming asked, extending a sweaty palm.

Clay returned the handshake. "Clay Holt, Lieutenant. I'm here on behalf of Tom Fitzpatrick. I'm to deliver some papers for him to the officer in command."

"You've found him, Mr. Holt." Fleming indicated a chair to Holt and settled back in his own. "Nichols . . ." he called to the young private hovering near the door, "a drink for Mr. Holt here and pour me another while you're at it."

While Nichols was pouring, Clay withdrew the packet of papers from inside his shirt and laid it on the desk.

"Damn shame about Fitzpatrick," Fleming said, opening the packet and scanning the contents. "Heard about his dying in Washington this year. Savages trusted him as much as they trust any white man."

Clay's jaw tightened. "He was a man of his word," he agreed, sipping the whiskey Nichols handed him. "Indians respect honor, Lieutenant Fleming. This report is Tom's last. Just before he died, he was working toward the repeal of the Indian Removal Act."

Fleming refolded the report, then dabbed his forehead with a linen hanky. "I must say I'm curious. How is it that you delivered these and it wasn't done through ordinary military channels?"

"I happened to be in Washington when Tom was dying. We were old friends and he asked me to deliver them as a favor to him when he heard I was headed this way." Clay glanced pointedly at Fleming's cluttered desk. "He didn't hold much stock in military channels."

Fleming lifted an amused brow and tossed back a slug of whiskey.

"Tell me something, Lieutenant. Are you in the habit of sending your patrols out armed with howitzers?"

Fleming straightened in his chair. "If you're referring to the patrol that just left, Mr. Holt—"

"I am."

"That was a disciplinary action—"

"Disciplinary," Clay interrupted, setting down his glass with a thud. "On whom?"

"On an Indian named High Forehead, of the Miniconjou Sioux," Fleming told him warily. He got up from his desk and paced to the glass-paned window.

"For what offense?"

Fleming stared out into the fort's courtyard. "He killed a cow from a Mormon train. Butchered the poor beast and ate it. It's a crime to steal cattle, Mr. Holt. We intend to bring the man to justice."

Clay blinked at the man in disbelief. "Are you aware that the Treaty of '51 makes no provisions for such an action?"

Surprised by Holt's audacity, Fleming turned to face him. "I'm aware that you're overstepping your bounds, Mr. Holt."

"Have you even bothered to read it, Lieutenant? The taking of prisoners is strictly forbidden. The treaty's quite clear on that. Withholding annuities until restitution is made is your only recourse and you know it."

"Sir, this is not a simple case of—"

Clay got to his feet. "The hell it isn't," he snapped. "We're talking about a goddamned *cow*, Lieutenant, and a tribe of hungry, and from what I hear, *unhappy* Sioux. Is it worth risking the lives of your men over something as petty as a cow?"

Fleming's face reddened with anger. "Who the hell do you think you are coming in here and questioning my judgment?"

Towering over the young second lieutenant, Clay chose his words carefully. "When you send twenty-some green men out on a fool's mission into an armed Sioux encampment—*on foot*, no less—someone better damn well question your judgment. *Sir.*"

"If you were a soldier, I'd have you court-martialed for that remark," Fleming gritted impotently.

"I've done my time in the army, Lieutenant. Long enough to see how many men get killed because of senseless orders like these. What did you hope to accomplish?"

Fleming backed down and poured himself a drink. He drank it before speaking. "I was against it from the first," he admitted grudgingly, "but Brevet Lieutenant Grattan was anxious to teach these Sioux a lesson. The Miniconjou have been stirring up trouble for more than a year. He persuaded me . . . he felt —"

"Call them back."

Fleming's mouth dropped open. "What?"

"Send a man out. Do it, Fleming."

"Impossible."

Clay narrowed his eyes and took a step closer.

"I d-didn't order those men out," Fleming sputtered. "They're all volunteers under Lieutenant Grattan's authority. I've given him complete —"

"If they press this thing, they'll all die. You know that, don't you?" Disgust laced Clay's tone.

Fleming swallowed hard. "I trust Lieutenant Grattan will know where to draw the line."

"And will you be able to live with yourself if he doesn't?" At the lieutenant's stubborn silence, Clay snatched his hat from Fleming's desk and slammed out of the office.

Once outside, he swore and took several deep draughts of air to calm himself down. It wasn't his problem, he told himself. It was an army problem. He could just walk away. Any white man within miles of those twelve-pounders could be considered fair game if this thing got out of hand. He had other things to consider now.

Kierin, for one.

Clay scanned the fort's interior, searching for a glimpse of her. The fort was crowded with people but she was nowhere in sight. He headed to the sutler's store, the most promising possibility, he decided. As his

241

long-legged strides covered the distance, his imagination formed pictures of the likely consequences of the coming confrontation.

He was constantly amazed at how little the army understood of Indian ways. No training was offered at their revered West Point, where most of these stiff-necked officers were emerging from. They came out here as green as sprouting buffalo grass and nearly as dumb. Glory-hungry idiots like Lieutenant Grattan were the worst of the lot.

At the Post store, Clay's search came up empty. *Where the hell did she go?* he wondered. He leaned a shoulder against the adobe wall outside the store and massaged the bridge of his nose between his thumb and forefinger, weighing the odds.

Should he follow his conscience or cold reason? And if he chose reason, would his conscience let him forget it if this all came out badly? He'd never been one to run from trouble before. Pushing away from the wall, he decided he wasn't about to start now.

Clay spotted Susan Thorp as she was coming out with her arms full of packages.

"Mrs. Thorp?" Clay touched the sleeve of her dress.

"Oh, hello, Mr. Holt. How are—"

"Could you do me a favor?" he asked, cutting her off.

She shifted her grip on the packages, and squinted at him through the sun's glint. "Of course, what is it?"

"I can't seem to locate my wife and there's something I need to do. It won't bear waiting. Would you see if you can find her and tell her I'll be back as soon as I can?"

"Certainly," she replied agreeably, "but where shall I tell her you went?"

Clay was already moving toward his tethered horse. "Just tell her I went out to have a talk with the soldiers who left earlier," he called, already back-pedaling toward his tethered horse. He could only hope Kierin would understand. "And, Mrs. Thorp," he added with

242

a forced smile, "tell her not to worry."

"Miss McKendry, are you all right?" the sergeant asked. "Maybe you should sit down."

The blood had siphoned from Kierin's face and she swayed against the counter. The sergeant hurried around the barricade and helped her to the bench beside the door.

"A-are you sure there's no mistake?" Her voice sounded small and far away. Shock stripped her of tears and she sat rigid as a church pew, staring blankly ahead of her.

He squatted down in front of her. "Sure as anyone can be, ma'am."

Her gaze slid to his. "Wh-what do you mean?"

He dropped his chin to his chest and heaved a long sigh. "Just that most of the bodies were recovered and buried, but some were never found. Considering the time that'd passed, it'd be pretty nigh impossible to make any kind of . . . identification."

"But my brother was just a boy," she said, grasping at the small remaining hope. "Did they find any bodies of children?"

"It wasn't in the report we got back, ma'am. But from the records, there were several families with children along."

She pressed her steepled fingers against her lips. "I see. Well," she said, clearing her throat, "thank you for all your help, Sergeant." Standing stiffly, she edged toward the door.

He rose beside her, concern etched on his face. "Are you sure you're all right, miss?"

"Yes, I'll—I'll be fine," she answered, letting herself out the door. The little bell jangled again, just as it had before, yet this time the sound was more ominous, final.

She closed the door behind her and leaned against

the jamb, hand to throat, gulping air.

"Why, there you are, Kierin!"

Kierin's eyes flew open at the sound of a woman's voice. Susan Thorp was staring at her strangely.

"I've been looking all over for you," she said. "Good heavens, dear, are you all right? You're pale as ashes."

Kierin pushed away from the wall. "I . . . I have to find Clay."

"Well, that's what I came to tell you. He had to leave and he asked if I'd find you."

Kierin blinked at her. "What? Clay left? When?"

"About five minutes ago. He said not to worry . . . that he needed to talk with some soldiers . . . or something like that, and that he'd be back soon. I assumed you'd know what he meant."

"Oh, no . . ." What little color she had left fled Kierin's face. Her gaze snapped to the spot where they'd tethered his horse. Another stood in its place. With a sinking feeling, she realized it was true. Dizziness assailed her and she leaned back against the jamb for support.

"Kierin, is everything all right?" she heard Susan ask.

A cold dread fingered up her spine. This couldn't be happening. She wouldn't let it. Strangely, her desperation gave her courage.

"Kierin?"

Leaving Susan staring after her, she strode up the walkway to the commander's office. Her heels beat an angry rhythm against the wooden boards. She flung open the office door, startling both the young private and the lieutenant behind the desk. They stared at her in open-mouthed silence.

"I want to know where my husband has gone, Lieutenant, and I want to know now," she demanded.

The lieutenant looked at her as if she were touched in the head. "Madam, I don't know who your husband *is*, but—"

"Clay Holt."

The name erased Fleming's smug expression.

"He just rode off after your troops—"

"He *what?*" Fleming sputtered.

"And you're going to tell me why." She glared at him, a mother lion protecting her own. "Now, Lieutenant."

Wisps of fog, like ghostly fingers, slunk along the shoreline of the Platte, and obscuring the fort's view of the river's glassy surface. The rising three-quarter moon—alternately cloaked behind fast-moving clouds then gilding their leaden edges silver—gave testament to the lateness of the hour.

Heartsick, Kierin sat watching the blue flame dance above a nest of coals at the center of the fire. Waiting. The warmth of the fire taunted her, but it was unable to quell the chill that had settled like a fist of ice around her heart.

Her talk with Lieutenant Fleming had proved to be both pointless and frustrating. Refusing to spare any more men from the post, Fleming told her it had been Clay's choice to follow the detachment and that he had no intention of stopping him.

For one desperate moment, she'd thought of stealing Jacob's horse and riding to find him herself, but stopped short of doing it. He was a grown man who had made a choice of conscience. His sense of honor, the very thing that had impelled him to follow the soldiers, was also the thing she loved most about him. She could only wait. And pray.

She had not told anyone what she'd learned about her father and brother. She couldn't bear to give voice to something her heart still could not accept. All these months . . . wouldn't she have known if her brother were dead? Could God be so cruel as to take away both the people she loved in the same day?

Beside her, Jim Kelly refilled Jacob's tin mug of coffee and gestured the pot toward her, breaking the long silence that had stretched between them. "Coffee, Kierin?"

She shook her head.

"You oughta put something in your stomach. You haven't eaten all day."

The thought of coffee made her nauseous. "I'm not hungry, Jim. Thanks, anyway."

The orange-red light of the fire cast flickering shadows on the faces of her companions. Little Ben whimpered in his mother's arms. Cooing to the babe, Dove shifted her garments and tucked him inside to give him suckle. Only a tiny coppery fist showed beneath the blanket and he made small gurgling noises of satisfaction as Dove's milk let down. Jacob looked on with something in his eyes akin to awe.

The fort was quiet, despite the numbers within its gates. Trappers, soldiers, and travelers mingled inside the stockade, waiting for the return of the overdue soldiers. Word had spread quickly. Reverend Beaker had held a small prayer service for the men and now sat around another fire with the Thorps, the Watkinses, and several other families. Parents spread sleeping rolls on the ground for their sleepy children. It had been too long and everyone knew it.

"Someone's coming, Lieutenant!" shouted the man on watch in the south turret.

Lieutenant Fleming, who was keeping watch with the men on the north side of the fort, made for the rough wooden ladder which led down to the courtyard. "Is he mounted or on foot?" he called.

"On foot, sir. He looks to be wounded."

Kierin closed her eyes and inhaled sharply.

"Jenkins! O'Halloran!" Fleming called. "See to that man and help him in. Watch yourselves."

The two men disappeared into the darkness. Minutes dragged by and finally they reappeared with the wounded man slung between them. His head drooped down between his shoulders, his dark hair obscuring his face. When they eased him down near the fire, Kierin finally got a good look at him. Her heart sank.

It wasn't Clay.

She wasn't sure whether to be grateful or disappointed. The man had been shot with arrows. One broken-off shaft protruded from his shoulder and another from his thigh. The gold stripe down the leg of his trousers was stained a deep crimson. That the man had made it this far on foot was a miracle.

"Get the surgeon over here, on the double," Fleming called as he knelt down beside the man. The lieutenant's horrified gaze scanned the ruined body of the soldier. "Cuddy, what in the hell happened?"

Cuddy opened his eyes with an effort. "They're dead, sir . . . all of 'em."

Fleming dropped his face into his hand. "Good God . . ."

"The place wuz crawlin' with Sioux," Cuddy continued, pain slurring his words, "hundreds of 'em, all over us like ants . . . couldn't . . . get away."

"Grattan?"

"Dead."

"But . . . what happened?"

"That Frenchman, the interpreter, Auguste . . . was drunk. Kept shoutin' insults at 'em in Sioux. The traders up the river warned Grattan to get him out of there . . . didn't listen . . . got them redskins all worked up. Grattan wouldn't stop, even when they come out with war paint on." Cuddy moaned and fingered the arrow in his shoulder. "Said he'd . . . take High Forehead or . . . die tryin'. The Sioux wouldn't give him up . . ."

Kierin dropped to her knees beside him. Her eyes felt raw with held-back tears. "My husband—did you see him, Private?"

Cuddy blinked, trying to refocus on her.

"Clay Holt," she insisted. "He rode out to meet you."

"Yeah," Cuddy told her, letting his eyes slide shut

247

with exhaustion. "He tried to talk sense to the lieutenant . . . didn't help." He was slipping into unconsciousness.

Desperate, Kierin shook the man. "Private! What happened to him? You have to tell me!"

Muddled by the pain, Cuddy shook his head. "Didn't see him after the fightin' started. But all of 'em wuz dead . . . ever' one . . . but . . . me."

The army surgeon arrived and knelt down beside Private Cuddy, nudging Kierin aside. She staggered to her feet. Shock settled like a heavy snow on her limbs, making her movements dull and spasmodic. *Clay dead? It's not possible. It can't be.* She shouldered past the crowd near Cuddy and took two faltering steps toward the gate. *I'll go find him myself,* she thought in a daze. *He's not dead. He's out there somewhere . . .*

But the night seemed to close in on her. Past the crowds, a spot of blackness grew in an ever-widening circle, engulfing first the gates, then the people, and finally, Kierin herself. As the ground tilted up crazily to meet her, she gave herself over to the tumbling black void of oblivion and forgetfulness.

Chapter Seventeen

"I'm coming with you," Kierin said unequivocally, matching Jacob's angry stride, step for step.

Jacob shook his head, his ample lips compressed in a stubborn line. "No you ain't." He didn't even look at her when he said it. Just kept walking. Dawn had cut a swath of pink across the dark morning sky, lighting their way.

"You can't make me stay behind," she called after him. "I'll take a horse. I'll follow you."

Jacob stopped in his tracks and grabbed her by the shoulders. "I think that faintin' spell addled your brains, woman! You gots any idea what be out there? You ever see'd what an Indian do to a white man after he kills him?"

She faltered back a step, but he kept talking.

"You ever smell a body ripenin' in the sun, or see the buzzard's helpin' themselves to a man's eyes? Is that what you wants to see? *Death?* 'Cause that's what's out there."

"No," she answered in a small voice. "I . . . just want to find Clay."

"And what if he's out there wid the others? Dat how you wants to remember him?" Jacob's eyes softened after he'd said it and he bowed his head. "Stay here, Kierin. If Clay's out there alive, I'll be findin' him. I promise you that." Jacob turned on his heel and strode off to meet the others.

Tears of frustration leaked from the corners of her eyes, but she capitulated. Watching Jacob ride off with the others, Kierin felt a helplessness well deep inside her. And even though he was going to search for Clay, she knew Jacob felt it, too. She looked on until the patrol of men became specks on the horizon. When she turned, she found Dove, with little Ben, standing silently at her shoulder.

"Oh, Dove . . ." Kierin dropped her forehead to the other woman's shoulder.

"Hatáka mitáwa," she whispered, wrapping her free arm around her, "my sister, it is in the hands of the All-Father. We know only this."

Kierin glanced over her shoulder at the disappearing men, remembering only that she had once entrusted her brother to the same merciful God.

A hot, dry wind blew across the flat sweep of prairie, sucking the moisture from everything in its path. A small cloud of dust, drawing steadily nearer to the fort, announced the return of the burial detail which had left hours earlier.

Kierin waited, hugging her arms across her chest, cold in spite of the fierce heat. The five soldiers, Jacob, and Jim Kelly had been gone since dawn, and now the sun hung overhead like a fiery ball.

All morning, the fear had festered and grown inside her. What if they found him dead? — the litany repeated itself in her head — his body riddled with arrows like the soldier who'd returned last night. And if, by some miracle, he was alive, why hadn't he returned? Even more agonizing was the thought that he could be lying wounded somewhere, dying by inches, without her beside him.

Dry-eyed, her mouth set in a determined line, Kierin

250

took a deep breath of the parched, sage-scented air, shaking loose such thoughts. There would be time enough to grieve if they found him dead. *But they wouldn't,* she told herself over and over. She couldn't allow herself to believe it was so.

The distant wagon rattled over the rutted ground as the detail approached. Shimmering waves of heat played tricks on her eyes, making it harder to see them clearly. She shaded her eyes with her hand, straining to focus. There were two on the benched seat driving the team. Five, no, six others rode alongside. Another riderless horse appeared to be tethered behind. Eight men altogether.

Eight! Her heart leapt into her throat. Not seven. She started to run, leaving the towering log gates of the adobe fort behind her. *Oh, God, please, let it be him.* Ahead, a rider spurred his horse forward, putting distance between himself and the wagon. Kierin let out a cry as she recognized his silhouette. There was no mistaking the fluid grace of the man in the saddle.

Clay was off his horse before it completely stopped, and scooping her into his outstretched arms, he twirled her around and around. Kierin released all the tears she'd been holding back in a torrent of happiness.

"Clay! Oh, Clay!"

Still suspending her in the cradle of his embrace, he covered her mouth with a kiss as fraught with relief as her own. His arms cinched around her, pulling her closer, ever closer. She felt his fingers in her hair, stroking and rediscovering it at once. When the kiss ended, his breathing was as ragged as her own.

"God, it feel's good to hold you again," he whispered.

She pulled away slightly so she could see his face. A day's growth of beard shadowed his jaw and fatigue lined his eyes. "They s-said you were k-killed."

He pressed a kiss in her palm before he replied, "You shouldn't believe everything you hear."

She caught sight of the bloodstained rag tied around

251

his arm. "Clay — you're hurt!"

"It's nothing," he said, pulling her into his arms again. "Just a graze, that's all. I'm all right."

Kierin bowed her head against his chest. "I wanted to believe you were, but that soldier came in last night and said —"

"Jacob told me." Tracing a thumb across her cheek, he wiped at her tears. "I managed to make it to a trader's cabin when the killing started. I was lucky. I had a horse." He closed his eyes at the memory. "Christ. It was awful. The men were all on foot. A soldier grabbed onto Taeva and I yanked him up. But he'd already taken two arrows and was bleeding badly. We made it back to Bordeau's, a trader who lives near the encampment, but the Sioux were threatening to burn his cabin down all night."

He shook his head. "Bordeau felt it would be best if the soldier parted company with his cabin as soon as humanly possible."

Clay motioned his head back to the approaching wagon. "He's still alive, but thank God I ran into the patrol with the wagon on the way back to the fort. I don't think he could have made it much farther on horseback."

Clay stooped and picked up his forgotten hat from the ground where it had fallen. Together, they walked to retrieve Taeva, who stood cropping at the brownish grass nearby.

Jim Kelly and Jacob rode up beside them. Jacob's relieved expression was tempered by what he'd been through himself that morning. "I tol' you I'd find him."

Kierin touched his hand. "Thank you, Jacob."

Flanked by the two, she and Clay walked back. Inside the gates, several men were helping the wounded man from the wagon. Lieutenant Fleming looked at the body beneath the canvas tarp. Fleming's face turned a sickly white and he rocked back a step.

"A-are you sure this is Grattan?" he asked one of the soldiers as he dropped the tarp. "How . . . how can you tell?"

"Yes, sir. It's Grattan, all right," the soldier answered with downcast eyes. "We, ah, identified him by the pocket watch he was wearing. It was — inscribed."

Fleming cleared his throat. "Very good, Corporal. See that he gets a proper box. We'll, ah . . . be sending his body back to Fort Leavenworth."

As the detail pulled the body from the wagon, Fleming turned to Clay. "I'd like a word with you, Mr. Holt."

Clay turned a disparaging look on the sandy-haired lieutenant. "Later." He took Kierin's arm and started to go.

"Holt—"

Clay turned sharply on the lieutenant. "I *said* later. Right now, I'm gonna clean up, talk to my wife." He glanced at Kierin, who was watching him with a proud smile, then at the blazing sun overhead. "I'll be back in two hours. That soon enough?"

Fleming, aware that he was drawing an audience, pursed his lips and nodded curtly. Then, he turned on his polished boot heel and strode away.

The sergeant Kierin had met in the records office yesterday approached them. "Mr., ah, Holt?"

Clay glanced inquiringly at him.

"Sergeant Damon," the man said, extending his hand. "I wanted to thank you for what you tried to do out there." Emotion cracked his voice. "Most of those men were friends of mine."

Clay's weary glance followed the soldiers carrying Grattan's shrouded body away. "I'm sorry I wasn't able to do more."

"Yes, sir." Damon pushed his spectacles back into place with his finger. "I just thought . . . well, with the Sioux still a threat, you might like to use my quarters to clean up instead of going back to the wagons. I'm on duty this afternoon." He sensed Clay's hesitation. "It's not much, but it's private."

Clay looked at Kierin and her smile convinced him.

"Thank you, Sergeant. I think we'll take you up on that."

Damon instructed a private to see to Clay's horse, then walked them over to the two-story, wood-framed "Old Bedlam." Green shutters at the windows and bi-level verandas gave the building a strangely homey appeal in contrast to its desolate surroundings.

The sound of their heels on the wooden floor echoed down the cool, vacant hallways. The heat of the day hadn't yet penetrated the first floor of the building.

Damon's room was small, Kierin noted, but as clean and orderly as his office had been. A small bed occupied one corner and a washstand and chair backed up against the far wall. A worn pair of regulation-issue trousers hung neatly from a peg on the wall near the door.

Damon turned to Kierin before leaving. "My condolences again about your family, ma'am." He glanced at Clay. "I'm glad it turned out better for you this time."

Kierin gulped back the tears that gathered at the back of her throat. Avoiding Clay's questioning stare, she gave the other man a wan smile. "Thank you, Sergeant."

When he had left and they'd closed the door behind them, Clay took her by the shoulders. "What was that all about?"

Haltingly, she told him what she'd learned about her brother and father — about another massacre, another time. "I still can't believe it's true," she said, shaking her head. "I'm not sure I ever will."

Clay held her tightly, allowing her anguished tears to dampen his shirt. "I'm so sorry, love."

"All I want to think about right now is having you back in my arms," she replied. "I was so afraid they'd killed you."

"I'm right here," he soothed, stroking her hair and pressing a kiss against her forehead.

She leaned into his comforting touch, glad for its solid strength. She couldn't think about her brother now. She had Clay, alive, in her arms. Her moments with him were too precious to waste on tears.

Tilting her head up, she reached for him on tiptoe until their mouths met in a fire storm of passion. His body fused with hers like heated metal, throbbing with need and wanting. Clay's hands massaged her back in long sensuous strokes, sending currents of desire through her. Then, he cupped her buttocks in his hands and dipped his knees, so his hips fit tightly against hers. She felt him there against her, pressing his swollen need into her abdomen. She wanted him inside her. She longed to be a part of him, in body as well as spirit.

Their clothes quickly became an obstacle to the burning need to touch each other, skin to skin. Wordlessly, they stripped off the hindering articles until they stood naked before one another. Clay's gaze roamed over the ivory perfection of her body, stunned, as always, by the power she had over him. He scooped her into his arms, savoring the soft silk of her skin against his.

The bed springs sang out as he dropped a knee to the mattress and gently lowered her down. When he'd covered her with his body, his mouth rained moist kisses across her face.

"Ah, Kierin," he whispered, "all I could think of when the shooting started was that I might never see you again." His lips brushed against hers as he spoke. "This face . . ." He trailed small kisses across her cheek. "These eyes . . ." Her lids fluttered closed as he kissed them, one at a time. "I couldn't bear the thought of that."

"Don't ever leave me again, Clay," she begged, combing her fingers through the dark curls at the back of his head. "Promise me . . ."

His soul-reaching kiss answered her, and her questions fell away into the abyss of his lovemaking. His lips burned a path down the hollow of her throat and onto the curve of her breasts. She shivered as he teased her sensitive, swollen nipple with his tongue, first caressing it, then taking it fully into his mouth. She arched up to meet him and let out a soft moan of pleasure.

Her hands moved up and down the sleek warmth of

his back, feeling the ripple of his muscles as he consumed her. He was her fire, her life, her reason for being. Her fingers traced a path down his ribs, feeling him quiver in response, until her hand met the fierce warmth of his swollen manhood and she closed her fingers around it. She felt his body jump as if from an electric shock and he buried his face in the valley between her breasts with a groan.

Stroking, gently stroking, she felt the fire build within him. His hand dipped to the small triangle of down at the juncture of her legs. Kierin was wet and ready for him, yet he stoked her desire with a practiced hand until she was nearly out of her mind with wanting.

"Now . . . please, Clay . . . I . . . want you . . . inside me," she begged.

He poised himself above her and entered her in one swift stroke, making her gasp with pleasure. Pushed beyond the brink of control, his body moved with hers in a rhythm old as time. The world fell away as they clung to each other. Heartbeat to heartbeat, silk against steel, they drowned in the waves of passion that flooded over them like a violent, sprawling tide. It drew them in and spiraled them up as one toward the crest of rapture. At last, exploding together, his groan of release mingled in the still, dry air with her strangled cry. It was a fulfillment so fierce, it left them both gasping for breath.

He slumped heavily against her, and she felt his heartbeat gradually slow from a furious pounding to a steady thud.

"Is it like this for everyone?" she wondered. Only after she heard his husky chuckle did she realize she'd spoken the question out loud.

"No, Princess. Not by a long shot." Clay wasn't a man to make comparisons. He rarely did it, and for good reason. But he did know he'd never felt so utterly complete, so balanced, as he did when he was with her. He was experienced enough to know that what they shared was rare and precious. It was a gift he vowed never to take lightly.

His body was damp with a sheen of perspiration, and reluctantly, he peeled his weight off her. She tightened her arms around him, afraid he would leave her.

"I'm not going anywhere, love," he soothed with a chuckle. "You've left me too weak to walk."

"Good," she said, laughing. "Perhaps I should keep you this way. Then you can't get into trouble."

His flattened palm teased her nipple again. "If that's what it takes, madam, I'm at your service."

She let out a throaty chuckle and reached down for his fingers, bringing them up to her lips. "Shall we test out my theory now?"

Clay sighed. "Woman, you may not know this but a man has his limits. It's . . . too soon."

Kierin's fingers inched down his chest, then to his stomach, sending exquisite ripples of pleasure to the taut pectorals of his abdomen.

"You're sure?" she queried with feigned innocence, her hand traveling lower. Her touch had an expanding effect on him and he let out a low growl.

"But you must be too tired," she teased.

"Mm-mm, exhausted."

"Mm-mm . . ." she agreed, stroking him slowly, maddeningly. "I should probably . . . let you . . . get some sleep."

His hand closed around her wrist, holding it in place. "Don't you dare," he warned, teasing one dusky peak with the tip of his tongue. He glanced up at her through a fringe of dark lashes, heavy lidded and languid with the pleasure of her touch. "As you can see, I'm not nearly as tired as I thought."

The next hour or so was spent in feverish verification of that fact, and when at last replete, they collapsed upon each other and slept.

A persistent knock on the door woke them. Clay sat up, startled and disoriented. "Who is it?"

"It's Sergeant Damon, Mr. Holt. Lieutenant Fleming

sent me over to get you, sir. It's past three."

Clay ran a hand through his wild hair and cleared his throat. "Tell Fleming I'll be there directly, Sergeant."

"Yes, sir." They heard his footsteps disappearing down the hallway.

"Do you have to go?" Kierin asked.

"I told him I would." Clay threw his legs over the side of the bed and pulled on his pants. "I won't be long." He poured some water from the pitcher into the bowl on the washstand, splashed it over his tired eyes, and ran his wet hands through his hair.

She reached for her discarded clothes. "Let me come with you."

"It's not something I want you to hear, Kierin," he said, drying his face on a thin linen towel.

"It can't be worse than what my imagination conjured up last night," she protested.

Clay sent her a look as he shrugged on his deerskin shirt and belted it with his holster. "Yes, it can. This is business. It's better if you stay here."

She frowned at him as she slipped her camisole over her head. "That business almost got you killed." She looked at him stubbornly. "I'm not letting you out of my sight again, Mr. Holt."

He understood her need to be with him. He felt it, too. But he wanted to protect her from the ugliness of what had happened, and was determined to do it.

He bent down and kissed the top of her head. "I promise not to go anywhere this time. I'll leave you with Jacob and Dove if you don't want to stay here. Believe me, it's better this way. Fleming won't let you in on this anyway."

Kierin regarded him for a long moment before reaching up to pull his head down to hers and kissing him soundly so he wouldn't forget the promise he'd just made. "All right," she said resignedly. "But hurry. The sooner we're out of here, the better I'll feel."

Clay slipped his knife into its sheath, thinking he couldn't agree more.

Fleming had a double shot of whiskey in his hand as Clay entered his office. He tipped the glass toward Clay. "Like one?"

"No. I didn't come here to drink with you. What's on your mind?"

Fleming shrugged. "You don't mind if I do?" Without waiting for an answer, he tipped his head back and downed the drink. "I'm glad to see you made it back in one piece, Mr. Holt."

"I'm sorry the rest of your men didn't," Clay answered, glaring at him.

Fleming stared into his empty glass. "So am I. I'd like to know what the hell happened out there."

"Exactly what I told you would happen, Fleming. Your West Point lieutenant had about as much savvy about the Sioux as a tree stump has of the axe that's about to cut it down. He wouldn't listen to reason. Just kept pressing them. The Brule chief, Bear, parlayed with him — even offered to pay for the damn cow with two horses — but Grattan refused it. He insisted on taking High Forehead prisoner.

"From the start, your interpreter, Lucien Auguste, was drunk as a coot, flinging insults at the Sioux. The trader, Bordeau, and I tried to smooth their ruffled feathers, but Grattan kept at 'em, making it worse.

"Finally, one of his men jumped the gun and killed one of the braves." Clay shook his head with disgust. "At that point, nothing in hell would have stopped what was coming. When it broke loose, Bordeau and I managed to get out with our lives. Damn few others did."

Fleming sat down heavily in his chair, eyeing Clay warily. "Where are the Sioux now?"

"Gone. Packed up in the night. Lock, stock, and te-pee."

"Do you know where they went?"

Clay's expression hardened. "I wouldn't tell you if I

259

knew, you bastard."

"No, I don't suppose you would," Fleming allowed. "Just what do you intend to do now?"

"I think you probably have a good idea."

"If you're considering implicating me in this, Mr. Holt, think again."

"And just how are you going to stop me?"

Fleming opened his desk drawer, pulled out a sheet of paper, and handed it to Clay. "With this."

Clay looked down at the paper and felt the color drain from his face. It was a Wanted poster. His name was emblazoned across the top and it bore a crude likeness of him. There was a two-thousand-dollar reward on his head.

Chapter Eighteen

"Where did you get this?" Clay demanded.

Fleming's mouth took on an unpleasant twist. "I received it in a supply shipment from Leavenworth a few days before you arrived," Fleming answered. "After you left yesterday, I remembered it. It says you killed a man in Independence."

With a sinking feeling, Clay realized the poster mentioned only one man, Kyle Jessup. Not John Talbot. *I should have known.* "It was self-defense," he replied flatly.

Fleming tipped his head, allowing for that possibility. "Nonetheless, you're a marked man, Mr. Holt, with quite a reward on your head. I could have you arrested right now if it suited me." He paused. "But as it happens, I have something else in mind."

Clay regarded the man as one would a coiled snake, while his mind raced with alternatives. "What do you want, Fleming?"

"First, your silence about what happened."

Clay's bark of laughter was humorless. "You actually believe you can keep this thing quiet? You're more of a fool than I thought. There are twenty-nine men out there whose families are going to ask questions."

A muscle tightened in Fleming's clean-shaven jaw. "Those men will be remembered as heroes, Mr. Holt. Your side of the story can only muddle things."

"The truth, you mean?"

Fleming gave Clay a warning look. "Do I have your word?"

Clay's expression was dangerously clouded. "What else?"

"I've heard you're friendly with the Dull Knife's band who summer up near the Wind River. I want you to go and have a parley with them. No doubt they'll have heard of this by the time you reach them. I want you to send my reassurances that this was an isolated incident—that the army has no intentions of warring against them."

"You want me to lie to them," came Clay's bitter retort.

"No. Granted, the army won't take what's happened lying down, you can be sure of that. The Sioux will pay for the lives they've taken here," Fleming answered. He braced his flattened palms on the top of his desk. "But we have no argument with the Cheyenne. If they should join forces against us with the Sioux, there will be considerable bloodshed. Avoidable bloodshed. Wouldn't you agree?"

Bloodshed wouldn't begin to cover what Clay was sure would follow this little transgression. "Avoidable? You really don't get it, do you?" He leaned across the desk angrily. "Lieutenant, this incident has started something you won't be able to stop. Do you think it will end there? They kill a few of us . . . we kill a few of them? You broke the treaty with Grattan's little stunt. Not to mention gunning down the Brule's chief. This won't just affect the Sioux. It will mean blood spilled for every man with red skin, because that's all people like you see when you're staring down your sights."

Fleming slammed his hand down on the desk. "What's done is done. If it's a war they want, then they'll have it. Now, do you agree to my terms or not?"

Clay swung around and stalked to the window. For a long moment he was silent, considering how he could fight the murder charges from the cell of Fleming's stockade. "Yes, dammit, I'll talk to them," Clay answered at last, snatching his hat from the desk. "But not for your sake. For theirs. And for the rest of the unsuspecting settlers who believe men like you are protecting them."

Fleming's face reddened.

"And you can keep your damn poster. There are probably a hundred more just like it floating around. Yours won't make one bit of difference to my neck after I leave here."

"Make it soon," Fleming snarled, slamming the desk drawer shut.

"It'll be my pleasure, Lieutenant." Clay opened the door, but turned after fitting his hat on his head. A hard-bitten smile played across his mouth. "Oh, and better protect that pretty hair of yours, Fleming. I'd be willing to wager any Sioux warrior worth his salt would go to great lengths to hang it from the end of his lance." He stalked out of the office and left the door rattling in its frame.

His angry strides drove him past Kierin, who was waiting for him outside the office.

"Clay . . ." she called. "What's wrong? I heard shouting."

Clay's mood was black as pitch and he stalked past her.

"Clay. Stop—talk to me."

He spun around and took her by the shoulders. The look in his eyes was bleak and desperate. "Talbot's alive."

"Wh—?" Kierin's body stiffened in shock.

"He's got a two-thousand-dollar bounty out on my head."

"My God—"

"Do you understand what this means?"

Numb with fear, she could only stare at him.

"It means I'll never be safe," he told her, shaking her by the shoulders. "*We'll* never be safe until I clear my name. If I don't get my head blown off by some bounty-hunting scavenger, the law will find me sooner or later. Or men like Fleming will blackmail me with what they know."

"F-Fleming blackmailed you?"

"He threatened to put me away where I couldn't do him any damage." Clay raked both hands through his hair and told her the rest of it.

When he'd finished, Kierin pressed her fingertips to her throbbing temples. *Would this nightmare never end?* She turned bleak eyes once more on Clay. "And after you talk with the Cheyenne? What then?"

Clay let out a long breath and bent his head. "I don't know. I . . . need some time to think."

A sudden choking fear curled around her throat. She knew what he was considering. "Clay — you're not thinking of going back to Independence, are you?"

Clay's mouth was set in a grim line and he refused to meet her eyes.

"Talbot will kill you," she said in a voice flattened with fear. "I know him. He owns half the town and certainly the sheriff. It won't do you any good —"

"Scudder Brown was a witness," he argued. "Maybe I can convince him to testify."

"He's got a family, Clay. And what if he's left Independence already? Please, think about this," she pleaded. "We can wait until we get out to Oregon. Write letters. They can't hang a man for defending himself. And *I'm* a witness. I'll swear to it."

"You think a bounty hunter will stop to ask for character references?" His huff laughter was harsh and unforgiving. "For that kind of money they'd as soon bring me in over the back of a saddle as alive."

His stricken eyes burned into hers. "You won't be safe with me either. What kind of a husband can I be to you? What kind of security can I give you?" He saw his plans for the future crumbling before his eyes and he was helpless to stop it.

"I don't care about that. Clay, you wouldn't get within

ten miles of Independence without someone recognizing you from that poster," she said. "Is that what you want?"

In frustration, he turned on her. "I didn't *want* any of this, but I've damn well got it, haven't I?" He started to walk away but she caught him by the sleeve.

"And you're all alone in this I suppose?" she accused, making him stop short. "What about me? What about us? I . . . I love you, Clay. Doesn't that mean anything to you?"

Clay stopped and bent his head. "Yeah," he answered slowly. "That's what makes this whole situation so damned impossible."

She shook her head at his logic. "Impossible? Don't you see that's the only thing that makes it bearable?"

His look to her was fierce and foreboding. "But it doesn't change the facts, does it?"

"If you're determined to go, I'm coming too."

"No! If I do this, I do it alone. I'm not going to get you any more involved than you already are."

She stamped her foot, sending up a cloud of reddish dust into the stifling air. "Involved? Ooh-h, you're a stubborn, bull-headed mule, Clay Holt, and you can't see the desert for the *sand*. I'm already involved up to my eardrums, in case you hadn't noticed!"

Clay glanced at the people hovering nearby and pulled Kierin off beside the front gates of the fort where they could have more privacy. "You're not coming. You'll stay with Jacob and Dove until I get back."

His commanding attitude irked her and she raised her chin defiantly. "*If* you get back. And what shall I do while you're gone?" she argued, fighting the tears of frustration that burned behind her eyes, "Spend the next year worrying that Talbot has had you killed? Didn't he come close enough the first time?"

He took her shoulders in his hands. "Don't you see I'm doing this for you? For us?"

"No," she replied, with a despairing shake of her head.

"I don't. And I think . . . you're wrong."

He dropped his hands — resigned, but determined. "Maybe I am. I don't know. I guess I won't until I get there. I just know I can't live my life this way, dodging the law and always looking over my shoulder. For the past year or so, I've had two hired guns after me, because I was getting too close to the man they worked for — the bastard who killed my wife. Obviously," he sighed, "never close enough.

"They even tried to bushwack me in St. Louis, just before I came to Independence, but I managed to get away. I'm tired of living this way, Kierin. I won't ask you to do it either."

Kierin frowned as the realization dawned on her. She looked up at him. "Did you say . . . two men?"

Clay nodded silently.

"Was one tall, prematurely gray and the other short and paunchy?"

Clay stared at her. "How did you know that?"

She shook her head. "It's probably nothing."

"What?"

Visibly shaken, she went on. "The same day you won me in that game, I accidentally overheard a conversation going on in Talbot's office between him and two men he'd hired to . . . kill someone. They'd botched the job in St. Louis for him and he was furious. He fired them on the spot and told them . . . well," she amended, "I won't repeat what he said.

"He was very angry with me when he realized I'd overheard it. He . . . he hit me." She focused on a button in the middle of his shirt. "It wasn't the first time, but he scared me. I guess I'd tried to put it out of my mind, but . . . is it possible they're the same men who were after you?"

"It's more than possible." Clay turned away, absorbing the implications. He plunged his fingers through his long hair. "He recognized my name. I remember now . . . his reaction at the table when I said it. He practically choked on his cigar. Damn! How could I have missed it? It was Talbot all the time. He was trying to kill *me* . . . he wasn't after you at all . . ."

"You said your wife was killed three years ago. Talbot only settled in Independence a little over two years ago."

"It all makes sense now. It *had* to be him. Damn it! If I'd only known . . ."

"You'd have done what?" Kierin asked. "Killed him? Is that what you planned to do?"

With his back still to her he answered, "Yes."

"How does that make you any different from him?" she asked.

Clay whirled on her. "I didn't burn his goddamned house down around his wife, did I?"

Kierin took a steadying breath. "No. And that's my point. You're not a murderer. I know this thing has eaten you up for three years, but vengeance won't take it away. It won't bring back your wife."

Pain flitted across his expression. "I know that. But I can't risk losing you the way I did Amanda. I want us to be free to live the way we want. Without fear. Now that I know he's still alive, I have no choice but to finish it with him."

Kierin turned away and looked out on the flat sweep of prairie outside the fort's gates. "And if he kills you?"

He hesitated for a long moment. "Then . . . you'll be taken care of. I'll make sure of that." He swallowed and looked away. "At least . . . I won't leave you a widow."

She shook her head in disbelief. "Is that supposed to make me feel better about all of this? Do you think I'll grieve any less without that certificate in my hand?"

His pain-filled eyes rose to meet hers, but he couldn't answer her.

She glared at him, knowing that to fight him was to do battle with a wall of granite. Yet, with her last available weapon, she had to try.

"Perhaps, if I'm lucky," she said, pressing a hand to her woman's womb, "you will leave me with something more

267

than a piece of paper to remember you by."

Clay didn't miss her meaning and she left him staring after her as she stalked out the fort gates toward the wagons.

It was decided that Clay would stay with the wagons until they neared the South Pass, for between there and Laramie was a difficult stretch of land that rose steadily upward toward the craggy peaks of the Great Divide. It took nearly three weeks of grueling travel to get there—past the Black Hills, whose starkly silhouetted buttes were often lined with Sioux keeping a keen eye on the wagoners' progress; past Poison Springs and a vast alkali flat which, despite their best efforts, claimed several head of cattle from the train. They stopped at Independence Rock, or as some called it, "The Great Register of the Desert," where they added their names to the thousands already inscribed on the great sandstone monolith.

Farther on came Devil's Gate, a nearly perpendicular gash in a towering rock which marked the headwaters of the Sweetwater River. A few of the emigrants fell sick with mountain fever, but remarkably, they dug no new graves on its account.

The days spun by, and she and Clay continued to share a bed, but they'd not made love since that last day at the Fort. He'd watched her carefully for signs that she was with child. Her hopes soared as first one week passed then two, with no sign of her monthly flow. Dove had counseled her about the signs of pregnancy. She waited anxiously to feel the first signs of morning sickness or dizziness that were wont to accompany it. The thought that she might bear Clay's child even took some of the sting out of Matthew's death.

During the third week, without warning, her flow began and she knew she'd lost him. Clay's obvious relief at seeing the flutter of white rags drying in the wagon only served to darken her mood. She watched the bond of love between Dove and Jacob grow stronger with each passing day, while she and Clay grew more distant.

Bit by bit, she'd watched him withdraw emotionally from her. And while she yearned for the closeness they'd shared in those first days together, she understood his wisdom in doing it. Leaving would be a hard thing. Letting him go, she knew, would be nearly impossible.

Soon, the rugged terrain funneled the wagons into the welcoming valley of the Sweetwater River, making traveling considerably easier. Kierin's heart grew heavier with each passing day because Clay's certain departure loomed ever closer.

Ringing the sheltered headwaters of the Sweetwater were the towering jagged peaks of cold, blue-gray granite that reached toward the sky like ancient claws. The wagons had made camp here, among the sliver-leafed Aspen and squat stands of hearty pine. Water and grass were bountiful and the animals and the travelers took a much needed break from the grueling climb.

On the morning Clay was to leave, dawn stole over the camp like a thief. The pink-tinged light filtered into the wagon, urging Kierin from a fitful sleep. One glance told her Clay was already up. Despair weighted her movements as she dragged herself from the comforting warmth of the blankets.

It was cold. So cold, she guessed there would be ice on the top of the water bucket again today. The air was pungently scented with pine and she could hear the rushing sound of the Sweetwater nearby as it tripped along its banks. Outside, she found Clay, tying his saddlebags to the cantle of Taeva's saddle. A mule Dove had given him stood alongside, packed for the trip. The stallion blew out a clouded breath, announcing her, and she pulled Clay's oversized wool coat tightly around her.

"Were you going to leave without saying good-bye?"

Clay turned at the sound of her voice. "You know I wouldn't."

"Maybe it would have been easier," she allowed, staring at the frost-tipped grass at her feet.

Clay drew her against him. "There's nothing easy about this."

She wrapped her arms around him tightly. "Is there nothing I can say to change your mind?"

Clay shook his head slowly. "I've looked at it from all the angles and it always comes out the same. I have no choice. I have to go."

"I wish . . ."

Clay dropped a kiss on the top of her head. "So do I, Princess, so do I." His chest tightened with regret.

Jacob ducked out of the tent he now shared with Dove and rubbed his hands in the morning chill. He stopped mid-yawn when he saw Clay already packed and ready to go and he crunched across the frosty grass to meet them.

"You fixin' to light out now?" he asked, reaching his hand out to Clay.

Clay nodded grimly. "I guess I am." He clasped Jacob's forearm in a two-handed gesture that bespoke the powerful emotion behind it.

"You thinkin' to make the Wind River by nightfall?" Jacob asked.

Clay looked at the jagged walls of stone behind him. Just beyond them lay the snow-capped peaks of the Wind River range. "I'm hoping to."

The darker man nodded, scuffing the toe of his boot into the nearly frozen ground. "Good luck, then. Watch your backside, you hear?"

"I will. Tell Dove good-bye for me and thanks for the mule. Tell her I'll be paying her back next spring."

"I'll do that."

Clay gave Kierin's shoulders a squeeze, and a tacit look of understanding passed between the two men. Clay was counting on his friend to make sure no harm came to her until he could clear up this mess back East.

"Well," Jacob drawled awkwardly, wiping at his nose,

270

"I'll be lettin' you two get your good-byes said. Take care, Clay-boy."

"You too," he said, lifting his chin in a final salute. He didn't want to say the words that made the parting seem so final. *Why did it have to be so damned hard?*

When Jacob had left them to tend to the stock, Clay looked down at Kierin again. Her nose and cheeks were rosy with cold, but her expression was grim. "I left Jacob with enough money to see you through the year."

She pulled away, not wanting to hear the way he'd so carefully arranged her life.

"We need to talk about this," he insisted, forcing her to look at him. "If you decide you don't want to live with Jacob and Dove, there should be enough for you to rent a little house in town until I get back. If anything should happen to me, the ranch will be in your name. Jacob has the papers on it."

Kierin pressed her head against his chest miserably and tears wet her cheeks. "I don't want your money, or your ranch." *All I want is you,* she thought, but her pride kept her from saying it.

Clay swallowed the lump at the back of his throat. "It's your security. I have to know you'll be all right, whatever happens to me. Promise me you'll do as I ask."

Her jade eyes glittered with sudden anger. "Will you promise to come back to me?" she asked.

He stared at her, hemmed in by his impotence. "I promise to do my damnedest," he said finally.

Her head snapped down. "Then, so do I."

He lifted her chin with a forefinger, tears burning at the back of his eyes. "I know what this is doing to you because, God knows, it's doing the same thing to me. Don't leave it this way. Kiss me. Just once before I go."

His mouth hovered inches away from hers, waiting for acquiescence. It came when her tortured eyes met his in the cloud of mingled breaths that stirred the air between them. She reached up to meet his waiting lips and he pulled her into a tight embrace. His kiss, like hers,

271

was urgent and hungry, not gentle at all. It symbolized everything they'd left unsaid over the past weeks and all the things they would never say.

He wrenched his mouth suddenly from hers and he searched her eyes for a long, painful moment. Their breaths came in short ragged puffs and hung in the air between them like the misery they felt. "I love you, Kierin, and I'll be back for you." With those words, he turned, gathered up the reins, and mounted Taeva.

"Clay — wait."

From her pocket, she pulled something and pressed it into his hand. It was the gold locket she'd recovered at Henri's store. He stared at it in his open palm, knowing how precious it was to her.

"For luck," she told him, with a tremulous smile.

"For luck," he repeated, closing it in his fist. He picked up the mule's lead rope, nudged Taeva forward, and disappeared into the lonely vastness of the mist-shrouded mountains.

Fort Hall lay on the arid eastern edge of Oregon Territory, where it served as a junction between the Oregon and California trails. The wagons pulled in as the sun sank behind a bank of lead-bellied cumulus clouds on the western horizon.

In the dying light, Kierin squinted at the wooden structure from her seat at the helm of Dove's mule-drawn cart. By anyone's standards, Fort Hall could barely be called an outpost of civilization. It had once been a minor trading post and, evidently, the presence of the military hadn't much improved its status. A simple rough-hewn stockade of timber surrounded the meager log buildings within the confines. Alongside the fort ran the swift-flowing Raft River and acres of sweet grassy meadows. At least, it would provide a good grassy place to rejuvenate the weary teams and take a much-needed rest for a day or so.

Behind them were two weeks of grueling travel, including the sun-parched forty-five-mile stretch of desert known as Sublette's Cutoff—a hellish pull for both livestock and people. Kierin and Jacob mourned the loss of Mose, one of their favorite oxen, whose brave heart had given out halfway across. Still, they considered themselves lucky, for others had lost considerably more stock in the beastly heat.

Past that fearsome leg of the journey were the more hospitable waters of Soda and Steamboat Springs—aptly named for the chugging sound its waters made. The respite there had been as welcome and much needed as this one.

Jim Kelly gave the signal to circle up and Kierin flicked the reins over the backs of the team, clucking to them with her tongue. Jacob had taken over the full job of driving the ox-pulled wagon she and Clay had shared, while Dove and she shared the responsibilities of the mule-drawn cart.

It had taken nearly a week to build up calluses on her palms to tolerate a full day of holding the stiff leather traces without pain. Now, as she guided the team expertly into the circle of wagons, she realized, with a certain degree of pleasure, she'd become quite adept at it.

Beside her, Dove nursed little Ben, who cooed and smiled at his mother with sparkling obsidian eyes while his chubby fist circled her copper finger. With a grunt of satisfaction, the child returned his attention to Dove's brown-tipped nipple.

"He doesn't look finished yet," Kierin observed wryly, tying off the reins on the hand brake.

Dove laughed at the boy's voraciousness. "He would suck all day if I let him." She started to disengage the child, but Kierin stopped her.

"Never mind," she told Dove. "I'll see to the team tonight. You finish up there and get the fire started for supper."

"I have dried corn soaking for *washtunkala,*" Dove replied with a mischievous waggle of her eyebrows.

Kierin's eyes lit at the prospect of the savory stew. It was an old Sioux recipe Dove had taught her to make from jerked buffalo, wild onions, dried prairie potatoes, and rehydrated corn. "I want to stop in at the post and buy a few things," she said. "I'll be back in time to help you get it ready."

After unharnessing the team, she set them loose with the other stock in the grassy pasture on the fort's west side. She watched as they dropped their shaggy heads hungrily to the rich graze, cropping at tufts of bluebunch wheatgrass with greedy tugs.

Dusk had deepened the sky a mauvish-gray, washing the rolling hills with color. A breeze stirred the tips of grass and she hugged her arms around her. This was the time of day she missed Clay most. She missed his careless hugs and the feel of his lips whispering in her hair and the way this kind of light turned his eyes violet. She missed having him beside her at the evening fire, and by her side at night in her cold bed. It had been two long weeks since she'd seen him last. Two miserable weeks.

There were so many things they'd left unsaid. She wished now she'd told him she loved him that last morning. Did he know she did? Had he known what was in her heart?

Beside her, Jacob loosed the oxen with a wave of his hat and came to stand beside her.

"I miss him, too," he said.

Kierin looked up at him. "Am I that obvious?" she asked.

Jacob laughed softly. "I reckon Clay got's that same look in his eye right now."

"I should have gone with him."

Jacob shook his head. "He be wantin' you safe, not in the line of fire. You done the right thing, lettin' him go."

"I wish I could believe that, Jacob." She patted his arm and shook off the foreboding feeling she had. "I'm going to the sutler's to buy a new needle and some sturdy

274

thread. Feel like coming?"

"Ain't no need to twist my arm. I'm outta smoke and candy, too. Dove's taken a likin' to my peppermints," he returned with a grin.

With the exception of liquor, which appeared plentifully on the shelves and on the crude bar near the front of the room, the store's supplies were low. Two gaming tables full of men were set up near the front door. One table full of scruffy-looking gamblers argued loudly about a hand of cards.

Kierin was glad Jacob had come with her and she stayed near him until they'd found what they'd come for. Jacob paid the sutler and popped a peppermint stick in his mouth while he held the door open for Kierin.

Once outside, they were stopped in their tracks by the crash of breaking glass. A man flew out the sutler's window beside them in a tumble of splintered glass and dirt.

". . . and stay out, you cheatin' bastard!" a voice shouted from inside the store.

"Damn you," came another voice, which Kierin recognized as the sutler's. "It'll take me months to get new panes for that window. Why didn't you just toss him out the door?"

The muffled reply was lost to her. The shadowed man on the ground cursed roundly and rolled to his knees with a groan, brushing the shards of glass from his faded red hair.

Jacob took her elbow, urging her away, but something about the man's voice stopped her.

"Louts . . ." he muttered, staggering to his feet "I was'na cheating!" he shouted, raising his fist to the shattered window. "Clabberheaded bast—" He blinked and did a double-take as his gaze fell upon Kierin. He staggered a step, arms swinging like clock pendulums searching for rhythm. "Well I'll be—"

Kierin's eyes widened with disbelief. "Papa?"

Chapter Nineteen

"Aye, lass, it's yer old man. Well, if this don't beat all!" Asa McKendry's ruddy face broke into a smile and he wrapped his stout arms around his daughter.

Kierin went hot, then cold, with shock. It rushed through her limbs, making her weak-kneed. *He's alive.* Tightening her arms around the man who'd abandoned her more than a year ago, she put all those thoughts aside and buried her face against his barrel chest.

"Oh, Papa . . . But how—? I thought . . . they told me—"

"Tha' I was dead?" Asa gave a scoffing laugh, and pulled her away slightly so he could see her face. "Not Asa McKendry. I've got too many fish to fry to let a few Indians be the end of me." He dabbed at the small bleeding cut on his forehead with the tip of one finger.

His Scot's brogue always became more distinct when he'd been drinking. She could smell liquor on his breath. "But . . . have you been here all along?" she asked. "Why didn't you write to tell me you were safe? I never heard from you. Not once."

He looked stricken. "You didn't get my letters?"

"No. Her eyes were stormy and doubtful "They told me at Fort Laramie that everyone on your train had been murdered." Another thought made her pull away from Asa with a quick in-drawn breath.

"Matthew!" Her gaze swept the small enclosure be-

276

hind him. "Where is he? Is he with you? What—?"

"Whoa, lass. One question at a time."

"Papa!"

Asa cleared his throat. "He's . . . fine, but he's not here."

Matthew's alive! Like a litany, the words repeated over and over in her head. "Thank God," she murmured tearfully. "But where is he?"

Her father rubbed a hand over his mouth and stubbled chin. "He's back in San Francisco with a friend, waitin' for ye."

"For me?"

"Aye. Ye see, I was comin' east to get ye, lass, like I said I would when I struck it rich."

Kierin closed her eyes and shook her head. "You were coming back without Matthew?"

Asa clapped an arm around her shoulder. "Well, it's . . . it's a long trip back, as ye well know. California is a growin' place. Full o' opportunity. And I like livin' out here. Matthew's better off stayin' put back there than traipsin' across the country again."

"Why d-didn't you just send for me?"

Asa gave her an affronted look. "What? And have ye travel without a chaperon? Unthinkable."

His sudden concern for her honor almost made her laugh out loud. "Do have any *idea* what I've had to do in the year since you left?"

Asa swallowed and color crept up past his collar. "Aw, don't be too hard on yer old man for his shortcomings, darlin'. Ye think a day's gone by I haven't regretted leavin' ye back there? It was a poor thing I did and I'm ashamed of it. I'm hoping ye can find it in yer heart to forgive me." He bowed his head. "I've missed ye, Kiery."

His plea for forgiveness caught her off guard. She was prepared for denial or, at the very least, indifference to what she'd been through. Was it possible he'd changed? Looking again at the shattered glass at his feet, she doubted it. But there was more at stake here than restoring her broken trust in him. There was her brother.

As if reading her thoughts, he said, "Matthew's missed you somethin' dreadful, too."

She knew Asa thought she could be swayed by the mention of Matthew's name. The truth was—she could. With a sigh, Kierin let the subject of forgiveness go for now and wiped at the moisture in her eyes. "Is Matthew all right? How did you manage to escape the Crow?"

A relieved smile softened the worried lines around Asa's eyes. He patted her arm. "There's time enough for that story and all the others I have to tell you. Where are ye stayin' and who's this?" he asked, gesturing at Jacob.

Jacob frowned slightly as he held out his hand to Asa. "Name's Jacob." He shook Asa's hand briefly then stuffed his hands into his back pockets. "Your daughter's been travelin' with us since Independence."

Asa blinked at the black man and then back at Kierin. "Oh?"

"It's a long story, too," Kierin interjected. "Why don't you come back to our camp. I'll clean up that cut for you and you can have some *washtunkala*."

Asa gave her a puzzled look. "Washtu-what?"

"Stew, Papa. Stew."

Dove ladled yet another serving of the savory corn stew into Asa's bowl while Jacob and Kierin exchanged looks. She wondered how long it had been since her father had had a decent meal. He never could find his way around a kitchen, she mused.

"Thank ye," Asa mumbled, digging into his third helping. The fire had died down to a mellow glow that warmed their feet and sent fragrant pitch-scented smoke spiraling into the star-studded sky. "So," he continued, looking up at Kierin, "where is this fellow, Clay Holt, now?"

She hesitated, knowing she could not tell him the truth. She'd already told him about Clay's winning her contract in a game of cards and she'd decided, in spite of Jacob's disapproving frown, to keep the whole truth about what had happened back in Independence from Asa—including her attempt to kill her former boss and Clay's being wanted for murder.

If she'd learned anything in the last year, it was to rely on her own instincts about whom she could trust. She didn't trust Asa any more now than she did a year ago—and certainly not with any knowledge that could endanger Clay's life. A two-thousand-dollar reward would be a temptation her father might not be able to resist.

Dove and Jacob watched her closely, waiting to hear her response. Jacob's expression was dark and unreadable.

Kierin smiled politely at her father. "Clay had some business to tend to with the Cheyenne. He's planning on meeting us back on the trail north of here in a few weeks," she lied.

Asa shook his head thoughtfully. "Don't seem like he should 'a left you in the middle of the wilderness to your own resources."

Kierin's chest tightened. Like an old wound torn open, resentment festered anew. "I'm hardly alone as you can see, and that's an odd statement coming from you, don't you think?"

"Aye." He nodded meekly. "You're right. I deserved that. You've every reason to hate me, Kiery. But as ridiculous as it may seem to you, I'm . . . askin' you not to. For Matthew's sake. He needs you Kiery. Needs yer firm hand. I'm afraid he's felt the lack of yer motherin'."

"He's all right isn't he? He's not sick?"

"No, nothin' like that. But he misses you. I was wrong to separate ye."

"Yes. You were." She tipped her chin up defiantly. "But it was my fault for letting you do it to me."

Surprise and relief chased the worry from his face. "You've changed, darlin'. My girl's growin' up."

"I'm not a girl anymore, Papa. I'm a woman. Don't

279

ever make the mistake of thinking you can take advantage of me again."

He stared at her thoughtfully for a long moment, as if he were about to tell her something. But he changed his mind, scuffling his heels in the dirt. If he'd wondered what she'd meant about being a woman, he didn't ask. She felt Jacob's eyes on her and decided she and her father had aired enough dirty linen for one night.

"You were going to tell me how you and Matthew got away from the Crow."

"So I was," he agreed, clearing his throat "Well it was like this. It was early in the mornin' when the bloodthirsty savages hit the train."

Kierin shot a look at Dove, who sat listening with a carefully blank expression.

"Me an' Matthew," Asa continued, "an' a Norwegian fella, named Kip Johanssen, were, by the Grace o' God, down by the river, a hundred yards or so from camp, gettin' water. All of a sudden, we heard a ruckus that curdled the blood in our veins.

"Most of them in camp were still abed when it happened," he continued. "They didn't even have time to load their guns. There were war whoops and screams . . . gunshots . . . 'twas terrible to hear.

"We were lucky enough to find cover there in the bushes," he went on, visibly shaken by the recollection. "There was nothin' we could 'a done for any of those poor souls, except die with 'em. So, we kept to ourselves until the Crow finished their nasty business and left. They burned the wagons, stole the stock and all the food and guns they could carry. They lifted the scalps of every man, woman, and child they left behind." Asa swallowed hard then, lost in the recollection of his own private version of hell.

"We laid low for a whole day, until we were sure they weren't watchin' our camp. Johanssen's partner died in the battle, but Kip managed to rescue the money they'd hidden in a strong box in the bottom of their wagon. At night, we lit out on foot for the Little Sandy, where we met up with another train headed for Fort Bridger."

Kierin put down the untouched bowl of soup she held. Her stomach was already tied in knots and her father's tale had just taken her appetite away altogether. The thought of her little brother facing such ugliness and terror broke her heart. "It's a miracle they didn't see you."

"Aye."

"You walked out on foot?" Jacob asked.

"One scrawny mule got missed somehow by the heathens," he replied. "Maybe he was too sorry-lookin' for them to take, but we caught him and took turns ridin' him down the mountain."

"You said you left Matthew in San Francisco. Is that where you went?"

"Aye. The goldfields of the mother lode were pretty near played out, so we went to the city to see what was what. I tell you, that town is growing so fast it would make your head spin. Fires burn it down every time they get the damn thing built, but they just keep rebuilding, bigger and better. Johanssen had been a sawyer in Minnesota, and with the money he had, we went into partnership in a small saw-mill operation." Asa's eyes lit up. "We made a killing in lumber, Kiery. More money than you ever saw. And when Kip decided he could spare me, I decided to come for ye." He spread his hands in a magnanimous gesture. "And here I am."

The only response was the crackling of the fire and the lowing of an oxen in the distance. He dropped his hands with a shrug and licked his dry lips. "My wagon's ready to pull out. I figure we can hook up with the folks on your train headed for California tomorrow. How long will it take you to pack, Kiery?"

His question made her feel suddenly sick. It was as if he were asking her to pack a Sunday picnic, for heaven's sake! She'd known the question was coming. She'd been preparing for it all evening. But when it came, she had no idea what to say. *Can I just leave Jacob and Dove?* she wondered. *And what about Clay? What would he do if he returned to find me gone? Would he understand my need to be with my brother? To protect him?*

How different was this from what he was doing? Riding off in search of vindication, she reasoned stubbornly. Misery struck her again at the thought of leaving without knowing what had happened to Clay. She had no choice. He must know what finding her brother meant to her. She would write to him and explain. If he still wanted her, she'd come back to him. With Matthew.

She was about to say as much, but Jacob's deep baritone voice stopped her.

"Miz Kierin, can I talks to you—alone?"

Kierin swallowed, guessing what was coming. But she owed it to him to explain. "Of course, Jacob. Excuse us, Papa, Dove."

When he'd drawn her away from the circle of light, Jacob bowed his head and sighed heavily. "It prob'ly ain't my place to be sayin' this to you, Kierin, but Clay gave me a responsibility fo' you. An I means to hold up my end of the bargain. I don't reckon Clay figured on nothin' like this comin' up . . . but I gots to say, I don't like it. I knows he's your pa, but I knows, too, what he done to you before."

"Jacob—"

He held up his large hand. "Let me say what I gots to say. I understands 'bout your brother an' all, but I don't like this. You just seen your pa throw'd out a barroom window fo' cheatin'. Don't that tell you nothin'?"

Kierin steepled her fingers against her lips. "Yes. It tells me that he hasn't changed and that's the very reason I have to go."

Jacob shook his head in confusion.

"I'm not a fool, Jacob. Not anymore. And I'm not as easily taken in as you might think. I don't know if my father's telling the truth about the saw mill or about the character of that Johanssen fellow. I hope it's the truth.

282

Nevertheless, I've made a promise to find Matthew, and now I have. My father's not fit to raise him, and right now he's all Matthew's got. My brother needs me. Don't you see?"

"So you just gonna hop in his wagon an' ride off wid him?" he asked with a helpless shake of his head. "What am I gonna tell Clay? He's gonna be madder'n a hornet."

"I'll leave a letter for him explaining everything. When he comes back"—she hesitated,—"*if* he comes back, you can give it to him."

"He's comin' back, Kierin," Jacob said with an assurance that made her wonder if he knew something she didn't. "An' when he does," he continued, "he'll be comin' after you."

Her throat constricted with tears she refused to shed. In the distance she heard the mournful yip of wolves. They mated for life, Clay had told her once. She understood it now. Mating for life. There would never be another man for her if Clay didn't come for her. Of that she was utterly certain.

Jacob's words echoed in her head. *He'll be comin' after you. God, I hope you're right, Jacob,* she thought. *I truly do.*

Clay eased Taeva and the pack mule out of the dappled shadow of a stand of aspen, into the fast-moving, frigid waters of the Greybull. The sharp scrape of hooves against the river rocks echoed off the shale wall above him like rifle shots. The shallow river mirrored the startling azure blue of the cloudless sky and the jutting snow-capped summits the Wind River Mountains above. The snow never melted completely up there, and even in August at 7,500 feet, the air still held the bite of winter. His breath formed little clouds as he blew into his hands to warm them.

There was an ethereal quiet to this place, he mused, urging the stallion onto the far bank. Something holy. Though God, per se, was a concept with which he'd lost touch long ago, it was easy to understand the Cheyennes' belief in the benevolence of the All Father when he was here amid the pristine beauty of the mountains. It went beyond human understanding, beyond mere mortal imagination. If there was a God, he thought, he was right here in this spot.

Above him, he caught the flash of white on the wingtips of a young golden eagle as it sailed on the aircurrents. It was the first game he'd seen for days and he hoped it meant he was getting closer to a decent meal. His stomach growled in response to the thought. He was headed to lower altitudes today, as soon as he found what he'd come for.

He broke the cover at the edge of the tree line and the Big Horn Basin spread out below him. A hundred shades of green shadowed the valley. White pine, aspen, and Douglas fir carpeted the floor. To the east, the Bighorn Mountains curved protectively around the valley like a cradling arm. To the north loomed the snow-capped peaks of the impressive Absarokas. Farther than these, the granite summits of the Pryors.

He pulled the brim of his hat down against the sun's glare and scanned the valley below. A smile eased the corners of his mouth when he found what he'd been seeking. Wisps of smoke curled from the cookfires of an Indian camp, not half a day's ride away. Many Horses' camp. He hoped.

Clay nudged Taeva forward, eager to make the camp by nightfall. It had been more than a week since he'd seen another human being. It had been startling to discover how much he missed human contact. He smiled again. One human, specifically.

As he eased down the mountain, Clay allowed his thoughts to drift to Kierin, as they had so many times since he'd left her behind. She'd laid claim to his heart as he thought no woman ever could again. A dull ache had settled in his chest the day he'd left and hadn't gone away since. Clay let out an audible breath, fingering the warm metal of the locket he kept fastened around his neck.

God he missed her.

Taeva and the pack mule dropped their big heads to crop at some tender cranesbill and mule's ear blossoms that dotted the slope. Clay let them have their heads for the moment, while he stared off into the distance.

For the hundredth time, he questioned whether he was doing the right thing in going back to Independence. Maybe he *was* bull-headed and stubborn as she'd said, though he preferred to call himself *practical*. He only knew that there were times when life narrowed a man's choices down to one. This was one of those times for him. He'd been running away from commitment for years — commitment to his own life, his need to be committed to someone else. That was all over now. Kierin had taken up permanent residence in his heart and he'd have her back, freely, or die trying.

By late afternoon, he crossed the first sign of unshod Indian ponies and he knew he was close. He pulled up on Taeva, laying a soothing hand on the horse's smooth black flank.

"What do you think, boy?" he asked, no longer bothered that he'd taken up talking to his horse for lack of other company. "Does this smell like home to you?"

Taeva's ears were pitched forward alertly and he stomped an anxious foot against the soft carpeting of pine needles. Clay surveyed the area carefully for signs of lookouts. Chances were, they'd already seen him coming, he thought, nudging Taeva forward. He straightened in the saddle and released the lock over his rifle scabbard. He was fairly sure this was Many Horses' camp, but better to be safe than sorry. It had been a long time since he'd shared a fire with the Cheyenne. He was *vé-ho-e* — a white man — and that fact alone could make him unwelcome these days.

Clay heard the camp before he saw it. The roar of excited voices was alarming and he wondered what the hell was going on. It didn't take him long to notice, with some relief, that the extra shadows he'd acquired since crossing the creek were lookouts posted at the outskirts of camp. If they were following him, he reasoned, nothing too serious could be happening in camp.

As he approached, he could see that the tepees were set up around a beaver-dammed stream, sheltered perfectly by the same white pine and mountain ash he'd been riding through for hours. The morningstar symbols painted on the tepees assured him that he'd found the Northern Cheyenne.

Clay spurred his horse forward and found himself joined by the two shadow-riders whom he immediately recognized as Spotted Frog and his older brother, Sees the Sky.

Spotted Frog, a tall, lanky warrior, whose youthful body already bore the scars of battle, grinned at him in silent greeting. Except for the small feathered braid alongside his face, his ebony hair flew behind him like a shiny black raven's wing.

Sees the Sky, a shorter version of his brother, raised his lance in greeting, then brought his horse to a jog beside Clay's.

Clay kept his eyes on the crowded circle of people ahead and he realized he'd ridden into the middle of a rollicking game of Buffalo Pound. Having no desire to interfere with the game, he motioned to Spotted Frog to pull up just short of the clearing, so they could watch the end of the game unobtrusively.

He'd seen it played before and could understand now why there was such a commotion. It was a game of skill, speed and wit in which the "hunters" try to corral the "buffalo" without either side making bodily contact. The goal was a three-foot gate through which the "buffalo" had to be herded.

This time, the players were young boys. They all looked to be near ten or twelve, dressed only in breechclouts and headbands, and covered head to toe with dirt.

Clay could easily see why the boy who played the buffalo had been chosen. He was fast, with a long-limbed grace that belied his obvious youth. Chasing him were six other young warriors, who, though agile, couldn't match his dexterity or speed.

The crowd cheered him as he feinted right when the others went left, rolling nearly beneath their feet to escape.

"Ee-yii!" came the boy's crow of success as he raced ahead. At the head of the circle, Clay's old friend, Many Horses, kept score, tallying the winning two points for the "buffalo" with a pair of smooth round river rocks. Each hunter, respectively, lost two of his.

A cheer went up for the boy who'd eluded his captors and won the game. The crowd closed in around him, offering their appreciation. Clay wondered if he knew the boy — if he was an older version of one of the children he'd come to know six years ago. It was hard to tell with all that dirt, he thought with a speculative grin.

Spotted Frog nudged his pony forward with a nod to Clay, and together the three rode into the clearing. Many Horses was the first to spot him riding between his two braves. One by one, heads turned in Clay's direction. Reaction, he noted, ranged from surprise to downright hostility, but all comments were silenced with a slashing gesture from Many Horses.

Clay stopped his stallion before the chief, whose solemn expression betrayed nothing of his thoughts. Many Horses was a young chief, one of several in the tribe. His strong body was that of a warrior, though in practice, he counseled his people in peace.

"Haáhe, hóovehe." Clay spoke in the other man's tongue as he dismounted. "Hello, my friend. It has been a long time since we have looked into each other's eyes."

"Yours have grown older, *vé-ho-e,*" Many Horses observed, a sad smile softening his strong features. "And wiser, I think."

Clay tipped his head in agreement. "Time changes a

287

man," he allowed.

"You are still a brother to the People, Sacred Bear Killer," Many Horses replied, using the name that had been given him years ago. "That has not changed."

"Your words honor me, Many Horses," Clay answered, relieved and grateful that he'd been welcomed. "It is good to be back among the People again. I have missed being here."

The chief motioned to Spotted Frog. "Stake his stallion beside my lodge where the grass is thick. Sacred Bear Killer will be my guest."

Spotted Frog led Clay's horse and mule away. The crowd began drifting off as it became apparent that the *vé-ho-e* posed no immediate threat, though it was obviously some were disappointed that his appearance hadn't occasioned more excitement.

Clay scanned the retreating faces. Some were familiar. Many more were not. The dirt-encrusted boys from the Buffalo Pound game watched him from a short distance away. The tall one—the "buffalo"—cast a suspicious glance at Clay through narrowed eyes. Something about the boy bothered Clay, but he couldn't put his finger on it. Clay tipped his chin up at the boy in silent acknowledgment. The boy's eyes widened, revealing, to Clay's utter surprise, eyes the color of new green shoots of grass. Clay's lips parted in astonishment and the boy turned and bolted away, disappearing into the crowd.

Clay turned to his friend, who had watched the exchange. "He's not Cheyenne?"

Many Horses shook his head. "Forgive him. He has become one of us now. He has much to prove."

Clay had known that the Cheyenne sometimes took white children captive and adopted them into the tribe. He'd simply never seen one in this camp before. "Prove? To whom?"

Many Horses started walking slowly toward his tepee. "To the others. To himself. But his heart is brave and he will make a good Cheyenne."

288

"Where did he come from?"

He gave Clay an inquiring look. "South. A hunting party found him. He was close to death. His people were killed by Crow raiders. It was many suns before he spoke of it."

The hairs on the back of Clay's neck bristled with cold suspicion. He thought again of the green eyes, so like Kierin's. *It couldn't be,* he thought, fingering the locket at his neck. *Could it?* "Did he tell you his name, Many Horses? His *vé-ho-e* name?"

Many Horses nodded. "He called himself Mat-hew."

Chapter Twenty

Clay's face went pale. "Oh, my God."

Many Horse's brows drew together in a frown. "You know this boy?"

"No . . . not personally," came Clay's slow response. "He may be the brother of my woman."

"Is this why you have come?"

Clay glanced up at his old friend. "No," he answered, but he wondered, ironically, if it was.

"Come into my lodge. We shall talk of this later."

With a nod, Clay followed Many Horses back to his tepee, still shaken by his discovery. If it *was* Matthew, it would change everything and his plans to return to Missouri were about to go all to hell.

The pair walked through the village, past the isolated camp of the *Ma-o-hóohevase*, the Red Shields — the elite warriors who lived apart from the rest of the village and lived by their own rules; past dozens more tepees, all set up so their entrances faced east, toward the dawn.

There were other societies — The Dog-men, the Bowstrings, the Wolf Warriors. All had different rules within the structure of the tribe. Like Spotted Frog and Sees the Sky, Clay remembered many of the braves he passed and they saluted to him with a nod as he walked by.

Many Horses' lodge was set up in the center of the village along with the other chiefs of the People. Stepping inside, Clay noted it was as spacious and orderly as it always had been. Sleeping robes occupied the sides of the

290

lodge. Beside these, neatly stacked, were Many Horses' weapons and medicine bundle. Corn Woman, Many Horses' only wife, was stirring something in a skin pot suspended above the slow-burning cook fire.

She was still as beautiful as Clay remembered. In spite of a thin strand of pure white that streaked her hair in front, she was younger by a few years than her husband — his guess was close to thirty. When she straightened, he saw that she was once again heavy with child. She smiled broadly when she saw Clay enter behind her husband.

"I had a dream that you would return soon, Sacred Bear Killer," she said with some satisfaction. "You are too thin."

Clay laughed softly at her bluntness. "It is good to see you, too, Corn Woman. The memory of your cooking still sweetens my dreams. Perhaps you can fatten me up while I am here."

She chuckled, pleased by his compliment. The two had shared a special bond since the time seven years ago when Clay had saved the life of her only son.

"Where is Lame Beaver?" he asked. "He must be nearly fourteen summers by now."

"He hunts with the men now," she said proudly. "He has grown handsome and strong like his father." She glanced with obvious love at her husband.

"*Saaaa!* Woman," Many Horses grumbled as he pulled his pipe from its intricately beaded sheath. "Your mouth runs like a creek in spring. Leave us now, so we might smoke in peace."

Corn Woman grinned knowingly and gave him an affectionate touch on the shoulder before waddling out the tepee flap.

"You are a lucky man, my friend," Clay told him, leaning against the willow backrest. "You must be the envy of many braves to have such a wife."

Many Horses' expression softened. "It is good to have a woman who admires you. Yours is such a woman?"

Clay pulled a packet of tobacco from within his shirt

and handed it to the other man. "Yes," he said, and his chest squeezed painfully at the thought of her. *When she's not fighting me.*

"But you are not with her, my brother. Why is this?"

"There is much to tell you. Let us smoke first."

Many Horses lit the pipe and tipped it in all four directions—north, south, west and east—before drawing the blue smoke into his lungs. He handed it to Clay, who repeated the gesture before taking his turn. Smoking the pipe was a gesture of peace and symbolized the long-standing friendship they shared.

He told Many Horses about Kierin, about their escape from Independence. And he told him about the massacre. Lieutenant Fleming had been right in thinking the Cheyenne would hear of it by the time Clay got there. Word had reached them already and anger ran rife through the hot-blooded braves who were hungry to set the Whites straight. As he had in the past, Many Horses had preached peace, but all feared the worst because of what had happened.

"Our brothers, the Sioux, will meet something very hard now," Many Horses said with a shake of his head. "But none can blame them for what they did. Conquering Bear, their chief, was killed that day. Many of his warriors are thirsty for the blood of the Yellow Legs. They say there are not many—it would not be hard to wipe them out."

"They are wrong." Clay searched Many Horses' obsidian eyes. "If the Sioux attack them, the Yellow Legs will send more. And more. They will come until they cover the prairies like blades of buffalo grass. And they will wipe out all the tribes from the Plains."

Many Horses looked at him skeptically, then drew a long pull on the pipe. "Many are hungry. Many of our people have been wiped out already by their sickness. The *vé-ho-e* in the rolling things drive the buffalo from our hunting lands or leave their flesh rotting in the sun." He shook his head sadly. "My brothers ask if we should let this thing happen."

"I cannot tell you what is right, Many Horses. I can tell you there are some honorable white men, even as there are dishonorable ones. The one who started this fight with the Sioux did not understand honor. He knew only his own hunger for power. And there are many like him.

"You must follow what your heart tells you. But if you choose to fight the Yellow Legs soldiers, I tell you this: Many Cheyenne will die."

"I will think on this," Many Horses said, putting the glowing tip of a burning twig to the bowl of his pipe. He took a long draw, filling his lungs with the fragrant smoke. He handed the pipe to Clay and leaned back against his willow backrest.

"The boy . . ." Clay asked, leaning back, too. "Whose lodge does he sleep in?"

"The lodge of my wife's sister, Buffalo Wallow Woman. It makes her heart glad to have a child in her tepee again. Her son died of the *vé-ho-e* sickness two winters ago. Little Fox brings her much happiness."

Little Fox. A name befitting a survivor like Matthew. "If he is my woman's brother, she will want him back." Clay paused. "And I will have to take him."

A frown played at the corners of the other man's mouth. "Speak with him first, before you decide. If he is the one you seek, and he wishes to go with you, there will be time to talk to Buffalo Wallow Woman."

Clay unfolded his legs and stood in the spacious tepee. "Do you know where I will find him?"

"He has been gentling a gelding pony for himself in the meadow to the north of the creek," Many Horses said. "He is a fast learner. Someday, he will be a great leader. But the lessons come hard for him."

"Life has been hard for him, I think," Clay replied. With a sigh, he lifted the flap of the tepee and headed out into the waning daylight to find him.

Dark spires of pine and Douglas fir silhouetted themselves against the vermillion evening sky as Clay left the circle of tepees behind and made his way around the edge of the dammed-up pond. The thick carpet of fragrant pine needles absorbed the sound of his footsteps. Not far from the camp, a clearing opened into a grassy meadow where Clay spotted the herd of horses grazing in the natural enclosure.

From where he stood, he could see the boy, clad now in deerskin leggings and shirt, nose to nose with a handsomely proportioned pinto gelding. The boy made soothing noises with his tongue and spoke to the horse in soft tones. Behind his back, he gripped a handful of purple clover. Smelling the sweet stuff, the pinto nudged him for it, shoving the boy backward, and again, until the boy relented with a laugh and fed it to him.

"He's a fine-looking horse, Little Fox," Clay observed, speaking in Cheyenne.

The boy jumped at the sound of Clay's voice and turned to face him, glaring at the intrusion.

"Is he yours?" Clay asked, approaching the pair. The boy had washed the grime from his face, leaving behind the fair but tanned skin of his Scottish ancestry. His dark hair was tied back from his face with a leather thong. The resemblance to Kierin, now that Clay had a good look at him, was astonishing.

The boy nodded silently and turned back to his pony, scratching it absently behind its ears. The pinto snorted a steamy breath and blinked at Clay.

"It looks like you're friends already," Clay said. *"E-pe-va?e.* That is good. Have you ridden him yet?"

The boy nodded and looked at him obliquely. "He's faster than all the others," he boasted.

The horse seemed a safe subject, Clay thought. "A man needs a fast horse."

The youth's proud green eyes darted up to Clay's blue ones. Watching. Waiting. Clay reached out and smoothed a hand over the animal's well-muscled hindquarters. The boy didn't succeed in hiding his surprise when the pony didn't skitter away, but stood enjoying

Clay's touch.

"You speak Cheyenne well for being here such a short time, Matthew." This time his words were spoken in English. Clay saw the boy's Adam's apple bob in his throat.

"H-how do you know my name?" He spoke in his native tongue now, too.

"I know a lot more about you than you think."

Matthew moved so the horse stood between them. "Who are you?"

"A friend."

"I don't know you."

"Your sister does."

Matthew's eyes flew open and a rush of memories clouded them. "M-my sister?"

Clay smiled. "She's been looking for you for a long time."

His expression sank again into mistrust. "I don't believe you. Why should I believe you? She's—"

"Kierin's told me all about you. About how you love the stars, and how you used to sit on your roof poring over astronomy charts . . ." This peaked the boy's interest. "About how she helped raise you when your mother died. And how it broke her heart when your father took you West without her . . ."

Matthew peered intently at the Pinto's soft coat, emotion riding the rims of his eyes. "She doesn't even know—"

"What happened to you? No, you're right. She doesn't. They told her you were killed in that attack in the South Pass."

Matthew's doubtful eyes met his again. "Then how did you—?"

"Blind luck," he answered. "I'm here on other business. Many Horses is an old friend of mine. So is his son, Lame Fox."

The boy hesitated. "I've heard the story of how a white man saved him from a grizzly. W-was that . . . you?"

"Knowing the Cheyenne, I'm sure the story's grown some in the telling," he answered with a soft laugh.

295

Wide-eyed, Matthew stared at him with new respect. If this was Sacred Bear Killer, perhaps he could trust him after all. Didn't his Cheyenne uncle speak of this man like a brother?

"Still have your doubts?" Clay undid the locket around his neck and handed it to the boy. "Maybe this will convince you."

Matthew's mouth dropped open. "How did you get this? M-my father sold it at—"

"Fort Kearny," Clay finished. "That's where we found it. Kierin gave it to me to carry when I left her a few days ago."

Questions spun around in Matthew's head like a whirlwind as he pried open the locket. Where was his sister now? How did this man know her? What did he want of him? He held his tongue, knowing that answers to all those things would come in time. That was what Buffalo Wallow Woman had taught him.

Beside his picture, inside the gold locket, was Kierin's. Tears burned the backs of his eyes, but he blinked them back. He'd worked too hard this year to become a man to let it all fall apart now. "If I believe you," he asked, "what then?"

"Then," Clay answered with a smile, "we need to talk."

Matthew shared the cook fire that night with Many Horses, Corn Woman, and Clay. Buffalo Wallow Woman and her husband, Gray Wolf, joined them for a feast of roast rabbit and fragrant soup. Buffalo Wallow Woman made fry bread and brought fresh, tart huckleberries for desert. It was the best food Clay had in days and he ate ravenously.

Matthew was quiet as was his adoptive mother, Buffalo Wallow. Clay had put his proposition to them both. He wanted to take Matthew back to his sister. It was to be Matthew's decision and he could see it would be a difficult one.

There was no question, by the look he saw in the boy's eyes when he spoke of Kierin, that he loved and missed her. But, he'd become attached to Buffalo Wallow and her husband, and had carved a niche for himself here among the Northern Cheyenne. It was a hard decision, and Clay said he would give him the night to think about it.

Morning mist still shrouded the camp when Clay stepped out of the warm confines of Many Horses' lodge the next morning, carrying a towel from his saddlebags and a bar of brown soap. He needed a bath after a week on the trail and preferred to do it privately.

The camp was still silent. Asleep. A few dogs stirred from their nightly repose, sniffing his heels, then wandered away, satisfied he was not a threat.

When Clay reached the pond, he stripped his clothes off and, with a quick in-drawn breath, waded into the frigid water. He ducked beneath the surface, every nerve alive as the cold water sluiced past his body. He hadn't slept much last night and his body felt the lack. Matthew's decision preyed heavily upon him. If the boy decided to return to Kierin, it meant Clay would have to give up the notion of returning to Independence for now. How ironic, that a boy could hold so much power over his life.

But did he? Clay wondered as he surfaced. Perhaps that was what Many Horses had meant last night when he'd reminded Clay that *Ma?heo?o*, the All Father, had his own plans for us while we were busy making our own. Was he talking about Fate? Clay had never been a believer in the word but he was beginning to doubt his own convictions.

What were the odds against finding Matthew here among his friends? What were the odds that Matthew had survived that attack at all? Astronomical, he supposed.

He smiled, imagining Kierin's reaction when he returned with her brother. He smiled just thinking about seeing her face again. A fresh pang of loneliness constricted his throat and he dove beneath the water again, pushing the feeling back.

He surfaced to the sight of Matthew, squatting near the bank of the pond watching him. Silently, the boy proffered the bar of brown soap to him.

"Pave-vooná?o," Clay said. Good morning.

"Morning," Matthew answered with a tentative smile.

It was good to see the grim look of suspicion gone from his eyes, Clay thought, taking the soap from him. "You're up early."

"I didn't sleep much," the boy admitted.

"Funny, neither did I."

Matthew swallowed hard. "You said I could tell you my decision this morning."

Clay waited.

"I've decided to go back."

Clay ran a wet hand down his face. "It was a man's decision, Matthew, any way you slice it. I know it wasn't easy for you to make it. But I know, from personal experience, you'll always have another home here if you want it. To the Cheyenne, you're family now. Time won't change that."

"Gray Wolf said the same thing to me." Matthew tipped his head down, his freckles more evident in the morning light. "Buffalo Wallow cried when I told her." He rubbed at his nose with the back of his hand. "When will we go?"

He'd planned on spending a week or so with the Cheyenne to rest up before going on. Now, that time could only work against them. "The sooner the better. Kierin's not getting any closer to us here. We should be able to catch up with the train in a couple of weeks on horseback."

Matthew gave a curt nod and stood, unfurling his lean, coltish legs. "I'll get my things together then. We'll leave today."

As he watched Matthew walk away, Clay decided he wouldn't regret spending the next two weeks getting to know the boy. Matthew reminded him a little of himself—the boy he'd been, years ago. He smiled at the bittersweet memory of his own youth.

Clay knew that the boy who'd become Little Fox would live on in Matthew even after he'd left the Cheyenne and what he'd learned here would hold him in good stead for the rest of his life.

He'd forgotten the water's chill until a shiver raced down his back and he ducked down under the water again to finish his bath. It was no use wondering what he'd do after he saw Matthew safely to Kierin. He'd learned a long time ago to do what was in front of him. Right now, that was getting Matthew home. After that? Perhaps, he sighed, the same force that seemed to be guiding his life now would lead his footsteps again.

Buffalo Wallow Woman and Corn Woman together packed enough food to last weeks and Clay carefully stowed it beneath the duck covering on his pack mule. Matthew had donned his best deer-hide shirt and leggings for his departure. The shirt was intricately quilled, a gift, Clay guessed, from Buffalo Wallow Woman.

At his side was a finely beaded sheath with a large bone-handled knife. With his long hair held back with a strip of tanned leather, Matthew looked every bit the part of the Cheyenne he'd become.

"Nё-sta-vä-hóse-vóomatse," the boy told Buffalo Wallow Woman and Gray Wolf. "I'll see you again." Corn Woman's sister embraced the boy, holding back her own tears.

When they parted, Gray Wolf pressed a small, fur-wrapped bundle into Matthew's hand. "Do not forget what I have taught you, Little Fox," he said. "May the All Father guide your path."

Matthew swallowed hard and nodded, squeezing the medicine bundle in his hand. "Good-bye, Gray Wolf. I will not forget you."

Clay said his farewells to Many Horses and Corn Woman and mounted Taeva. Matthew swung up on the back of his steady Pinto and glanced at Clay.

"Ready, boy?"

Silently, Matthew nodded. Without looking back, he nudged his pony forward with the touch of his moccasined heels. Clay did the same and together, with the sun on their backs, they galloped out of the village of their brothers, the Northern Cheyenne.

"What do you mean she's *gone?*" Clay exploded, sending Jacob stumbling back a step. With nearly two weeks of grueling riding behind them, Clay was in no mood for guessing games. Blind anger overrode the panic welling in Clay's chest on hearing the bombshell Jacob had just dropped in his lap. "Where the hell is she?"

"I be *tryin'* to tell you . . ." Jacob's expression revealed what it had cost him to tell Clay this news. "She left more'n a week ago."

"Where? Where'd she go?"

Dove moved protectively toward her man. Jacob's arm went around her and his uneasy glance flicked back and forth between the boy and Clay. "To California . . . wid her pa."

"Her *pa?*" came Matthew and Clay's stunned echo.

Clay shook his head with disbelief. "What the hell — ? I thought he was killed in the massacre." He glanced at Matthew, the other unexpected survivor, whose worried expression now rivaled his own.

Matthew had told him as much as he could remember about the massacre — which wasn't a lot. He'd been in shock and most of it remained simply a shadowy nightmare for him. But one thing was certain now, Clay thought. If Asa McKendry *had* lived through it somehow, he sure as hell hadn't bothered to go back to see if his son had, too.

"You're *sure* it was him?"

Jacob nodded reluctantly.

"Damn it!" Clay whirled around and slammed his open palm against the side of the wagon. "Damn it to hell!" He and Matthew had pushed hard for nearly two weeks to get back here. They'd damn near worn out their horses and themselves in the process. And she'd left him. Just like that.

Gone.

He knew she'd been angry when he'd left. He thought she'd get over it once she thought about it rationally; thought she'd see he'd had no other choice but to go. But he'd never expected something like this. Betrayal settled like a cold winter snow around his heart.

Jacob cleared his throat. "That ain't all of it, Clay."

Clay turned on Jacob, an angry light burning behind his steely eyes. He gave a short, bitter laugh. "It's worse?"

"Well, it ain't what you be thinkin'. I tell you, she wouldn'a gone wid him at all, 'cept'n he told her Matthew be waitin' for her in San Francisco."

Clay's jaw dropped open. "He . . . *what?*"

"I had a bad feelin' 'bout the whole thing," Jacob told him with a regretful frown. "I tried to tell her . . ."

Like a sail suddenly stripped of its wind, Clay slumped against the wagon with a groan. He stared out onto the sage-covered bottomland of the Raft River without really seeing it. What kind of a father—hell, what kind of man—manipulated his daughter with such blatant lies? And to what end? What could he want with her in San Francisco? He closed his eyes against the fearful hollow pounding of his heart.

"It sounds just like something he'd do," Matthew commented bitterly.

Clay put an arm around the boy's shoulders. "Maybe we'd better hear this from the beginning, Jacob."

Shaking his head sadly, Jacob said, "She be a grow'd woman wid a mind o' her own. But I swear, I wish I'da hog-tied her an' kep' her here."

The image of that brought a reluctant smile to Clay's lips and he wondered how many times he'd thought of doing the same thing himself.

An hour later, the fire popped and sizzled as Dove turned a pair of rabbits skewered on stripped green sticks over the flame. The smokey aroma drifted over the campsite, teasing Clay's growling stomach even when he'd thought he wasn't hungry. He turned to Jacob. "You said this Kip Johanssen fellow has some kind of a lumber operation on the Sacramento River?"

"That's what McKendry *say*, but even Kierin had her doubts 'bout it," Jacob answered. "She just be so all-fired set on findin' her brother again . . ." His voice drifted off.

Matthew was silent, grim, poking a stick into the edge of the fire. Clay could only guess what the boy was feeling. It made him all the angrier that Matthew's father was using his son as a pawn in whatever game he was playing. After hearing Jacob's side of it, Clay felt sure that the meeting at Fort Hall had been no coincidence. But if it wasn't, what was Asa McKendry doing there and what kind of trouble had Kierin fallen into?

"They have a nine-day head start on us. Was he pulling with oxen teams or mules?" Clay asked Jacob.

"Mules."

"Damn. They'll move faster with mules." Clay stared at the plate Dove handed him. "Well, so be it. I'll be leaving at first light."

Matthew's head jerked up. "I'm going with you."

"No, you're not. You're staying right here where Jacob and Dove can keep an eye on you."

"Oh, no I ain't," he answered stubbornly, crossing his arms across his chest. "I'm coming. She's my sister and I'm gonna help you find her."

Clay scowled at him. "Look. I have no idea what I'm getting into here. All I know is I'm going to be riding hard and fast to catch up with your sister and I can't afford to be slowed down."

Matthew's chin went up in a way that was irritatingly familiar. "Have I slowed you down yet?"

Clay rolled his eyes heavenward. "Lord, deliver me from stubborn McKendrys," he muttered.

"Well, have I?"

Clay stared at him silently, knowing it was true. Not

302

only had he never slowed them down on the way here, but he'd proved himself to be quite handy with a bow and arrow. Over the past couple of weeks, he'd come to enjoy Matthew's company.

Still, he didn't know what he'd find when he finally caught up with Kierin. She would never forgive him if anything happened to her brother, and the very real fear that she was walking into something dangerous clawed at his gut like some wild animal. *Oh hell,* he thought. *You tried this tack once before with his sister and look how far it got you.* "No, you haven't slowed me down, boy, and I was wrong to say it," he admitted with a sigh. "If you're determined to go, I don't suppose there's much I can say to stop you."

"Hena?haanehe," Matthew said, slipping back into the familiar Cheyenne tongue. "That's the end of it, then. I'm going."

Clay arched a dark brow. "Right."

"It looks like you met your match, Clay boy," Jacob said with easy grin.

"It appears that way," he agreed. "It's that blasted McKendry logic. Gets me every time. Your sister is just as proficient at it as you seem to be."

Matthew smiled knowingly. "She was a good teacher."

"She's good at a lot of things," Clay replied as her face crept back into his mind. Besting him in arguments was only one of them, he thought with a grin. He watched Matthew dig into the food Dove had placed before him with renewed relish, his youthful appetite restored with the settling of their argument. Clay forced himself to eat, knowing his body required the food. But his mind was elsewhere. On the woman who possessed a piece of his soul.

If it had been practical to ride off tonight after her, he would have. Nine days' head start. Damn, he thought, they could be a hundred and seventy-five miles ahead of him by now. *If anything's happened to her, I'll kill McKendry with my bare hands.* Clay closed his eyes, willing himself to stay calm, rational. For her sake, he'd need to.

Lost in thought, he jumped when Jacob touched him on the shoulder.

"Clay, Kierin left this for you when she left for California. She wanted me to give it to you when you come back from Independence."

Clay hesitated a moment before taking the letter Jacob offered him. "Thanks," he said. His hand shook slightly as he broke open the envelope and he angled it closer to the firelight. It read:

Dearest Clay,

By now Jacob has told you where I have gone and why. I hope you can understand my need to do this, just as I've tried to understand your need to go back to clear things in Independence. My own stubborn pride kept me from saying this before you left, Clay. But pride seems so unimportant in the face of things, so I'll say it now. I love you and, in spite of everything that's come between us, I always will.

My fondest hope is that you are safe and well, my darling. I will get in touch with Jacob after we are settled in San Francisco with Matthew.

All My Love,
Kierin

Clay stared at the letter for a long minute before refolding it and slipping it back in its envelope. He blinked and swallowed hard, trying to relieve the burning lump of emotion at the back of his throat. *I'll find her,* he thought. *I swear to God I will. And when I do I'll never let her go again.*

Chapter Twenty-one

A heart-wrenching scream shattered the night's stillness and tore Kierin from a deep sleep. She sat bolt-upright in the small tent she shared with her father, her heart pounding like a caged wild thing within her breast. Blindly, she searched for her father's hand.

"Papa!" In the inky blackness, she could hear Asa thrashing, still in the throes of a nightmare. "Papa, wake up," she demanded, shaking him. "It's all right, it's only a dream. Wake — ungh-h —" His brawny arm connected with her jaw, knocking her backward, sprawling her against the side of the canvas tent.

"No! Let go!" he yelled, still gripped by the night terror. "I have t' . . . go back . . ."

Momentarily stunned, Kierin blinked back the dizziness from the blow and struggled back up to her knees. It wasn't the first time she'd seen him like this since they'd started out together nearly three weeks ago. His nightmares were becoming more and more frequent as the days passed. And more violent, she mused, rubbing her tender jaw.

"Papa, it's Kierin. It's all right." She pinned his arm down this time and soothed the hair off his damp forehead. "It's all right now."

Asa awoke with a start. He stiffened and blinked, trying to focus on the face hovering above him.

"It's Kierin, Papa."

"Ach-h . . . Kiery . . ." he breathed, tightening his hand around her arm. "Oh-h-h . . . sweet God in heaven. I thought—"

"It was only a dream. You're right here with me now."

"Aye, that's good . . . that's good . . ." He pulled a sweaty hand down his damp face. "I . . . I'm sorry, darlin'." He reached up and touched her face. "Did I . . . did I hurt you?"

"It's nothing," she reassured softly. "You didn't mean to. But these dreams you're having are worrying me, Papa. They're happening more and more. Maybe if you talk about them, they'll—"

"No." He sat up abruptly. "I mean, I don't even re-member what it was about now. Better to leave dreams in their place. It's all they are anyway. Just dreams."

"Bad dreams," she said, unconvinced.

"Aye," he sighed. "Go back to sleep now, lass. We've got a long day in front of us tomorrow."

Kierin hesitated, then lay back down on her pallet, staring into the darkness. She listened to the steady rushing sound of the nearby Humbolt River and the rhythmic thudding of her heart.

Asa, too, listened to the uneven rhythm of his heart. It thumped painfully against the wall of his chest and felt as if it had a steel band tightening around it. He lay per-fectly still waiting for the pain to pass.

It always did.

He flexed the fingers of his left hand, which felt char-acteristically numb. The attacks were getting worse all the time, just as that doctor in San Francisco had warned they would. He wondered just how long he had. Not long by his calculations. Long enough, he hoped, to get Kierin to San Francisco and settled with the security for her he'd been promised.

He squeezed his eyes shut, taking long slow breaths. He hoped to God he hadn't made a mistake tricking her this way. But it was the only way she'd have come with him, after the way he'd left her behind in Independence. He only hoped she'd forgive him the lie when she found out the real reason he'd come for her. It was for her own good, he told himself for the hundredth time. After he was gone, she'd be taken care of in a style he'd never been able to give her. After what he'd put her through, God knew, she deserved it.

Aye, it was the right thing, he decided. But, he wondered, why then was he plagued by these nightmares? Over and over in his dream, he'd see Matthew being murdered at the hands of the Crow—his scalp lifted, his face battered beyond recognition. Helplessly, he'd watch Kierin run toward her brother, to help him, only to be set upon by the savages as well. He blinked back the recurrent images.

It was his conscience that plagued him, he knew. He hadn't seen Matthew die, of course. His imagination generously supplied all the horrible details his eyes hadn't witnessed. In fact, he hadn't been able to find his body and could only assume that the red savages had dragged him off to torture and kill him somewhere else. He groaned silently, thinking of it.

His son. His boy.

He'd failed both his children miserably. No one would argue that point, he thought with a grimace of pain which was as much physical as mental. He'd made his share of mistakes in his life. Mostly, he had to admit, because of his love of a bottle. It had taken his health, his home, and worst of all, his children. But he meant to do what he could to change that. God help him, though, if the dreams that tormented him at night didn't stop, they would surely be the death of him.

Beside him, he could hear his daughter's restless breathing, telling him she was no more asleep than he.

"Kiery?"

She turned her head in the darkness. "Mm-hm?"

"Do you remember your ma much?"

"Course I do." It had been ten years since she'd died,

307

but her face was still as vivid in Kierin's mind as if it were yesterday. "Why?"

"Ach-h, ye remind me of her sometimes, ye know."

She could hear the smile in his voice as he said it. "I do?"

"Aye. Sometimes yer eyes flash the way hers did — all green like the sea in a storm. Sometimes . . . it's the way ye talk, like ye could forgive me anything. She was like that, ye know." His voice cracked with emotion. "I — I was never worthy of her."

Kierin swallowed hard, surprised to hear him speak of her. It had been years since he'd allowed himself to do so. It was common knowledge that her mother had married beneath her station — all grist for the gossip mills of Independence where she'd grown up, she recalled bitterly.

Sarah McKendry's family, the grandparents Kierin had never known, hadn't forgiven her for falling in love with a working-class Scotsman who had nothing more than his dreams to offer her. Though Sarah had forgiven him everything, Kierin knew he'd never forgiven himself for the life of privilege he'd stolen from her.

The night sheltered the two of them and the words they had never spoken to each other before. It cloaked expressions best left unseen.

"She loved you, Papa," Kierin told him simply.

"Aye, and more's the pity. I want better for ye, Kiery. Better than just a living eked out of the land like I gave yer ma. Ye know that, don't ye?"

Kierin frowned, turning toward him again. "What's this all about, Papa?"

He was silent for a long minute. "I haven't done too well keeping the promises I made yer ma when she died. I told her I'd raise ye up right and keep ye headed in the right direction. An' look what I've done to ye . . ."

"Pa . . ."

"But that's all gonna change when we get to San Francisco, lass," he told her. "Things'll be better for us, ye'll see."

308

She reached over, took his hand, and gave it a squeeze. He'd always been full of dreams—dreams and promises that he'd make everything better for them.

Someday.

For as long as she'd known him, he'd promised her those things. It was the only way he had of loving her, she realized now. They weren't lies. They were his truth. His reason for going on.

She found, at last, she could forgive him that fatal flaw as her mother before her had. She felt him squeeze her hand back, and suddenly she knew—for just this moment in time—the differences separating them had narrowed to the space between their fingertips.

"Good night, Papa."

"G'night, Kiery."

It was mid-October before she and Asa drove their weary team of mules through the outskirts of the city of San Francisco. With nearly two thousand long miles behind Kierin, the city—rough and hastily erected as it was—looked like heaven. Left behind at places like Sutter's Fort, Sacramento City, and Marysville were most of the people and wagons they'd traveled with from Fort Hall—seekers of gold and quick fortune. Their own destination, Kierin mused, was more modest but, for her, a hundred times more exciting.

Matthew was here!

As the day of their arrival drew nearer, her anticipation had grown, helping to ease the constant and irreconcilable pain of missing Clay. He was in her thoughts even now as they edged into the city and she wished she were seeing it for the first time with him beside her.

Wishing would get her absolutely nowhere, she reasoned pragmatically. Clay was, by all estimates, nearly back to Independence by now—back to the town and all the troubles it held for him. Kierin sent up another of her hundred daily prayers for his safety. A helpless sense of dread filled her whenever she thought of him, and she gave herself a mental shake, determined to make her homecoming with her brother a happy one.

Indian summer had descended upon the land of the Golden Gate. A warm breeze blew across the clumps of wild mint, or yerba buena, that grew along the sides of the road, filling the air with its sweet tangy scent. Though the town of San Francisco no longer bore the name "Yerba Buena," it was easy to see why the Californians had originally called it that. The mint seemed to be everywhere.

The wagon wheels crunched rhythmically along the rutted, heavily used dirt road. Beside her on the swaying wagon seat, her father peered straight ahead, the traces hanging loosely, distractedly, in his hands. His mouth was narrowed to a grim slash across his face.

It was an expression with which she'd become disturbingly familiar in the last few days. As their approach to the city had loomed closer, her father seemed to be growing more and more restless and withdrawn. She attributed it to the long trip, and the fact that he was obviously feeling unwell. He had lost weight in spite of her cooking and all his denials that it wasn't true. A fine sheen of perspiration now glistened on his forehead.

She laid a hand on his arm. "Are you feeling all right, Papa?"

Startled out of his thoughts, his head jerked around to face her. "What?"

"I asked if you were all right. You look—"

"Aye, girl, I'm fine," he told her curtly, with a slap of the reins.

"Well, I don't care what you say, you're going to see a doctor as soon as we get settled," she told him in a voice that would brook no arguments.

He gave her none. Instead he sank back to the slump-shouldered stare he'd had earlier.

Kierin slipped her jittery hands beneath her thighs and decided to try a new tack. "How far is it from here to

310

your friend Kip Johanssen's?"

Asa cleared his throat but took a long time to answer. "Not far."

Kierin settled back to wait. She wouldn't allow her father's mood to dull her spirits. Her eager eyes took in the sights. Fire-purged hillsides — treeless now — but studded with newly erected houses and businesses dotted the landscape. Landaus, surreys, and dog carts crowded the wide dirt-paved streets of the city.

A thrill chased through her at the sight of the Long Wharf, stretching out some two thousand feet into the San Francisco Bay. It was crowded with steamers, packets, and three-masted sailing ships unloading passengers fresh from Panama.

Asa turned the wagon down Montgomery Street, past the formidable stone masonry of the Bank of California and the Wells Fargo Express Building. They followed Kearny Street, with its string of false-fronted buildings to the bustling hub of Portsmouth Square. Long shadows carved by the late afternoon sun sheltered the crowds milling through an open-air market. The pungent smell of fish mingled with the scent of fresh-cut flowers, and the raucous sound of caged, squawking chickens. Young boys hawked the latest issue of the newspapers — *Alta California* and *The California Star* — from every street corner.

It was so wonderful, Kierin could hardly take it all in. Her head was still spinning with excitement as Asa pulled the wagon to a stop in front of a well-kept three-story townhouse at the edge of the square.

Asa reached behind him and pulled a nearly empty bottle of whiskey from beneath a sack and took a long pull on it — for courage, he told himself — before tying the traces around the handle of his brake.

"Is this it?" Kierin asked.

"Aye, this is the place," he answered, considering the possibilities of turning his back on this venture all together. A sharp pain pounded between his temples at the

311

prospect of telling her the truth. Why hadn't he worked up the nerve to tell her about Matthew earlier? He told himself it was because he couldn't bear to spoil the new kinship they'd come to share since they'd come together. Because the truth would shatter that bond forever. *Because,* a voice reminded him, *you're a weak, sniveling old wreck of a man, Asa McKendry, and you'll never amount to more than that.*

Tell her now, he coached himself, *before it's too late.* A weariness settled upon his bones. It was too late already, he knew. "Kiery . . . there's somethin'—"

"What are we waiting for?" she asked, leaping from the wagon seat.

"Wait," he warned, following her down off the wagon. He had to tie the mules to the hitching post and she was already bounding up the steps. "Kiery—"

Kierin raised her fist to knock on the door but the door swung open before she could.

A young woman in a stunningly low-cut solferino pink silk gown pulled back a step in surprise. She cocked her head sideways, causing an ermine-colored curl to bounce appealingly against her rouged cheek. She gave Kierin a once-over with a slow sweep of her luminous brown eyes.

Kierin was suddenly aware of how scruffy she must look in her worn blue calico and her hair pulled back stylessly in its leather thong.

"Deliveries are around back, at the kitchen door," the woman announced, about to dismiss her.

Kierin's face reddened. "No, I—I'm not here to deliver anything."

The woman perused her again. "Well then? What can I do for you?" she asked with a twirl of her matching silk parasol.

"Ah . . . we're here to see Kip Johanssen. Is he in?"

The woman gave her a blank look. "Kip . . . who?"

"Jo-hanssen," Kierin repeated more slowly in case the girl was dull-witted.

312

The girl let out a trill of laughter. "You must be mistaken, there's no one by . . ." The girl's gaze lit on something behind Kierin's shoulder and her words trailed off.

Kierin turned to see her father gesturing wildly to the strange woman with his hands. Kierin's confused look stopped him abruptly.

Frowning, she turned back to the woman in pink, who was revising her denial even before getting the whole thing out.

"Oh, you mean *that* Kip Johanssen." She laughed again. "Of course, come in, come in."

The skin on the back of Kierin's neck crawled in warning. "Actually, it's Matthew McKendry we've come for. Is *he* here?"

The woman pasted a smile on her tinted lips and daintily took Kierin's elbow. "Of course. Why don't you both come in and sit down? I'll get them for you."

Kierin shrugged the girl's hand from her arm and tossed a narrow-eyed glance at Asa, who by now was standing on a step beside her. "What's going on?" she demanded.

Asa was sweating profusely and dabbed at his forehead with a cotton hanky. "I—"

"Who is this woman and where is Matthew?"

"Darlin', there's something I have to tell . . ."

"Well, what have we here?" came a man's voice from behind the girl.

Kierin's breath froze in her throat at the sound and she turned to see a man looming in the shadow of the doorway. She backed against the wrought-iron rail guarding the steps. *It couldn't be him,* she thought desperately. *It wasn't possible.*

As the man moved out of the shadow, the sunlight glinted off the shiny black eye patch he sported over his left eye and Kierin's heart sank to her toes. She recognized the ruined cheek, the sandy blond hair, the cold set to his jaw.

There was a thin-lipped smile on his mouth as John

313

Talbot's gaze fell on Kierin. "So I see you found her, Asa. My compliments on a job well done."

"You—how—?" Kierin gasped in a choked voice.

"Hello, Kierin. Surprised to see me? I'm afraid the wagon train is not the most economical means of transport to the West, my dear. The route through Panama cut my traveling time by nearly half."

She turned her angry glare on her father. "What have you done?"

"He's done what I told him to do," Talbot answered for him. "He's brought you back to me. Why don't we all go inside, instead of causing a scene out here on the stoop?"

Asa's eyes pleaded with her. "I did it for your own good, Kiery."

Kierin let out a disbelieving huff of breath. "My own—what are you talking about?" *This can't be happening.* She felt Talbot's fingers close around her arm, and instantly, she tried to lunge away from him.

"Come along, Kierin," he said, stopping her easily. "I've waited too long for this moment to let it slip away now."

"Let go of me, you bastard!" she screeched.

"Here now," Asa said, "don't be doin' that to 'er—" Talbot and the woman in pink silk succeeded in dragging her into the opulently appointed house, with Asa close behind. "Hey, wait just a minute now—"

"Have a drink, McKendry," Talbot invited, pointing at the table filled with decanters of liquor. "Cool your heels. You'll get your money." He shoved Kierin down onto a green velvet settee.

Kierin's stunned look shot to her father. *"Money?* He *paid* you to bring me here?"

"It's not what yer thinkin'." Asa's hands ground into fists at his sides. "He said he'd pay my expenses to go and find you. He told me . . . he said . . . he was in love with you and you with him—that he wanted to marry you."

"W-what?" Kierin's anger-flushed cheeks drained of color. Her head spun crazily, like an out-of-kilter top.

"He said ye'd been taken by a no-account drifter against yer will." Asa skewered Talbot with a hard look. "He told me you and he had some little spat before ye left Independence, but . . . he was sure ye'd be able to work it out once I brought ye back to him."

"And you *believed* him?" Kierin asked incredulously. Her gaze shifted back and forth between Talbot and her father.

Asa dragged a hand across his mouth, ignoring the others in the room. "Aye, lass, I did. That's why I didn't tell you about it all this time. I didn't want yer stubborn pride to get in the way of yer future."

"My future? With *him?*" She let out a harsh bitter laugh. "Did he neglect to mention that he tried to kill me the last time he saw me and nearly succeeded in killing Clay?"

Asa shot a look at Talbot. "What?"

"So, Holt's still alive, is he?" Talbot's lip curled into a snarl and he casually poured himself two fingers of scotch from the crystal decanter. He tipped the amber liquid down his throat with a grimace. "I might have known I wouldn't get that lucky. No matter. The law will catch up with him soon enough."

"You lied to me, Talbot," Asa said, taking a step toward him.

Talbot pointed at him accusingly with the empty shot glass, stopping the other man short. "You've been lying to yourself for years, McKendry. That's why you're such an easy mark. You heard what you wanted to hear . . . *all* you wanted to hear."

Asa staggered back as if struck. "You sonofabitch—"

"It's a bit late for all this fatherly protectiveness now, isn't it, McKendry? I'll pay you what I promised. That should keep you in whiskey for the next year."

Asa grabbed Kierin's arm. "C'mon. We're getting out o' here."

Just as fast, Talbot stopped him. "No, you're not."

"The hell you say . . ." Asa brushed the other man's

315

hand off his arm.

"Don't push me, McKendry," Talbot warned. Two other men — who seemed to fill the room — entered from the other doorway, both with guns drawn. "As you can see," he said, glancing at the brawny men behind him, "I'm not without a means of persuasion."

"You d'na scare me with yer strong-arm tactics. A plain coward is what ye are, hidin' behind the likes of them. You want a fight?" he asked, holding his fists up near his face. "Let's see what ye got."

Talbot shook his head with a snort of disgust, then reached into the vest pocket of his tailored coat and withdrew a small leather drawstring pouch. He tossed it carelessly toward Asa. It landed with a thud at his feet. "Pick it up, old man," Talbot ordered. "Cut your losses and get out while you've still got two good legs under you."

The threat sent a cold chill up Kierin's spine, but Asa ignored the money and pulled her close to him. "I'm not leavin' without her."

Talbot laughed again. "You think she'll still want to go with you when you tell her how you lied about her brother?"

With a sinking feeling of dread, Kierin looked up at her father. The color had siphoned from his ruddy face. "W-what does he mean?" she insisted. "Where's Matthew?"

Asa squeezed his eyes shut and dropped his hold on her arm.

"Tell her, McKendry . . ." Talbot snarled. "Tell her how you lied to her about him being here. About how her brother's young scalp is dangling off the tip of some Crow warrior's lance."

"No-o-o!" The half-cry, half-scream of denial tore from her throat and she stumbled backward, away from her father. "It's not true. Tell him it's not true."

"He can't. Can you, McKendry?" Talbot baited.

Asa's guilt-ridden eyes slowly rose to meet Kierin's.

His face was the color of ashes, and his lip beaded with perspiration. "I — I'm sorry, Kiery."

Bile rose in her throat and her stomach lurched threateningly. She groped blindly for the seat of the settee behind her and sat down hard. Her insides ground together like bits of shattered glass. It hurt too much to cry, too much to even breathe. How could she have been such a fool? So utterly gullible?

Asa took a step toward her and anger surged inside her. "Don't touch me!" she snapped, knocking away from his outstretched hand. *Just leave me alone.*

"Kiery . . ."

Tears glistened on her cheeks and slid in tiny rivulets past her jaw. "Don't you ever call me that again. I hate you! Do you hear me? *I hate you!*"

Asa swallowed hard and backed up a step. His mouth opened and closed like a land-locked fish.

"Get out, McKendry," Talbot said with a pleased smile tipping the corners of his mouth. "Your daughter doesn't need you anymore."

Asa's whole body vibrated with the shock waves of what had just happened. He'd been duped, but it would do him no good to try to explain his way out of this with Kiery. His own stupidity had gotten him here. He didn't need to hear the words she'd just flung at him to know how she felt about him. She hated him and, he reasoned, she had every right to.

You're a miserable excuse for a man, Asa McKendry, he berated himself, *and a poorer excuse for a father.* If he thought he had a chance of saving her now, he'd try to overpower one of those louts with the Colt dragoons in their hands. But he was unarmed.

He needed a gun and he needed it fast.

Asa massaged his left arm, which had gone almost completely numb. Maybe it was a fool's errand, but he had one chance left to help his only daughter and he decided to take it.

Straightening, he shot Kierin a scornful look. "Ach —

the hell with it, then. Stay here with him if that's what ye want. Ye've always been a thorn in my side, girl, and the truth is, I'll be glad to be rid of ye."

Kierin's head came up with a snap and she sent him a scorching look that singed his resolve, but didn't stop him.

He bent down to retrieve the pouch of gold that lay on the floor. "I might as well have somethin' for my trouble," he said, offhandedly. "You're welcome to her, Talbot. She's a hard one, that girl."

Perched on the edge of the velvet settee, Kierin watched him walk toward the door and felt all emotion drain from her. In its place came a strange sense of calm and resolve. It didn't really surprise her that her father was leaving her here without a fight. It was his way. The truth was, he'd quit on her and Matthew long ago. Why should now be any different?

Keep your wits about you, Kierin, she warned herself. *You'll need every one of them to get out of this alive.* Clay's face swam in her memory, filling her up, giving her a reason to fight. *Oh, Clay,* she thought, with a longing that tore at her heart, *will I ever see you again?*

Asa turned one last time before going out the door. Kierin's chin hitched up a notch and she glared at him, her eyes the color of a storm-tossed sea.

Asa swallowed hard and his hands gripped the gold-filled pouch until his knuckles turned white. "I was wrong about yer bein' like yer ma, Kierin," he told her with a quivering lip. "Yer nothin' like her. Ye never will be."

Something snapped in Kierin. She grabbed the first thing she could lay her hands on: an etched-crystal egg poised on a small teakwood stand on the low table in front of her. Her fist closed around it and she flung it with all the force she could muster toward her father.

Asa saw it coming and ducked, but not before the glass shattered against the doorjamb beside him and sent a piece splintering into his cheek. Stunned, he reached up and touched the tiny trickle of blood that traveled down his cheek.

"You go to hell!" she shouted at him as one of Talbot's men hurried to her side and grabbed her arms.

"Aye. No doubt," he replied, and without another word, he walked out the door. The heavy oak portal rattled in its frame with all the finality of a jail cell door.

Kierin winced at the tight grip of the man who held her. One tree-limb-sized arm was wrapped around her chest, flattening her breasts and cinching her arms at her sides. "Let me . . . go," she cried. Twisting in his arms, she struggled to free herself but he only tightened his hold on her.

"What a little wildcat you've become, Kierin," Talbot said, grinning at her. "I've always liked my women feisty. The West seems to agree with you."

"You can go to hell, too," she snapped. "Why don't you call off this grizzly bear of yours and tell me what it is you want with me." Talbot threw his head back and laughed. The man holding her gave her a punishing little squeeze and she let out a coughing gasp.

Suddenly, her fingertips brushed the butt of the gun the goliath wore strapped to his thigh. It was just within her reach. Adrenaline pumped through her bloodstream as she considered her chances to grab it before she was discovered.

"I've got what I want," Talbot replied, laconically. "Well, part of it anyway."

"Me." It was a statement, not a question.

"Yes," he replied, brushing his fingers in an absent gesture over the black patch on his eye. As he drew nearer, Kierin could see the puckered scar that ran across his cheek where the poker had burned his skin.

"And the rest?" she asked, forcing her gaze from the ugly scar.

"Do you see this?" He pointed to the patch.

"It's hard to miss," she taunted with a smile.

Talbot's good eye narrowed. "True. And I have you to

319

thank for it."

Kierin tipped her head cockily and clucked her tongue. "And I thought the patch looked rather rakish."

Talbot's hand snaked out and he slapped her hard across the face. Her head snapped to one side and black spots swam before her eyes. Blinking slowly to clear them, Kierin lifted her head to glare at him. She could taste the blood on her lip.

Kierin let out a harsh breath. "You are a coward, Talbot. What's the matter? Are you afraid of the wildcat's claws? You need a big strong man like this to hold me back from you?" Her fingers poised above the butt of the gun.

Talbot smiled savagely and he gestured for the man to release her. The moment his arms loosened, her fingers closed around the butt of the revolver and she yanked with all her strength. She spun out of the arms of her jailer and pointed his gun directly at Talbot's heart.

Talbot's eyes widened with surprise. "What the—"

The man started to rush her but she'd already cocked the pistol and tightened her finger on the trigger. "Don't!" she warned. "I'll kill him. I swear to God I will."

Talbot jerked his hand up and backed up a step. "Get back, Belson," he ordered. "She means it." At the other side of the room, Talbot's other lackey, Cain, kept his hands carefully away from his gun.

"Damn right I do," she agreed, "and at this range, I could hardly miss." Kierin sidestepped the table and kept her eyes glued to Talbot. "I'm leaving now. Don't try to stop me." Her heart pounded like thunder against her ribs.

"At the moment, you seem to be holding all the cards . . ." Talbot's eyes flicked for a fraction of a second to a point behind her.

Too late, she saw the violent sweep of pink silk out of the corner of her eye. Too late, she tried to dodge the inevitable blow. She felt a crushing pain at the back of her head and—as if from a long distance off—she heard

320

the shattering of glass. Like sand through her fingers, the gun slipped from her hand and a profound darkness closed in around her. And as she slid into that numbing void, she knew with utter certainty that she had lost.

Chapter Twenty-two

Clay and Matthew made a striking pair as they loped their horses down the central corridor of Kearny Street into Portsmouth Square. Dressed in beaded buckskins and riding with the savage grace they'd each acquired at the hands of the Cheyenne, the two ignored the outright stares they drew from the pedestrians crowded onto the boarded walkways of the street. Instead, their focus was directed toward the three-story brick building at the center of the Plaza: a gambling hall called El Dorado.

Clay pulled his Appaloosa to a stop and dismounted. Beside him, Matthew climbed off the pinto and tied his reins to the hitching rail under the gold-painted sign announcing the establishment they sought.

Clay tipped his hat off, raked a hand tiredly through his dark hair, then settled the sweat-soaked band over his brow again. A day or two's growth of whiskers shadowed his jaw. Fatigue etched dark blue smudges beneath his eyes. Gaunt and weary, Clay's body betrayed the evidence of the punishing weeks of travel behind them.

Twenty-four hours in San Francisco hadn't put them any closer to finding Kierin than they had been yesterday. It was obvious they'd either missed Kierin and Asa somehow back on the trail in one of the gold-mining camps, or the pair had beaten them to San Francisco.

Either way, finding them in a city this size was like looking for a needle in a haystack.

Clay had been forced to take a room at the Parker House out of deference to an equally exhausted eleven-year-old. Matthew had fallen asleep before his head even hit the pillow. Clay had paced the room like a caged animal until the early hours of the morning when his body had forced him, at last, to sleep.

In the morning, after locating Johanssen's mill on the east end of town, they'd questioned the man Asa had claimed was his partner.

"Ja, he *was* my partner," Johanssen had replied, shaking his head, " 'til he started losing the company's money gambling—four, maybe five months ago. He wagered his way right out of the business."

"Do you have any idea where he might have gone?" Clay had asked. "Was there someplace he went regularly, where people might have known him?"

The blond-haired man scratched his head. "I ain't laid eyes on him since he left. But if a man's serious about the gambling, there's only one place worth going to. That's El Dorado."

Clay pushed away from the hitching post and headed toward the louvered doors at the entrance to the saloon. Matthew was close at his heels. He'd come to respect Kierin's brother too much to even suggest that he stay behind, but from the sound coming from inside the saloon, it wasn't the place for a young boy.

Evening had only just begun, yet El Dorado was filled with men eager to lose what they'd worked so hard for in the goldfields. Green-topped poker and craps tables crowded the room alongside shiny roulette wheels. Scantily clad women acted as dealers.

Clay and Matthew approached the long polished bar where a heavy man with a well-trimmed beard stood wiping glasses out with a questionable rag.

"What'll it be, gentlemen?" he asked with a twinkle in his eye for Matthew.

Matthew pulled himself up straighter to appear taller. "Sarsaparilla."

"Make that two," Clay added, not wanting to muddle his foggy brain with alcohol.

When the barkeep set the drinks before them, Clay pushed a ten-dollar gold piece toward him.

The man's eyebrow went up. "That the smallest you got?"

"If you've got the information I want, you won't have to change it for me," Clay replied.

"What kinda information?"

"I'm looking for a man by the name of Asa McKendry. I was told he spent a lot of time here. Do you know him?"

"I might," the man answered, stroking his beard. "As you can see, we stay pretty busy here. Lotta folks drift in . . . drift out. McKendry, you say? Had a fella used to come in here regular until a few months ago by that handle. Reddish hair, not too tall, bit of a brogue . . ."

"That's him," said Matthew.

"Like I said," the man repeated, going for the coin, "I haven't seen him for months now."

Clay flattened his hand over the gold piece. "What can you tell me about him? Where was he living? Did he meet anyone here regularly?"

The bearded man frowned. "Nope. In a place like this, nobody knows too much about nobody else. Folks like it that way."

Clay cursed under his breath.

"Why are you looking for him anyway?"

Clay sent him a chilling look. "He took my wife."

"Shee-it! You don't say?" The barkeep picked up the coin and fingered it absently in his hand. "Ya know, come to think of it, you ain't the first to come looking for this McKendry fella."

Clay's head shot up. "We're not?"

"Nope. About the time McKendry disappeared, a fella come askin' for him just like you. I knew right off

324

he was the kinda hombre you don't wanna tangle with. Mean as sin, but smooth as Kentucky bourbon. Wore a black patch over his eye and had a nasty-looking scar on his cheek. Had him a couple of big fellas with —"

Clay straightened abruptly. A sick feeling twisted his gut. "Did you say a *patch?*"

"Yeah — black patch."

Clay swallowed hard. "What did he look like?"

The other man shrugged. "Tall, good-looking — except for the eye — sandy hair . . ."

"Oh, Christ —" *It couldn't be.* His skin broke out in a cold sweat. "Did he tell you his name?"

The bartender scratched his head thoughtfully. "He's been comin' in here pretty regular since then. It's Talbin . . . or Tolbert . . . something like that."

Clay's voice was flat, emotionless. "Talbot? John Talbot?"

The barkeep's face flattened with surprise. "That's it."

"Oh, no," Matthew moaned. "Is that the same — ?"

Clay nodded. He'd told Matthew all about Talbot and now imagined the boy's pale expression was a perfect mirror of his own. Clay turned back to the man. "Any idea where he lives?"

"I heard he lives somewhere around here, in Portsmouth Square."

"That's *it?*"

"Yup. That's all I know."

Clay shoved away from the bar. "Thanks . . ."

"Hey, good luck," the man called after them.

Clay barely heard him as he pushed through the saloon doors again. Once outside, he took deep gulps of air to try to combat the ragged fear inside him. *Talbot here in San Francisco?* he thought. *It doesn't seem possible. He must have come through Panama,* he reasoned, *the bastard. What if he has Kierin already? How will we find her?*

"W-what does it mean, Clay?" In spite of the boy's outward calm, his voice trembled.

Clay rested a hand on the boy's shoulder. "If Talbot's

325

involved . . . we've got to find your sister. Fast."

"First, we've got to find Talbot," Matthew returned, staring out into the crowded street.

"Right." Clay glanced back into the saloon at the women dealing cards. It was a long shot, but maybe one of those woman had made Talbot's acquaintance. "I'll be right back, son—"

Matthew's hand on his arm stopped him. "Clay . . ."

Clay turned around. "What is it?"

Matthew was staring at a drunk old man stumbling up the street. The boy swallowed hard. "It's . . . it's my father."

Matthew was already off the boarded walkway and into the street before Clay realized what the boy had said. A quick scan of the area told him Kierin wasn't with her father. With his heart pounding in his chest like a fist, Clay was off the portico in one long stride and right behind Matthew.

Asa's lurching run kept him close to the wall of the building beside him and his hand was stretched out at arm's length to keep from careening into it.

"Pa!" Matthew called from a few feet away. "Pa! Stop!"

Asa's head came up in bewilderment and he stumbled to a stop. His eyes blinked in confusion as his gaze fell upon his son, but Asa hardly had time to speak before Clay seized his sweat-soaked shirtfront and slammed him up against the wall.

"Where is she, you sonofabitch?"

Asa grunted as he connected with the bricks behind him.

"Where's Kierin, you bastard? *Tell me!*"

"Clay," Matthew interceded, wrestling with the steely muscles of Clay's arm. "Stop it. He'll never tell you anything if you kill him!"

Asa's eyes were wide open and panicked. Clay noticed that the old man's skin was the color of dried mud and wondered dispassionately if he'd already hurt him.

Clay took a deep breath and reluctantly released his hold on the trembling man. He *wanted* to kill him. But not before he got some answers.

Asa's knees gave way and he slid partway down the wall before Clay swore and caught him, easing him to the ground.

"I don't think he's drunk," Matthew said, unfastening his father's collar, "I think he's sick."

Looking at him, Clay had to agree.

Asa blinked at the beads of sweat rolling into his eyes.

"Matthew?"

"Yeah, Pa, it's me."

"You're alive . . . Sweet Jesus . . . I don't . . . believe it . . ."

"Pa—where's Kiery? What have you done with her?"

Asa grimaced and rubbed his chest. "Got to help her . . . can't let them—"

"Where is she, Asa?" Clay demanded. "Tell us."

"Talbot . . . Talbot's got her." He licked his dry lips. "I was such a fool . . . I thought he wanted to . . . marry her."

"Marry her." Clay stared at the man, incredulous. "What's he done with her? Is she hurt?"

"Don't know . . ." Disoriented, he struggled to get up. "I have to get help . . . need a gun. I had nothing . . ."

Clay pushed him back down again. "You're in no shape to help anyone, McKendry. Tell me where she is."

"Not far down Kearny. Tall brick townhouse . . . picket fence . . . number forty-seven . . ."

Clay was already on his feet, sprinting toward his horse.

"There's two men with him," Asa called after him. "They're armed."

Matthew watched Clay go, torn between helping him and staying with his father.

"Matthew."

327

Asa's voice brought the boy's gaze around to his father's face.

Asa started to reach up to touch Matthew's face, but stopped short of doing it when the boy flinched. "I looked for ye. I swear I did, but . . . couldn't find ye anywhere. Thought they'd kilt ye. Sorry, boy. I've . . . made such a mess of things."

Was his father actually asking him for forgiveness? Matthew wondered. As he looked into Asa's eyes, all the pain of those first few months returned like a wave of frigid water. He wasn't sure he'd ever be up to forgiving him. And certainly not now, with Kierin in so much trouble. "I know, Pa. I have to go help Kiery. You stay here, you hear me? You're sick."

"I've got to help her," Asa argued. "She's got to know I didn't mean the things I said. Only said them so I could get out to help her. Give me a hand up, boy."

Matthew shook his head. "Pa, I'm going now. You stay. You'll only slow us down. When we find her, I'll bring her back to you. That's a promise." He walked backward a few steps then turned and ran to his pinto.

Asa watched him spur the horse down the street, with the certain knowledge that later would be too late for him. Bracing his hand on the wall behind him, he edged up from the ground and headed for the sorrel horse tied not far away on a hitching rail. *Add horse stealing to my crimes,* he thought grimly, checking the old Sharps rifle cradled in the scabbard. Hauling himself into the saddle, he set his sights for Talbot's house. He'd find the man and kill him if it was the last thing he did. With a grimace of pain, he reflected that it very likely would be.

Clay flattened himself against the rear door of the townhouse, listening to the unexpected sound of a woman humming in the kitchen. His Colt hovered near his cheek, his finger poised over the trigger. He heard the heavy footsteps of a man enter the room and then the woman's enticing giggle.

"Cain! You scared me," the woman"s sultry voice scolded. "Now, stop that, you devil—ooh-hh . . ."

"That was some stunt you pulled with that girl," the man growled, his voice muffled against her skin. "You're somethin' else, Suzanne. It made me all . . . hot . . . and bothered."

She laughed throatily. "What would your boss say if he saw you with me like this?"

"Like to kill us both, I reckon. Mm-mm . . . he's got other things on his mind right now," the man answered.

"El Dragón, for instance?"

"That pimp's been waiting two weeks for Talbot's shipment to arrive. From the looks of her, he ought to turn a pretty profit on her, too."

"Is . . . Belson there with him? Waiting?"

"Mm-mm, yeah, honey. We're all alone h—"

An ominous click beside the man's ear silenced his words. "Not anymore, you're not," Clay told him, pressing the barrel of his gun against the man's cheek.

"Shit."

"Move real slow, both of you, back against the wall." Clay eased his gun away from the man's ear and nudged it against his throat. The brown-haired woman named Suzanne inched away from her lover and flattened herself up against the wall, her brown eyes wide with fear.

Cain stood a good four inches taller than Clay's considerable height and peered down his nose at Clay through slitted eyes. "What do ya want?"

"First, your gun. Hand it to me. Real slow."

Cain two-fingered the stock of his pistol and dangled it in front of Clay.

He took it and slipped it into the wide leather belt at his waist. His voice was low, unmistakably dangerous. "Now . . . tell me where she is."

The barrel of Clay's gun rippled with the movement

of Cain"s Adam's apple. "She?"

He nudged the gun harder, cutting into Cain's flesh. "I'd like nothing better than to blow your goddamned brains out, you bastard, and you've got exactly five seconds to change my mind."

Sweat trickled down Cain's cheek.

"One . . ."

"I—I don't know who you mean, mister."

"Two . . ."

"I—"

"Three . . ."

"If you mean that girl—"

"Four . . . sometimes I miss five altogether—"

"Wait! I'll tell you. The McKendry girl. Is that who you mean?"

"Keep talking."

"Talbot's took her down to a warehouse—by the docks."

"Who's this El Dragoń?" Clay demanded.

Cain's tongue flicked over his lips. "He's a whore-monger from Sonora, Mexico, up here buyin' women for his brothels."

Clay's jaw tightened. "Are you telling me Talbot's planning on selling Kierin to him?"

The big man swallowed painfully. "Uh-huh. Got some kind of personal grudge against her, I think. He don't talk about it, but I think it has something to do with the scar on his face."

Clay took a deep breath. His eyes glittered like blue ice. "How far is it?"

"Huh?"

"The warehouse."

Cain hesitated. Clay shoved the gun tighter.

"Only a b-block or two from here, on Commercial Street. The Long Wharf," Cain answered.

Peripherally, Clay caught the subtle movement of Suzanne's arm as she eased a drawer open behind her. Before he could react, Matthew was beside him with a knife blade at her throat. Suzanne gasped and pressed her head back against the white cupboards, taking in the sight of the savage-looking boy threatening her. "My God, it's an *Indian!*"

"Put it down," Matthew ordered. When she made no move to comply—only widened her eyes—he said, "I may be young, but don't doubt that I know how to use this." He pressed his blade harder against the white skin of her throat. The sharp knife she'd managed to pilfer from the drawer fell to the floor with a clatter.

"Boy," Clay said admiringly, "you move like a Cheyenne."

Matthew's drawn expression softened slightly at the praise. "Is she here?" he asked, not taking his eyes off his prisoner.

"No," Clay answered. "But this gentleman is going to take us to her. Aren't you, Cain?"

Cain's eyes widened in response.

"Matthew, lock our troublemaking lady in the pantry over there," he said, indicating the small room off the kitchen. "I don't want her getting into any trouble while we're gone."

Matthew nudged her into the room. He turned the skeleton key in the lock behind him, then slipped it into his knife sheath for safekeeping.

"Let's go, Cain," Clay said, urging the brawny man out the back door with the gun at his back. "Show us the warehouse. If anything's happened to her . . . you're a dead man."

The trio mounted their horses tethered at the front of the house. They headed southeast, toward the Long Wharf, with Clay holding the reins of Cain's horse. They failed to notice the man hunched over the saddle of a sorrel horse who followed at a safe distance.

Voices. A dull, throbbing ache at the back of her head. The scratch of straw against her cheek. Kierin's muted senses registered all these things one by one as she awoke. Her hands were twisted up behind her and she winced, realizing they were bound tightly with some kind of rope. Something warned her to keep her eyes closed. It was too painful to think about opening them anyway, her fuzzy brain reminded her. She lay like that, listening, trying to reorient herself.

Mingled with the scent of the straw beneath her face, she could smell the ocean; hear its constant surge close by, punctuated by the distant cry of seabirds.

Kierin focused on the sound of voices a few feet away. Men's voices. One sounded familiar. Were they talking about her? Realization came with a sickening rush of adrenaline to her aching head.

John Talbot.

". . . have no way of knowing that," she heard him saying to the other man.

"Ah, señor—el precio es differente por cosas arinadas," the other man replied. "The price is different for damaged goods. My customers like *birgenes*— virgins. They pay a lot of money for them. Of course," he amended, "the American woman will bring a good price too, virgin or not. Such hair! The color of fire! You did not exaggerate when you spoke of her."

Kierin heard the crunch of straw as one of the men walked toward her. She lay perfectly still, feigning the deep, even breath of sleep. *Oh God, don't let him touch me.*

"There's only one way to be sure," came Talbot's voice close to her face. "But I want her awake when you do it."

She could hear the smile of anticipation in his voice.

The Mexican chuckled gruffly. "Whatever your pleasure, señor. Perhaps—if she is not in one piece, so to speak—we can have a little fun with *la señorita* before I take her."

"That," Talbot snarled, "would more than compensate me for the loss of a few dollars, Señor Dragón.

Kierin's heart pounded in her ears so loudly she thought they must be able to hear it, too. A booted toe nudged her roughly in the ribs and she couldn't help the sharp intake of breath that betrayed her.

Talbot laughed. "So, you're awake, my little wildcat. Why don't you open your eyes so we can have a little talk?"

Kierin squeezed her eyes shut tighter. "Go to hell."

His hand cinched around her upper arm and she felt herself being hauled up like a sack of grain. She cried as he wrenched her shoulder and a white hot pain traveled down her arm.

"Hell. That's just where you're heading, Miss McKendry," he said with a vicious smile after hauling her to her knees.

She blinked back the nauseating dizziness that made her rock unsteadily before him and she sat down hard on her heels. Her head felt swollen and pounded with every beat of her heart. She pressed her lips together against the pain.

When it passed, Kierin glanced at her surroundings for the first time. She was in some kind of storehouse. Crates and hogsheads were stacked everywhere and the floor was covered with a thin layer of straw. Above them, a shadowy loft, stacked with more crates and barrels. High on the far wall was a window, propped open with a stick of wood. Moonlight spilled through the dirty panes, mingling with the harsh yellow glow from the lantern hanging on the wall. Talbot's man, Belson, lounged languidly against an upright wooden beam, cleaning his fingernails with a piece of straw.

"*Ah, qué bonita . . .*" crooned the Mexican to Talbot. "Such a beauty is rare, *amigo*. She is even more beautiful awake than asleep, eh?" He reached down and tipped her chin to either side to get a better look. Kierin jerked her head from his grasp and fired an angry glare in his direction. Her auburn hair spilled across her face.

"And fiery, too? This is very good. We will tame those fires, señorita, and put them to good use."

333

Tears prickled the backs of Kierin's eyes, but she refused to let them see her cry. Hopelessness settled like a mantle of snow on her shoulders. She had no illusions that she'd be able to overpower these two. They could do whatever they wanted to her and she'd be helpless to stop it. *Oh, why didn't I listen to Clay and stay with Jacob?* she agonized. Clay's face swam up in her memory — the gentle handsome face she'd never see again. *Forgive me, my darling.*

There was no one now. No one who would help her. She was completely, utterly alone. *I'll die before I let them touch me,* she swore silently.

"El Dragón is very good at what he does, Kierin. I think you two will get along famously."

"Why?" The tremble in her voice betrayed her desperation. "Why are you doing this?"

He laughed in disbelief. He grabbed her hair and yanked her head back so she could get a good look at his face. *"Why?* You can look at this hideous excuse for an eye and ask me that question? Women used to beg to get into my bed. Now" — a shudder ran through him — "they turn the other way so they won't have to look at me. I have you to thank for that." He let her hair go with a shove.

"No, I've been looking forward to this moment for a long time." Talbot slipped his fine brown wool jacket off his shoulders and dropped it atop a crate beside him. "It was an easy matter to find your father once I got here and even easier to convince him of my honorable intentions toward you. One of my greatest talents has always been knowing a man's vulnerable spots. Your father's happens to be money. Or more specifically," he amended, "the lack of it.

"He was well paid to betray you, Kierin. Perhaps that thought will console you while you rot in one of Dragón's brothels in Mexico. I, for one, will think of you there often, with great pleasure."

Kierin choked back the tears that bunched in her

throat and tipped her chin up defiantly. "You think it's your eye that makes people turn away from you, Talbot? Well, you're wrong. It's that empty place inside you where a conscience should be. That's what frightens people. Oh, they'll come to your gambling house and your dens of sin. Some will even come to your bed if the price is right.

"But you'll never experience what it is to care about another person or to have that person care for you. Thank God I had it once in my life before this. With Clay. I'll always have that to hang on to, until the day I die. And you can never take that away, no matter what you do to me."

Talbot laughed as if her words hadn't affected him, but she could see they had. "Clay Holt — that cow pusher." Talbot rolled a sudden kink out of his neck as if it pained him. "He'll get what's coming to him, too."

"You were the one behind his wife's murder, weren't you?"

Talbot's eyes narrowed into a frown and his gaze shifted nervously to Dragón and Belson, who were watching him closely.

"Did you think he wouldn't put two and two together by now?" she asked, feeling suddenly lightheaded with the knowledge that she'd surprised him. "You're a dead man already and you don't know it, because when Clay finds out what you've done to me, he'll find you and kill you."

Talbot slapped her across the face, knocking her down to the straw floor. "Shut up!"

Kierin smiled up at him. "The truth hurts, doesn't it?"

Talbot started at her again but the Mexican stopped him. *"Muchacho,"* Dragón prodded gruffly. *"El tiempo buela.* Time flies. Let us settle our business."

Talbot shrugged, regaining his composure. "Ah, yes. There is that little matter of your virginity, Kierin. Bothersome, I know," he said with an indifferent smile,

335

"but it seems important to my friend here." Talbot started walking toward her.

Kierin frantically scuffled backward on her side. There was no more stalling for time. A sick feeling rose in her throat. She knew exactly what he wanted to do. She knew she'd rather die than let Talbot put his hands on her. "Don't you touch me . . ."

"You don't seem to understand, Kierin. I'm not asking your permission." With a tip of his head, he gestured to Belson and Dragón, who walked toward her.

"Please . . . don't . . ." She tried to get her feet under her but she couldn't.

Belson took her by the shoulders and forced her down so that her head knocked painfully against the floor. With her hands tied behind her back, she could only use her feet as weapons. She flailed them wildly, connecting twice with Talbot's shin before he grabbed her ankle and pinioned it to the floor.

Shock and pain staggered her senses. She felt hands groping with her skirts, heard the fabric of her under clothes rip. A wordless scream welled up from the depths of her being. Its throaty, desperate pitch shattered the still night air, silencing the seabirds and blotting out the sound of the waves.

Chapter Twenty-three

Cain raised his hand, signaling Clay and Matthew to stop. He pointed to a dimly lit building that sat on the edge of the waterfront. Anchored just off shore was a fine-looking two-masted sloop ready for sail. The boat rocked in the waves from side to side and the small lantern atop one mast swung gently back and forth like a soundless church bell.

"Is this it?" Clay's voice was low and harsh.

"Yeah," Cain answered.

"You sure?"

Cain nodded, squinting at the wooden structure in the shadowy light from the quarter-moon. "He's meeting El Dragón here. That's his sloop."

"Good." The butt end of Clay's pistol came down on the back of Cain's head with a dull thud. The man's eyes went wide for the moment it took his body to assimilate the blow, then he dropped from his horse to the ground like a fallen oak.

Clay glanced at Matthew, who was staring wide-eyed at the fallen man. "He'll live, don't worry."

"I don't care about him," the boy replied defensively. "You just took me by surprise is all."

Clay threw his leg over his horse's back and dismounted, thinking the boy wasn't as tough as he wanted everyone to think he was. "*That* was the idea." Clay spared the body of the giant sprawled on the ground a brief glance. "Surprised the hell out of him, too, I imagine."

He looped Taeva's reins around the branches of a nearby bush. Before he'd finished, Matthew had dismounted and done the same. Clay had serious reservations about involving Matthew in any of this, but from the looks of it, he'd need his help—if only to provide a distraction.

He took the boy by the shoulders. "This is going to get dangerous. I don't plan on letting Talbot walk out of there alive."

"I know."

"I don't want you in the middle of this when it happens, you hear?"

Matthew stared at him.

"You hear me?"

"I heard you. Are you going to stand here talking about it all night or are we going to go and get her?"

Clay let out a long shaky breath. Perspiration dotted his upper lip. *I should know better than to try to argue with a McKendry,* he mused with a surrendering smile. "Let's go."

They circled around the building silently. Clay had considered storming the building through the front door, but discarded the idea. He had no idea how many guns were in there and it would more than likely put Kierin directly in the line of fire. There'd be no second chances here, he thought grimly. The element of surprise would be his best weapon. He had to get a closer look to see what his best approach was.

Inside, where a light shone dimly through a propped window and the thin cracks between the planked wooden walls, they could hear the voices of two men talking. A small window opened onto each side of the large one-room building. From the ground, he caught sight of a partial loft over the right side of the room. His skin prickled. Where there was a loft, there was a door.

"C'mon," he whispered to Matthew.

Asa McKendry drew his horse to a stop beside the others and slid awkwardly off the animal. He pulled the rifle from its sheath noiselessly. His breath came in harsh rolling gasps, but he forced himself forward on legs that felt like river mud. His eyes focused only on the splinters of light coming from the barnlike building in front of him.

It was too late for him, he mused, stumbling ahead. Too late to recover the mistakes he'd made in his life. Too late to win his children back. But not too late to help them. He'd get Kierin out of there. Whether he survived it or not made no difference.

On the far side of the warehouse, Clay found what he was looking for. An L-shaped beam protruded from the center of the roof, beneath a squat triangular portico. Behind the block and tackle that dangled, suspended from the beam, was a rough wooden door leading to the loft. A sturdy wooden ladder was built against the wall.

As Clay's foot struck the first rung of the ladder, he heard the raised voices of a man and a woman. Adrenaline pumped through him at the sound of it.

Kierin!

He still couldn't make out her words, but he recognized the inflection. Her voice urged him on. *Hold on, honey, I'm coming.*

Matthew was right behind him by the time he reached the loft door. Carefully lifting the wooden latch, Clay prayed the door wouldn't squeak when he opened it. That thought went right out of his head at the sound of Kierin's gut-wrenching scream. Caution gone, Clay threw open the door and charged into the loft.

At the same moment, the front door crashed open

339

and the explosive roar of a discharged rifle thundered through the cavernous room. Clay slid to his knees at the edge of the loft just as a swarthy black-haired man flew backward from the force of the gunshot and landed in a lifeless heap on the straw-strewn floor. Clay saw another taller man duck low and roll behind a crate while drawing his gun.

At the wide-flung entry door, Asa lowered his smoking rifle disgustedly. "Ye bastard, Talbot!" his voice boomed on the heels of the shot. "I'll kill ye with my bare hands!"

"Papa!" Kierin screamed in warning, but it was too late. Talbot's own pistol screamed in retort. Asa slammed back against the door and crumpled to the ground, clutching his bleeding chest.

"No-o-o-o!" Kierin shrieked, and hurled herself at her father's murderer. She struck him from behind, causing Talbot's knees to buckle. The gun flew from his hand and landed a few feet away with a noisy clatter.

Then he landed on her—hard. The air rushed from her lungs in a painful whoosh. With her face pressed into the cold straw floor, she gasped for breath. She heard Talbot swear and roll his excruciating weight off her. Reflexively, she drew her knees up to her chest, in the vain search for air. Her chest ached and hammered and she writhed against the floor, trying to prime her deprived lungs.

Dimly, over the roar in her own ears, she heard another sound—a fierce growl, more animal than human—and caught the fleeting glimpse of buckskin and flashing gunmetal. The banshee dropped out of the loft above them, landing on Talbot with a bone-rattling thud. The two rolled across the floor, locked in a desperate, pummeling struggle.

Kierin coughed, then gasped as her breath returned in fitful choking puffs. Finally, her lungs sucked in deep draughts of life-giving air. Strength returned to her limbs. Spitting straw from her mouth, she rolled onto her side and, using her knees for leverage, struggled to sit up.

Shock raced through her as she caught sight of the men wrestling with each other. Her eyes fell to the long-legged man in buckskin whose face was hidden from her as the two men tumbled over and over. Yet she knew there was no mistaking the lean, powerful body which had become as familiar to her as her own.

Clay! Oh, Clay it's you! her mind screamed. She saw the flash of the gun Clay held tightly in his grip. Talbot ended up on top of Clay, fighting for possession of the weapon. He slammed Clay's wrist against the floor and simultaneously sent his right fist crashing into Clay's face. The gun sailed free and landed beneath a crate, out of reach.

Clay's fist returned the blow in kind, and sent Talbot rocking back off balance. Clay rolled the other man off him and grabbed him by the shirtfront. Savagely, he punished Talbot's jaw with another blow and the man flew backward, his face bloodied and battered.

Clay swayed on his knees, searching the ground for his gun. With his back to Belson, Clay didn't see the man taking a bead on him from behind the stack of wooden boxes.

"Clay, watch out!" shouted a warning voice from above them. Clay ducked, rolling to the ground and the shot went wild, slapping into a barrel of molasses. Thick brown liquid exploded from the hole and oozed down the side of the barrel.

Behind the crate, Belson was frantically reloading his pistol while trying to retreat from his position. A blood-curdling war-whoop rent the air as Matthew dropped from the loft down onto the man's back.

Belson's surprised yelp was cut short by a blow from the heavy handle of Matthew's hunting knife. The big man let out a grunt and sank like a stone to the floor.

The savage boy looked, at that moment, more like an Indian than her brother—with his long hair and beaded buckskins—but a rush of joy swept through Kierin at the sight of him. "Matthew!"

The boy tossed a brief victorious smile in her direction, then returned his attention to the men. In the middle of the floor, Talbot had gotten to his feet and was circling Clay. Kierin inhaled sharply when she saw the glittering knife blade in his hand. Unarmed, Clay hopped backward, arms outstretched for balance, barely avoiding the deadly swipe of Talbot's knife. Matthew edged toward them, with the large knife poised to throw.

"No, Matthew," Clay growled low, spotting him too. "I want the bastard." His face was slick with sweat and blood, his expression—fierce and deadly.

Matthew lowered his arm apprehensively. "Then take this, so it's even," he said, tossing the knife to him.

Clay caught the weapon easily and flicked it in Talbot's direction. "Okay, you son of a bitch," he said, his breath coming hard and ragged. "Let's end this." He swiped the blade at Talbot's chest, slicing his shirt and drawing blood.

Talbot drew in a hissing breath. Eyes narrowed, he swallowed hard. Blood flowed freely from his nose and mouth, spattering his crisp white shirt. "My pleasure, Holt." His blade snaked out again, grazing Clay in the arm. A crimson stain seeped through the buff-colored buckskin sleeve.

The two circled each other like stalking cats—watchful, poised to strike, neither giving ground to the other.

"I should have killed you years ago, when I had the chance," Talbot snarled.

"You were as much of a coward then as you are now," Clay taunted, feinting forward with his blade.

Talbot jumped back, eluding the thrust.

"Did it make you feel like a big man to kill my wife, Talbot?" Violence simmered in his voice.

Talbot's eyes widened with taunting innocence. "That was a mistake."

"A *mistake?*"

"She was in the wrong place at the wrong time."

"She was in her *home,* God damn you!" Holt lunged, but Talbot evaded him again, throwing him slightly off balance. He felt the sting of Talbot's blade as it sliced his arm again. He ignored the pain. He knew he was letting his emotions get in the way of what he had to do.

"Not that it matters now," Talbot continued, with a hint of a smile, "but we thought she'd gone with you. It was an accident."

It didn't matter. Not for a second. "This wasn't any accident, though, was it, Talbot? Taking Kierin? Making her beg you for her life?"

Talbot smiled. Blood tinged his teeth red. "No. Quite the opposite, in fact. How does it feel to know you've lost both of your women to me, Holt?"

"Not a prayer of that, you bastard . . ." Tired of the game of cat and mouse, Clay kicked Talbot's wrist with a stinging jab of his foot, knocking the blade from his hand.

Talbot only had time to stagger back a step before Clay launched himself at him, knocking him into a stack of crates that splintered beneath their combined weight. Talbot caught Clay's right arm with both of his, holding the deadly blade away from his face. They rolled off the crates and onto the floor, locked in a struggle they both knew only one would survive.

Clay saw the revolver at the same moment Talbot did. The gunmetal glinted in the lantern light. Wedged beneath the crate where it had been knocked in the scuffle, it was within the grasp of both men, but only Talbot had a hand free enough to grab for it. Talbot's fingers closed around the stock and drew the gun between them.

Hysteria rose in Kierin's throat. "Clay, watch out!" she screamed. She saw him drop his knife to focus all his strength and attention on the more lethal weapon. They rolled behind a barrel, out of sight.

343

Struggling to her feet, she yanked furiously at the bonds on her wrists. If only she could *do* something. Across the room, her frustrated gaze met Matthew's. His helpless expression was a mirror of her own.

The deafening crack of gunfire sent her heart leaping to her throat. She went stock-still, unable to move or even breathe. Seconds passed, but the silence stretched like minutes. Woodenly, she took one step closer, then another. "Clay?" Her voice was a hoarse whisper.

Nothing. Silence, except for the slamming of her heart in her ears.

There . . . the rattle of splintered wood. Someone moved. "C-Clay?" she called again, louder this time. An arm covered in buff-colored buckskin came up to brace against the barrel. A cry of joy tore from her throat as Clay straightened and stepped out into the room. His arms met and enfolded her as she collided with his solid strength.

"Oh, Clay, I was so afraid . . ." Tears of joy streamed down her face.

His body was taut and his hand trembled as he soothed his fingers over her hair but he murmured, "Sh-h, I'm all right, now. He's dead. It's all over now." He reached down behind her and untied her hands.

Kierin flung her arms around his neck and pulled his mouth down to hers. His answering kiss met the sweet urgency of hers and his arms tightened around her with a fierce possessiveness.

When they pulled back to look at each other, Matthew appeared beside them, head down with sudden embarrassment.

"Oh, Matthew," Kierin cried, shifting her embrace to include him. "Look how you've grown. But how did you find me?" She looked back and forth between him and Clay. "How . . . how did you two . . . ?"

"It's a long story." He and Matthew exchanged conspiratorial smiles.

"A very long story," Matthew agreed.

"What the hell is going on here?" called a deep voice from the doorway.

Clay whirled around, tucking Kierin and Matthew protectively behind him. Four men pointed guns at them from the open door. The one who'd spoken stepped over Asa's inert body and came closer. Thick gray hair peeked out from beneath his flat crowned hat and his barrel-chested body was exaggerated by a bulky sheepskin coat.

"Who are you?" Clay demanded.

"U.S. Marshal Clinton Richardson," the man replied evenly, his gaze taking in the sprawled bodies of El Dragón and Talbot lying nearby. "Who the hell are they?"

"That one's John Talbot," Kierin replied, stepping out from behind Clay. "And o-over there, a whore-monger from Mexico named El Dragón." She swallowed back the lump of pain as she looked at her father's body. Her whole body began to quake in delayed reaction. "They k-killed my father and were trying to kidnap me." She looked up at Clay with devotion in her eyes. "I-I'd be on my way to Mexico by now if it weren't for Clay and my brother."

Richardson whistled and lowered his gun a bit. "El Dragón, huh? We've been after that son of a gun for years. You sure it's him?"

"That's his boat docked out front," Clay said. "The big guy with the lump on his head outside will verify everything I'm saying . . . with a little persuasion."

One of Richardson's men hauled Cain through the door by his arm. The giant scowled thunderously at Clay. "You mean him?" the marshall asked.

Clay nodded. "There's another one nursing a head-ache over behind those crates. He was a witness to most of it."

"And what's your name, mister?" Richardson inquired.

"Holt. Clay Holt."

345

Richardson tipped the brim of his hat back with the barrel of his gun. "Well, Mr. Holt, if you've told me the truth, and it sounds like you have, it shouldn't take long to get to the bottom of this. If these two don't want the Vigilance Committee after their necks, they'll talk."

"While you're at it," Clay added, "there's a woman named Suzanne back at Talbot's house, locked up with enough food to last her a month. She was involved in this, too."

Richardson nodded and gestured to his men to start picking up the bodies. He frowned at Clay for a moment, then said, "You three best come back to my office with me 'til we get this all untangled. I think I'm gonna need a cup of coffee." Sizing up the blood on Clay he added, "And the doc's gonna want to take a look at those cuts."

One hour later, after the doctor had stitched and swabbed Clay's wounds, he and Kierin rose to meet the marshal as he walked back into his outer office. The man had spent nearly a half hour interrogating Cain, Belson, and Suzanne, and had returned wearing a scowl on his face. He dropped into his rolling desk chair and started sifting through a mound of paperwork on his desk.

"You're likely to find a Wanted poster in there with my name on it," Clay told him without preamble.

Standing by his side, Kierin let out a small gasp. "Clay . . ."

Richardson fell silent and looked at the pair.

"Clay, don't . . ." she begged in a throaty whisper.

"No," Clay argued, staring past her. The muscles in his jaw bunched with determination. "There's no use lying about it. I want it settled. If it means I have to go to jail then so be it. But I won't make you live with this cloud over our heads anymore."

"How can you say that after what we've just been through?" Kierin took his arms, forcing him to look at her. "Oh, Clay . . . don't you know you're the most im-

346

portant thing in my life? That I'd rather die than live without you?" Tears of desperation formed behind her eyes. "If you have to go to jail . . . I'll . . ."

Clay drew her against him and held her tightly. "Damn . . . I love you too," he whispered into her hair. "Nothing will ever change that." Kierin pressed her face miserably against his chest. "But you know I have to do this. I wouldn't be much of a man if I dragged you down with me."

Richardson threaded his fingers together across his ample chest and leaned back in his chair watching them.

Pulling herself from Clay's arms, she braced her hands upon the lawman's paper-scattered desk. "He didn't do anything wrong," Kierin pleaded. "I don't know what they told you in there, but it's not true. Kyle Jessup and John Talbot would have killed us both that night. It was self-defense . . ."

"I know," the marshal murmured.

"I swear it. He was only protecting me. I'll testify in—" She blinked, his words finally registering. "W-what did you say?"

The marshal smiled. "I said, I know."

Clay's lips parted in surprise. "You do?"

"Yup. But if you two ain't through, please," he invited, waving his hand good-naturedly, "be my guests. It's been a long time since I saw two people as dead set on loving each other as the pair of you appear to be."

"Marshal . . ." Clay warned in a low voice.

"Okay, okay." Richardson laughed and threw his hands in the air palms up. "I'll tell you then. I knew about the poster before you even told me. Knew about it when you told me your name back there in the warehouse. This desk may look completely disorganized, but I've got a mind like a steel trap when it comes to names.

"So I also remembered the second paper that come in on you, Holt. The one that counteracted the first

347

poster." He dug through the stack of papers, finally withdrawing the one he was looking for. "Ah, here it is." He scrutinized it for a moment, then handed it to Clay. "Seems a man named Brown, Scudder Brown, came forward and cleared your name. And several of Talbot's former employees backed Brown's story up. Charges against you have been dropped, Mr. Holt. You're a free man."

"Oh, Clay!" Kierin breathed.

Matthew let out a full-blooded Cheyenne whoop, and Clay grabbed Kierin and scooped her into his arms. Heedless of all the people around them, Clay dropped his mouth onto hers and kissed her with exquisite thoroughness.

Abruptly he pulled his lips from hers and dragged her over to the desk before the grinning marshal. "There's only one thing to do then," Clay announced.

Richardson's eyebrows lifted inquiringly while Kierin stared at him, her face still flushed from his kiss.

"Marry us," he told the marshal.

"W-what?" Kierin sputtered, astounded.

"Now. Tonight," Clay insisted. "You have the authority don't you, Marshal?"

"You're crazy!" she laughed.

"About you," he admitted, dropping a kiss on her blushing nose. He turned to the other man. "Well?"

"Hell yes, I've got the authority," Richardson replied with a broad smile. "Is that what you folks want?"

Clay turned to Kierin, bracketed her face in his large hands, and searched her eyes for the answer he hoped to find there. "I don't want one more day, one more minute to come between us, Kierin. I love you. God," he groaned, "I love you so much, I hurt. Say you will and we'll catch the next packet for Oregon. We'll be there within a week. I want to take you there as my wife." He glanced up at her brother. "We'll go there as a family." His eyes pleaded with her. "Say yes."

Stunned by his unabashed profession of love and devotion, Kierin didn't trust herself to speak. She tried to swallow the fist of tears in the back of her throat, but failed.

Clay's face fell when she didn't answer right away, mistaking her hesitation for reluctance. "Unless . . . you've got your heart set on a big wedding . . ."

"Oh, you!" Her laughter tumbled out and mingled with her tears. "Now I know you're crazy!" Throwing her arms around him, she plunged her fingers into the rich dark hair at the nape of his neck and pressed her cheek to his. She inhaled deeply of his wonderful, familiar scent.

"You're everything I've ever wanted," she told him, "and more than I ever dreamed I could have. I love you too, Clay, and if you wanted to marry me in the middle of a cow pasture, that would be just fine with me. Yes, yes," she murmured, planting small moist kisses on his cheeks, "Yes—I'll marry you. Tonight, tomorrow, any time you want."

The marshal grinned and disappeared into the back room, muttering something about marriage certificates.

"You won't be sorry, honey," Clay told her, holding her close. "I promise you, you won't. It won't be much to start with. We'll have to rebuild the ranch house."

"Fine."

"But I've got some of the finest timberland this side of the Rocky Mountains. Trees so tall you have to nearly break your neck to see the tops. We'll build a house with lots of rooms, and plenty of space for babies."

"Babies?"

"You want babies, don't you?"

Her eyes glimmered with love. "Absolutely."

"And I have the perfect spot picked out to rebuild. It overlooks the most spectacular view you've ever seen."

"Uh-huh." Her gaze traced the perfect shape of his mouth.

"I'll build our bedroom facing east, so we can lie in

349

bed and watch the sun come up every morning. And—"

"Clay?" she whispered.

"Huh?" His faraway expression returned to her.

"Remember when I complained about your being too close-mouthed? And that you only had one thing on your mind?"

"Yeah?"

She smiled. A woman's smile. "Well, forget what I said. If you don't kiss me right now, I'm going to have to do something desperate."

"Sounds serious." Clay shook his head slowly.

"Oh, it is. It definitely is."

She reached up to meet his kiss and he enfolded her in his arms, just as he intended to do for the rest of his life.

HISTORICAL ROMANCES BY VICTORIA THOMPSON

BOLD TEXAS EMBRACE   (2835, $4.50)

Art teacher Catherine Eaton could hardly believe how stubborn Sam Connors was! Even though the rancher's young stepbrother was an exceptionally talented painter, Sam forbade Catherine to instruct him, fearing that art would make a sissy out of him. Spunky and determined, the blond schoolmarm confronted the muleheaded cowboy . . . only to find that he was as handsome as he was hard-headed and as desirable as he was dictatorial. Before long she had nearly forgotten what she'd come for, as Sam's brash, breathless embrace drove from her mind all thought of anything save wanting him . . .

TEXAS BLONDE   (2183, $3.95)

When dashing Josh Logan resued her from death by exposure, petite Felicity Morrow realized she'd never survive rugged frontier life without a man by her side. And when she gazed at the Texas rancher's lean hard frame and strong rippling muscles, the determined beauty decided he was the one for her. To reach her goal, feisty Felicity pretended to be meek and mild: the only kind of gal Josh proclaimed he'd wed. But after she'd won his hand, the blue-eyed temptress swore she'd quit playing his game—and still win his heart!

ANGEL HEART   (2426, $3.95)

Ever since Angelica's father died, Harlan Snyder had been angling to get his hands on her ranch, the Diamond R. And now, just when she had an important government contract to fulfill, she couldn't find a single cowhand to hire on—all because of Snyder's threats. It was only a matter of time before she lost the ranch. . . . That is, until the legendary gunfighter Kid Collins turned up on her doorstep, badly wounded. Angelica assessed his firmly muscled physique and stared into his startling blue eyes. Beneath all that blood and dirt he was the handsomest man she had ever seen, and the one person who could help her beat Snyder at his own game—if the price were not too high. . . .

Available wherever paperbacks are sold, or order direct from the Publisher. Send cover price plus 50¢ per copy for mailing and handling to Zebra Books, Dept. 3111, 475 Park Avenue South, New York, N.Y. 10016. Residents of New York, New Jersey and Pennsylvania must include sales tax. DO NOT SEND CASH.

HISTORICAL ROMANCES BY EMMA MERRITT

RESTLESS FLAMES (2203, $3.95)

Having lost her husband six months before, determined Brenna Allen couldn't afford to lose her freight company, too. Outfitted as wagon captain with revolver, knife and whip, the single-minded beauty relentlessly drove her caravan, desperate to reach Santa Fe. Then she crossed paths with insolent Logan Mac-Dougald. The taciturn Texas Ranger was as primitive as the surrounding Comanche Territory, and he didn't hesitate to let the tantalizing trail boss know what he wanted from her. Yet despite her outrage with his brazen ways, jet-haired Brenna couldn't suppress the scorching passions surging through her . . . and suddenly she never wanted this trip to end!

COMANCHE BRIDE (2549, $3.95)

When stunning Dr. Zoe Randolph headed to Mexico to halt a cholera epidemic, she didn't think twice about traversing Comanche territory . . . until a band of bloodthirsty savages attacked her caravan. The gorgeous physician was furious that her mission had been interrupted, but nothing compared to the rage she felt on meeting the barbaric warrior who made her his slave. Determined to return to civilization, the ivory-skinned blonde decided to make a woman's ultimate sacrifice to gain her freedom — and never admit that deep down inside she burned to be loved by the handsome brute!

SWEET, WILD LOVE (2834, $4.50)

It was hard enough for Eleanor Hunt to get men to take her seriously in sophisticated Chicago — it was going to be impossible in Blissful, Kansas! These cowboys couldn't believe she was a real attorney, here to try a cattle rustling case. They just looked her up and down and grinned. Especially that Bradley Smith. The man worked for her father and he still had the audacity to stare at her with those lust-filled green eyes. Every time she turned around, he was trying to trap her in his strong embrace.